THE COLOSSAL COIN CALAMITY!

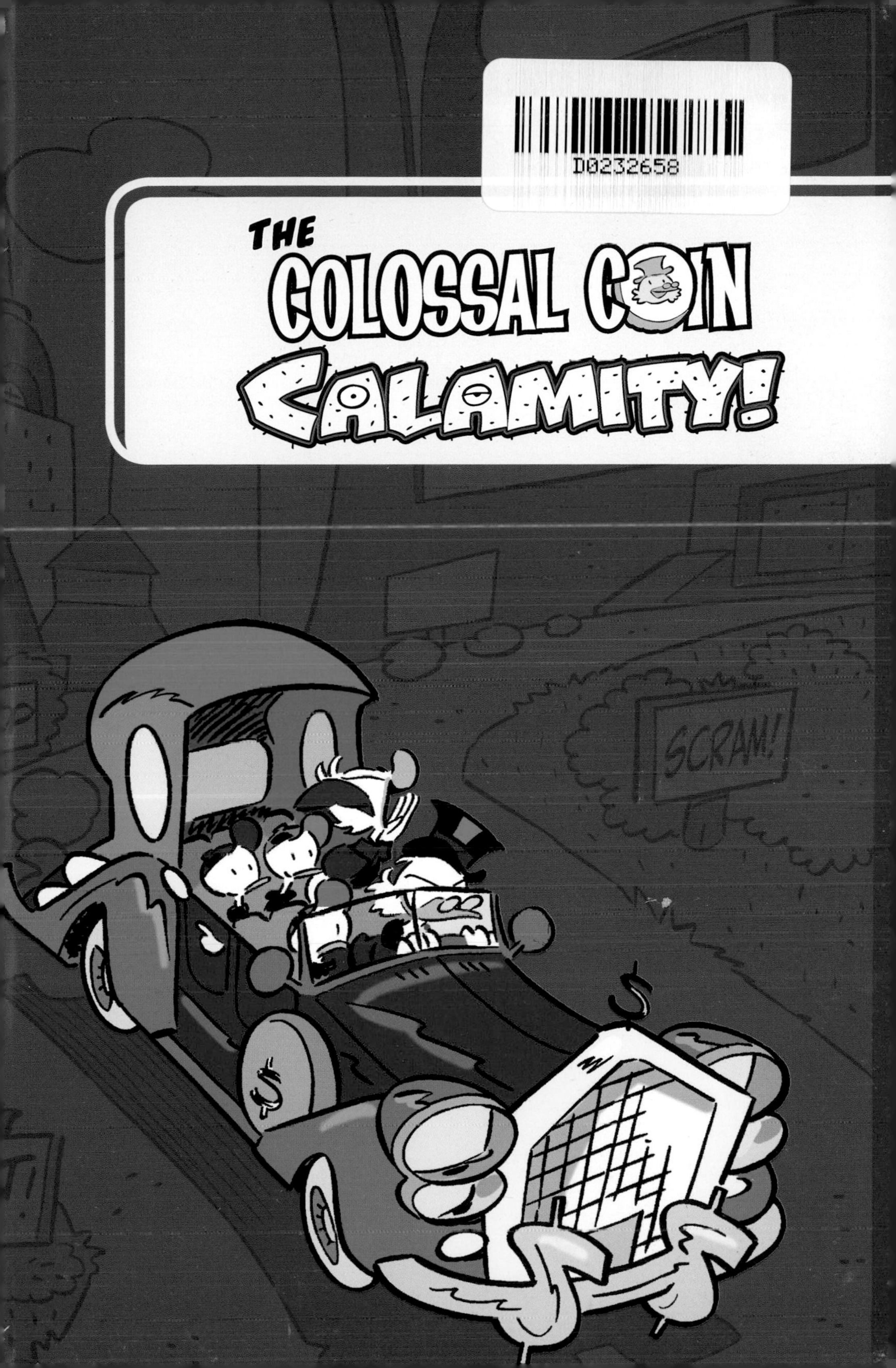
SCRAM!

Facebook: **facebook.com/idwpublishing**
Twitter: **@idwpublishing**
YouTube: **youtube.com/idwpublishing**
Tumblr: **tumblr.idwpublishing.com**
Instagram: **instagram.com/idwpublishing**

ISBN: 978-1-68405-510-4   22 21 20 19   1 2 3 4

COVER ARTIST
ANDREA FRECCERO

COVER COLORIST
MARCO COLLETTI

SERIES EDITOR
CHRIS CERASI

ARCHIVAL EDITOR
DAVID GERSTEIN

COLLECTION EDITORS
JUSTIN EISINGER
& ALONZO SIMON

COLLECTION DESIGNER
CLYDE GRAPA

Originally published as UNCLE SCROOGE issues #38–40 (Legacy #442–444).

Chris Ryall, President, Publisher, & Chief Creative Officer

John Barber, Editor-In-Chief

Robbie Robbins, EVP/Sr. Art Director

Cara Morrison, Chief Financial Officer

Matt Ruzicka, Chief Accounting Officer

David Hedgecock, Associate Publisher

Jerry Bennington, VP of New Product Development

Lorelei Bunjes, VP of Digital Services

Justin Eisinger, Editorial Director, Graphic Novels & Collections

Eric Moss, Senior Director, Licensing and Business Development

Ted Adams, IDW Founder

Special thanks to Stefano Ambrosio, Stefano Attardi, Julie Dorris, Marco Ghiglione, Jodi Hammerwold, Behnoosh Khalili, Manny Mederos, Eugene Paraszczuk, Carlotta Quattrocolo, Roberto Santillo, Christopher Troise, and Camilla Vedove.

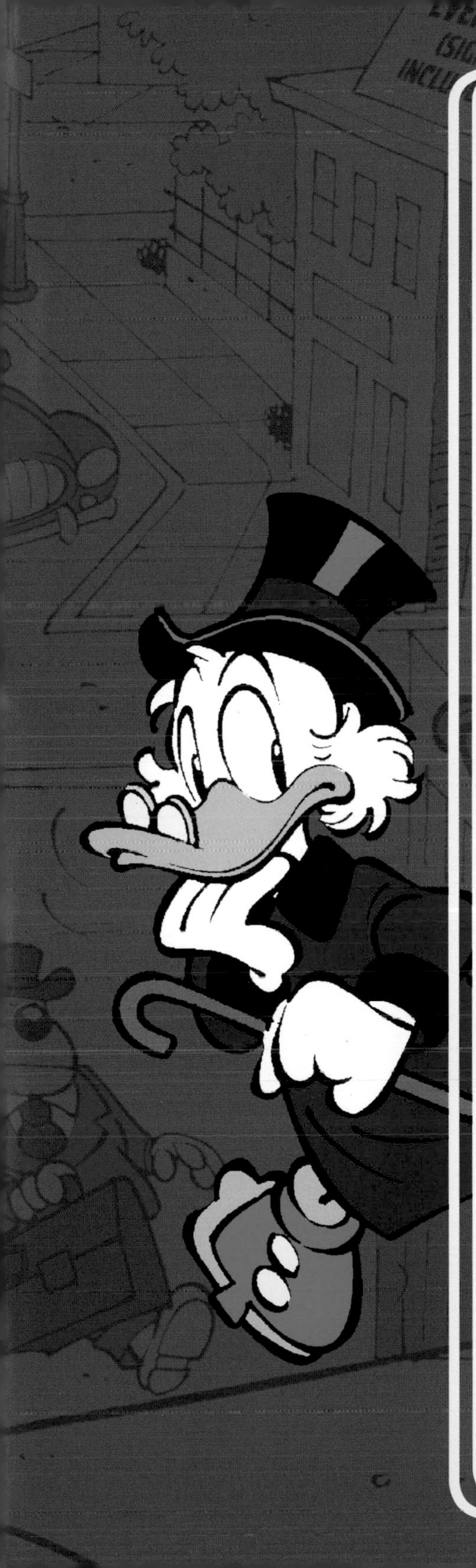

The Colossal Coin Calamity
From Italian *Topolino* #3141, 2016
Writer: Simone "Sio" Albrigi
Artist: Stefano Intini
Colorist: Disney Italia
Letterers: Nicole and Travis Seitler
Translation and Dialogue: Jonathan H. Gray

It's All Relative
From *Donald Duck* Sunday comic strip, 1962
Writer: Bob Karp
Artist and Letterer: Al Taliaferro
Colorist: Digikore Studios

Mismatched Mentors
From German *Lustiges Taschenbuch* #470, 2015
Writers: Pat and Carol McGreal
Artist: Giorgio Cavazzano
Colorist: Disney Italia
Letterers: Nicole and Travis Seitler

Bean Buffet
From Dutch *Donald Duck Weekblad* #41/2003
Writers: Frand Jonker and Paul Hoogma
Artist: Freddy Milton
Colorists: Sanoma with Nicole and Travis Seitler
Letterers: Nicole and Travis Seitler
Translation and Dialogue: Maura McManus

The Case of the Circulating Saucer
From Italian *Topolino* #1389, 1982
Writer: Carlo Chendi
Artist: Giorgio Cavazzano
Colorists: Mondadori and Digikore Studios
Letterers: Nicole and Travis Seitler
Translation and Dialogue: Joe Torcivia

Donald's First Million
From Dutch *Donald Duck Weekblad* #24/2017
Writer: Evert Geradts
Artist: Wanda Gattino
Colorist: Sanoma
Letterers: Nicole and Travis Seitler
Translation and Dialogue: David Getstein

So Dear To His Heart
From Danish *Anders And & Co* #42/2012
Writer: Maya Åstrup
Artist: Wanda Gattino
Colorists: Egmont and Digikore Studios
Letterers: Nicole and Travis Seitler

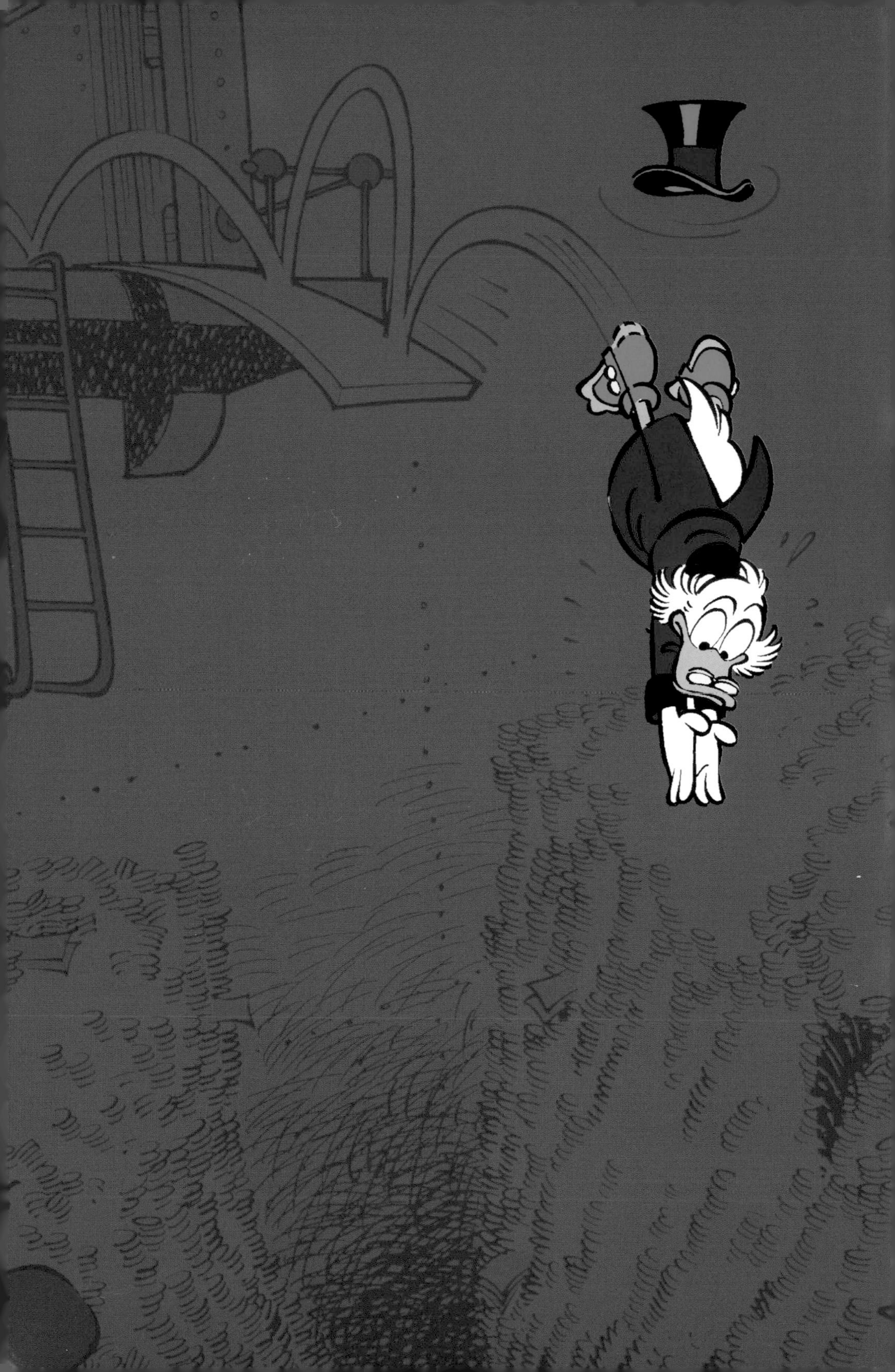

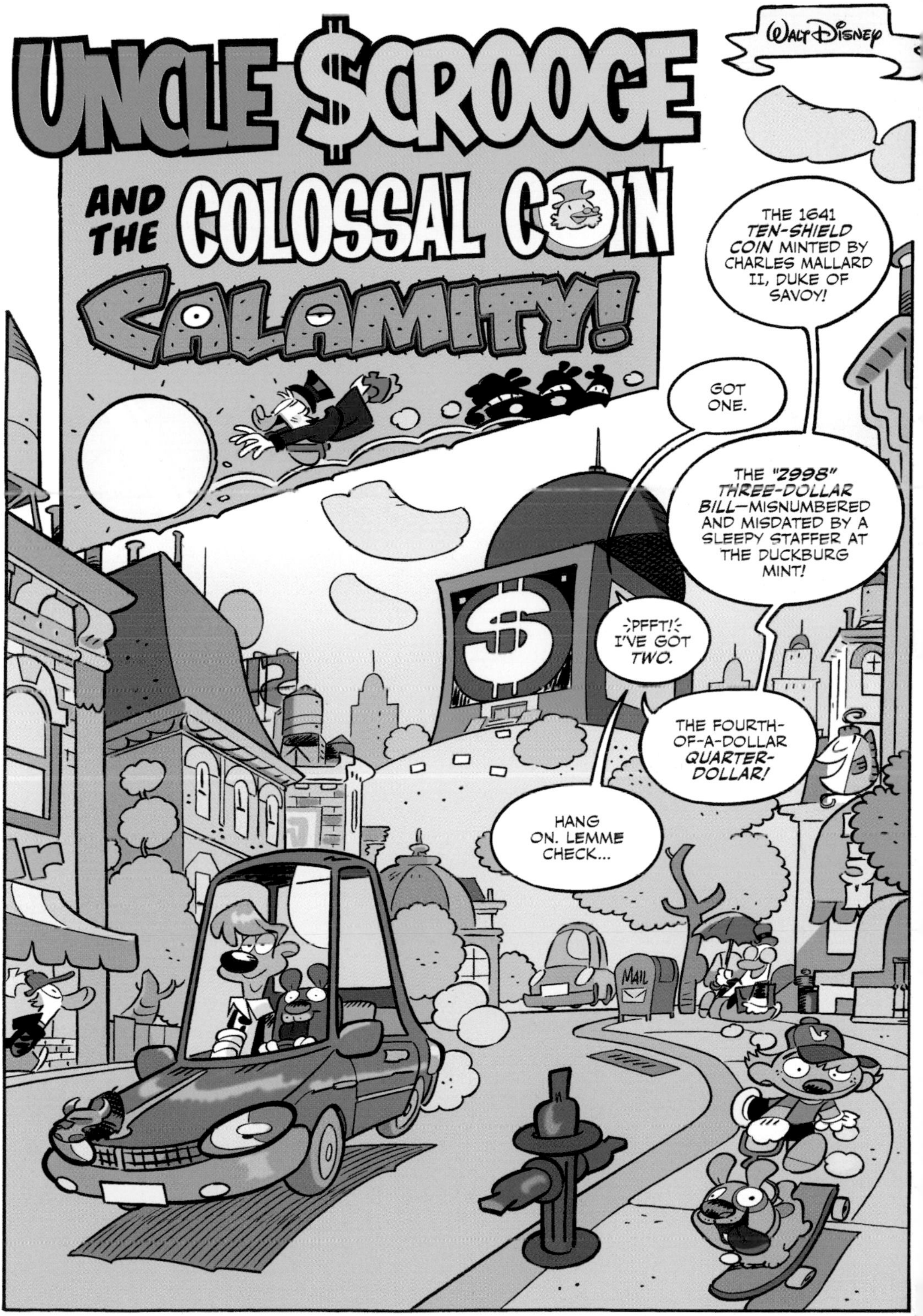
WALT DISNEY
UNCLE $CROOGE
AND THE COLOSSAL COIN CALAMITY!
THE 1641 TEN-SHIELD COIN MINTED BY CHARLES MALLARD II, DUKE OF SAVOY!
GOT ONE.
THE "2998" THREE-DOLLAR BILL—MISNUMBERED AND MISDATED BY A SLEEPY STAFFER AT THE DUCKBURG MINT!
PFFT! I'VE GOT TWO.
THE FOURTH-OF-A-DOLLAR QUARTER-DOLLAR!
HANG ON. LEMME CHECK...
MAIL

ORIGINALLY PUBLISHED IN TOPOLINO #3141 (ITALY, 2016) • FIRST USA PUBLICATION

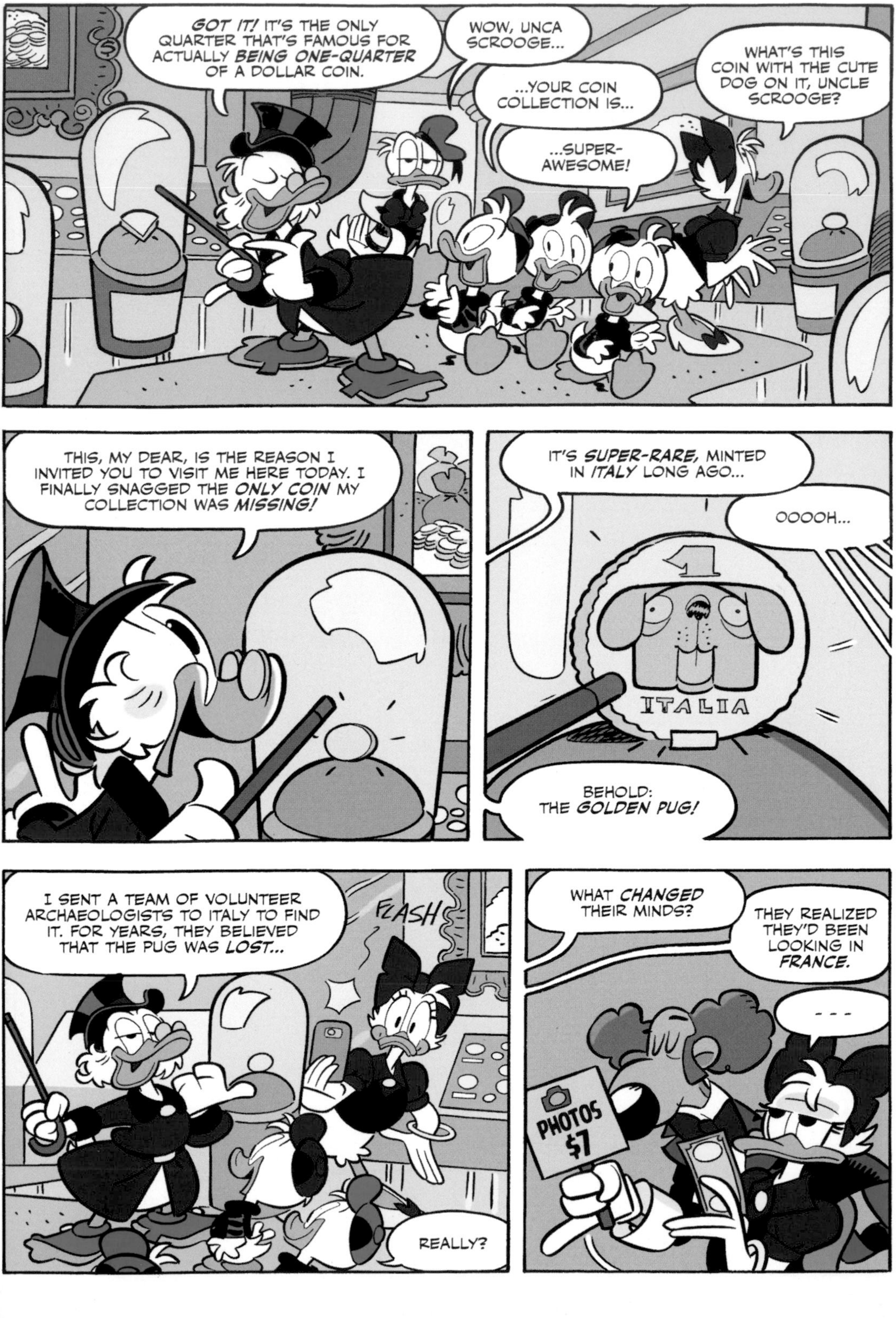

GOT IT! IT'S THE ONLY QUARTER THAT'S FAMOUS FOR ACTUALLY BEING ONE-QUARTER OF A DOLLAR COIN.
WOW, UNCA SCROOGE...
...YOUR COIN COLLECTION IS...
...SUPER-AWESOME!
WHAT'S THIS COIN WITH THE CUTE DOG ON IT, UNCLE SCROOGE?
THIS, MY DEAR, IS THE REASON I INVITED YOU TO VISIT ME HERE TODAY. I FINALLY SNAGGED THE ONLY COIN MY COLLECTION WAS MISSING!
IT'S SUPER-RARE, MINTED IN ITALY LONG AGO...
OOOOH...
1
ITALIA
BEHOLD: THE GOLDEN PUG!
I SENT A TEAM OF VOLUNTEER ARCHAEOLOGISTS TO ITALY TO FIND IT. FOR YEARS, THEY BELIEVED THAT THE PUG WAS LOST...
FLASH
REALLY?
WHAT CHANGED THEIR MINDS?
THEY REALIZED THEY'D BEEN LOOKING IN FRANCE.
- - -
PHOTOS $7

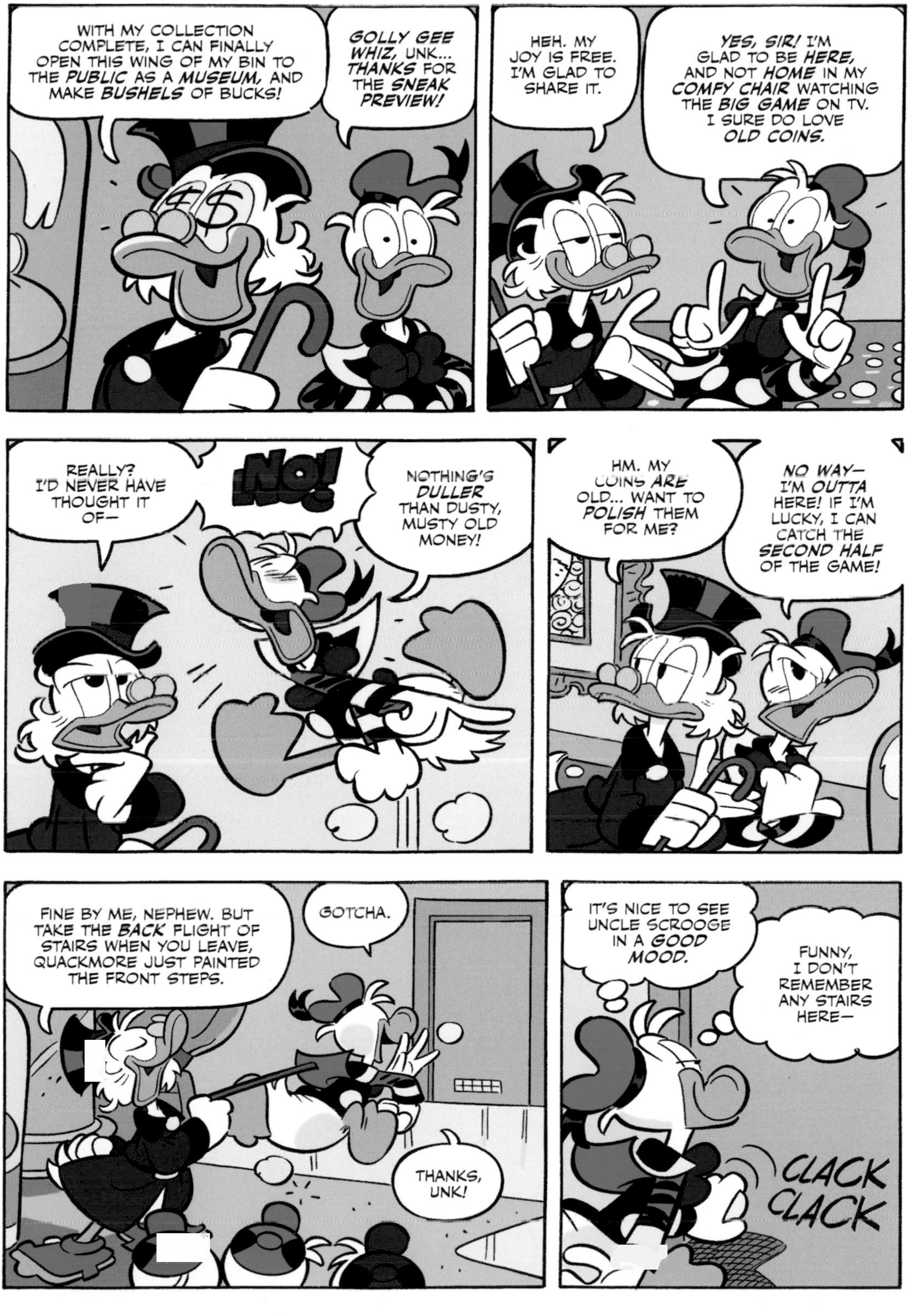

WITH MY COLLECTION COMPLETE, I CAN FINALLY OPEN THIS WING OF MY BIN TO THE PUBLIC AS A MUSEUM, AND MAKE BUSHELS OF BUCKS!
GOLLY GEE WHIZ, UNK... THANKS FOR THE SNEAK PREVIEW!
HEH. MY JOY IS FREE. I'M GLAD TO SHARE IT.
YES, SIR! I'M GLAD TO BE HERE, AND NOT HOME IN MY COMFY CHAIR WATCHING THE BIG GAME ON TV. I SURE DO LOVE OLD COINS.
REALLY? I'D NEVER HAVE THOUGHT IT OF—
¡NO!
NOTHING'S DULLER THAN DUSTY, MUSTY OLD MONEY!
HM. MY COINS ARE OLD... WANT TO POLISH THEM FOR ME?
NO WAY— I'M OUTTA HERE! IF I'M LUCKY, I CAN CATCH THE SECOND HALF OF THE GAME!
FINE BY ME, NEPHEW. BUT TAKE THE BACK FLIGHT OF STAIRS WHEN YOU LEAVE, QUACKMORE JUST PAINTED THE FRONT STEPS.
GOTCHA.
THANKS, UNK!
IT'S NICE TO SEE UNCLE SCROOGE IN A GOOD MOOD.
FUNNY, I DON'T REMEMBER ANY STAIRS HERE—
CLACK CLACK

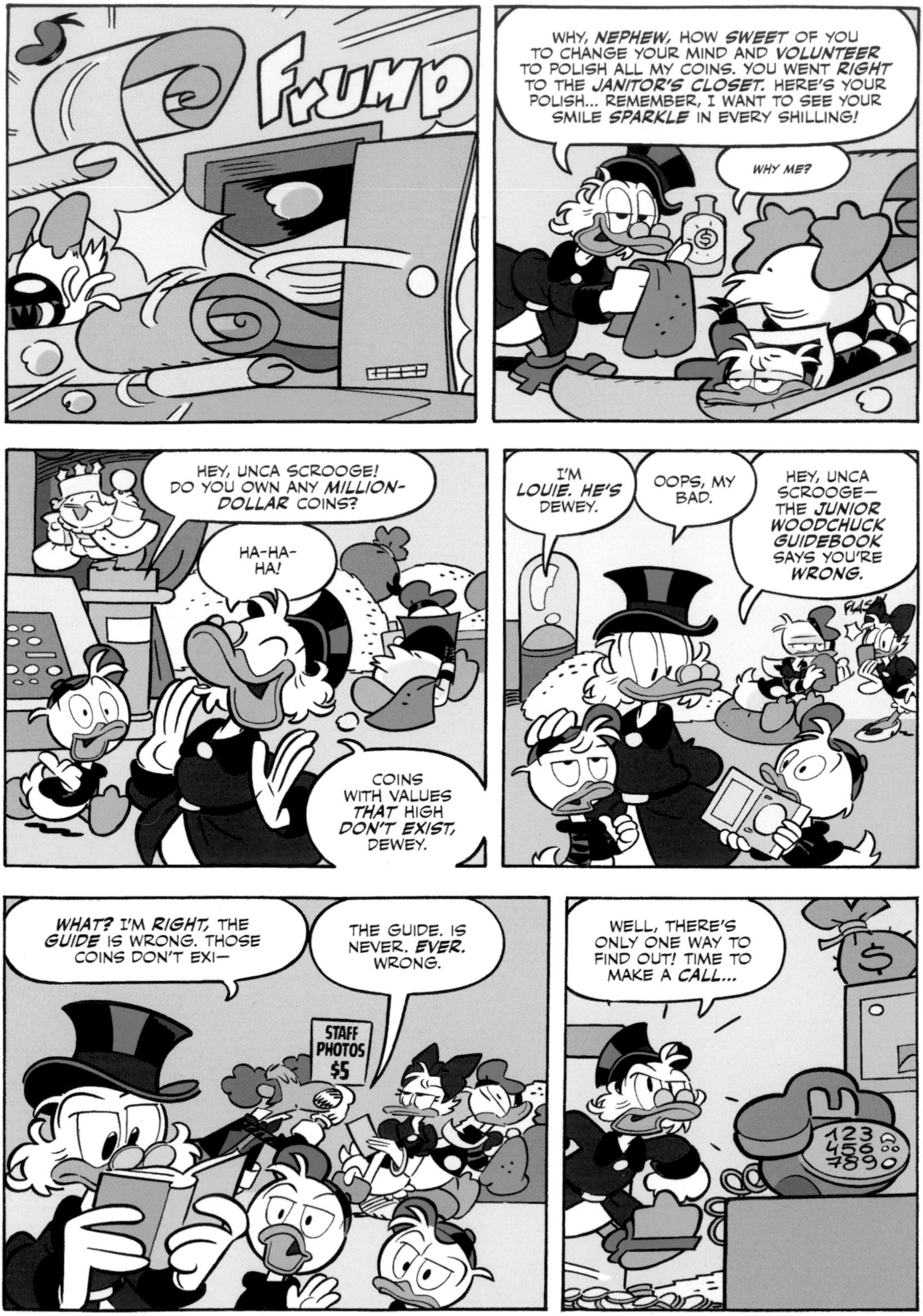
FRUMP
WHY, NEPHEW, HOW SWEET OF YOU TO CHANGE YOUR MIND AND VOLUNTEER TO POLISH ALL MY COINS. YOU WENT RIGHT TO THE JANITOR'S CLOSET. HERE'S YOUR POLISH... REMEMBER, I WANT TO SEE YOUR SMILE SPARKLE IN EVERY SHILLING!
WHY ME?
HEY, UNCA SCROOGE! DO YOU OWN ANY MILLION-DOLLAR COINS?
HA-HA-HA!
COINS WITH VALUES THAT HIGH DON'T EXIST, DEWEY.
I'M LOUIE. HE'S DEWEY.
OOPS, MY BAD.
HEY, UNCA SCROOGE— THE JUNIOR WOODCHUCK GUIDEBOOK SAYS YOU'RE WRONG.
WHAT? I'M RIGHT, THE GUIDE IS WRONG. THOSE COINS DON'T EXI—
THE GUIDE. IS NEVER. EVER. WRONG.
STAFF PHOTOS $5
WELL, THERE'S ONLY ONE WAY TO FIND OUT! TIME TO MAKE A CALL...
123
456
7890

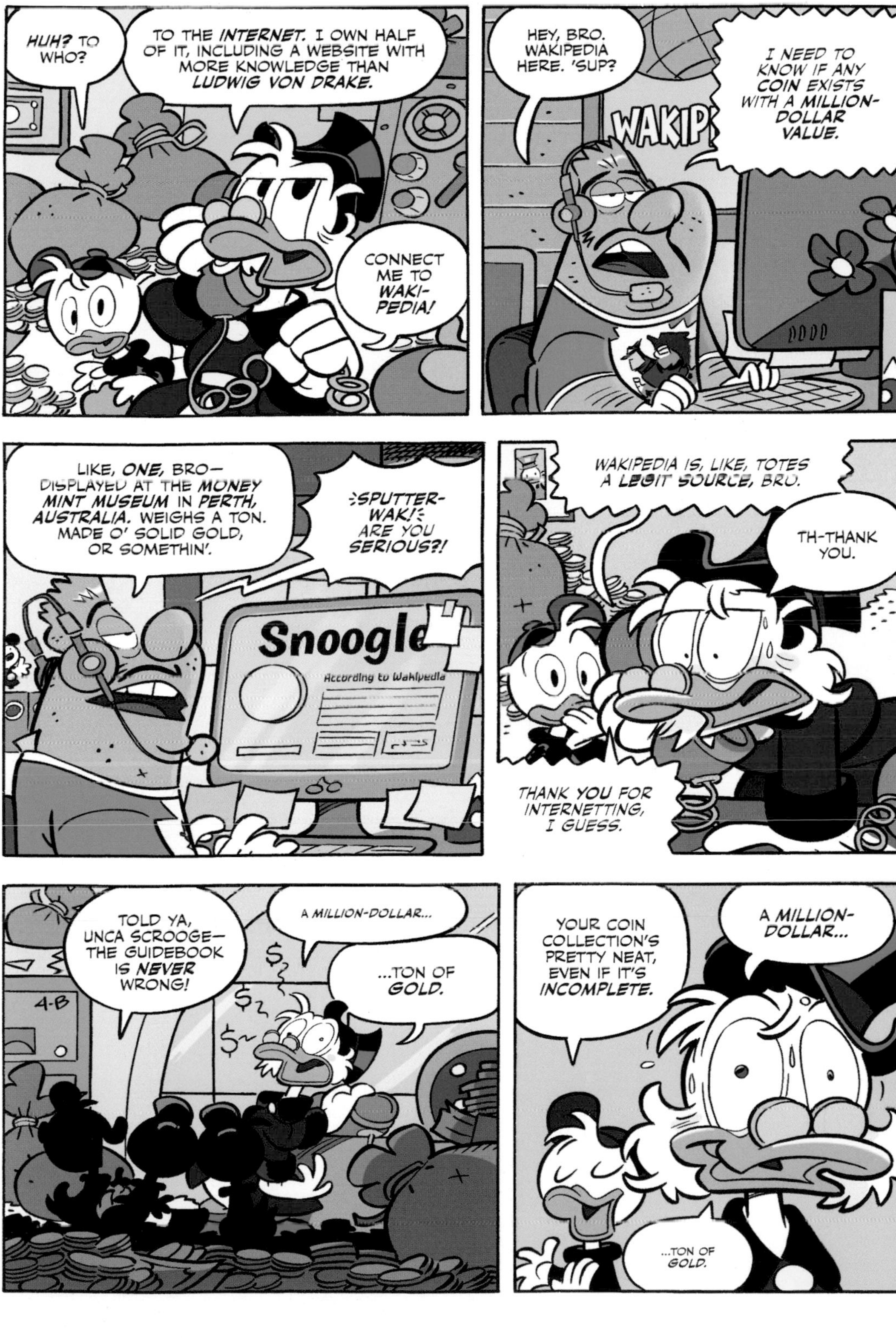
HUH? TO WHO?
TO THE INTERNET. I OWN HALF OF IT, INCLUDING A WEBSITE WITH MORE KNOWLEDGE THAN LUDWIG VON DRAKE.
CONNECT ME TO WAKI-PEDIA!
HEY, BRO. WAKIPEDIA HERE. 'SUP?
WAKIP
I NEED TO KNOW IF ANY COIN EXISTS WITH A MILLION-DOLLAR VALUE.
LIKE, ONE, BRO—DISPLAYED AT THE MONEY MINT MUSEUM IN PERTH, AUSTRALIA. WEIGHS A TON. MADE O' SOLID GOLD, OR SOMETHIN'.
SPUTTER-WAK! ARE YOU SERIOUS?!
Snoogle
According to Wakipedia
WAKIPEDIA IS, LIKE, TOTES A LEGIT SOURCE, BRO.
TH-THANK YOU.
THANK YOU FOR INTERNETTING, I GUESS.
TOLD YA, UNCA SCROOGE—THE GUIDEBOOK IS NEVER WRONG!
A MILLION-DOLLAR...
...TON OF GOLD.
4-B
YOUR COIN COLLECTION'S PRETTY NEAT, EVEN IF IT'S INCOMPLETE.
A MILLION-DOLLAR...
...TON OF GOLD.

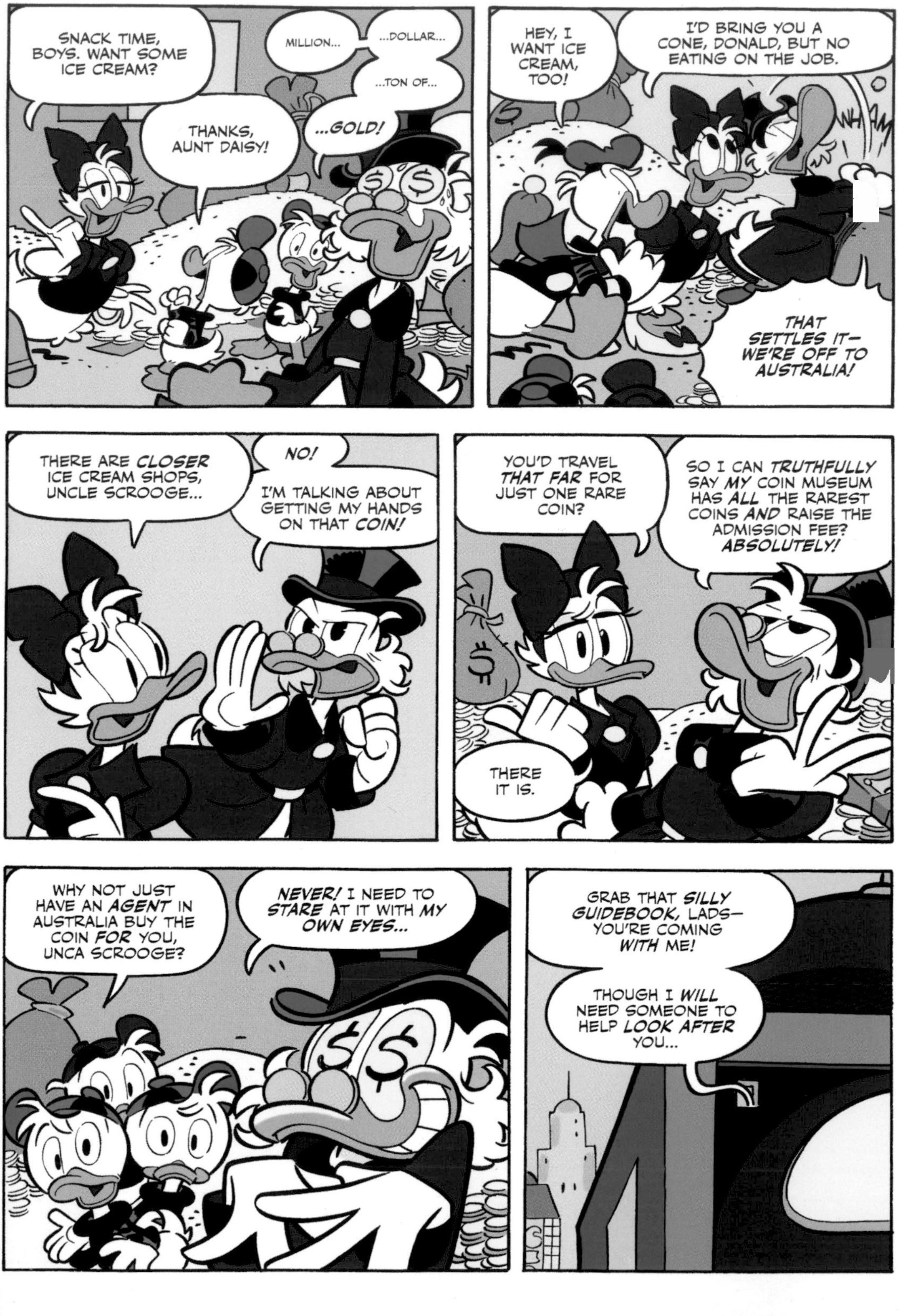
SNACK TIME, BOYS. WANT SOME ICE CREAM?
THANKS, AUNT DAISY!
MILLION...
...DOLLAR...
...TON OF...
...GOLD!
HEY, I WANT ICE CREAM, TOO!
I'D BRING YOU A CONE, DONALD, BUT NO EATING ON THE JOB.
THAT SETTLES IT— WE'RE OFF TO AUSTRALIA!
THERE ARE CLOSER ICE CREAM SHOPS, UNCLE SCROOGE...
NO!
I'M TALKING ABOUT GETTING MY HANDS ON THAT COIN!
YOU'D TRAVEL THAT FAR FOR JUST ONE RARE COIN?
SO I CAN TRUTHFULLY SAY MY COIN MUSEUM HAS ALL THE RAREST COINS AND RAISE THE ADMISSION FEE? ABSOLUTELY!
THERE IT IS.
WHY NOT JUST HAVE AN AGENT IN AUSTRALIA BUY THE COIN FOR YOU, UNCA SCROOGE?
NEVER! I NEED TO STARE AT IT WITH MY OWN EYES...
GRAB THAT SILLY GUIDEBOOK, LADS— YOU'RE COMING WITH ME!
THOUGH I WILL NEED SOMEONE TO HELP LOOK AFTER YOU...

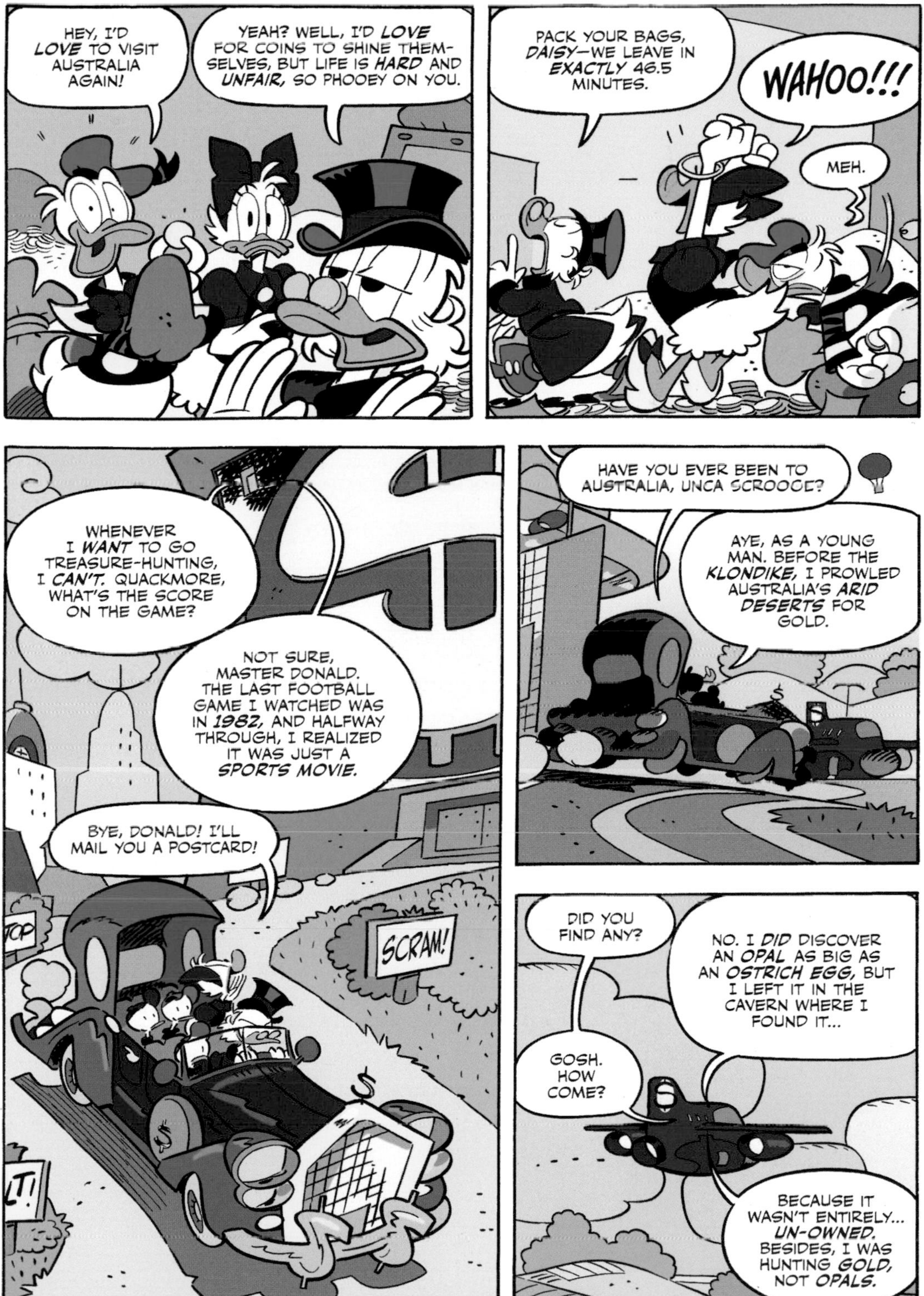

HEY, I'D LOVE TO VISIT AUSTRALIA AGAIN!
YEAH? WELL, I'D LOVE FOR COINS TO SHINE THEMSELVES, BUT LIFE IS HARD AND UNFAIR, SO PHOOEY ON YOU.
PACK YOUR BAGS, DAISY—WE LEAVE IN EXACTLY 46.5 MINUTES.
WAHOO!!!
MEH.
WHENEVER I WANT TO GO TREASURE-HUNTING, I CAN'T. QUACKMORE, WHAT'S THE SCORE ON THE GAME?
NOT SURE, MASTER DONALD. THE LAST FOOTBALL GAME I WATCHED WAS IN 1982, AND HALFWAY THROUGH, I REALIZED IT WAS JUST A SPORTS MOVIE.
BYE, DONALD! I'LL MAIL YOU A POSTCARD!
SCRAM!
HAVE YOU EVER BEEN TO AUSTRALIA, UNCA SCROOGE?
AYE, AS A YOUNG MAN. BEFORE THE KLONDIKE, I PROWLED AUSTRALIA'S ARID DESERTS FOR GOLD.
DID YOU FIND ANY?
NO. I DID DISCOVER AN OPAL AS BIG AS AN OSTRICH EGG, BUT I LEFT IT IN THE CAVERN WHERE I FOUND IT...
GOSH. HOW COME?
BECAUSE IT WASN'T ENTIRELY... UN-OWNED. BESIDES, I WAS HUNTING GOLD, NOT OPALS.

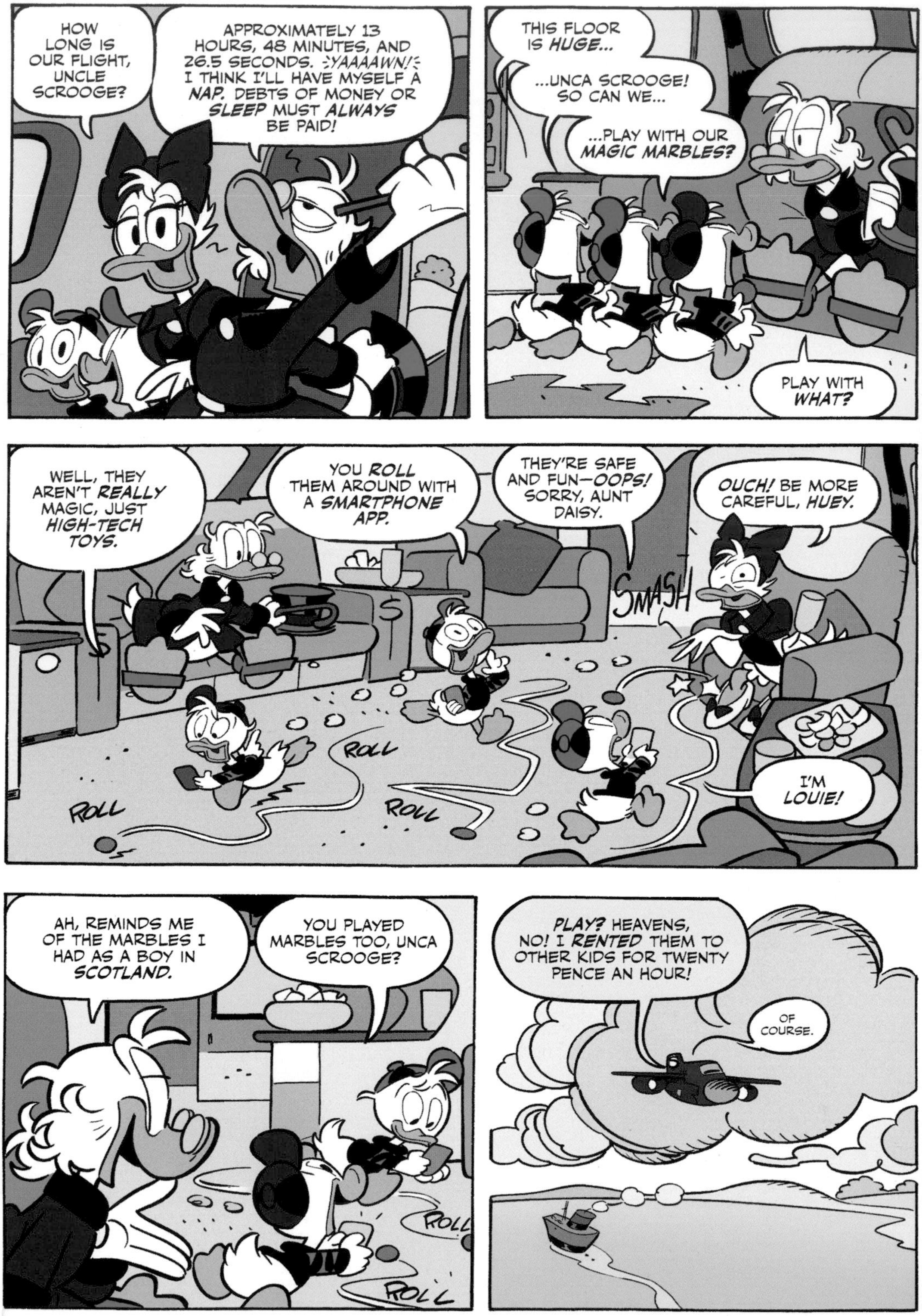
HOW LONG IS OUR FLIGHT, UNCLE SCROOGE?
APPROXIMATELY 13 HOURS, 48 MINUTES, AND 26.5 SECONDS. YAAAAWN! I THINK I'LL HAVE MYSELF A NAP. DEBTS OF MONEY OR SLEEP MUST ALWAYS BE PAID!
THIS FLOOR IS HUGE...
...UNCA SCROOGE! SO CAN WE...
...PLAY WITH OUR MAGIC MARBLES?
PLAY WITH WHAT?
WELL, THEY AREN'T REALLY MAGIC, JUST HIGH-TECH TOYS.
YOU ROLL THEM AROUND WITH A SMARTPHONE APP.
THEY'RE SAFE AND FUN—OOPS! SORRY, AUNT DAISY.
OUCH! BE MORE CAREFUL, HUEY.
SMASH
I'M LOUIE!
ROLL
ROLL
ROLL
AH, REMINDS ME OF THE MARBLES I HAD AS A BOY IN SCOTLAND.
YOU PLAYED MARBLES TOO, UNCA SCROOGE?
ROLL
ROLL
PLAY? HEAVENS, NO! I RENTED THEM TO OTHER KIDS FOR TWENTY PENCE AN HOUR!
OF COURSE.

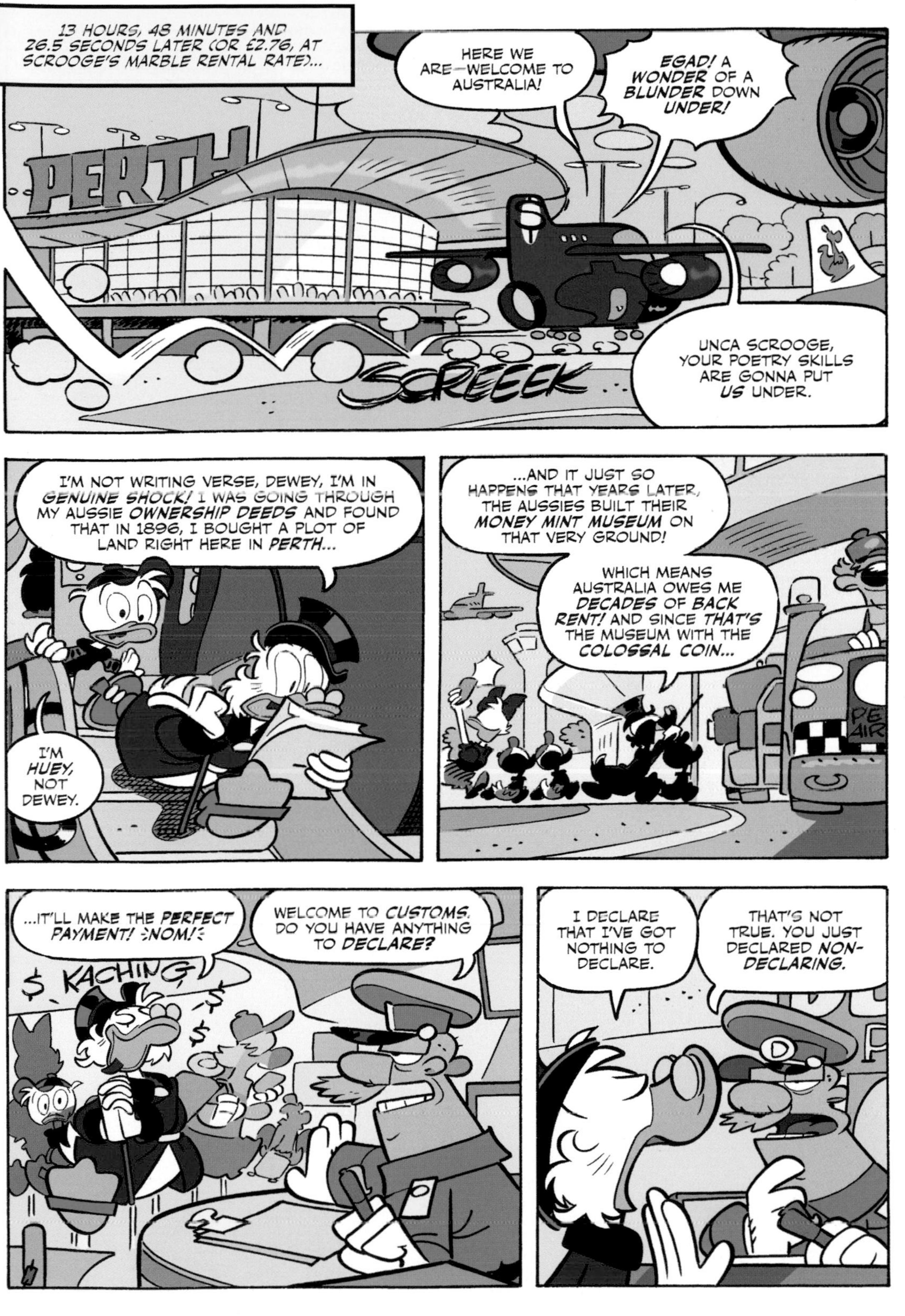
13 HOURS, 48 MINUTES AND 26.5 SECONDS LATER (OR £2.76, AT SCROOGE'S MARBLE RENTAL RATE)...
HERE WE ARE—WELCOME TO AUSTRALIA!
EGAD! A WONDER OF A BLUNDER DOWN UNDER!
PERTH
SCREEEK
UNCA SCROOGE, YOUR POETRY SKILLS ARE GONNA PUT US UNDER.
I'M NOT WRITING VERSE, DEWEY, I'M IN GENUINE SHOCK! I WAS GOING THROUGH MY AUSSIE OWNERSHIP DEEDS AND FOUND THAT IN 1896, I BOUGHT A PLOT OF LAND RIGHT HERE IN PERTH...
I'M HUEY, NOT DEWEY.
...AND IT JUST SO HAPPENS THAT YEARS LATER, THE AUSSIES BUILT THEIR MONEY MINT MUSEUM ON THAT VERY GROUND!
WHICH MEANS AUSTRALIA OWES ME DECADES OF BACK RENT! AND SINCE THAT'S THE MUSEUM WITH THE COLOSSAL COIN...
...IT'LL MAKE THE PERFECT PAYMENT! ;NOM!;
$ KACHING
WELCOME TO CUSTOMS. DO YOU HAVE ANYTHING TO DECLARE?
I DECLARE THAT I'VE GOT NOTHING TO DECLARE.
THAT'S NOT TRUE. YOU JUST DECLARED NON-DECLARING.

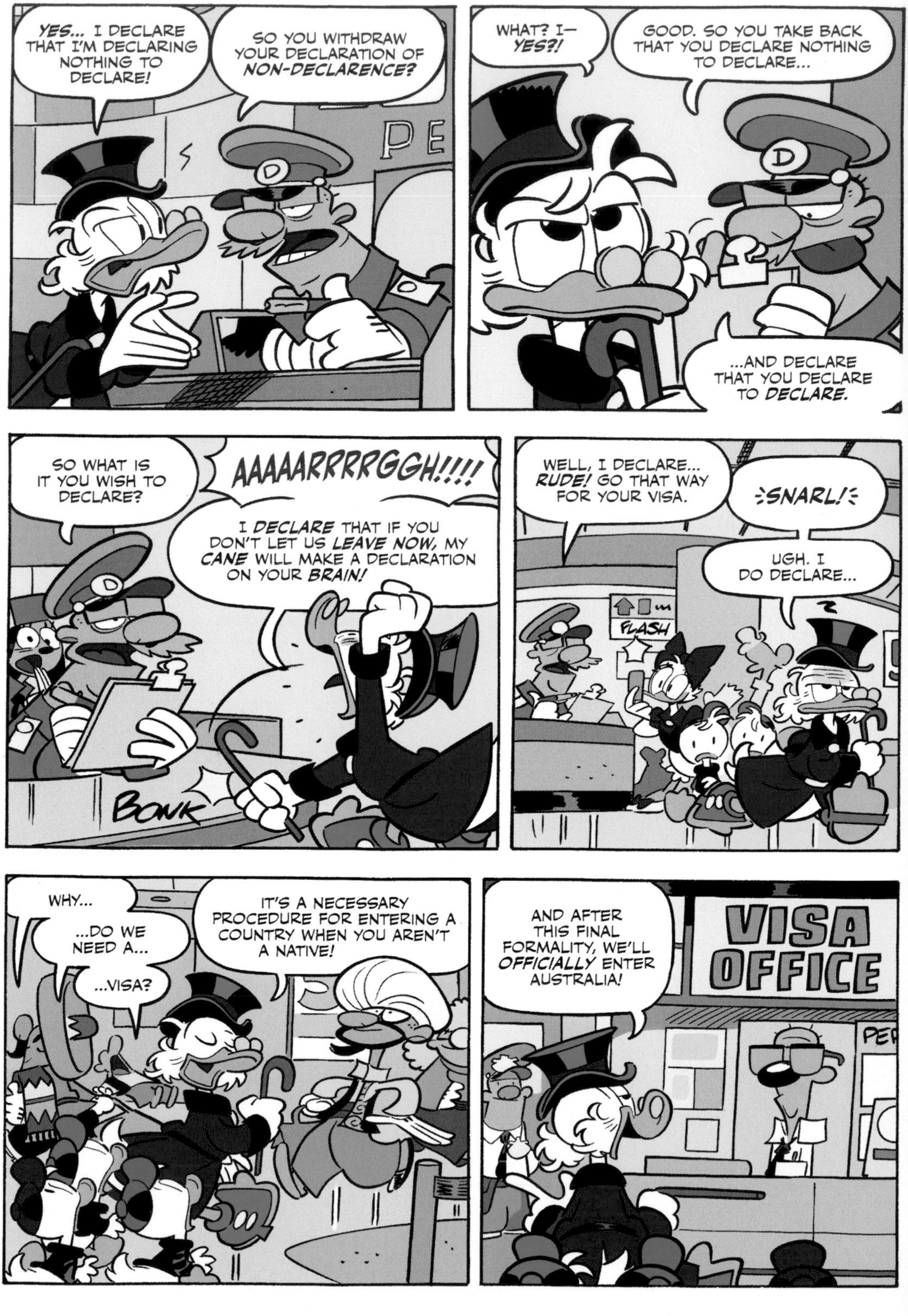
YES... I DECLARE THAT I'M DECLARING NOTHING TO DECLARE!
SO YOU WITHDRAW YOUR DECLARATION OF NON-DECLARENCE?
WHAT? I— YES?!
GOOD. SO YOU TAKE BACK THAT YOU DECLARE NOTHING TO DECLARE...
...AND DECLARE THAT YOU DECLARE TO DECLARE.
SO WHAT IS IT YOU WISH TO DECLARE?
AAAAARRRRGGH!!!!
I DECLARE THAT IF YOU DON'T LET US LEAVE NOW, MY CANE WILL MAKE A DECLARATION ON YOUR BRAIN!
BONK
WELL, I DECLARE... RUDE! GO THAT WAY FOR YOUR VISA.
SNARL!
UGH. I DO DECLARE...
FLASH
WHY...
...DO WE NEED A...
...VISA?
IT'S A NECESSARY PROCEDURE FOR ENTERING A COUNTRY WHEN YOU AREN'T A NATIVE!
AND AFTER THIS FINAL FORMALITY, WE'LL OFFICIALLY ENTER AUSTRALIA!
VISA OFFICE

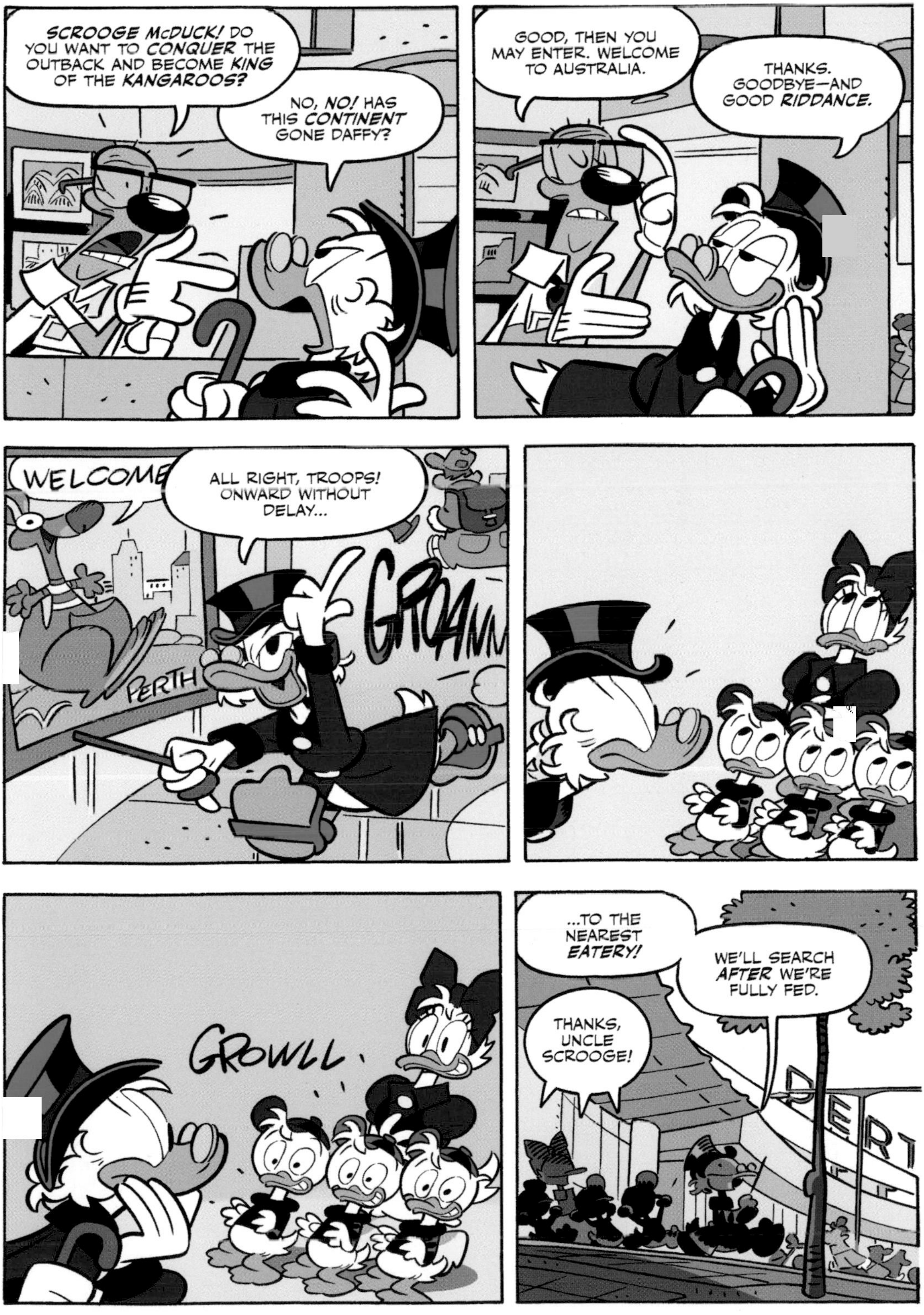
SCROOGE McDUCK! DO YOU WANT TO CONQUER THE OUTBACK AND BECOME KING OF THE KANGAROOS?
NO, NO! HAS THIS CONTINENT GONE DAFFY?
GOOD, THEN YOU MAY ENTER. WELCOME TO AUSTRALIA.
THANKS. GOODBYE—AND GOOD RIDDANCE.
WELCOME
PERTH
ALL RIGHT, TROOPS! ONWARD WITHOUT DELAY...
GROANN
GROWLL
...TO THE NEAREST EATERY!
WE'LL SEARCH AFTER WE'RE FULLY FED.
THANKS, UNCLE SCROOGE!
PERT

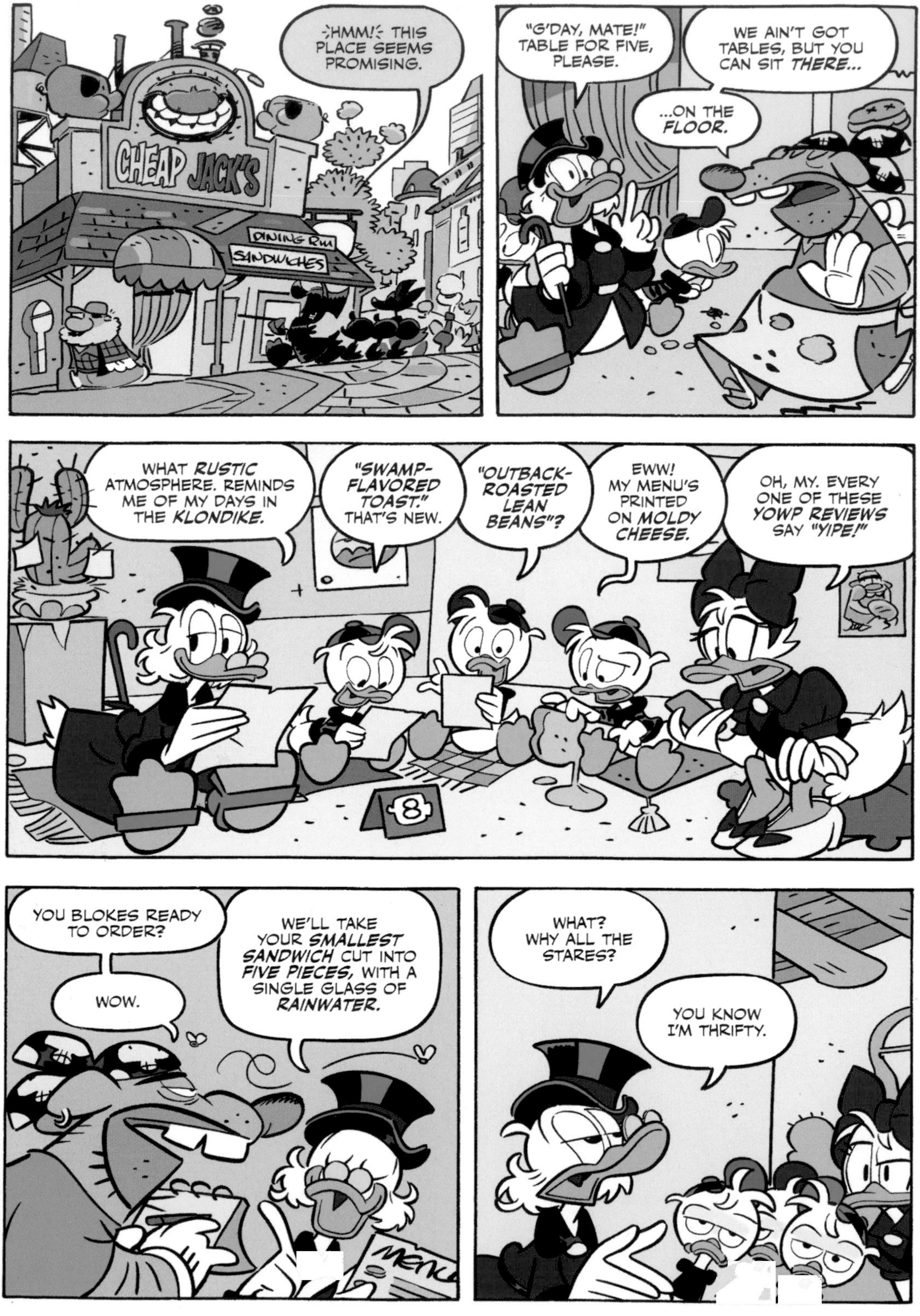
CHEAP JACK'S
DINING RM
SANDWICHES
-HMM!- THIS PLACE SEEMS PROMISING.
"G'DAY, MATE!" TABLE FOR FIVE, PLEASE.
WE AIN'T GOT TABLES, BUT YOU CAN SIT *THERE...*
...ON THE *FLOOR.*
WHAT *RUSTIC* ATMOSPHERE. REMINDS ME OF MY DAYS IN THE *KLONDIKE.*
"SWAMP-FLAVORED TOAST." THAT'S NEW.
"OUTBACK-ROASTED LEAN BEANS"?
EWW! MY MENU'S PRINTED ON *MOLDY CHEESE.*
OH, MY. EVERY ONE OF THESE *YOWP REVIEWS* SAY *"YIPE!"*
8
YOU BLOKES READY TO ORDER?
WOW.
WE'LL TAKE YOUR *SMALLEST SANDWICH* CUT INTO *FIVE PIECES,* WITH A SINGLE GLASS OF *RAINWATER.*
MENU
WHAT? WHY ALL THE STARES?
YOU KNOW I'M THRIFTY.

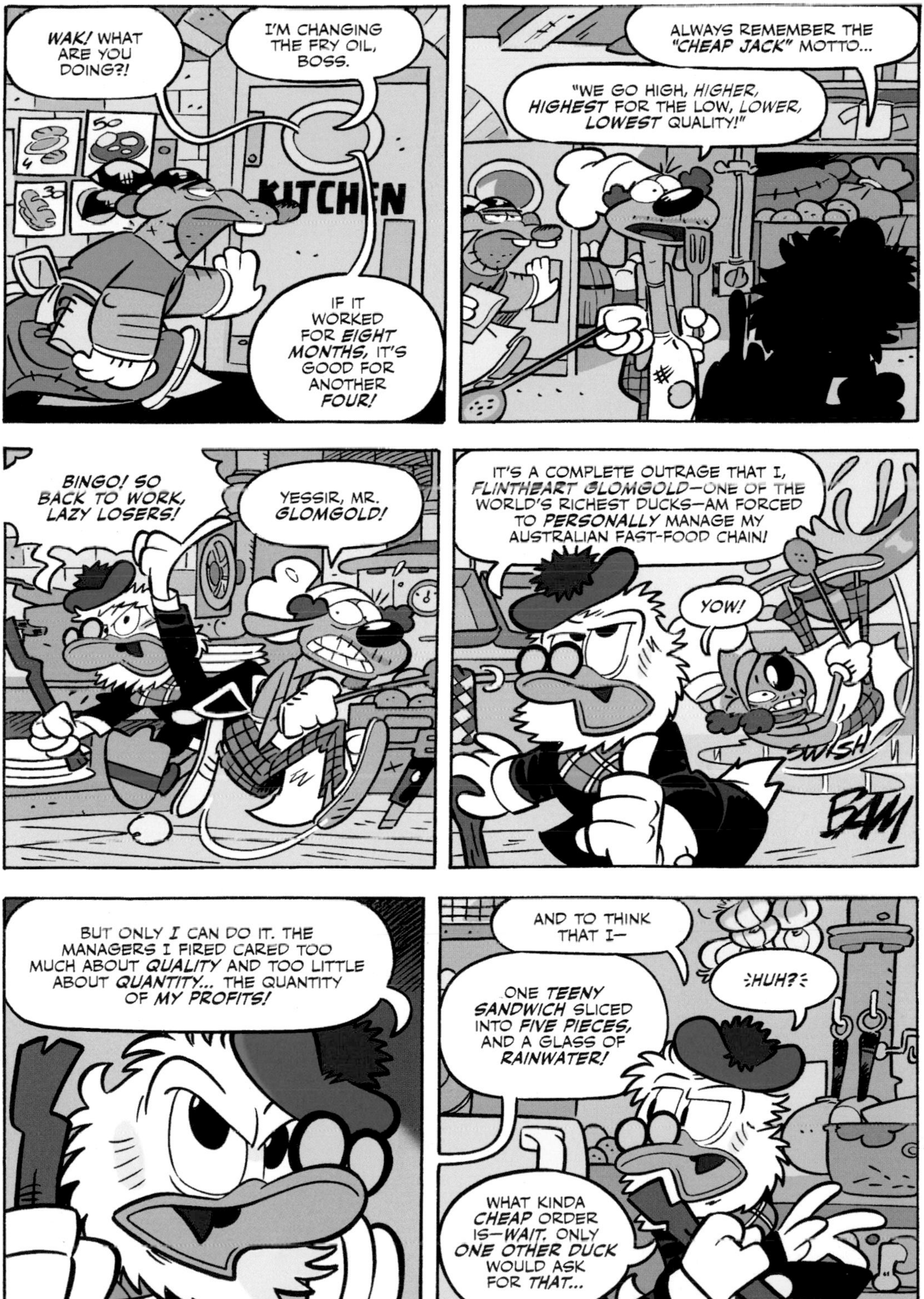
WAK! WHAT ARE YOU DOING?!
I'M CHANGING THE FRY OIL, BOSS.
IF IT WORKED FOR EIGHT MONTHS, IT'S GOOD FOR ANOTHER FOUR!
KITCHEN
ALWAYS REMEMBER THE "CHEAP JACK" MOTTO...
"WE GO HIGH, HIGHER, HIGHEST FOR THE LOW, LOWER, LOWEST QUALITY!"
BINGO! SO BACK TO WORK, LAZY LOSERS!
YESSIR, MR. GLOMGOLD!
IT'S A COMPLETE OUTRAGE THAT I, FLINTHEART GLOMGOLD—ONE OF THE WORLD'S RICHEST DUCKS—AM FORCED TO PERSONALLY MANAGE MY AUSTRALIAN FAST-FOOD CHAIN!
YOW!
SWISH
BAM
BUT ONLY I CAN DO IT. THE MANAGERS I FIRED CARED TOO MUCH ABOUT QUALITY AND TOO LITTLE ABOUT QUANTITY... THE QUANTITY OF MY PROFITS!
AND TO THINK THAT I—
ONE TEENY SANDWICH SLICED INTO FIVE PIECES, AND A GLASS OF RAINWATER!
HUH?
WHAT KINDA CHEAP ORDER IS—WAIT. ONLY ONE OTHER DUCK WOULD ASK FOR THAT...

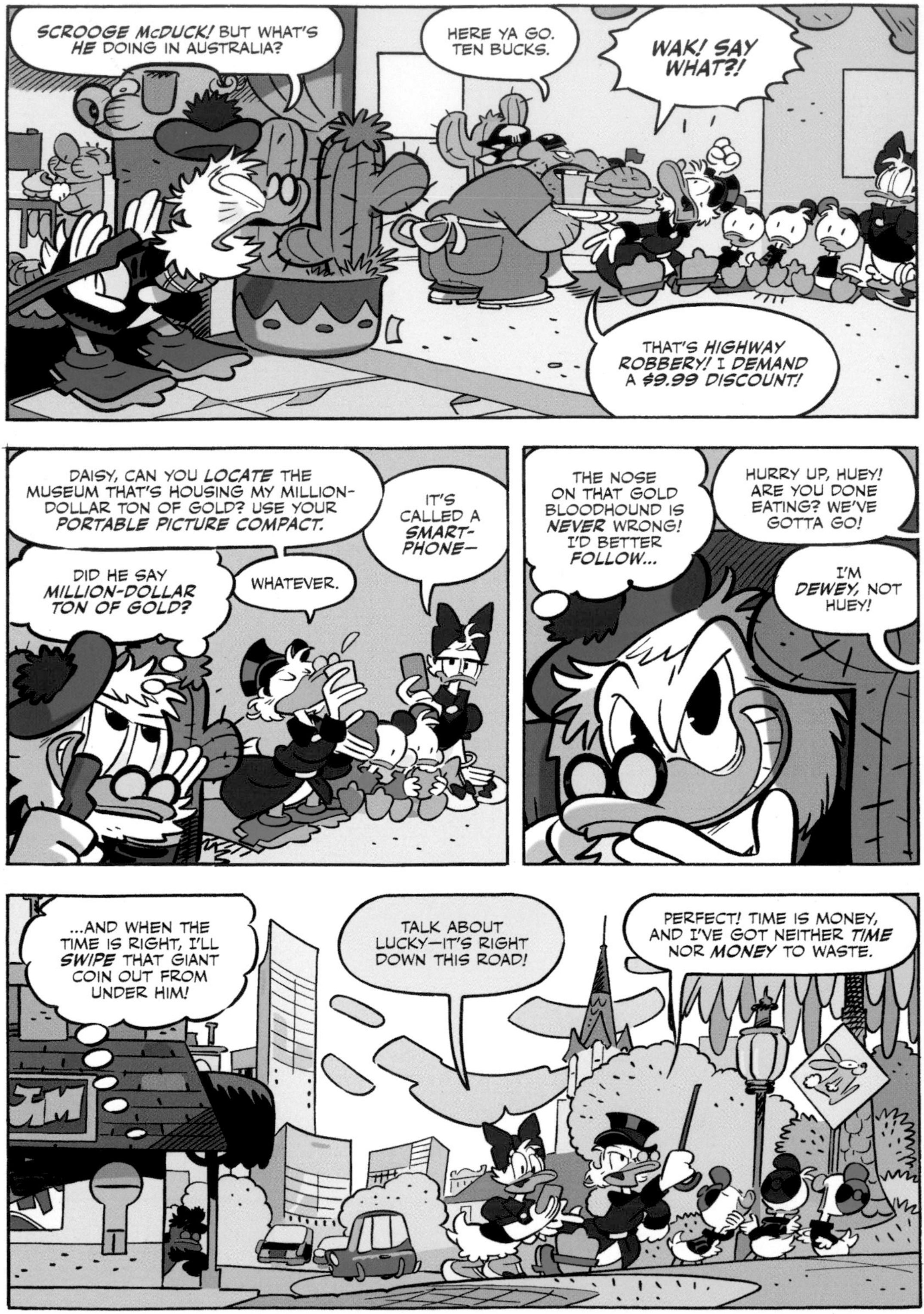
SCROOGE McDUCK! BUT WHAT'S HE DOING IN AUSTRALIA?
HERE YA GO. TEN BUCKS.
WAK! SAY WHAT?!
THAT'S HIGHWAY ROBBERY! I DEMAND A $9.99 DISCOUNT!
DAISY, CAN YOU LOCATE THE MUSEUM THAT'S HOUSING MY MILLION-DOLLAR TON OF GOLD? USE YOUR PORTABLE PICTURE COMPACT.
IT'S CALLED A SMART-PHONE—
DID HE SAY MILLION-DOLLAR TON OF GOLD?
WHATEVER.
THE NOSE ON THAT GOLD BLOODHOUND IS NEVER WRONG! I'D BETTER FOLLOW...
HURRY UP, HUEY! ARE YOU DONE EATING? WE'VE GOTTA GO!
I'M DEWEY, NOT HUEY!
...AND WHEN THE TIME IS RIGHT, I'LL SWIPE THAT GIANT COIN OUT FROM UNDER HIM!
TALK ABOUT LUCKY—IT'S RIGHT DOWN THIS ROAD!
PERFECT! TIME IS MONEY, AND I'VE GOT NEITHER TIME NOR MONEY TO WASTE.

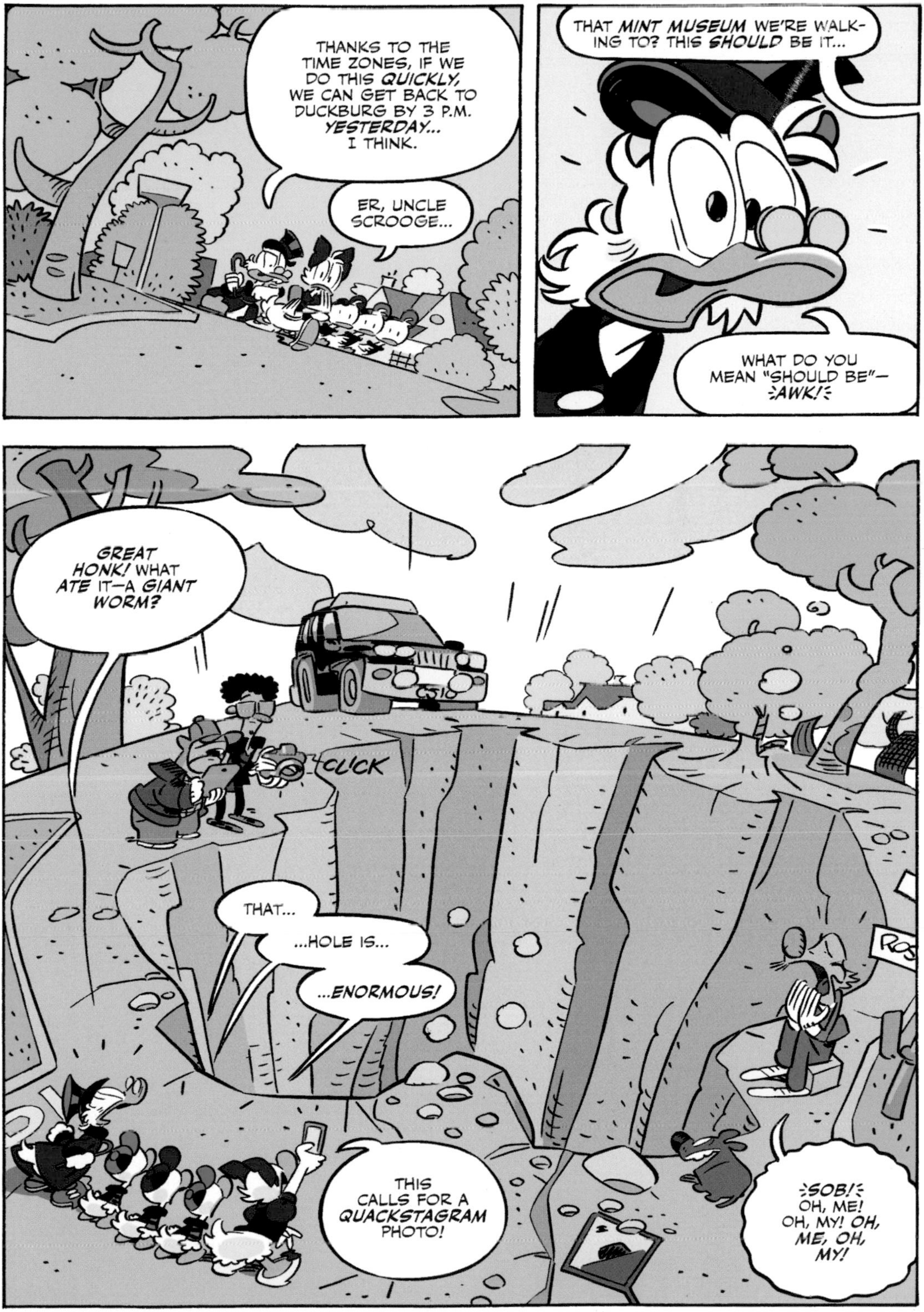
THANKS TO THE TIME ZONES, IF WE DO THIS QUICKLY, WE CAN GET BACK TO DUCKBURG BY 3 P.M. YESTERDAY... I THINK.
ER, UNCLE SCROOGE...
THAT MINT MUSEUM WE'RE WALKING TO? THIS SHOULD BE IT...
WHAT DO YOU MEAN "SHOULD BE"— AWK!
GREAT HONK! WHAT ATE IT—A GIANT WORM?
CLICK
THAT...
...HOLE IS...
...ENORMOUS!
THIS CALLS FOR A QUACKSTAGRAM PHOTO!
SOB! OH, ME! OH, MY! OH, ME, OH, MY!

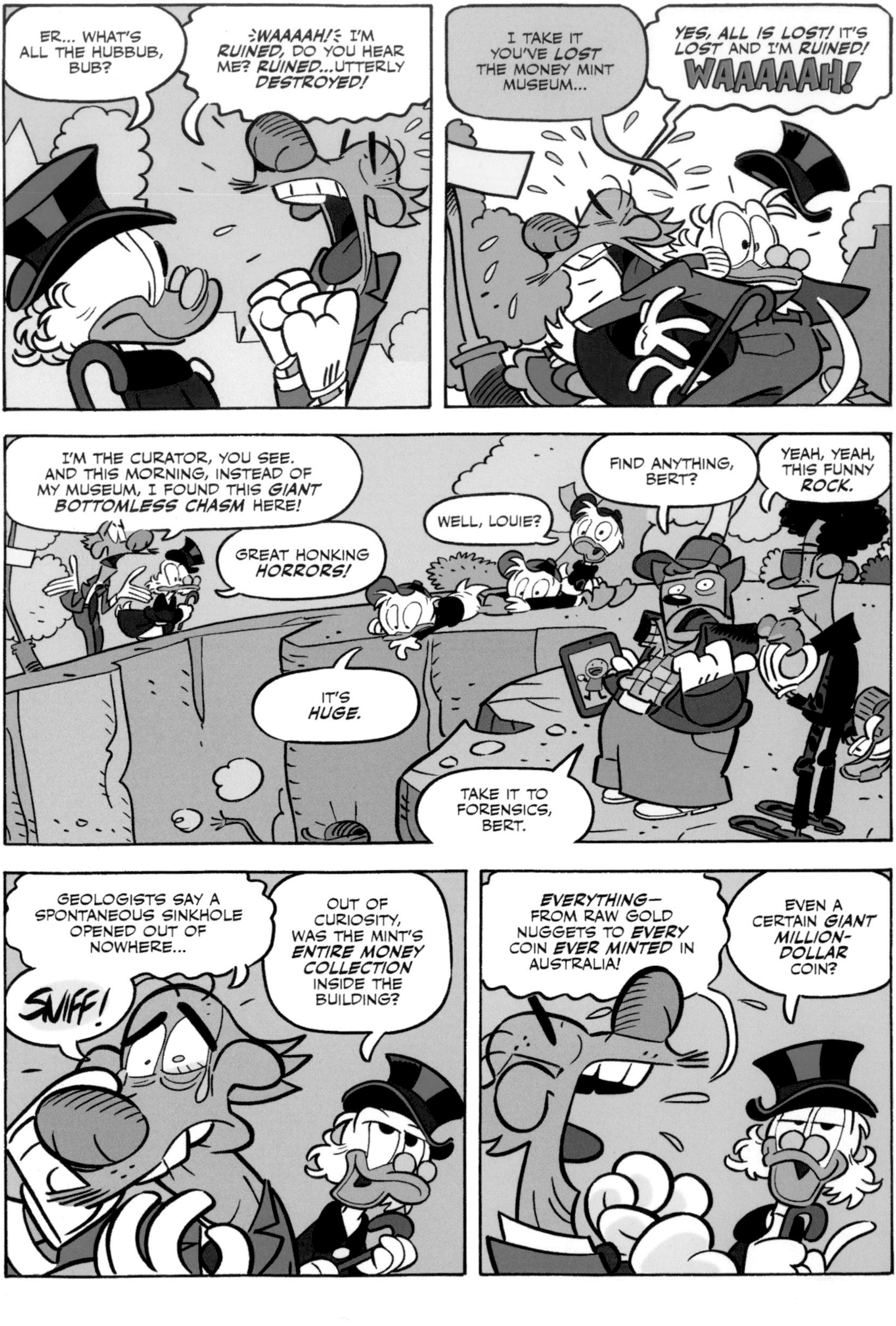
ER... WHAT'S ALL THE HUBBUB, BUB?
WAAAAH! I'M RUINED, DO YOU HEAR ME? RUINED...UTTERLY DESTROYED!
I TAKE IT YOU'VE LOST THE MONEY MINT MUSEUM...
YES, ALL IS LOST! IT'S LOST AND I'M RUINED!
WAAAAAH!
I'M THE CURATOR, YOU SEE. AND THIS MORNING, INSTEAD OF MY MUSEUM, I FOUND THIS GIANT BOTTOMLESS CHASM HERE!
GREAT HONKING HORRORS!
WELL, LOUIE?
IT'S HUGE.
FIND ANYTHING, BERT?
YEAH, YEAH, THIS FUNNY ROCK.
TAKE IT TO FORENSICS, BERT.
GEOLOGISTS SAY A SPONTANEOUS SINKHOLE OPENED OUT OF NOWHERE...
SNIFF!
OUT OF CURIOSITY, WAS THE MINT'S ENTIRE MONEY COLLECTION INSIDE THE BUILDING?
EVERYTHING— FROM RAW GOLD NUGGETS TO EVERY COIN EVER MINTED IN AUSTRALIA!
EVEN A CERTAIN GIANT MILLION-DOLLAR COIN?

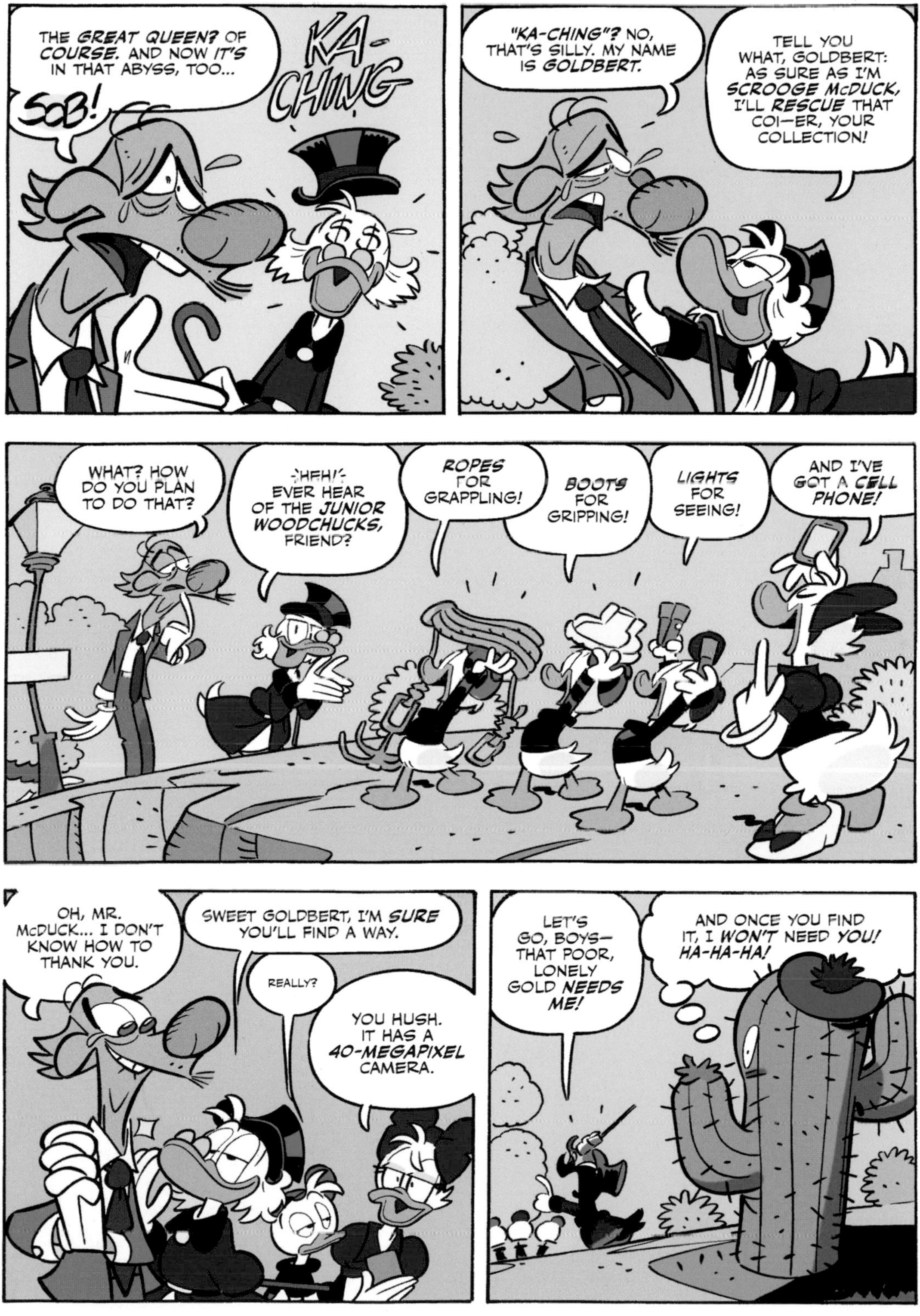

THE GREAT QUEEN? OF COURSE. AND NOW IT'S IN THAT ABYSS, TOO...
SOB!
KA-CHING
"KA-CHING"? NO, THAT'S SILLY. MY NAME IS GOLDBERT.
TELL YOU WHAT, GOLDBERT: AS SURE AS I'M SCROOGE McDUCK, I'LL RESCUE THAT COI—ER, YOUR COLLECTION!
WHAT? HOW DO YOU PLAN TO DO THAT?
-HEH!- EVER HEAR OF THE JUNIOR WOODCHUCKS, FRIEND?
ROPES FOR GRAPPLING!
BOOTS FOR GRIPPING!
LIGHTS FOR SEEING!
AND I'VE GOT A CELL PHONE!
OH, MR. McDUCK... I DON'T KNOW HOW TO THANK YOU.
SWEET GOLDBERT, I'M SURE YOU'LL FIND A WAY.
REALLY?
YOU HUSH. IT HAS A 40-MEGAPIXEL CAMERA.
LET'S GO, BOYS— THAT POOR, LONELY GOLD NEEDS ME!
AND ONCE YOU FIND IT, I WON'T NEED YOU! HA-HA-HA!

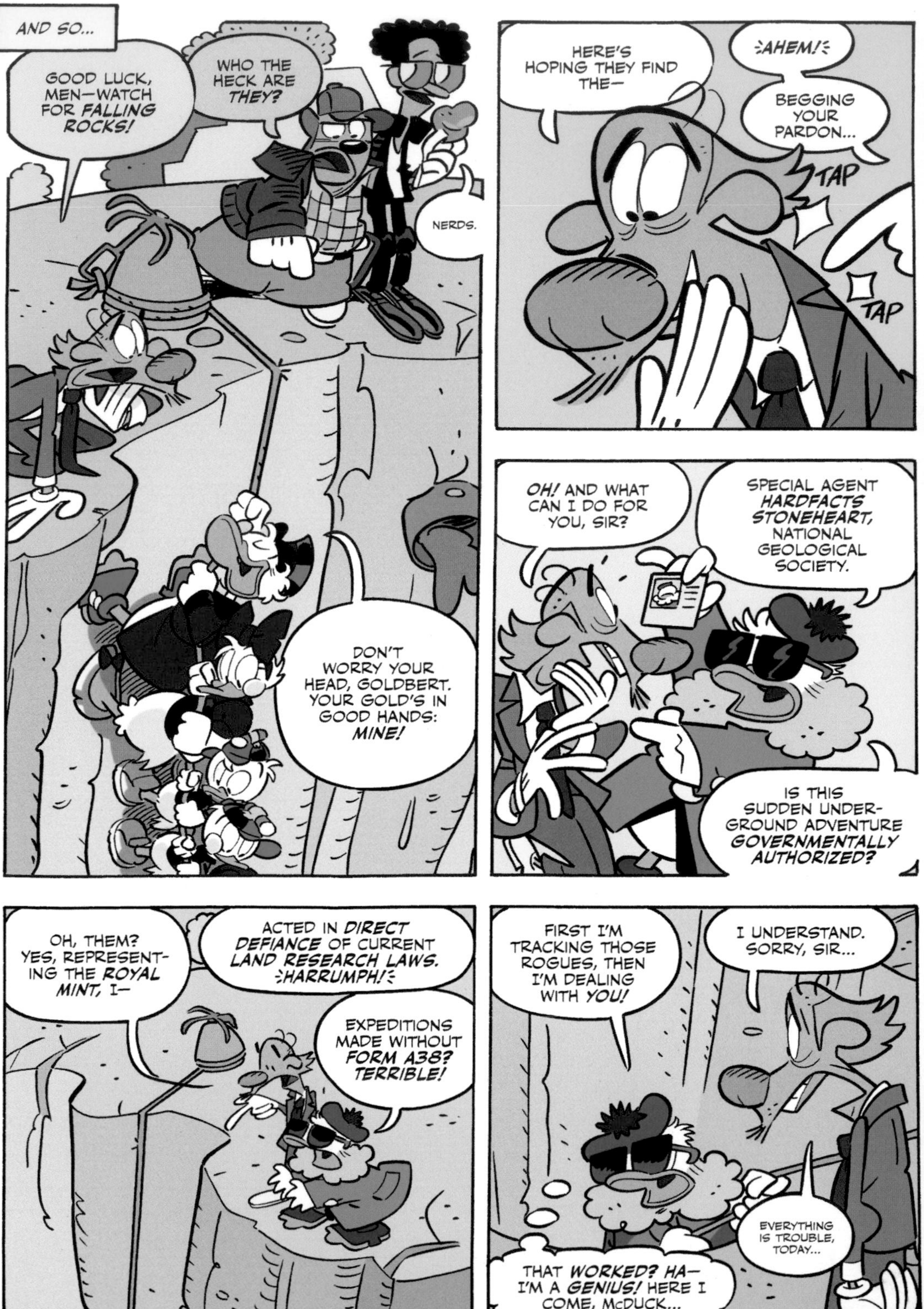
AND SO...
GOOD LUCK, MEN—WATCH FOR FALLING ROCKS!
WHO THE HECK ARE THEY?
NERDS.
DON'T WORRY YOUR HEAD, GOLDBERT. YOUR GOLD'S IN GOOD HANDS: MINE!
HERE'S HOPING THEY FIND THE—
AHEM!
BEGGING YOUR PARDON...
TAP
TAP
OH! AND WHAT CAN I DO FOR YOU, SIR?
SPECIAL AGENT HARDFACTS STONEHEART, NATIONAL GEOLOGICAL SOCIETY.
IS THIS SUDDEN UNDER-GROUND ADVENTURE GOVERNMENTALLY AUTHORIZED?
OH, THEM? YES, REPRESENT-ING THE ROYAL MINT, I—
ACTED IN DIRECT DEFIANCE OF CURRENT LAND RESEARCH LAWS. HARRUMPH!
EXPEDITIONS MADE WITHOUT FORM A38? TERRIBLE!
FIRST I'M TRACKING THOSE ROGUES, THEN I'M DEALING WITH YOU!
I UNDERSTAND. SORRY, SIR...
EVERYTHING IS TROUBLE, TODAY...
THAT WORKED? HA—I'M A GENIUS! HERE I COME, McDUCK...

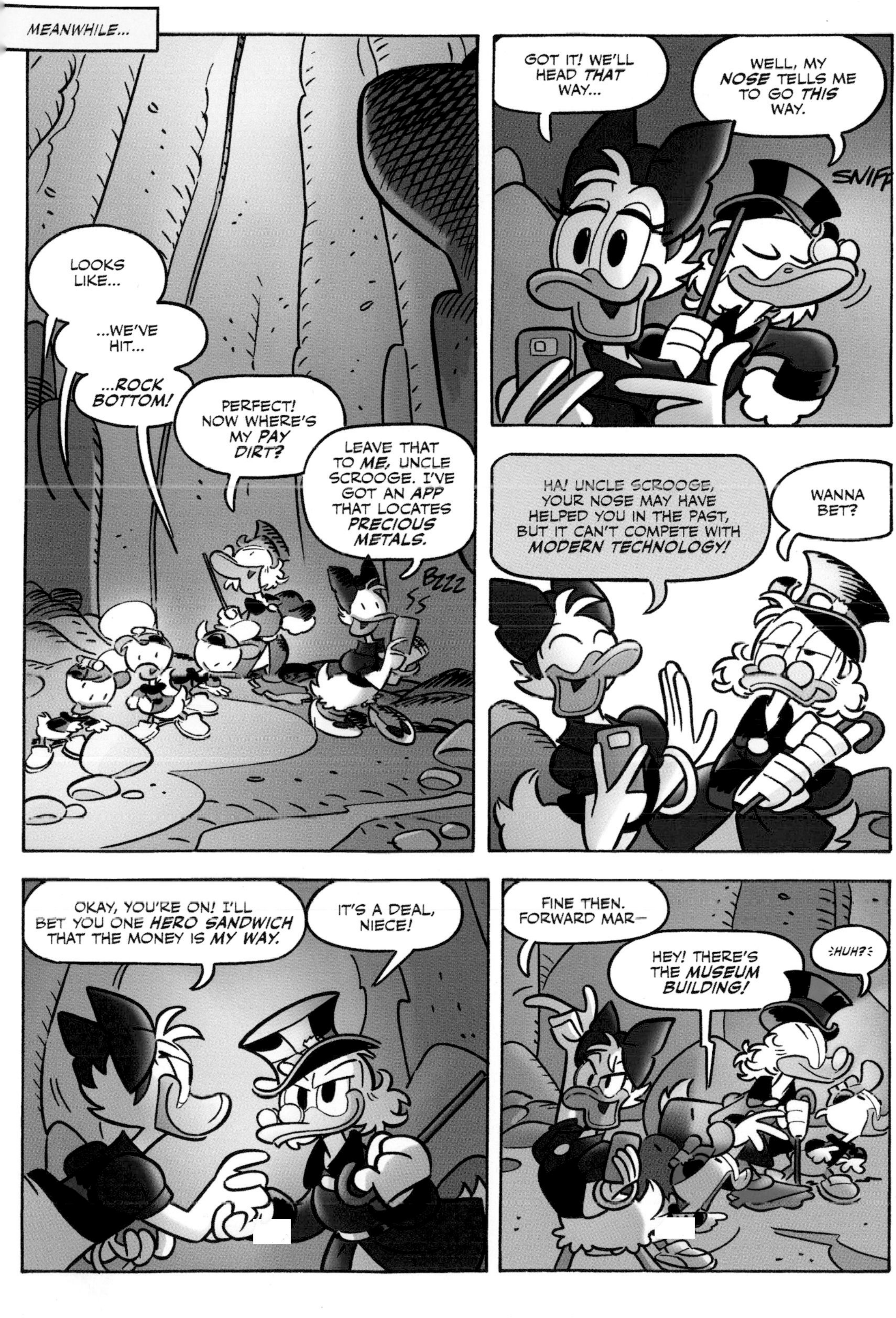
MEANWHILE...
LOOKS LIKE...
...WE'VE HIT...
...ROCK BOTTOM!
PERFECT! NOW WHERE'S MY PAY DIRT?
LEAVE THAT TO ME, UNCLE SCROOGE. I'VE GOT AN APP THAT LOCATES PRECIOUS METALS.
BZZZ
GOT IT! WE'LL HEAD THAT WAY...
WELL, MY NOSE TELLS ME TO GO THIS WAY.
SNIFF
HA! UNCLE SCROOGE, YOUR NOSE MAY HAVE HELPED YOU IN THE PAST, BUT IT CAN'T COMPETE WITH MODERN TECHNOLOGY!
WANNA BET?
OKAY, YOU'RE ON! I'LL BET YOU ONE HERO SANDWICH THAT THE MONEY IS MY WAY.
IT'S A DEAL, NIECE!
FINE THEN. FORWARD MAR—
HEY! THERE'S THE MUSEUM BUILDING!
HUH?

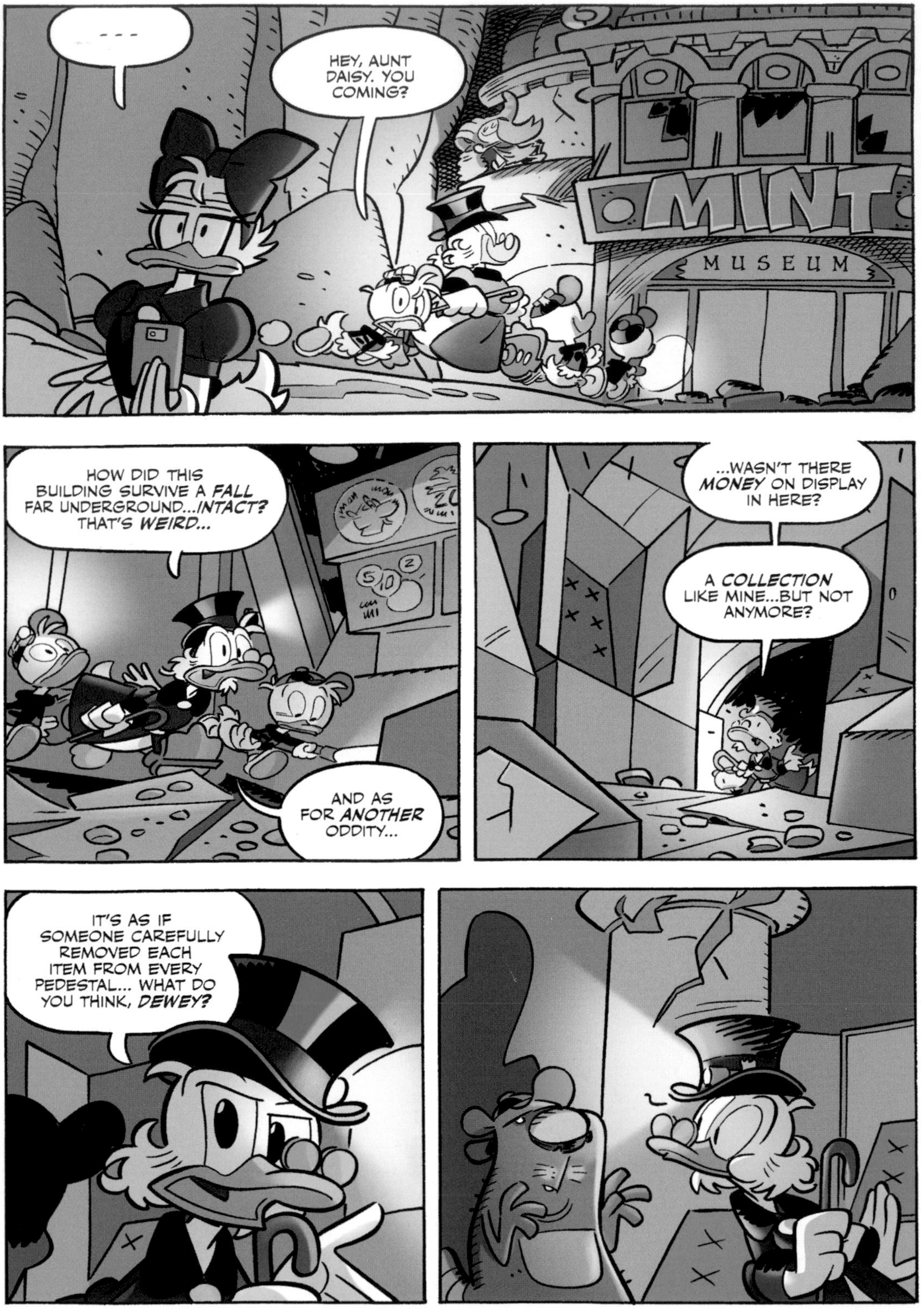
- - -
HEY, AUNT DAISY. YOU COMING?
MINT
MUSEUM
HOW DID THIS BUILDING SURVIVE A *FALL* FAR UNDERGROUND...*INTACT?* THAT'S *WEIRD...*
AND AS FOR *ANOTHER* ODDITY...
...WASN'T THERE *MONEY* ON DISPLAY IN HERE?
A *COLLECTION* LIKE MINE...BUT NOT ANYMORE?
IT'S AS IF SOMEONE CAREFULLY REMOVED EACH ITEM FROM EVERY PEDESTAL... WHAT DO YOU THINK, *DEWEY?*

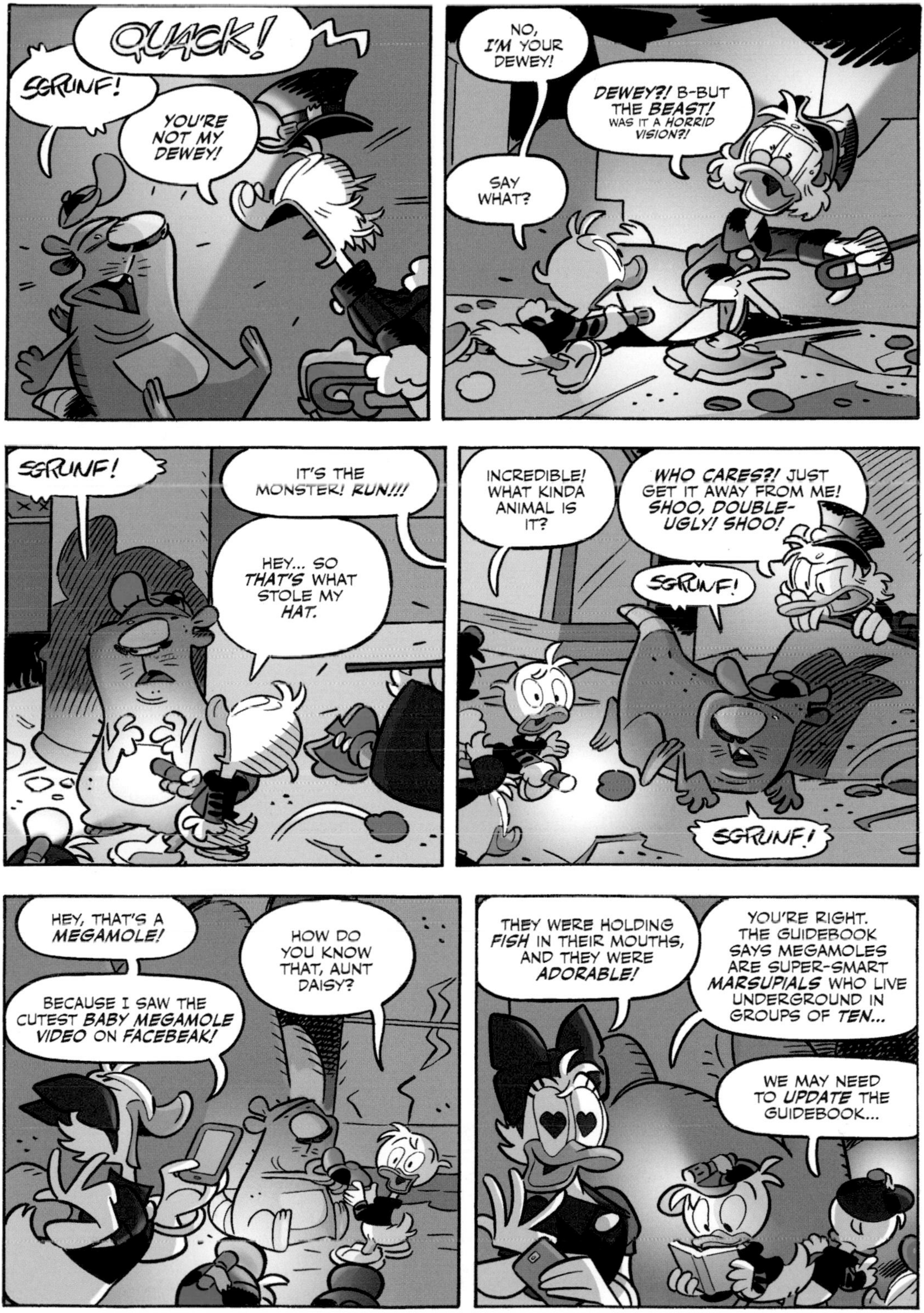
QUACK!
SGRUNF!
YOU'RE NOT MY DEWEY!
NO, I'M YOUR DEWEY!
DEWEY?! B-BUT THE BEAST! WAS IT A HORRID VISION?!
SAY WHAT?
SGRUNF!
IT'S THE MONSTER! RUN!!!
HEY... SO THAT'S WHAT STOLE MY HAT.
INCREDIBLE! WHAT KINDA ANIMAL IS IT?
WHO CARES?! JUST GET IT AWAY FROM ME! SHOO, DOUBLE-UGLY! SHOO!
SGRUNF!
SGRUNF!
HEY, THAT'S A MEGAMOLE!
HOW DO YOU KNOW THAT, AUNT DAISY?
BECAUSE I SAW THE CUTEST BABY MEGAMOLE VIDEO ON FACEBEAK!
THEY WERE HOLDING FISH IN THEIR MOUTHS, AND THEY WERE ADORABLE!
YOU'RE RIGHT. THE GUIDEBOOK SAYS MEGAMOLES ARE SUPER-SMART MARSUPIALS WHO LIVE UNDERGROUND IN GROUPS OF TEN...
WE MAY NEED TO UPDATE THE GUIDEBOOK...

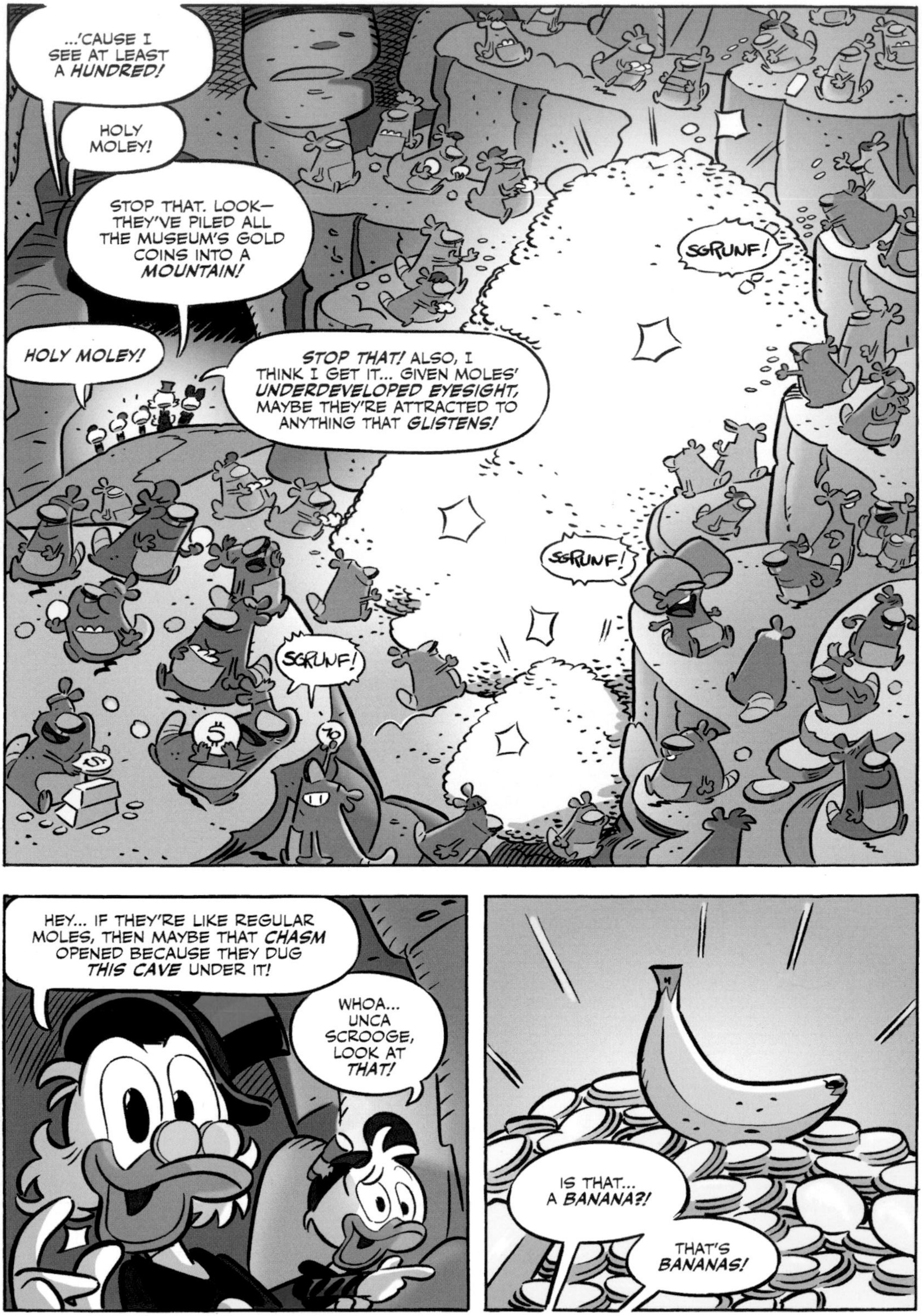
...'CAUSE I SEE AT LEAST A *HUNDRED!*
HOLY MOLEY!
STOP THAT. LOOK— THEY'VE PILED ALL THE MUSEUM'S GOLD COINS INTO A *MOUNTAIN!*
HOLY MOLEY!
STOP THAT! ALSO, I THINK I GET IT... GIVEN MOLES' *UNDERDEVELOPED EYESIGHT,* MAYBE THEY'RE ATTRACTED TO ANYTHING THAT *GLISTENS!*
SGRUNF!
SGRUNF!
SGRUNF!
HEY... IF THEY'RE LIKE REGULAR MOLES, THEN MAYBE THAT *CHASM* OPENED BECAUSE THEY DUG *THIS CAVE* UNDER IT!
WHOA... UNCA SCROOGE, LOOK AT *THAT!*
IS THAT... A *BANANA?!*
THAT'S *BANANAS!*

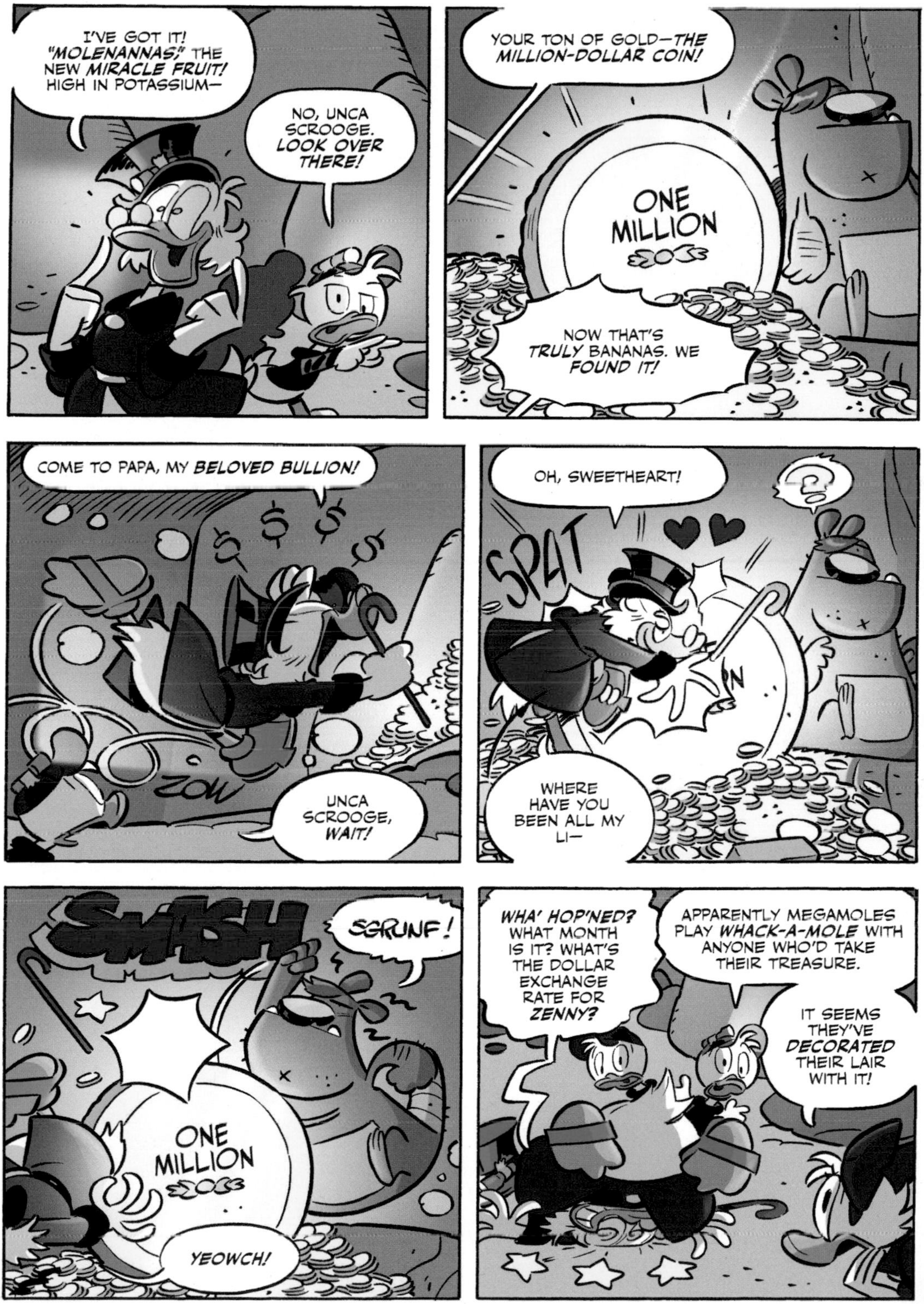
I'VE GOT IT! "MOLENANNAS," THE NEW MIRACLE FRUIT! HIGH IN POTASSIUM—
NO, UNCA SCROOGE. LOOK OVER THERE!
YOUR TON OF GOLD—THE MILLION-DOLLAR COIN!
ONE MILLION
NOW THAT'S TRULY BANANAS. WE FOUND IT!
COME TO PAPA, MY BELOVED BULLION!
ZOW
UNCA SCROOGE, WAIT!
OH, SWEETHEART!
SPAT
WHERE HAVE YOU BEEN ALL MY LI—
SMASH
SGRUNF!
ONE MILLION
YEOWCH!
WHA' HOP'NED? WHAT MONTH IS IT? WHAT'S THE DOLLAR EXCHANGE RATE FOR ZENNY?
APPARENTLY MEGAMOLES PLAY WHACK-A-MOLE WITH ANYONE WHO'D TAKE THEIR TREASURE.
IT SEEMS THEY'VE DECORATED THEIR LAIR WITH IT!

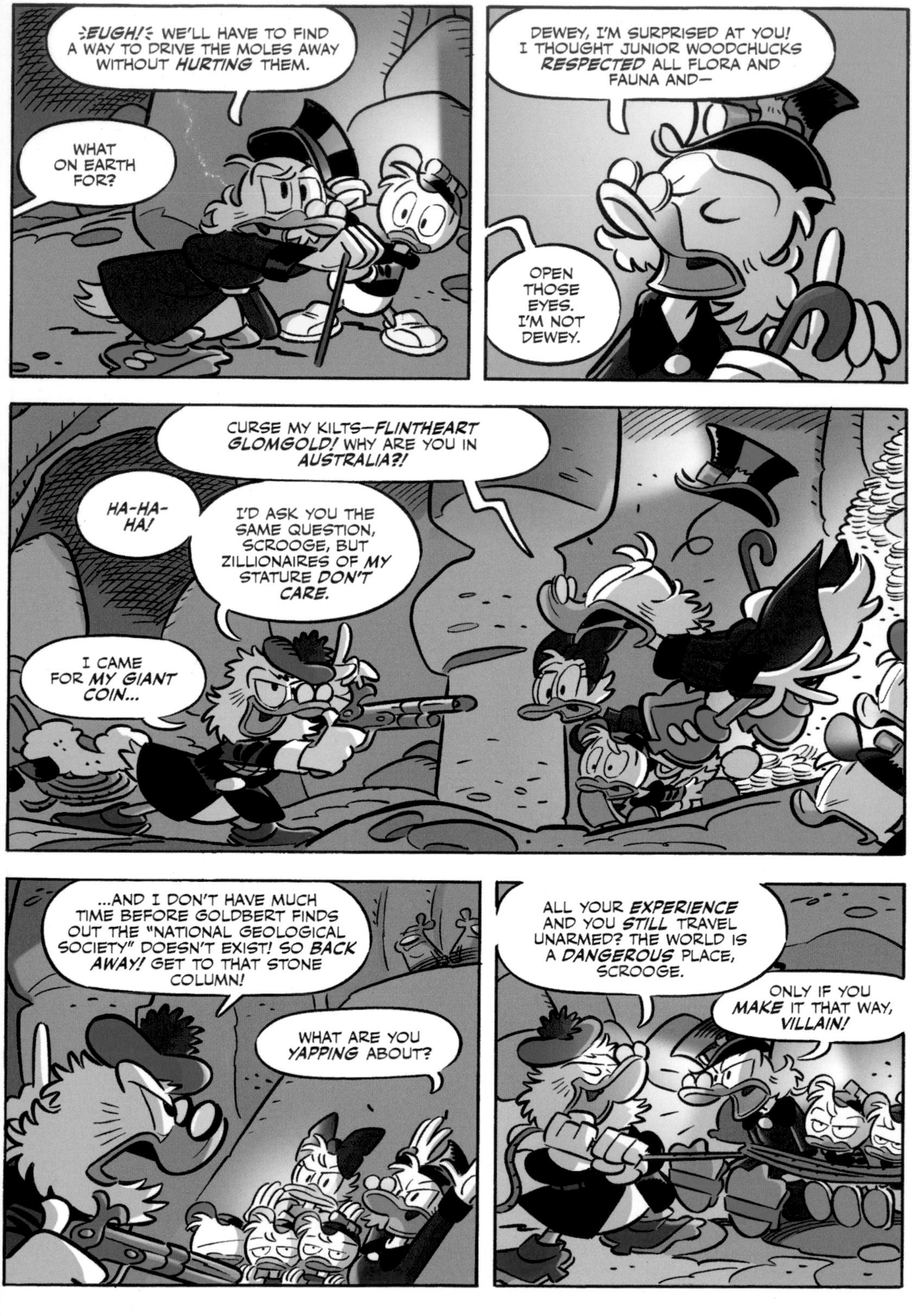

EUGH! WE'LL HAVE TO FIND A WAY TO DRIVE THE MOLES AWAY WITHOUT HURTING THEM.
WHAT ON EARTH FOR?
DEWEY, I'M SURPRISED AT YOU! I THOUGHT JUNIOR WOODCHUCKS RESPECTED ALL FLORA AND FAUNA AND—
OPEN THOSE EYES. I'M NOT DEWEY.
CURSE MY KILTS—FLINTHEART GLOMGOLD! WHY ARE YOU IN AUSTRALIA?!
HA-HA-HA!
I'D ASK YOU THE SAME QUESTION, SCROOGE, BUT ZILLIONAIRES OF MY STATURE DON'T CARE.
I CAME FOR MY GIANT COIN...
...AND I DON'T HAVE MUCH TIME BEFORE GOLDBERT FINDS OUT THE "NATIONAL GEOLOGICAL SOCIETY" DOESN'T EXIST! SO BACK AWAY! GET TO THAT STONE COLUMN!
WHAT ARE YOU YAPPING ABOUT?
ALL YOUR EXPERIENCE AND YOU STILL TRAVEL UNARMED? THE WORLD IS A DANGEROUS PLACE, SCROOGE.
ONLY IF YOU MAKE IT THAT WAY, VILLAIN!

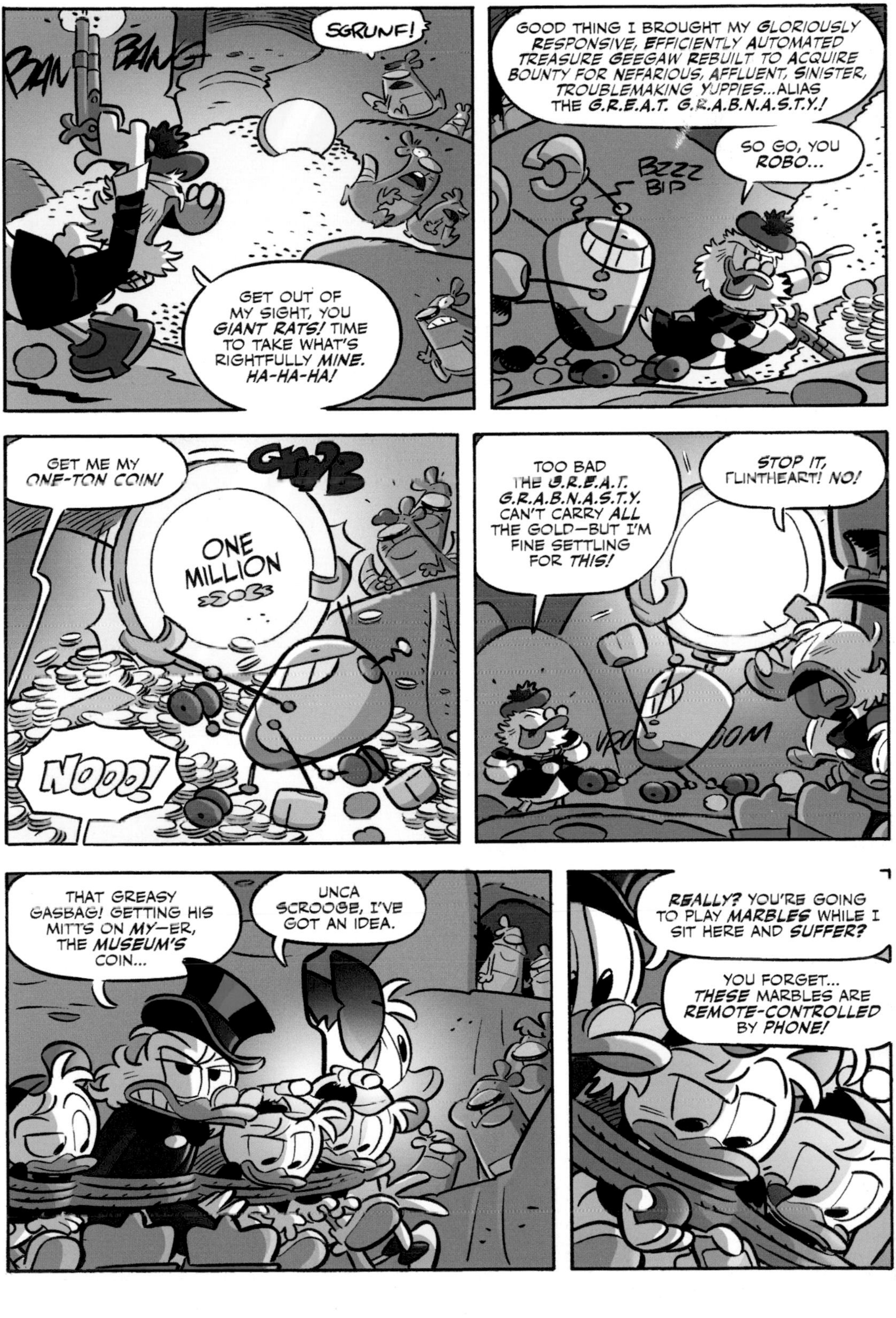
BAN BANG
SGRUNF!
GET OUT OF MY SIGHT, YOU GIANT RATS! TIME TO TAKE WHAT'S RIGHTFULLY MINE. HA-HA-HA!
GOOD THING I BROUGHT MY GLORIOUSLY RESPONSIVE, EFFICIENTLY AUTOMATED TREASURE GEEGAW REBUILT TO ACQUIRE BOUNTY FOR NEFARIOUS, AFFLUENT, SINISTER, TROUBLEMAKING YUPPIES...ALIAS THE G.R.E.A.T. G.R.A.B.N.A.S.T.Y.!
SO GO, YOU ROBO...
BZZZ BIP
GET ME MY ONE-TON COIN!
ONE MILLION
NOOO!
TOO BAD THE G.R.E.A.T. G.R.A.B.N.A.S.T.Y. CAN'T CARRY ALL THE GOLD—BUT I'M FINE SETTLING FOR THIS!
STOP IT, FLINTHEART! NO!
THAT GREASY GASBAG! GETTING HIS MITTS ON MY—ER, THE MUSEUM'S COIN...
UNCA SCROOGE, I'VE GOT AN IDEA.
REALLY? YOU'RE GOING TO PLAY MARBLES WHILE I SIT HERE AND SUFFER?
YOU FORGET... THESE MARBLES ARE REMOTE-CONTROLLED BY PHONE!

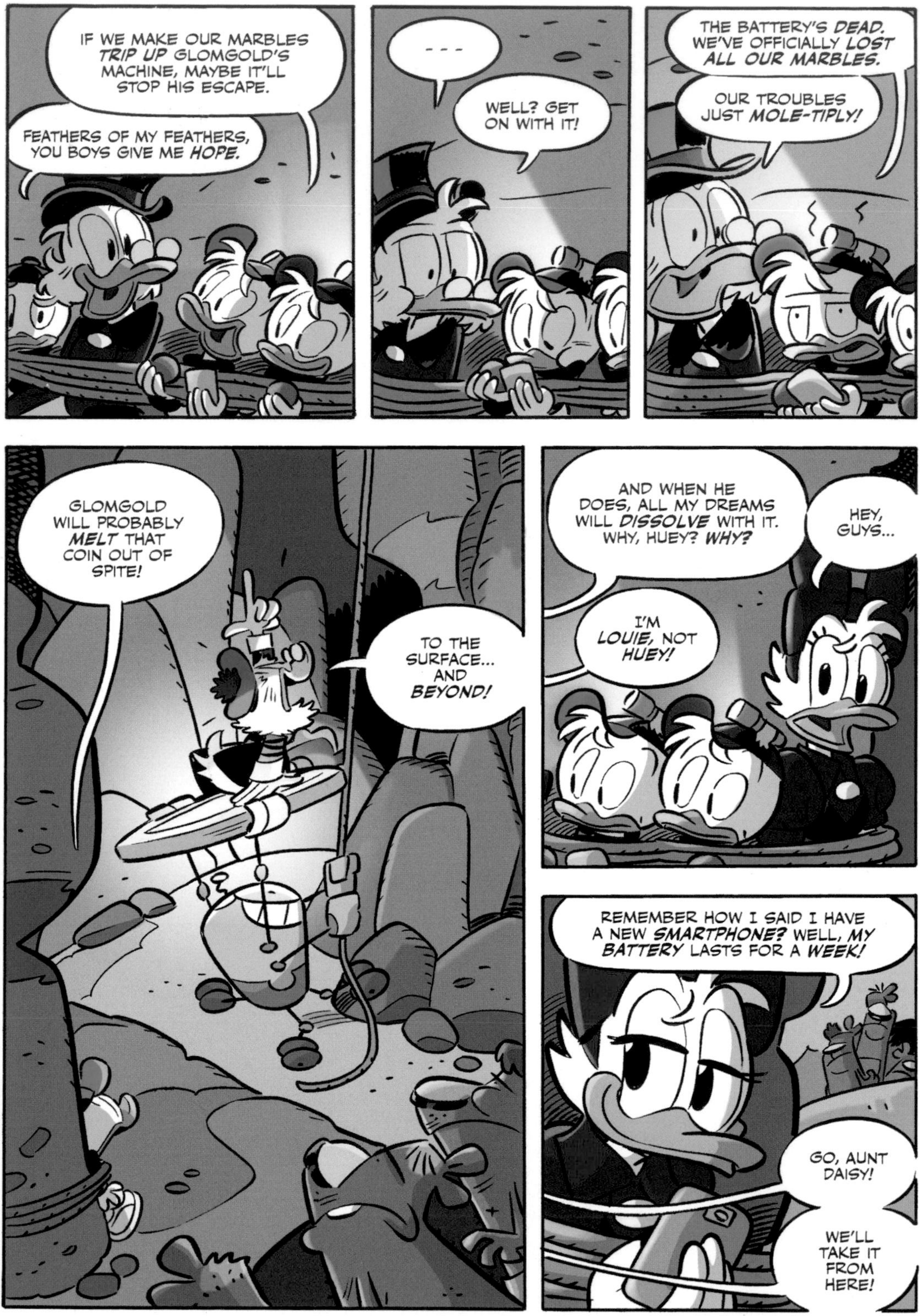
IF WE MAKE OUR MARBLES TRIP UP GLOMGOLD'S MACHINE, MAYBE IT'LL STOP HIS ESCAPE.
FEATHERS OF MY FEATHERS, YOU BOYS GIVE ME HOPE.
- - -
WELL? GET ON WITH IT!
THE BATTERY'S DEAD. WE'VE OFFICIALLY LOST ALL OUR MARBLES.
OUR TROUBLES JUST MOLE-TIPLY!
GLOMGOLD WILL PROBABLY MELT THAT COIN OUT OF SPITE!
TO THE SURFACE... AND BEYOND!
AND WHEN HE DOES, ALL MY DREAMS WILL DISSOLVE WITH IT. WHY, HUEY? WHY?
HEY, GUYS...
I'M LOUIE, NOT HUEY!
REMEMBER HOW I SAID I HAVE A NEW SMARTPHONE? WELL, MY BATTERY LASTS FOR A WEEK!
GO, AUNT DAISY!
WE'LL TAKE IT FROM HERE!

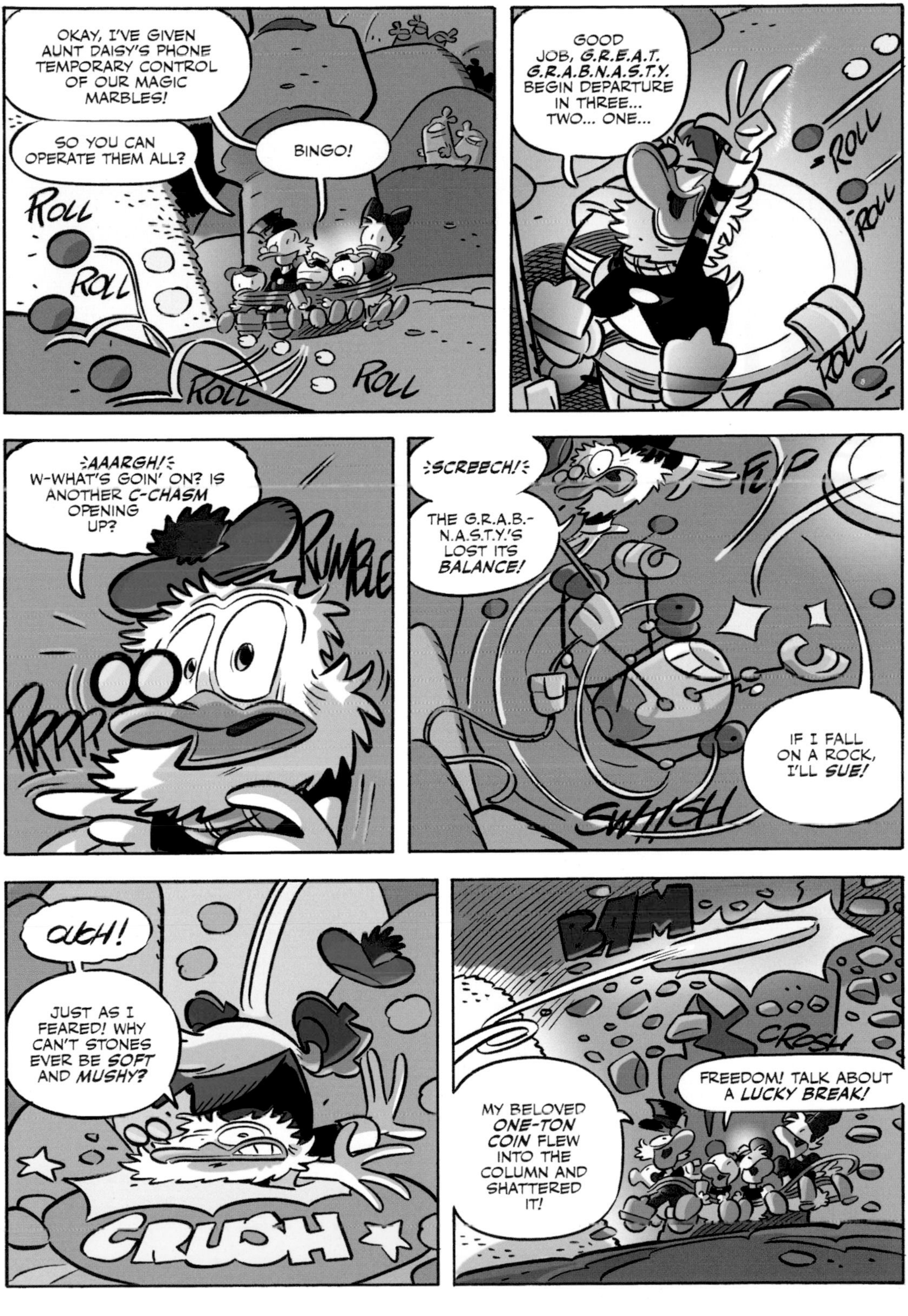
OKAY, I'VE GIVEN AUNT DAISY'S PHONE TEMPORARY CONTROL OF OUR MAGIC MARBLES!
SO YOU CAN OPERATE THEM ALL?
BINGO!
ROLL
ROLL
ROLL
ROLL
GOOD JOB, G.R.E.A.T. G.R.A.B.N.A.S.T.Y. BEGIN DEPARTURE IN THREE... TWO... ONE...
ROLL
ROLL
ROLL
AAARGH! W-WHAT'S GOIN' ON? IS ANOTHER C-CHASM OPENING UP?
RUMBLE
PRRRR
SCREECH!
THE G.R.A.B.-N.A.S.T.Y.'S LOST ITS BALANCE!
FLIP
IF I FALL ON A ROCK, I'LL SUE!
SWISH
OUCH!
JUST AS I FEARED! WHY CAN'T STONES EVER BE SOFT AND MUSHY?
CRUSH
BAM
CRASH
FREEDOM! TALK ABOUT A LUCKY BREAK!
MY BELOVED ONE-TON COIN FLEW INTO THE COLUMN AND SHATTERED IT!

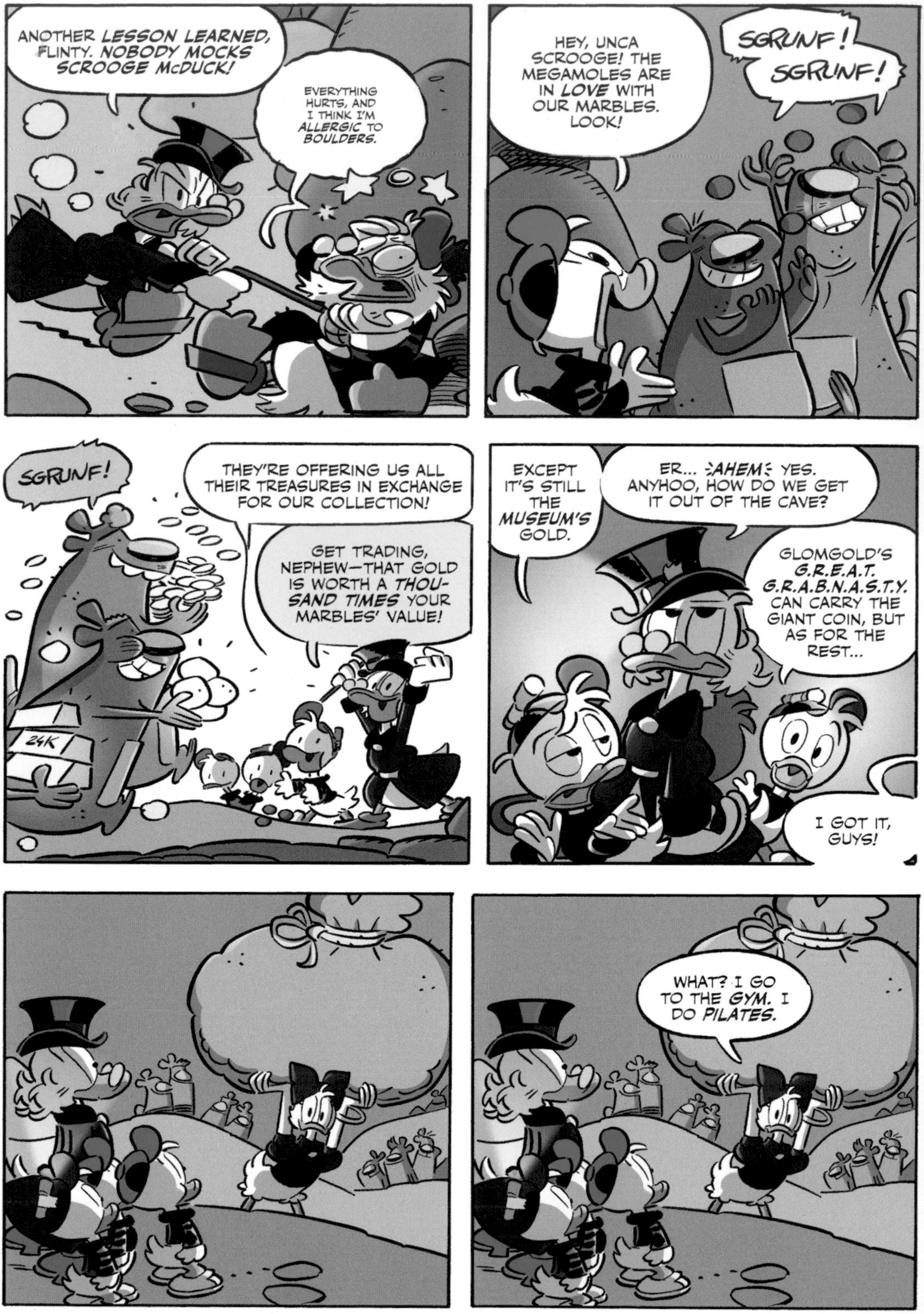

ANOTHER LESSON LEARNED, FLINTY. NOBODY MOCKS SCROOGE McDUCK!
EVERYTHING HURTS, AND I THINK I'M ALLERGIC TO BOULDERS.
HEY, UNCA SCROOGE! THE MEGAMOLES ARE IN LOVE WITH OUR MARBLES. LOOK!
SGRUNF! SGRUNF!
SGRUNF!
THEY'RE OFFERING US ALL THEIR TREASURES IN EXCHANGE FOR OUR COLLECTION!
GET TRADING, NEPHEW—THAT GOLD IS WORTH A THOUSAND TIMES YOUR MARBLES' VALUE!
24K
EXCEPT IT'S STILL THE MUSEUM'S GOLD.
ER... AHEM YES. ANYHOO, HOW DO WE GET IT OUT OF THE CAVE?
GLOMGOLD'S G.R.E.A.T. G.R.A.B.N.A.S.T.Y. CAN CARRY THE GIANT COIN, BUT AS FOR THE REST...
I GOT IT, GUYS!
WHAT? I GO TO THE GYM. I DO PILATES.

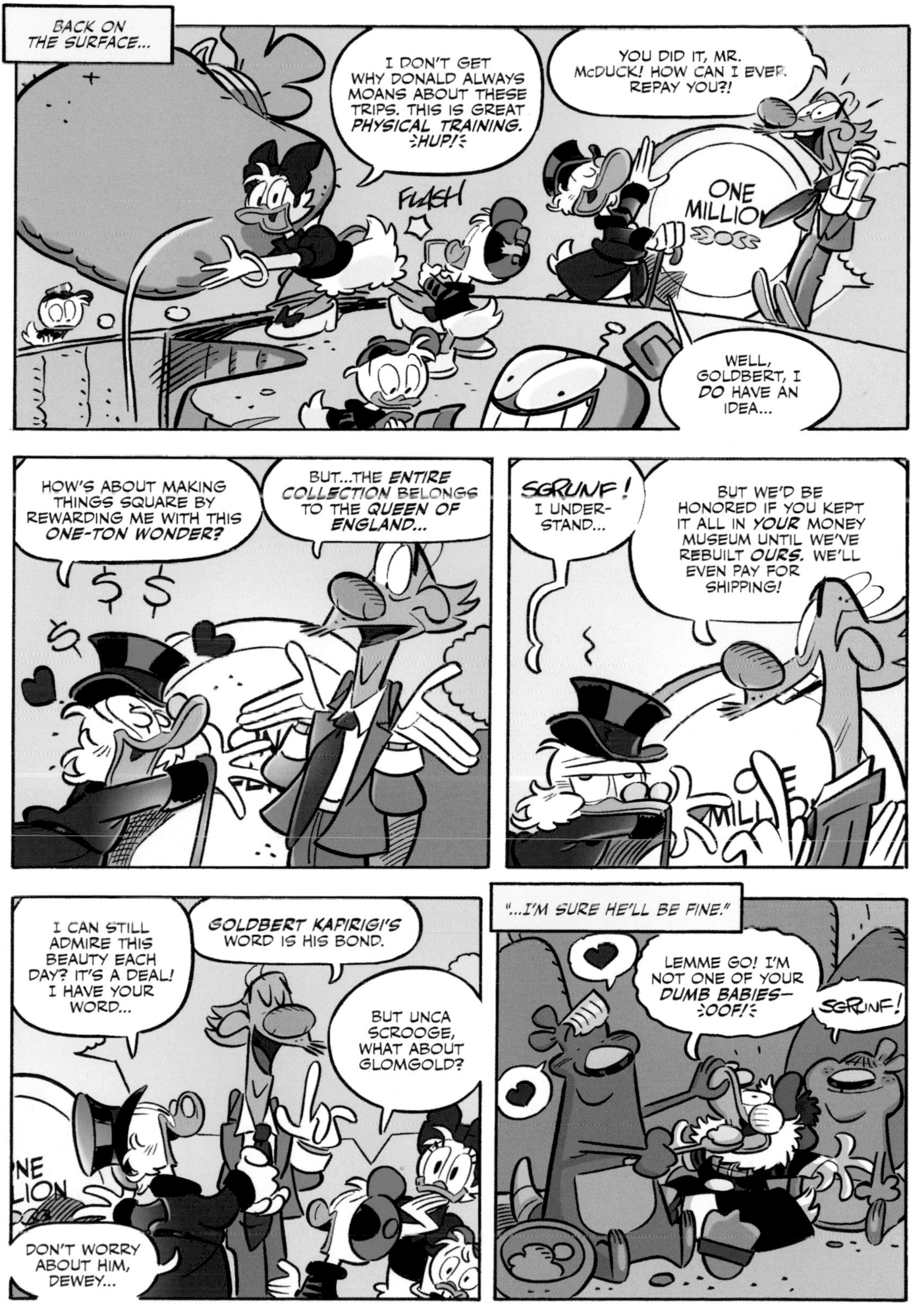
BACK ON THE SURFACE...
I DON'T GET WHY DONALD ALWAYS MOANS ABOUT THESE TRIPS. THIS IS GREAT PHYSICAL TRAINING. HUP!
FLASH
YOU DID IT, MR. McDUCK! HOW CAN I EVER REPAY YOU?!
ONE MILLIO
WELL, GOLDBERT, I DO HAVE AN IDEA...
HOW'S ABOUT MAKING THINGS SQUARE BY REWARDING ME WITH THIS ONE-TON WONDER?
BUT...THE ENTIRE COLLECTION BELONGS TO THE QUEEN OF ENGLAND...
SGRUNF! I UNDERSTAND...
BUT WE'D BE HONORED IF YOU KEPT IT ALL IN YOUR MONEY MUSEUM UNTIL WE'VE REBUILT OURS. WE'LL EVEN PAY FOR SHIPPING!
I CAN STILL ADMIRE THIS BEAUTY EACH DAY? IT'S A DEAL! I HAVE YOUR WORD...
GOLDBERT KAPIRIGI'S WORD IS HIS BOND.
BUT UNCA SCROOGE, WHAT ABOUT GLOMGOLD?
DON'T WORRY ABOUT HIM, DEWEY...
"...I'M SURE HE'LL BE FINE."
LEMME GO! I'M NOT ONE OF YOUR DUMB BABIES—OOF!
SGRUNF!

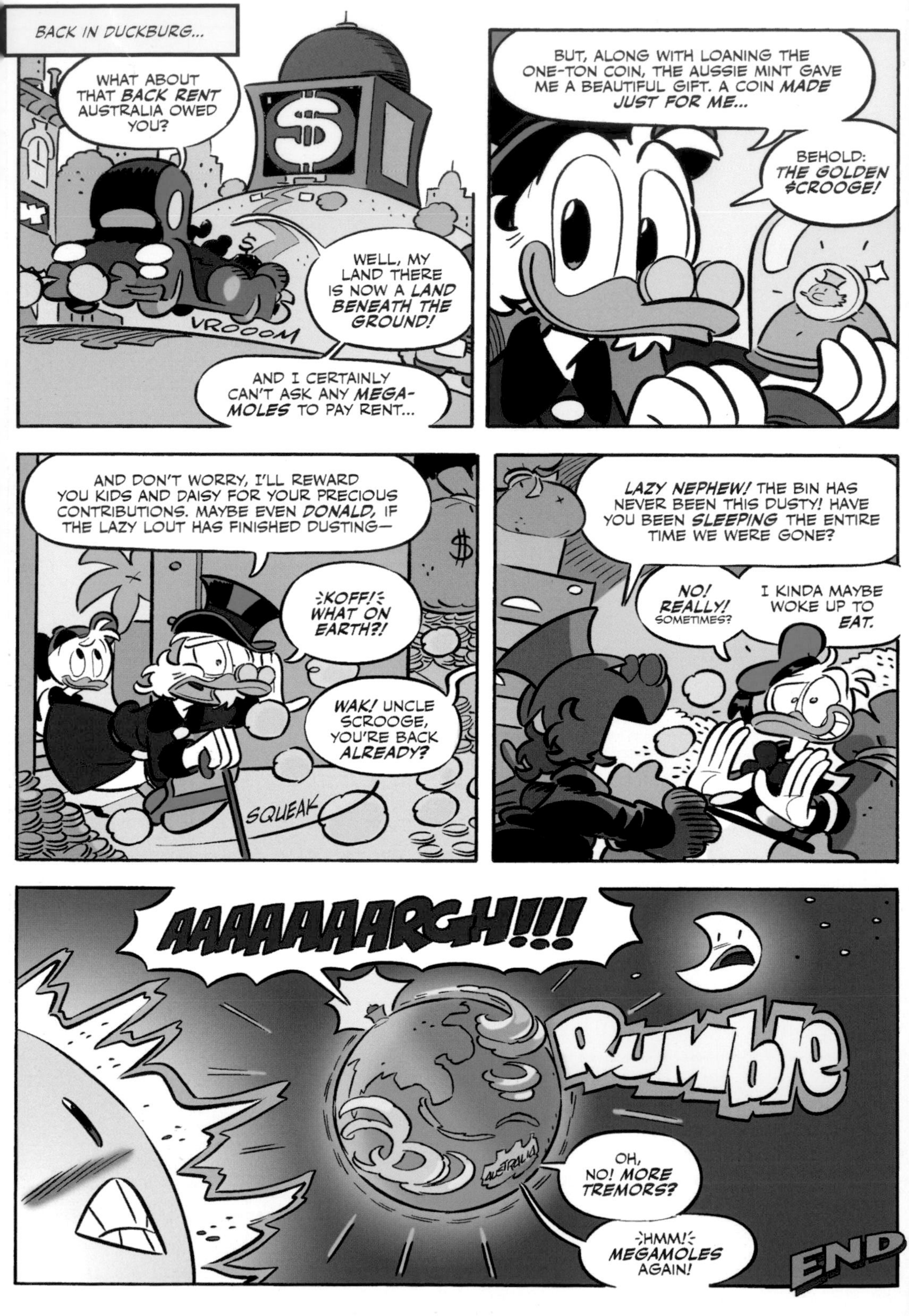
BACK IN DUCKBURG...
WHAT ABOUT THAT BACK RENT AUSTRALIA OWED YOU?
WELL, MY LAND THERE IS NOW A LAND BENEATH THE GROUND!
VROOOM
AND I CERTAINLY CAN'T ASK ANY MEGA-MOLES TO PAY RENT...
BUT, ALONG WITH LOANING THE ONE-TON COIN, THE AUSSIE MINT GAVE ME A BEAUTIFUL GIFT. A COIN MADE JUST FOR ME...
BEHOLD: THE GOLDEN $CROOGE!
AND DON'T WORRY, I'LL REWARD YOU KIDS AND DAISY FOR YOUR PRECIOUS CONTRIBUTIONS. MAYBE EVEN DONALD, IF THE LAZY LOUT HAS FINISHED DUSTING—
KOFF! WHAT ON EARTH?!
WAK! UNCLE SCROOGE, YOU'RE BACK ALREADY?
SQUEAK
LAZY NEPHEW! THE BIN HAS NEVER BEEN THIS DUSTY! HAVE YOU BEEN SLEEPING THE ENTIRE TIME WE WERE GONE?
NO! REALLY! SOMETIMES?
I KINDA MAYBE WOKE UP TO EAT.
AAAAAAARGH!!!
RUMBLE
AUSTRALIA
OH, NO! MORE TREMORS?
HMM! MEGAMOLES AGAIN!
END

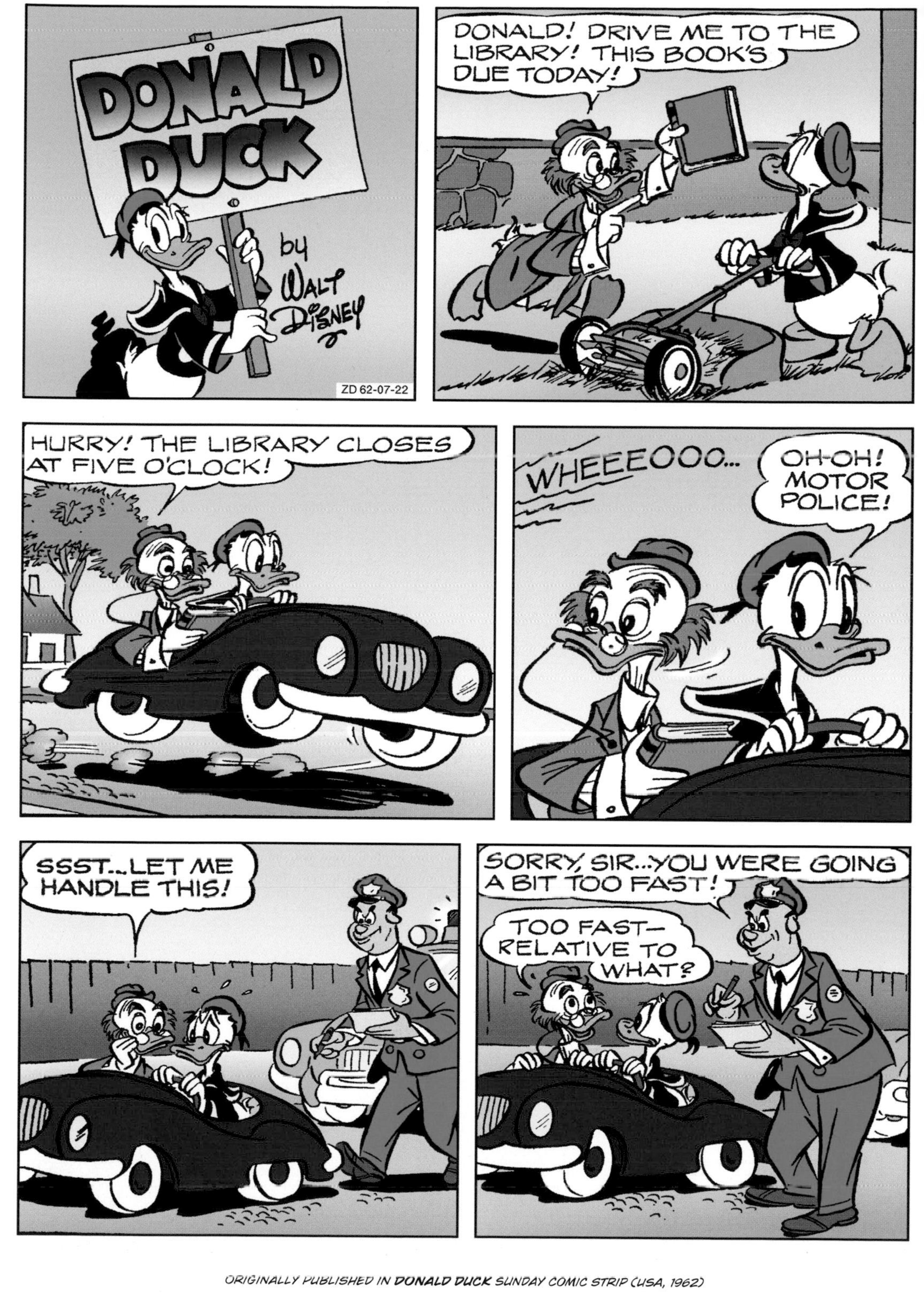
DONALD DUCK
by WALT DISNEY
ZD 62-07-22
DONALD! DRIVE ME TO THE LIBRARY! THIS BOOK'S DUE TODAY!
HURRY! THE LIBRARY CLOSES AT FIVE O'CLOCK!
WHEEEOOO...
OH-OH! MOTOR POLICE!
SSST...LET ME HANDLE THIS!
SORRY, SIR...YOU WERE GOING A BIT TOO FAST!
TOO FAST—RELATIVE TO WHAT?

*ORIGINALLY PUBLISHED IN **DONALD DUCK** SUNDAY COMIC STRIP (USA, 1962)*

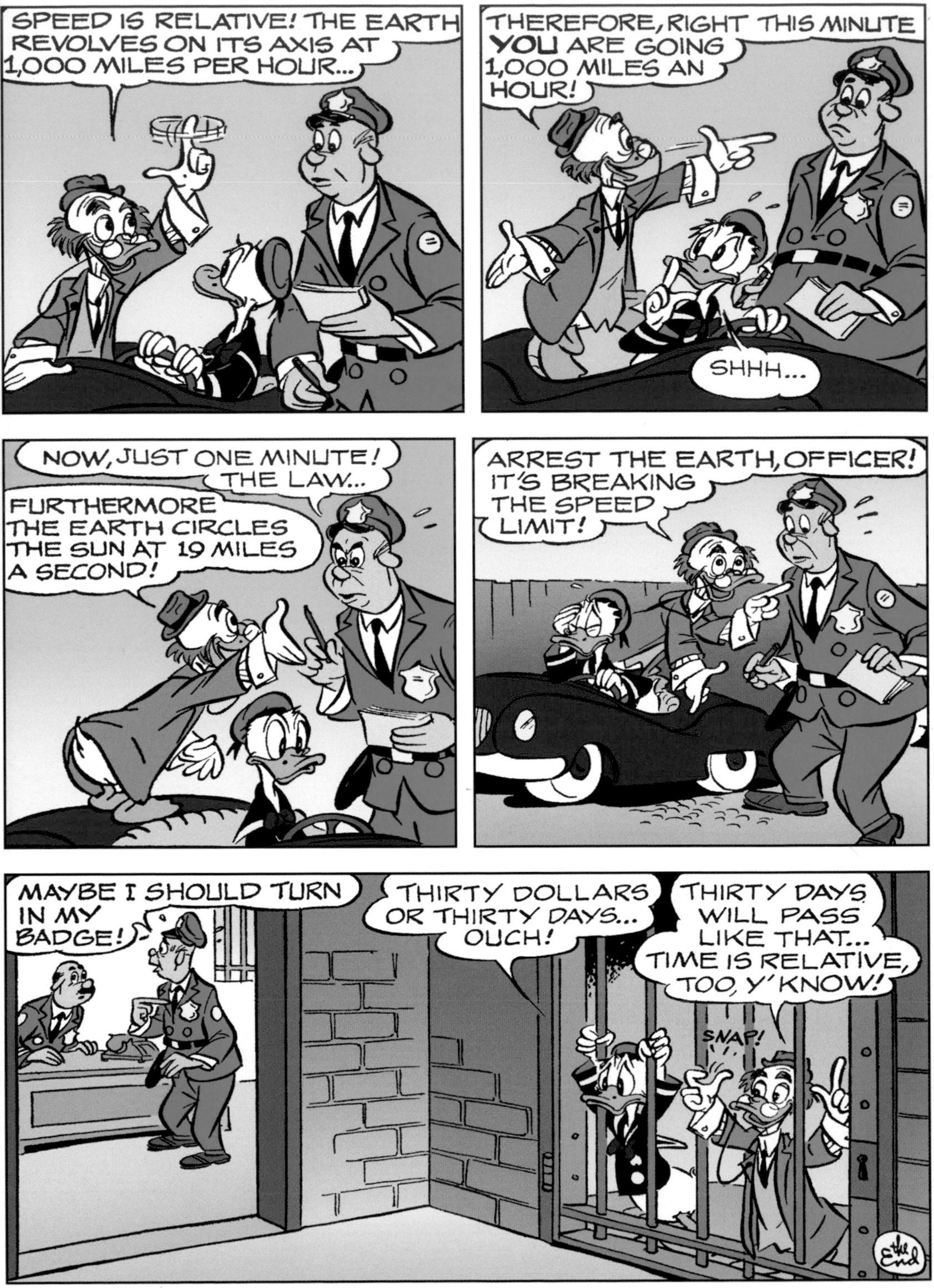

SPEED IS RELATIVE! THE EARTH REVOLVES ON ITS AXIS AT 1,000 MILES PER HOUR...
THEREFORE, RIGHT THIS MINUTE YOU ARE GOING 1,000 MILES AN HOUR!
SHHH...
NOW, JUST ONE MINUTE! THE LAW...
FURTHERMORE THE EARTH CIRCLES THE SUN AT 19 MILES A SECOND!
ARREST THE EARTH, OFFICER! IT'S BREAKING THE SPEED LIMIT!
MAYBE I SHOULD TURN IN MY BADGE!
THIRTY DOLLARS OR THIRTY DAYS... OUCH!
THIRTY DAYS WILL PASS LIKE THAT... TIME IS RELATIVE, TOO, Y' KNOW!
SNAP!
the End

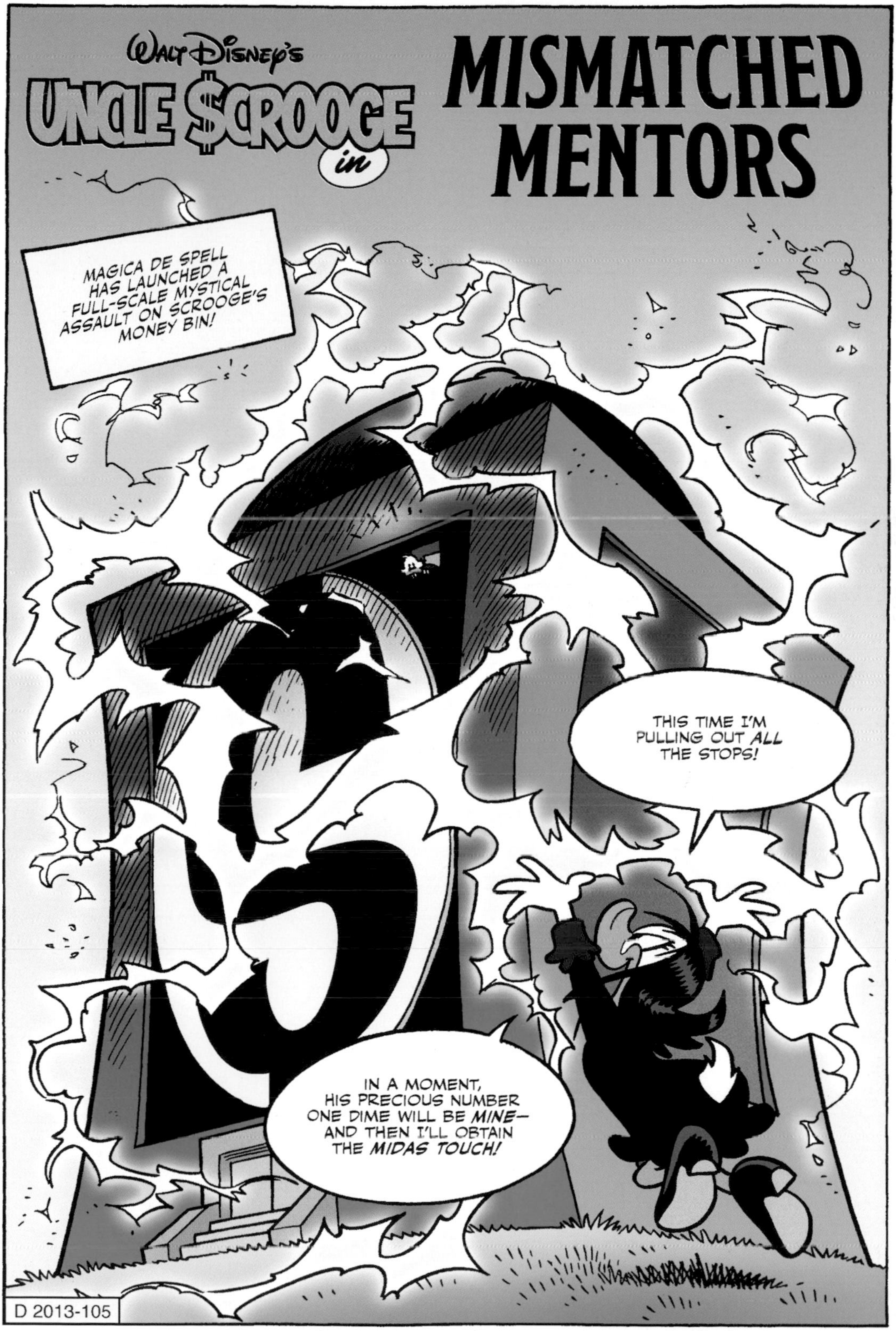
WALT DISNEY'S
UNCLE $CROOGE in
MISMATCHED MENTORS
MAGICA DE SPELL HAS LAUNCHED A FULL-SCALE MYSTICAL ASSAULT ON SCROOGE'S MONEY BIN!
THIS TIME I'M PULLING OUT *ALL* THE STOPS!
IN A MOMENT, HIS PRECIOUS NUMBER ONE DIME WILL BE *MINE*— AND THEN I'LL OBTAIN THE *MIDAS TOUCH!*
D 2013-105

ORIGINALLY PUBLISHED IN LUSTIGES TASCHENBUCH #470 (GERMANY, 2015) • FIRST USA PUBLICATION

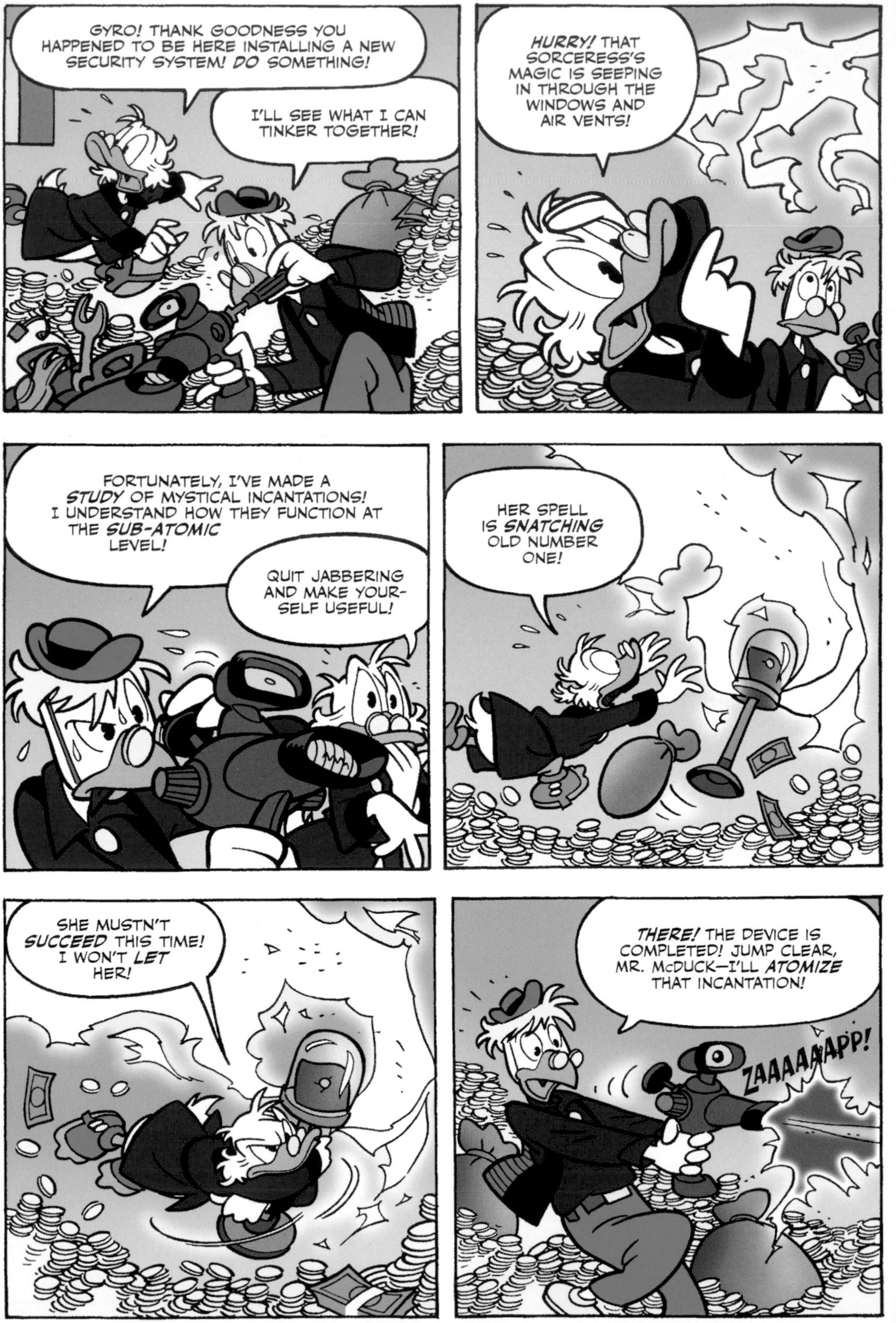
GYRO! THANK GOODNESS YOU HAPPENED TO BE HERE INSTALLING A NEW SECURITY SYSTEM! *DO* SOMETHING!
I'LL SEE WHAT I CAN TINKER TOGETHER!
HURRY! THAT SORCERESS'S MAGIC IS SEEPING IN THROUGH THE WINDOWS AND AIR VENTS!
FORTUNATELY, I'VE MADE A *STUDY* OF MYSTICAL INCANTATIONS! I UNDERSTAND HOW THEY FUNCTION AT THE *SUB-ATOMIC* LEVEL!
QUIT JABBERING AND MAKE YOUR-SELF USEFUL!
HER SPELL IS *SNATCHING* OLD NUMBER ONE!
SHE MUSTN'T *SUCCEED* THIS TIME! I WON'T *LET* HER!
THERE! THE DEVICE IS COMPLETED! JUMP CLEAR, MR. McDUCK—I'LL *ATOMIZE* THAT INCANTATION!
ZAAAAAAPP!

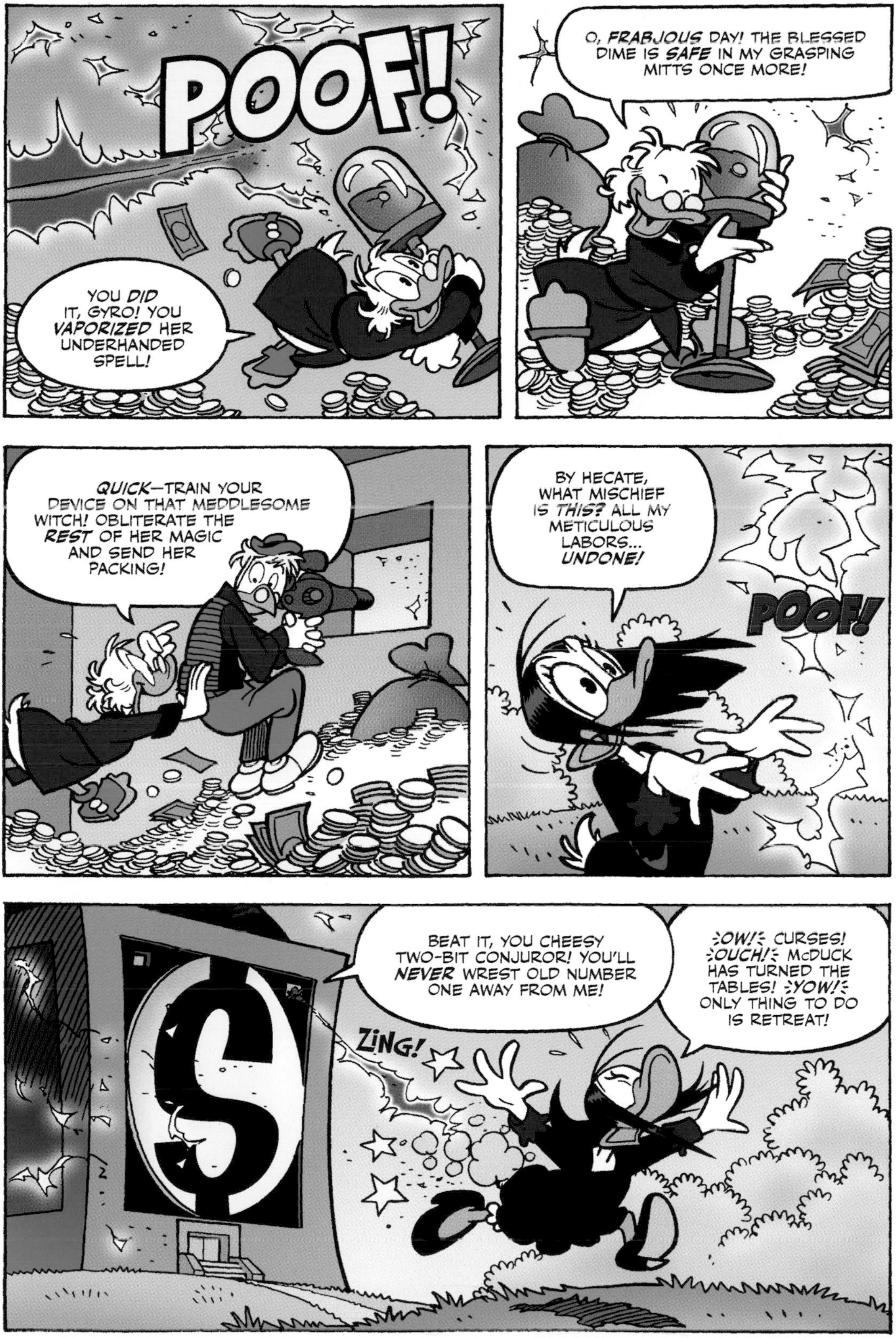
POOF!
YOU DID IT, GYRO! YOU VAPORIZED HER UNDERHANDED SPELL!
O, FRABJOUS DAY! THE BLESSED DIME IS SAFE IN MY GRASPING MITTS ONCE MORE!
QUICK—TRAIN YOUR DEVICE ON THAT MEDDLESOME WITCH! OBLITERATE THE REST OF HER MAGIC AND SEND HER PACKING!
BY HECATE, WHAT MISCHIEF IS THIS? ALL MY METICULOUS LABORS... UNDONE!
POOF!
BEAT IT, YOU CHEESY TWO-BIT CONJUROR! YOU'LL NEVER WREST OLD NUMBER ONE AWAY FROM ME!
OW! CURSES! OUCH! McDUCK HAS TURNED THE TABLES! YOW! ONLY THING TO DO IS RETREAT!
ZING!

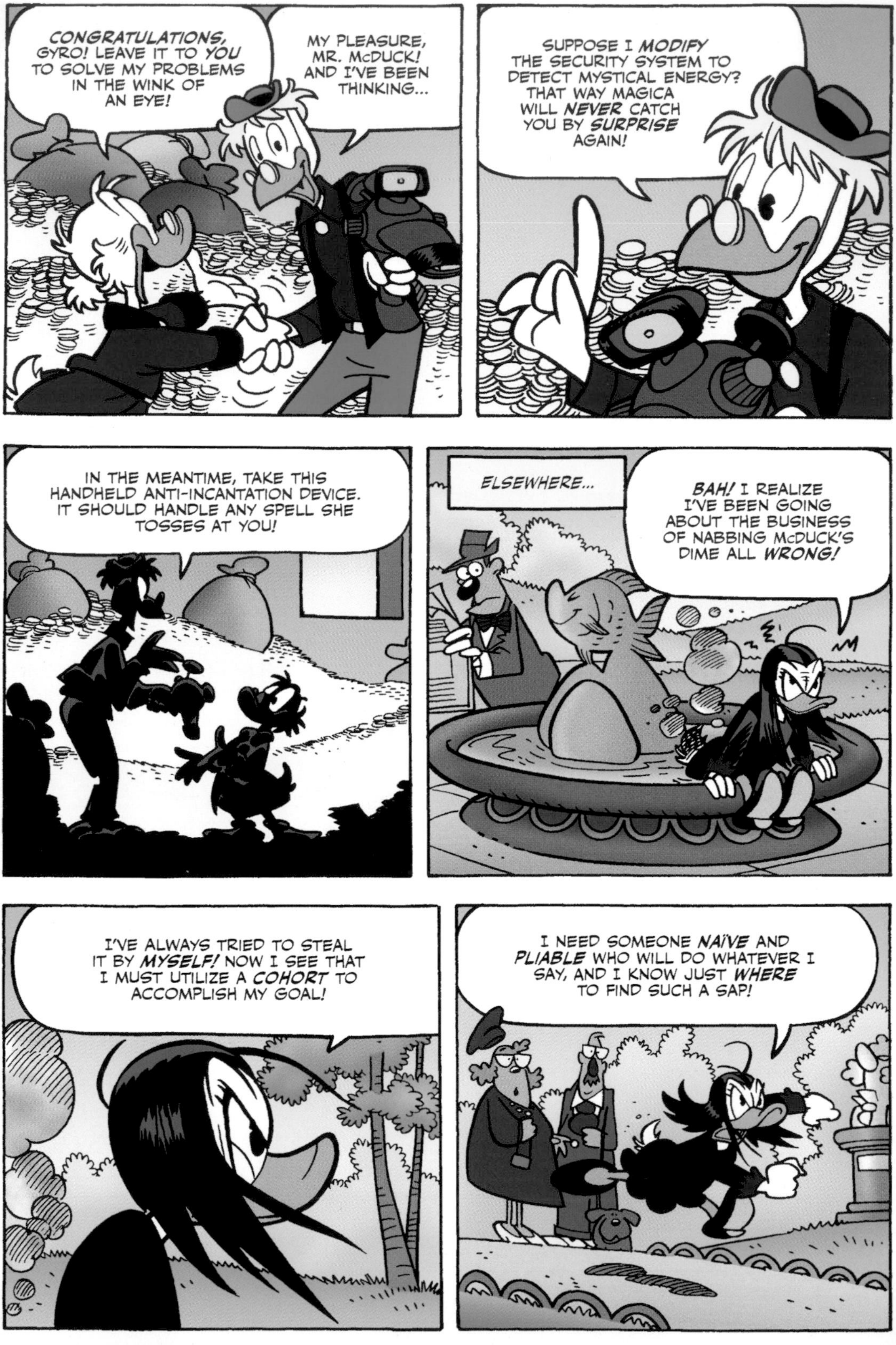
CONGRATULATIONS, GYRO! LEAVE IT TO YOU TO SOLVE MY PROBLEMS IN THE WINK OF AN EYE!
MY PLEASURE, MR. McDUCK! AND I'VE BEEN THINKING...
SUPPOSE I MODIFY THE SECURITY SYSTEM TO DETECT MYSTICAL ENERGY? THAT WAY MAGICA WILL NEVER CATCH YOU BY SURPRISE AGAIN!
IN THE MEANTIME, TAKE THIS HANDHELD ANTI-INCANTATION DEVICE. IT SHOULD HANDLE ANY SPELL SHE TOSSES AT YOU!
ELSEWHERE...
BAH! I REALIZE I'VE BEEN GOING ABOUT THE BUSINESS OF NABBING McDUCK'S DIME ALL WRONG!
I'VE ALWAYS TRIED TO STEAL IT BY MYSELF! NOW I SEE THAT I MUST UTILIZE A COHORT TO ACCOMPLISH MY GOAL!
I NEED SOMEONE NAÏVE AND PLIABLE WHO WILL DO WHATEVER I SAY, AND I KNOW JUST WHERE TO FIND SUCH A SAP!

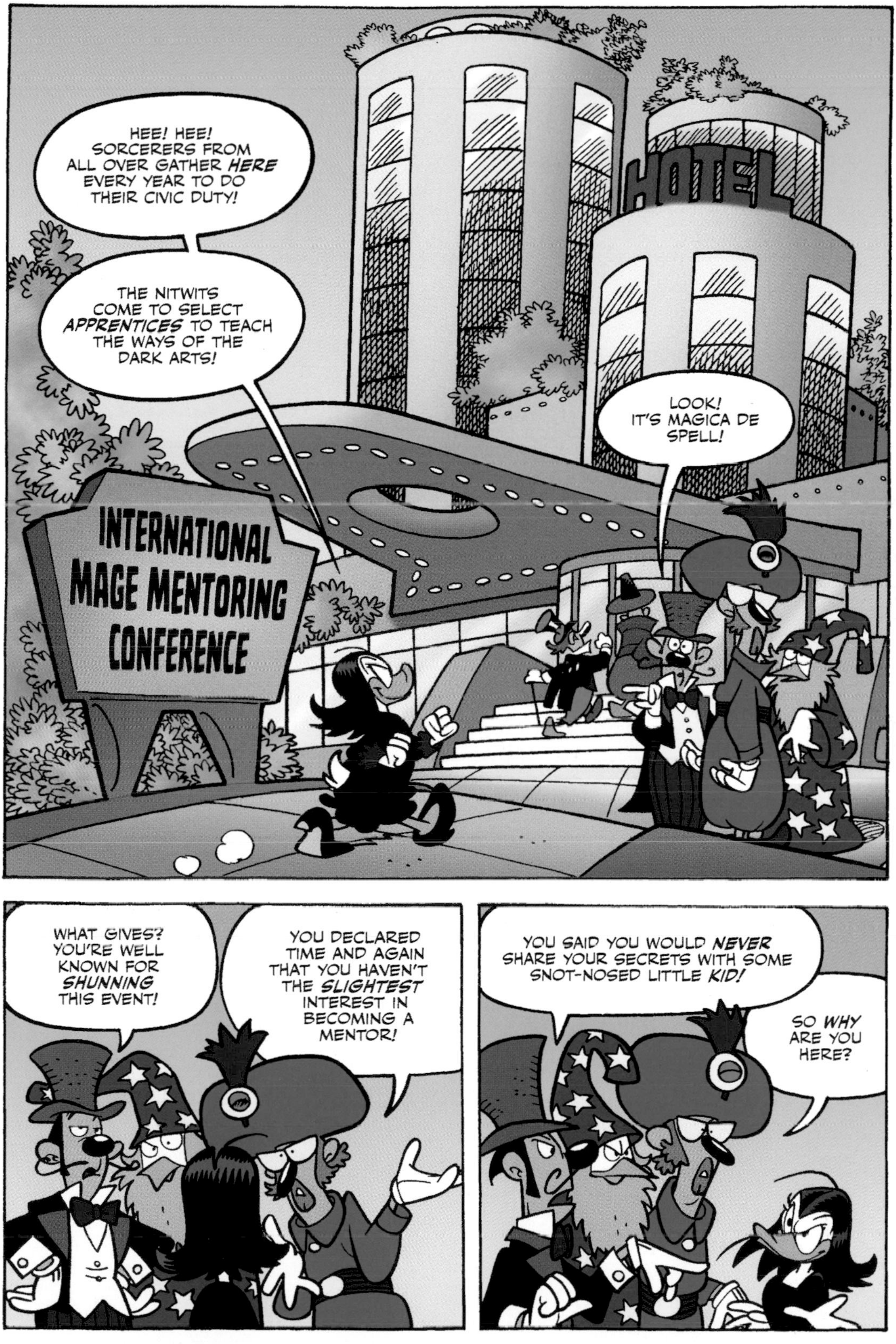
HEE! HEE! SORCERERS FROM ALL OVER GATHER HERE EVERY YEAR TO DO THEIR CIVIC DUTY!
THE NITWITS COME TO SELECT APPRENTICES TO TEACH THE WAYS OF THE DARK ARTS!
HOTEL
INTERNATIONAL MAGE MENTORING CONFERENCE
LOOK! IT'S MAGICA DE SPELL!
WHAT GIVES? YOU'RE WELL KNOWN FOR SHUNNING THIS EVENT!
YOU DECLARED TIME AND AGAIN THAT YOU HAVEN'T THE SLIGHTEST INTEREST IN BECOMING A MENTOR!
YOU SAID YOU WOULD NEVER SHARE YOUR SECRETS WITH SOME SNOT-NOSED LITTLE KID!
SO WHY ARE YOU HERE?

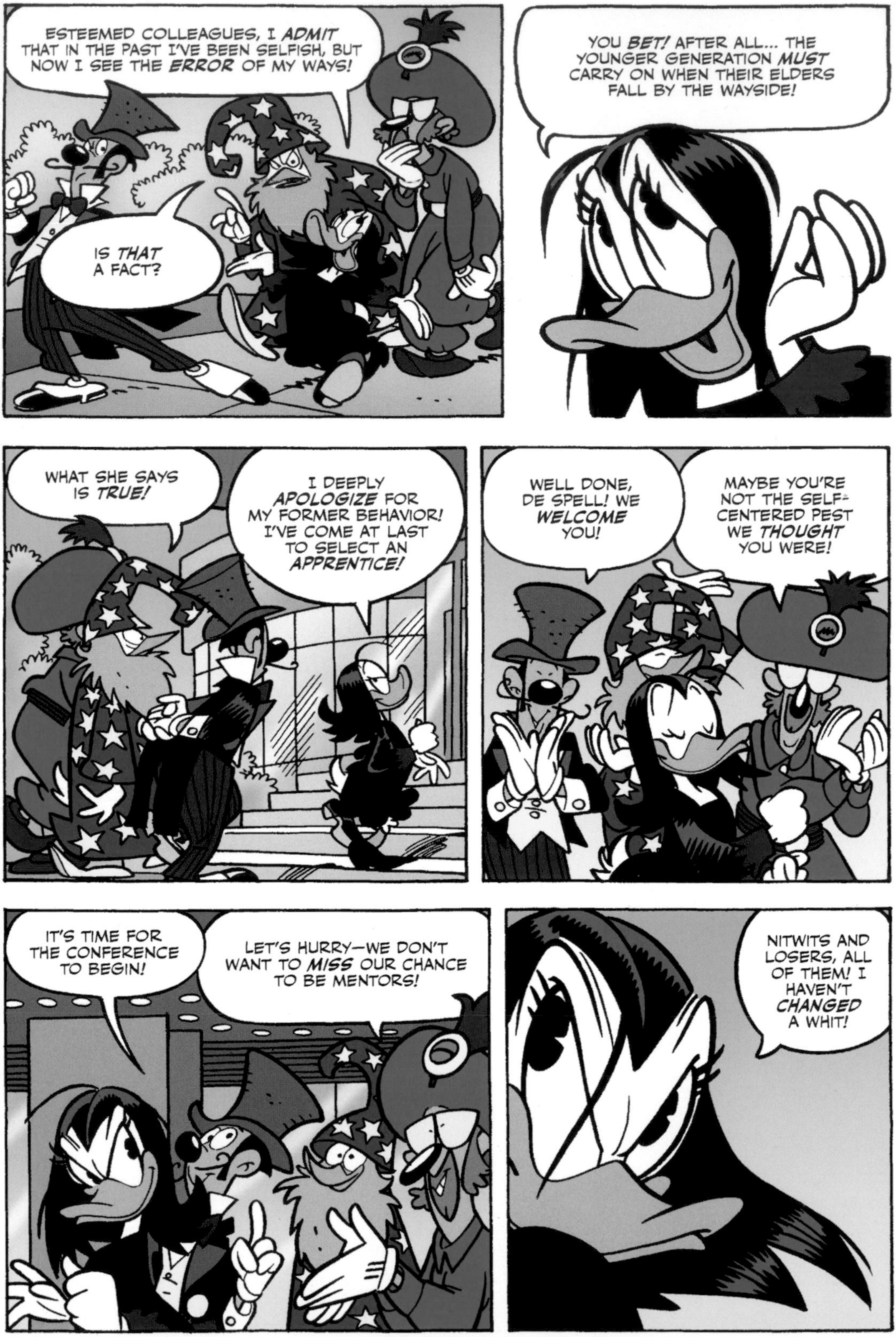
ESTEEMED COLLEAGUES, I *ADMIT* THAT IN THE PAST I'VE BEEN SELFISH, BUT NOW I SEE THE *ERROR* OF MY WAYS!
IS *THAT* A FACT?
YOU *BET!* AFTER ALL... THE YOUNGER GENERATION *MUST* CARRY ON WHEN THEIR ELDERS FALL BY THE WAYSIDE!
WHAT SHE SAYS IS *TRUE!*
I DEEPLY *APOLOGIZE* FOR MY FORMER BEHAVIOR! I'VE COME AT LAST TO SELECT AN *APPRENTICE!*
WELL DONE, DE SPELL! WE *WELCOME* YOU!
MAYBE YOU'RE NOT THE SELF-CENTERED PEST WE *THOUGHT* YOU WERE!
IT'S TIME FOR THE CONFERENCE TO BEGIN!
LET'S HURRY—WE DON'T WANT TO *MISS* OUR CHANCE TO BE MENTORS!
NITWITS AND LOSERS, ALL OF THEM! I HAVEN'T *CHANGED* A WHIT!

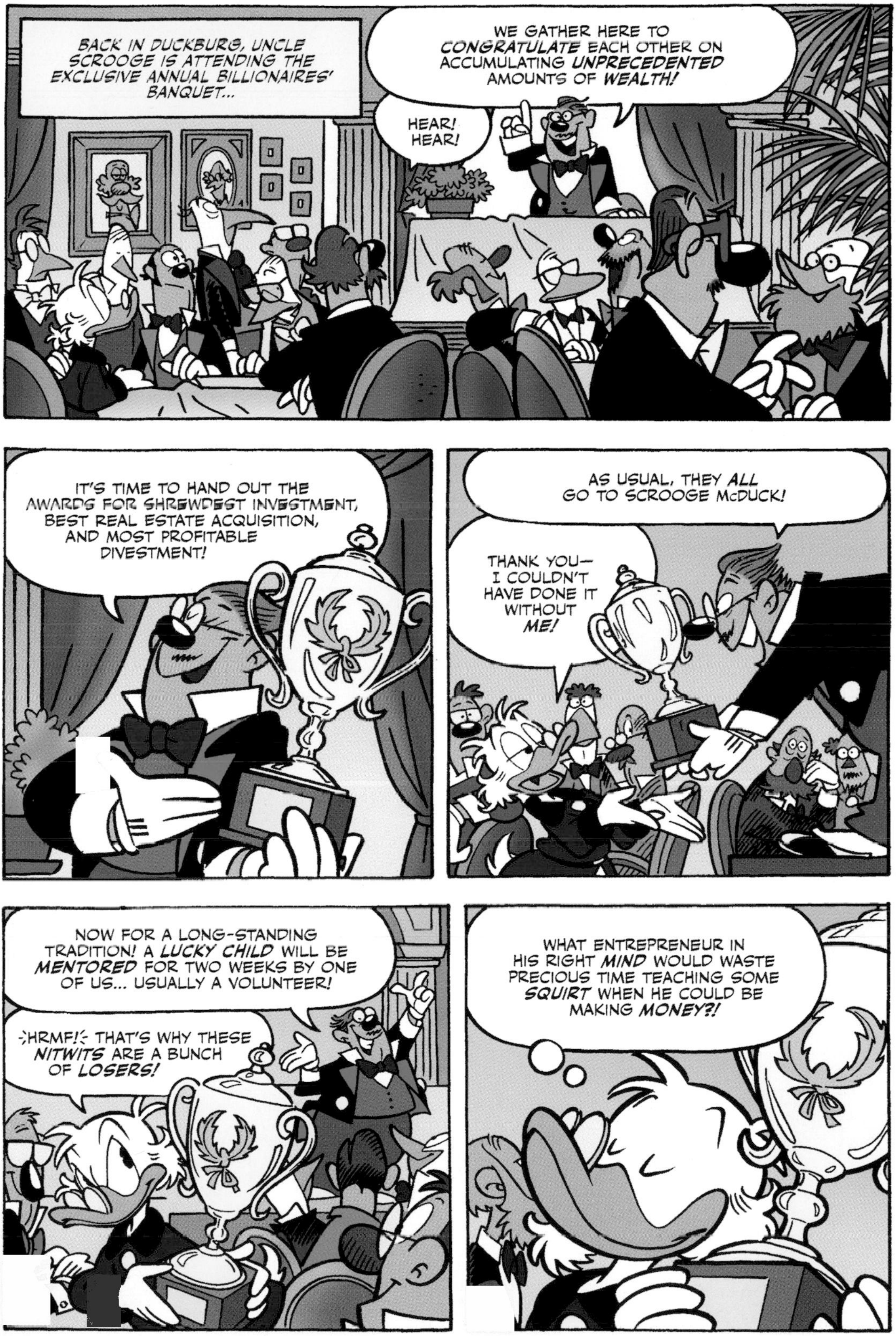
BACK IN DUCKBURG, UNCLE SCROOGE IS ATTENDING THE EXCLUSIVE ANNUAL BILLIONAIRES' BANQUET...
WE GATHER HERE TO CONGRATULATE EACH OTHER ON ACCUMULATING UNPRECEDENTED AMOUNTS OF WEALTH!
HEAR! HEAR!
IT'S TIME TO HAND OUT THE AWARDS FOR SHREWDEST INVESTMENT, BEST REAL ESTATE ACQUISITION, AND MOST PROFITABLE DIVESTMENT!
AS USUAL, THEY ALL GO TO SCROOGE McDUCK!
THANK YOU— I COULDN'T HAVE DONE IT WITHOUT ME!
NOW FOR A LONG-STANDING TRADITION! A LUCKY CHILD WILL BE MENTORED FOR TWO WEEKS BY ONE OF US... USUALLY A VOLUNTEER!
HRMF! THAT'S WHY THESE NITWITS ARE A BUNCH OF LOSERS!
WHAT ENTREPRENEUR IN HIS RIGHT MIND WOULD WASTE PRECIOUS TIME TEACHING SOME SQUIRT WHEN HE COULD BE MAKING MONEY?!

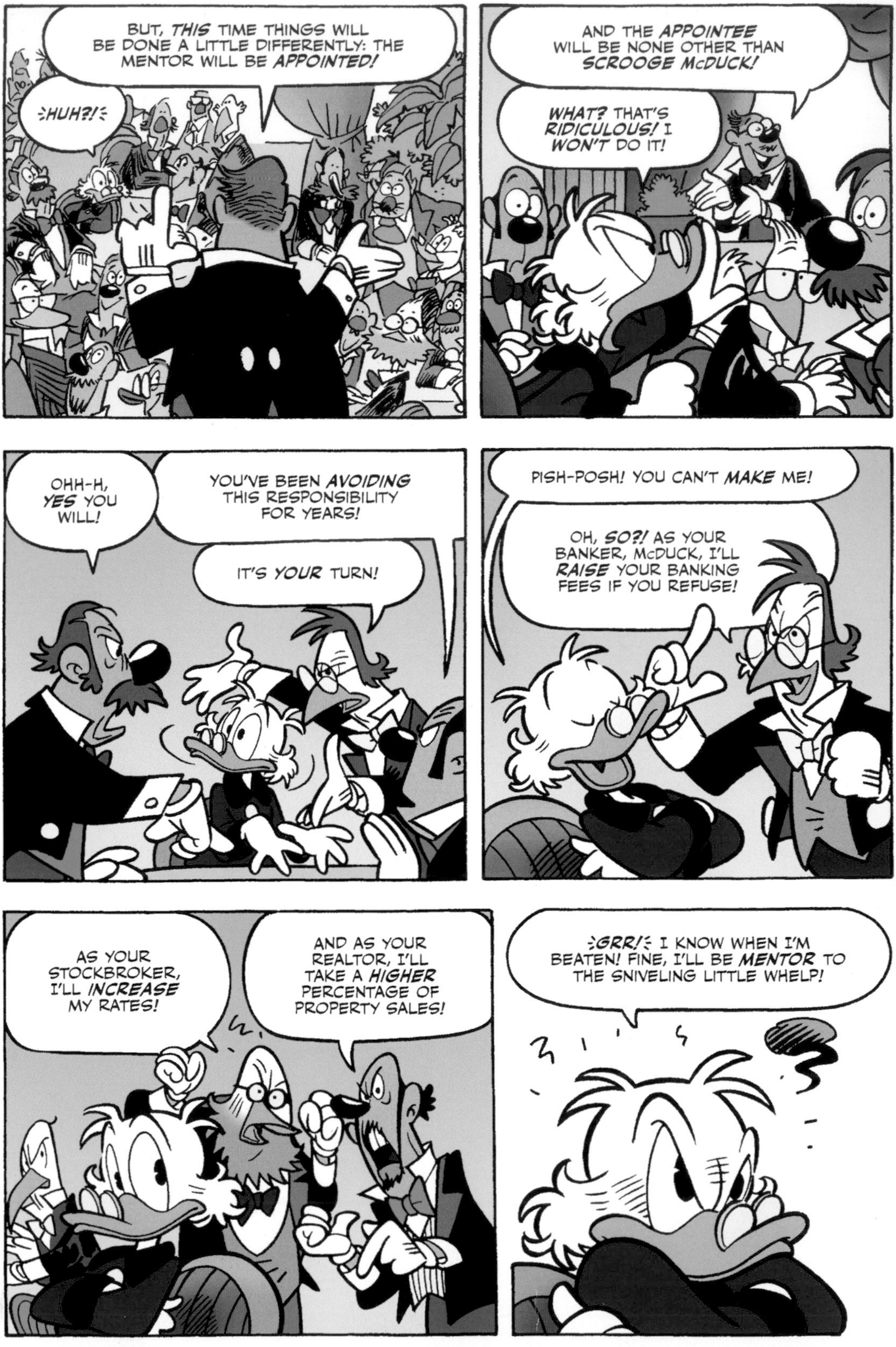
BUT, *THIS* TIME THINGS WILL BE DONE A LITTLE DIFFERENTLY: THE MENTOR WILL BE *APPOINTED!*
HUH?!
AND THE *APPOINTEE* WILL BE NONE OTHER THAN *SCROOGE McDUCK!*
WHAT? THAT'S *RIDICULOUS!* I *WON'T* DO IT!
OHH-H, *YES* YOU WILL!
YOU'VE BEEN *AVOIDING* THIS RESPONSIBILITY FOR YEARS!
IT'S *YOUR* TURN!
PISH-POSH! YOU CAN'T *MAKE* ME!
OH, *SO?!* AS YOUR BANKER, McDUCK, I'LL *RAISE* YOUR BANKING FEES IF YOU REFUSE!
AS YOUR STOCKBROKER, I'LL *INCREASE* MY RATES!
AND AS YOUR REALTOR, I'LL TAKE A *HIGHER* PERCENTAGE OF PROPERTY SALES!
GRR! I KNOW WHEN I'M BEATEN! FINE, I'LL BE *MENTOR* TO THE SNIVELING LITTLE WHELP!

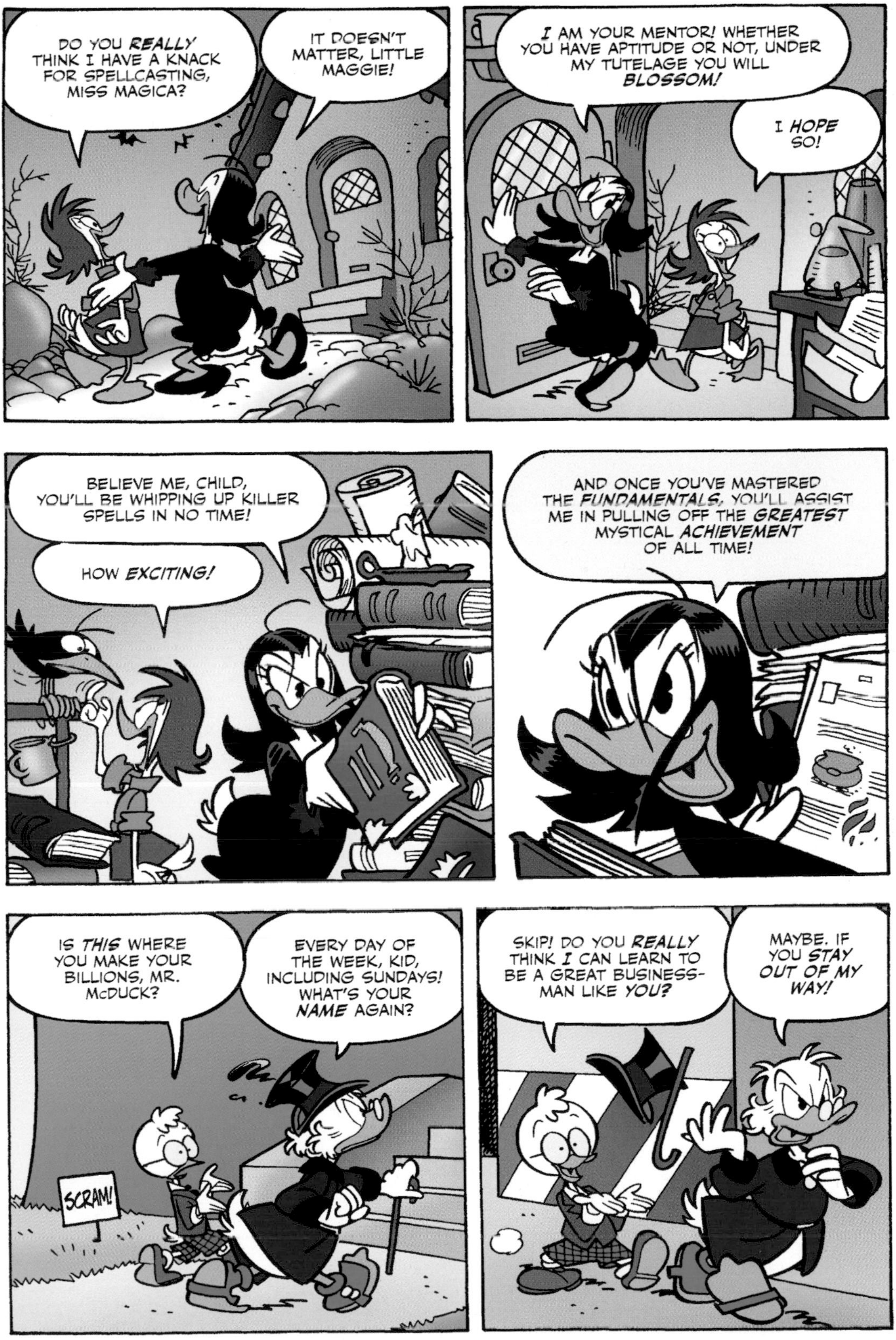
DO YOU REALLY THINK I HAVE A KNACK FOR SPELLCASTING, MISS MAGICA?
IT DOESN'T MATTER, LITTLE MAGGIE!
I AM YOUR MENTOR! WHETHER YOU HAVE APTITUDE OR NOT, UNDER MY TUTELAGE YOU WILL BLOSSOM!
I HOPE SO!
BELIEVE ME, CHILD, YOU'LL BE WHIPPING UP KILLER SPELLS IN NO TIME!
HOW EXCITING!
AND ONCE YOU'VE MASTERED THE FUNDAMENTALS, YOU'LL ASSIST ME IN PULLING OFF THE GREATEST MYSTICAL ACHIEVEMENT OF ALL TIME!
IS THIS WHERE YOU MAKE YOUR BILLIONS, MR. McDUCK?
EVERY DAY OF THE WEEK, KID, INCLUDING SUNDAYS! WHAT'S YOUR NAME AGAIN?
SCRAM!
SKIP! DO YOU REALLY THINK I CAN LEARN TO BE A GREAT BUSINESS-MAN LIKE YOU?
MAYBE. IF YOU STAY OUT OF MY WAY!

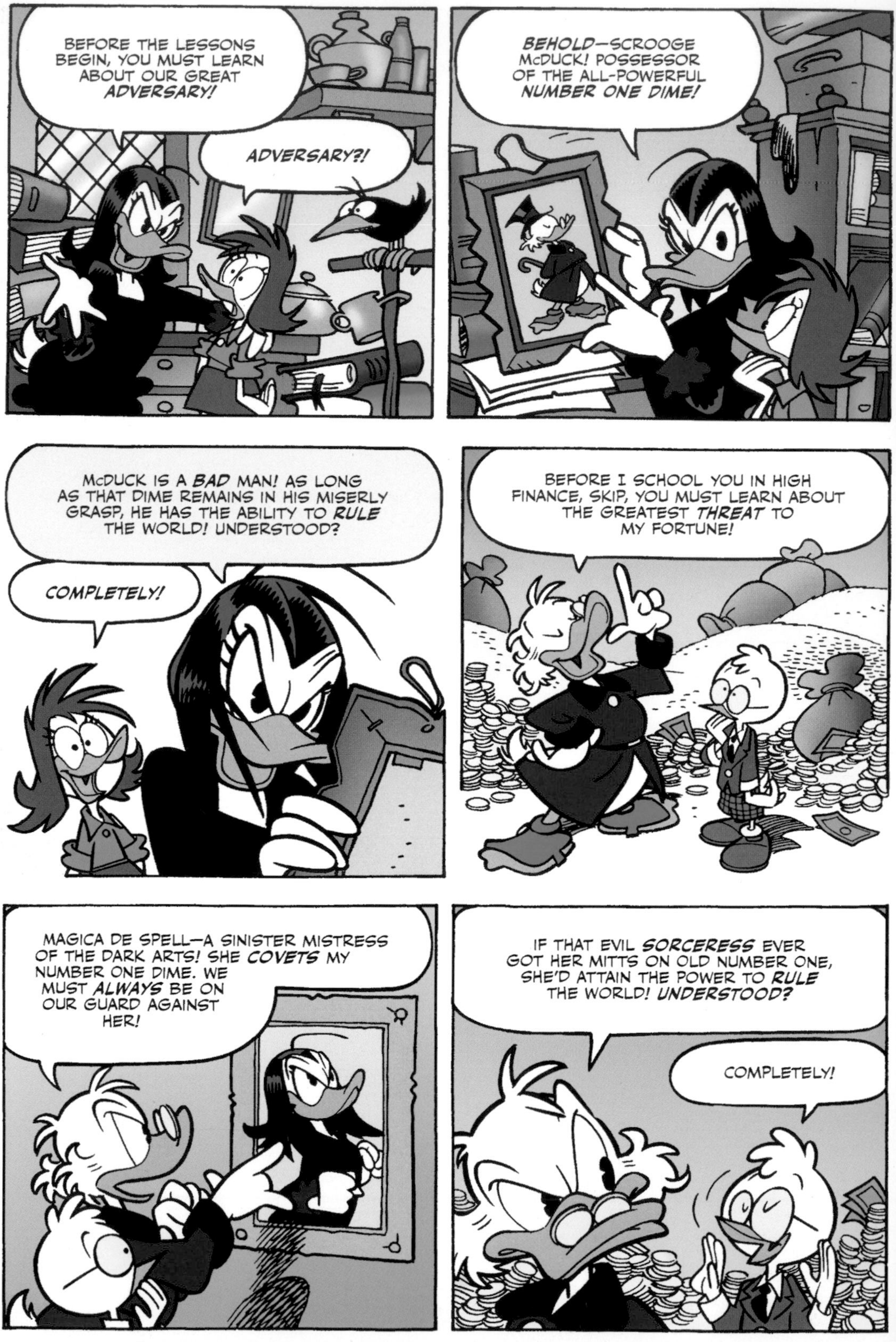
BEFORE THE LESSONS BEGIN, YOU MUST LEARN ABOUT OUR GREAT ADVERSARY!
ADVERSARY?!
BEHOLD—SCROOGE McDUCK! POSSESSOR OF THE ALL-POWERFUL NUMBER ONE DIME!
McDUCK IS A BAD MAN! AS LONG AS THAT DIME REMAINS IN HIS MISERLY GRASP, HE HAS THE ABILITY TO RULE THE WORLD! UNDERSTOOD?
COMPLETELY!
BEFORE I SCHOOL YOU IN HIGH FINANCE, SKIP, YOU MUST LEARN ABOUT THE GREATEST THREAT TO MY FORTUNE!
MAGICA DE SPELL—A SINISTER MISTRESS OF THE DARK ARTS! SHE COVETS MY NUMBER ONE DIME. WE MUST ALWAYS BE ON OUR GUARD AGAINST HER!
IF THAT EVIL SORCERESS EVER GOT HER MITTS ON OLD NUMBER ONE, SHE'D ATTAIN THE POWER TO RULE THE WORLD! UNDERSTOOD?
COMPLETELY!

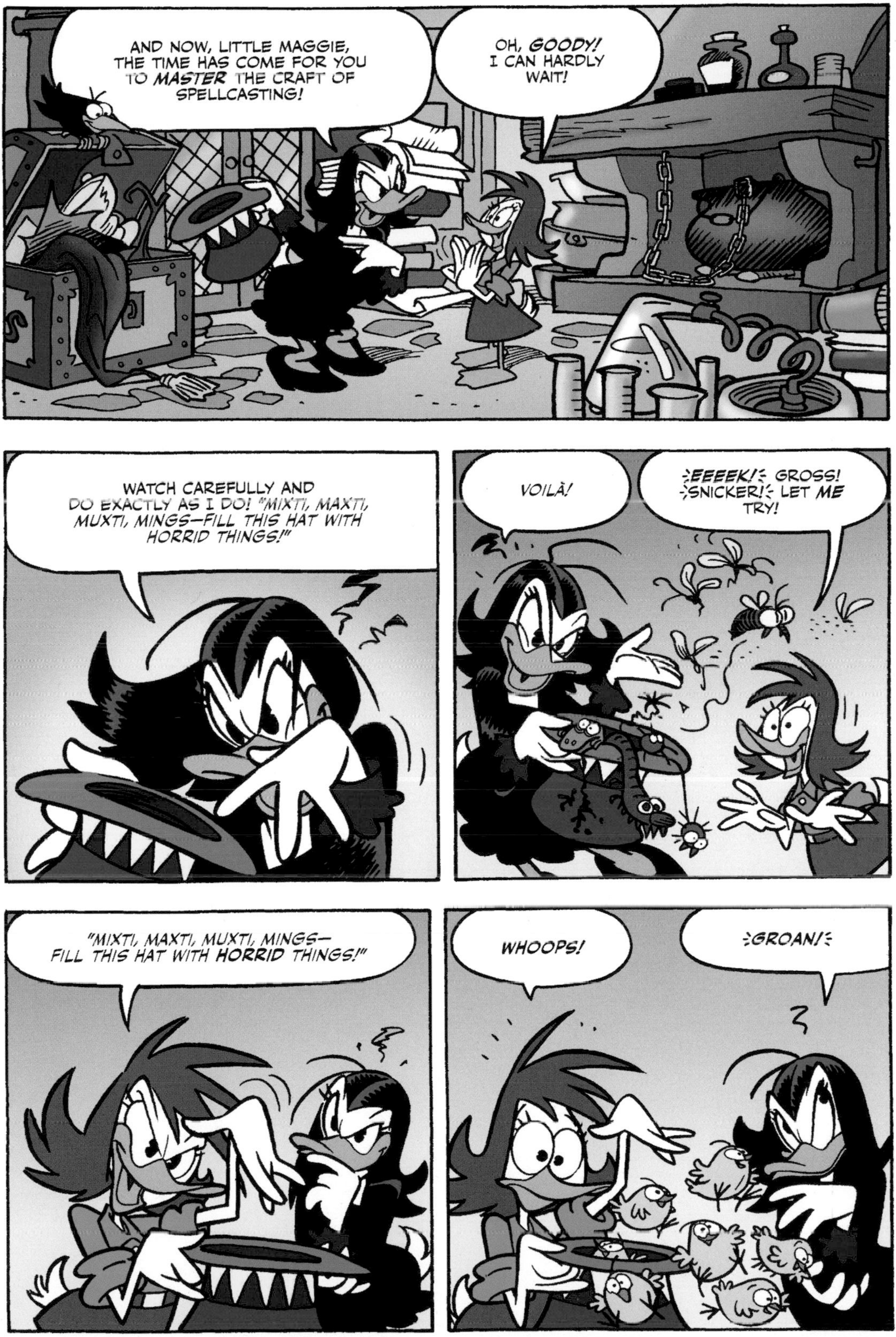
AND NOW, LITTLE MAGGIE, THE TIME HAS COME FOR YOU TO MASTER THE CRAFT OF SPELLCASTING!
OH, GOODY! I CAN HARDLY WAIT!
WATCH CAREFULLY AND DO EXACTLY AS I DO! "MIXTI, MAXTI, MUXTI, MINGS—FILL THIS HAT WITH HORRID THINGS!"
VOILÀ!
EEEEK! GROSS! SNICKER! LET ME TRY!
"MIXTI, MAXTI, MUXTI, MINGS— FILL THIS HAT WITH HORRID THINGS!"
WHOOPS!
GROAN!

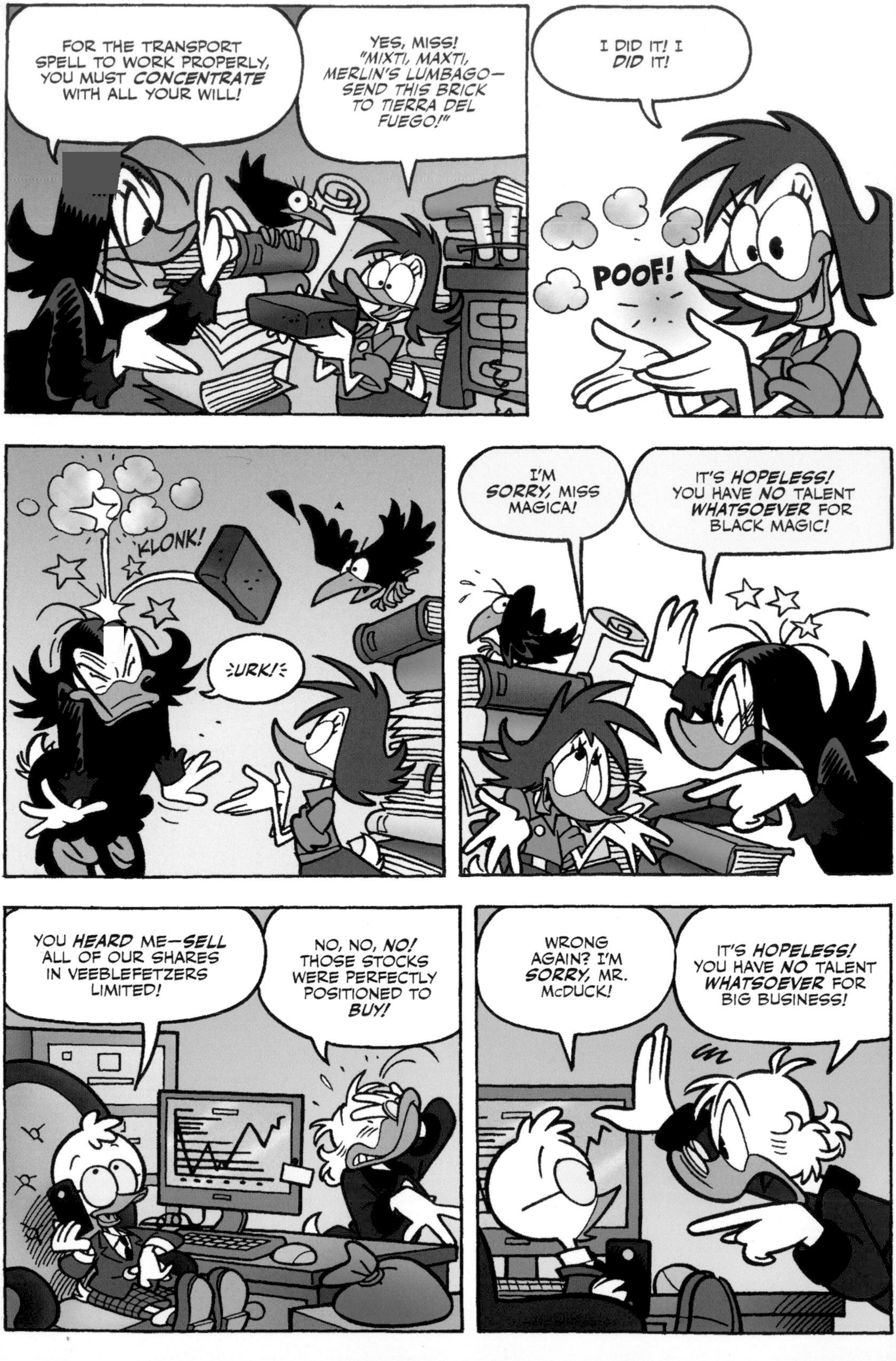
FOR THE TRANSPORT SPELL TO WORK PROPERLY, YOU MUST CONCENTRATE WITH ALL YOUR WILL!
YES, MISS! "MIXTI, MAXTI, MERLIN'S LUMBAGO— SEND THIS BRICK TO TIERRA DEL FUEGO!"
I DID IT! I DID IT!
POOF!
KLONK!
URK!
I'M SORRY, MISS MAGICA!
IT'S HOPELESS! YOU HAVE NO TALENT WHATSOEVER FOR BLACK MAGIC!
YOU HEARD ME—SELL ALL OF OUR SHARES IN VEEBLEFETZERS LIMITED!
NO, NO, NO! THOSE STOCKS WERE PERFECTLY POSITIONED TO BUY!
WRONG AGAIN? I'M SORRY, MR. McDUCK!
IT'S HOPELESS! YOU HAVE NO TALENT WHATSOEVER FOR BIG BUSINESS!

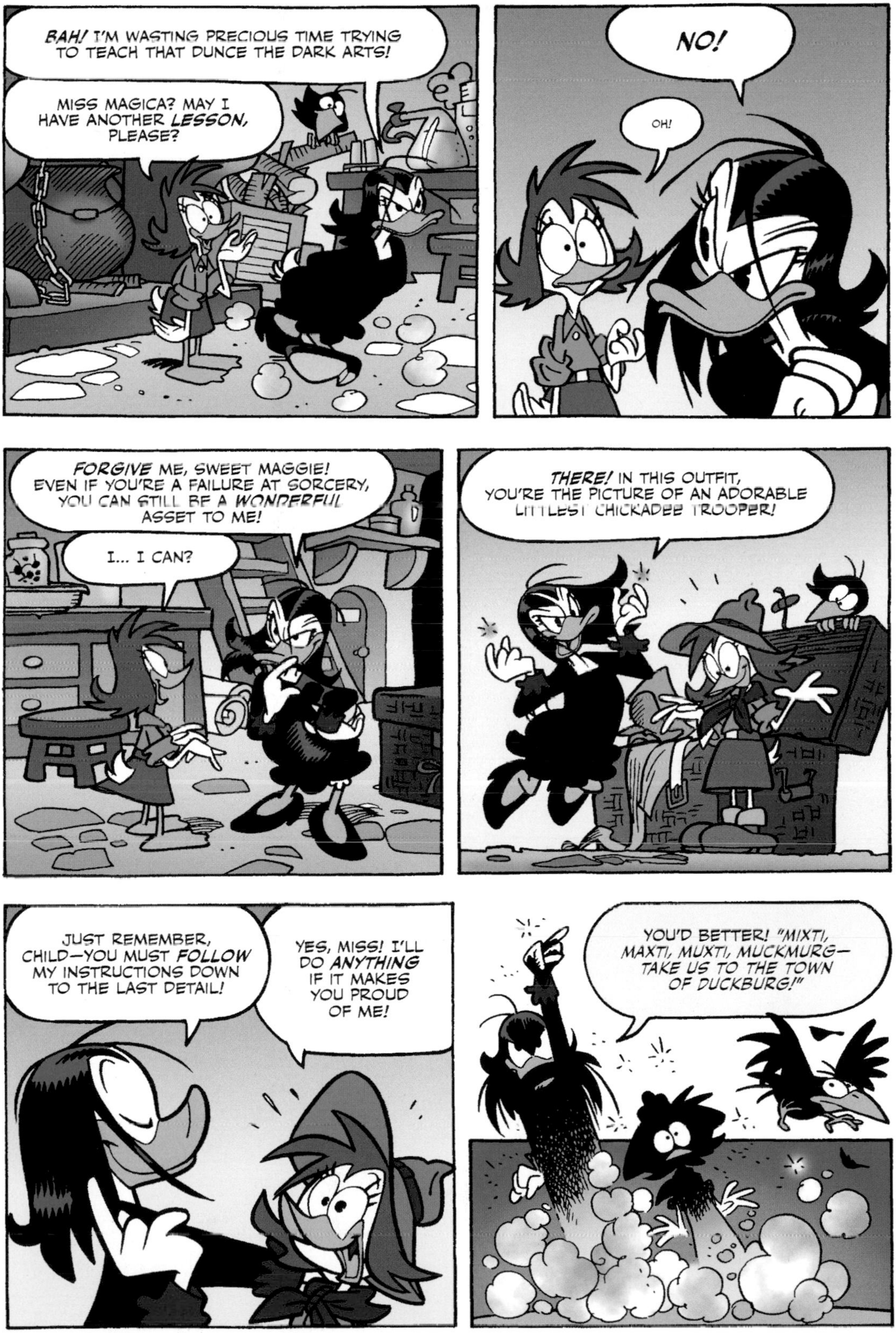
BAH! I'M WASTING PRECIOUS TIME TRYING TO TEACH THAT DUNCE THE DARK ARTS!
MISS MAGICA? MAY I HAVE ANOTHER LESSON, PLEASE?
NO!
OH!
FORGIVE ME, SWEET MAGGIE! EVEN IF YOU'RE A FAILURE AT SORCERY, YOU CAN STILL BE A WONDERFUL ASSET TO ME!
I... I CAN?
THERE! IN THIS OUTFIT, YOU'RE THE PICTURE OF AN ADORABLE LITTLEST CHICKADEE TROOPER!
JUST REMEMBER, CHILD—YOU MUST FOLLOW MY INSTRUCTIONS DOWN TO THE LAST DETAIL!
YES, MISS! I'LL DO ANYTHING IF IT MAKES YOU PROUD OF ME!
YOU'D BETTER! "MIXTI, MAXTI, MUXTI, MUCKMURG— TAKE US TO THE TOWN OF DUCKBURG!"

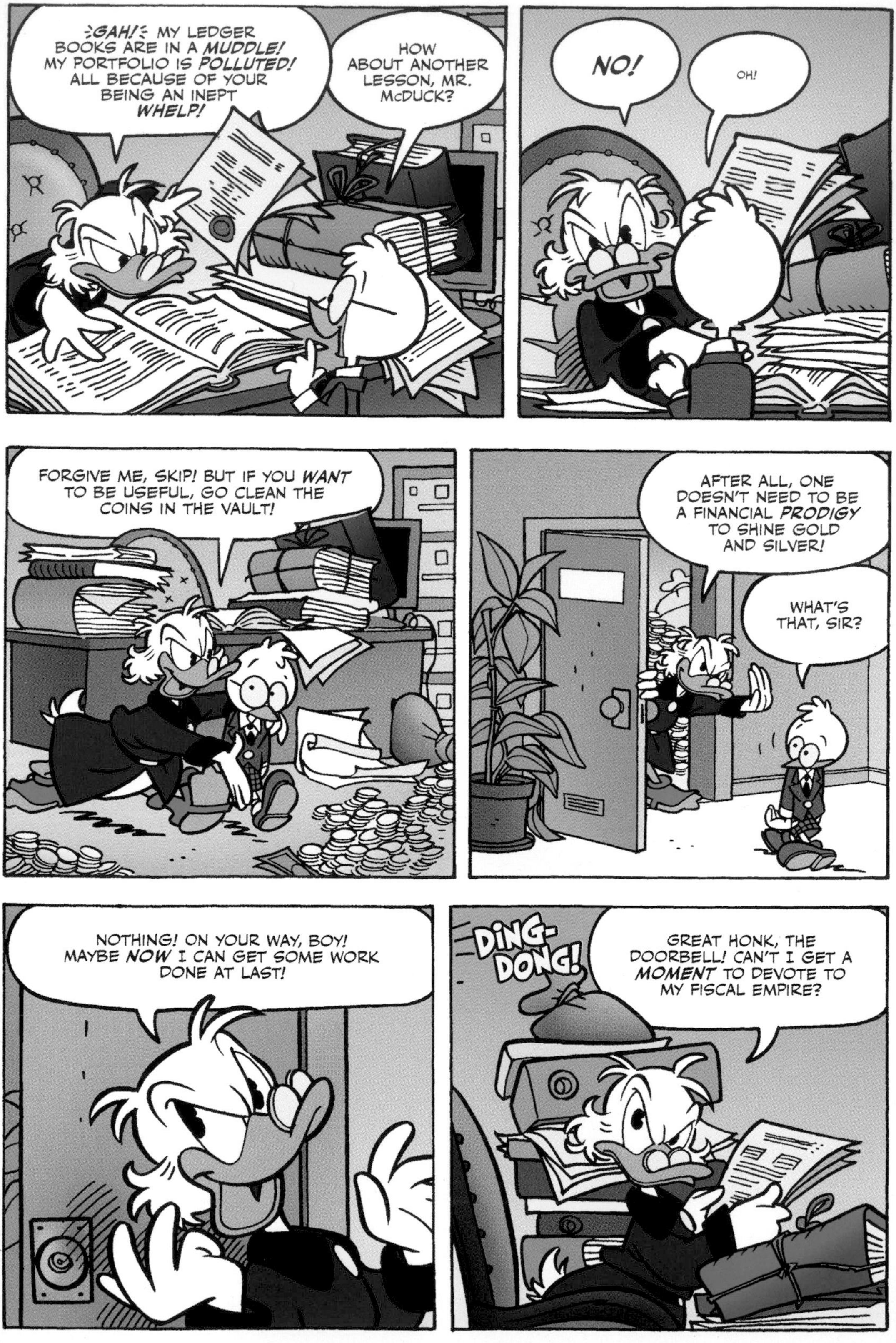

GAH! MY LEDGER BOOKS ARE IN A MUDDLE! MY PORTFOLIO IS POLLUTED! ALL BECAUSE OF YOUR BEING AN INEPT WHELP!
HOW ABOUT ANOTHER LESSON, MR. McDUCK?
NO!
OH!
FORGIVE ME, SKIP! BUT IF YOU WANT TO BE USEFUL, GO CLEAN THE COINS IN THE VAULT!
AFTER ALL, ONE DOESN'T NEED TO BE A FINANCIAL PRODIGY TO SHINE GOLD AND SILVER!
WHAT'S THAT, SIR?
NOTHING! ON YOUR WAY, BOY! MAYBE NOW I CAN GET SOME WORK DONE AT LAST!
DING-DONG!
GREAT HONK, THE DOORBELL! CAN'T I GET A MOMENT TO DEVOTE TO MY FISCAL EMPIRE?

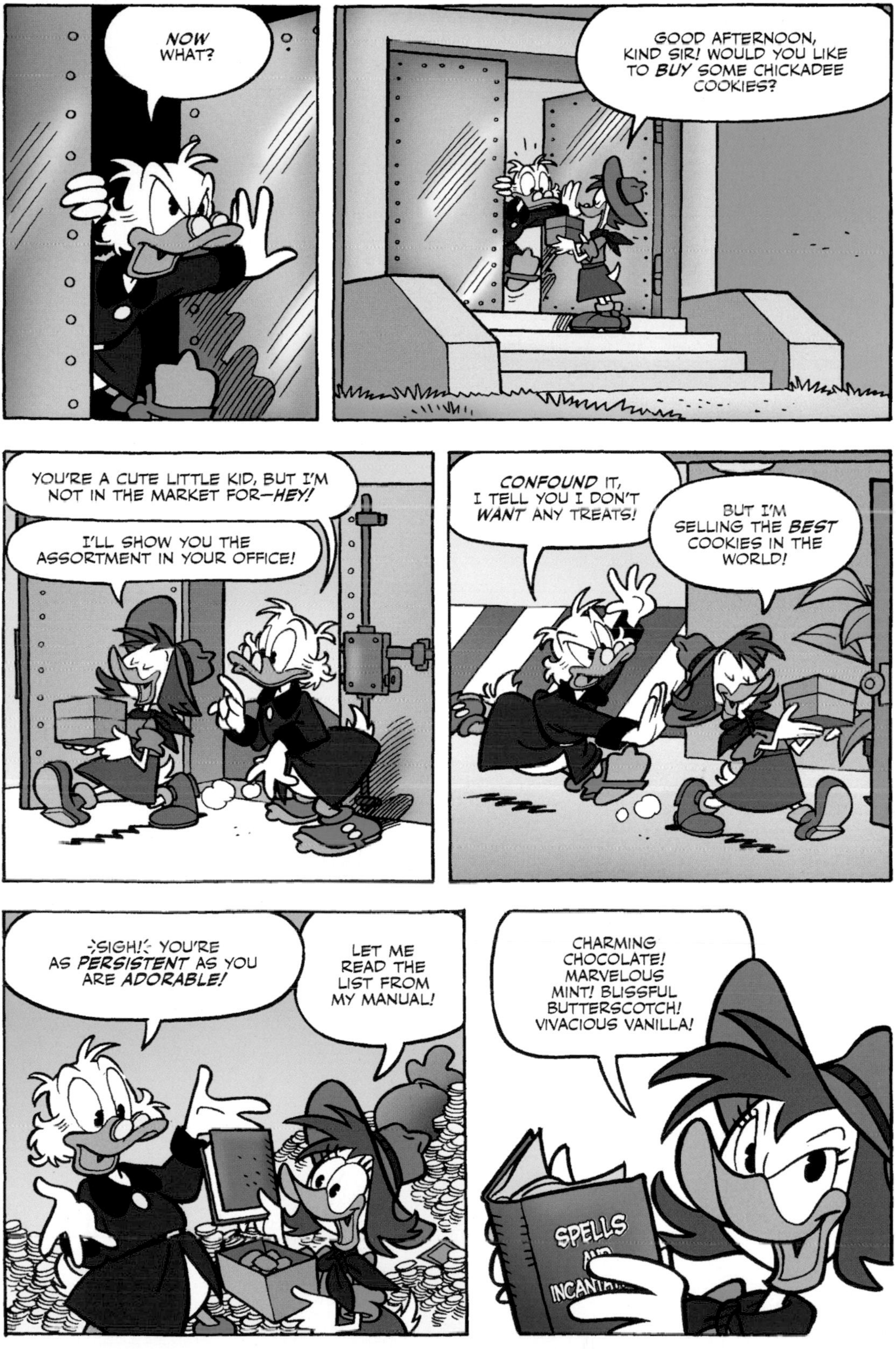

NOW WHAT?
GOOD AFTERNOON, KIND SIR! WOULD YOU LIKE TO BUY SOME CHICKADEE COOKIES?
YOU'RE A CUTE LITTLE KID, BUT I'M NOT IN THE MARKET FOR—HEY!
I'LL SHOW YOU THE ASSORTMENT IN YOUR OFFICE!
CONFOUND IT, I TELL YOU I DON'T WANT ANY TREATS!
BUT I'M SELLING THE BEST COOKIES IN THE WORLD!
SIGH! YOU'RE AS PERSISTENT AS YOU ARE ADORABLE!
LET ME READ THE LIST FROM MY MANUAL!
CHARMING CHOCOLATE! MARVELOUS MINT! BLISSFUL BUTTERSCOTCH! VIVACIOUS VANILLA!
SPELLS AND

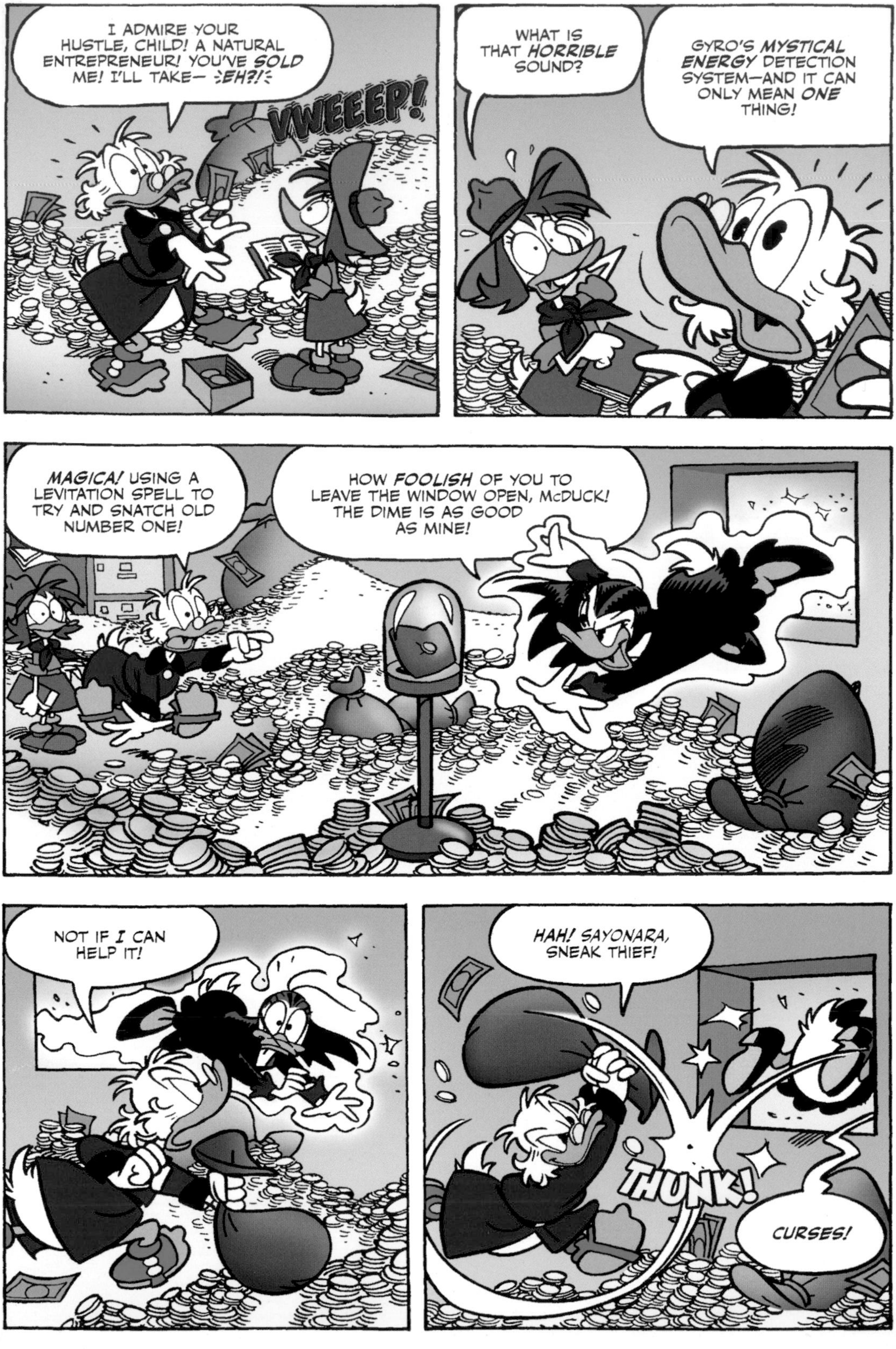
I ADMIRE YOUR HUSTLE, CHILD! A NATURAL ENTREPRENEUR! YOU'VE SOLD ME! I'LL TAKE— EH?!
VWEEEP!
WHAT IS THAT HORRIBLE SOUND?
GYRO'S MYSTICAL ENERGY DETECTION SYSTEM—AND IT CAN ONLY MEAN ONE THING!
MAGICA! USING A LEVITATION SPELL TO TRY AND SNATCH OLD NUMBER ONE!
HOW FOOLISH OF YOU TO LEAVE THE WINDOW OPEN, McDUCK! THE DIME IS AS GOOD AS MINE!
NOT IF I CAN HELP IT!
HAH! SAYONARA, SNEAK THIEF!
THUNK!
CURSES!

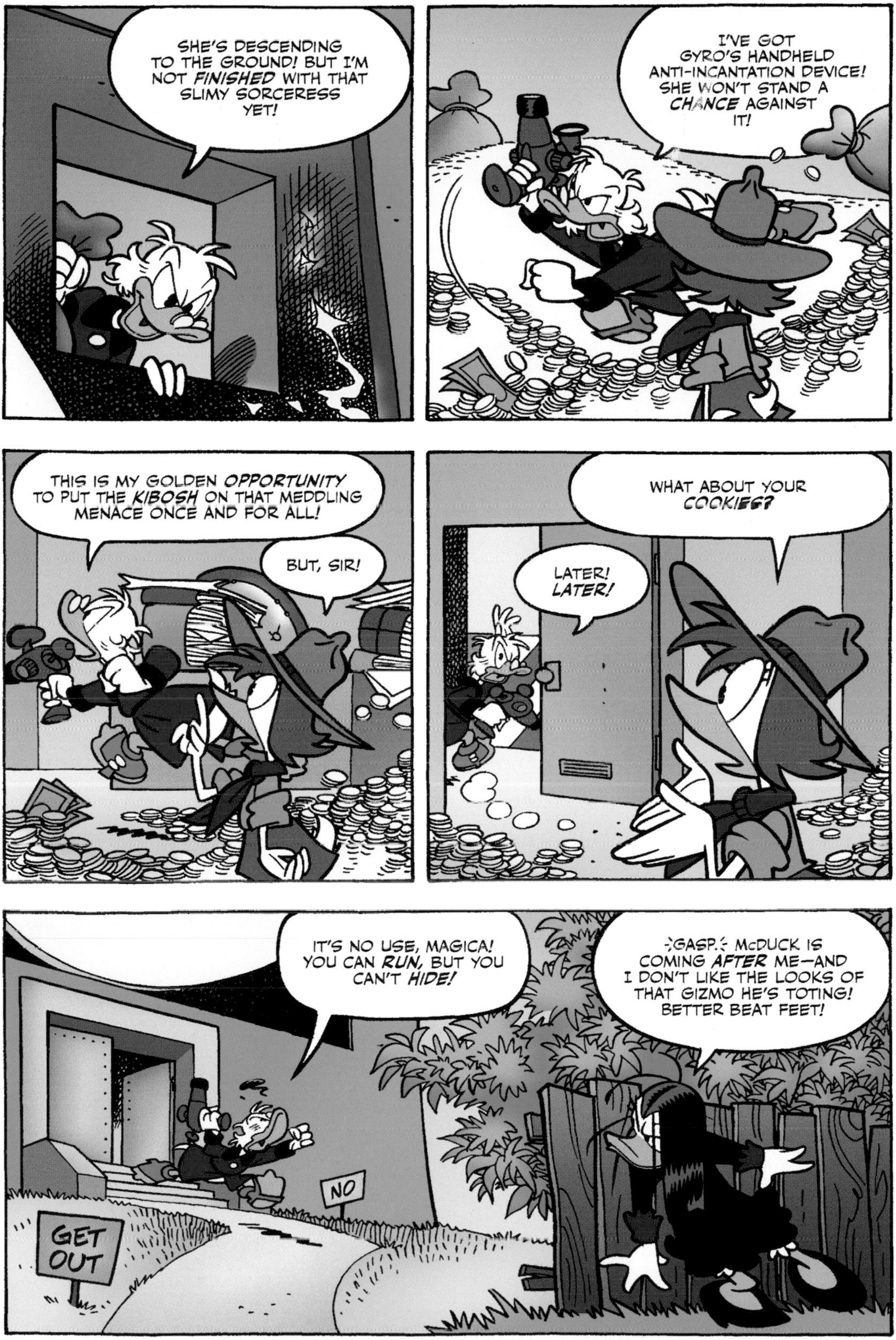
SHE'S DESCENDING TO THE GROUND! BUT I'M NOT FINISHED WITH THAT SLIMY SORCERESS YET!
I'VE GOT GYRO'S HANDHELD ANTI-INCANTATION DEVICE! SHE WON'T STAND A CHANCE AGAINST IT!
THIS IS MY GOLDEN OPPORTUNITY TO PUT THE KIBOSH ON THAT MEDDLING MENACE ONCE AND FOR ALL!
BUT, SIR!
WHAT ABOUT YOUR COOKIES?
LATER! LATER!
IT'S NO USE, MAGICA! YOU CAN RUN, BUT YOU CAN'T HIDE!
GASP. McDUCK IS COMING AFTER ME—AND I DON'T LIKE THE LOOKS OF THAT GIZMO HE'S TOTING! BETTER BEAT FEET!
NO
GET OUT

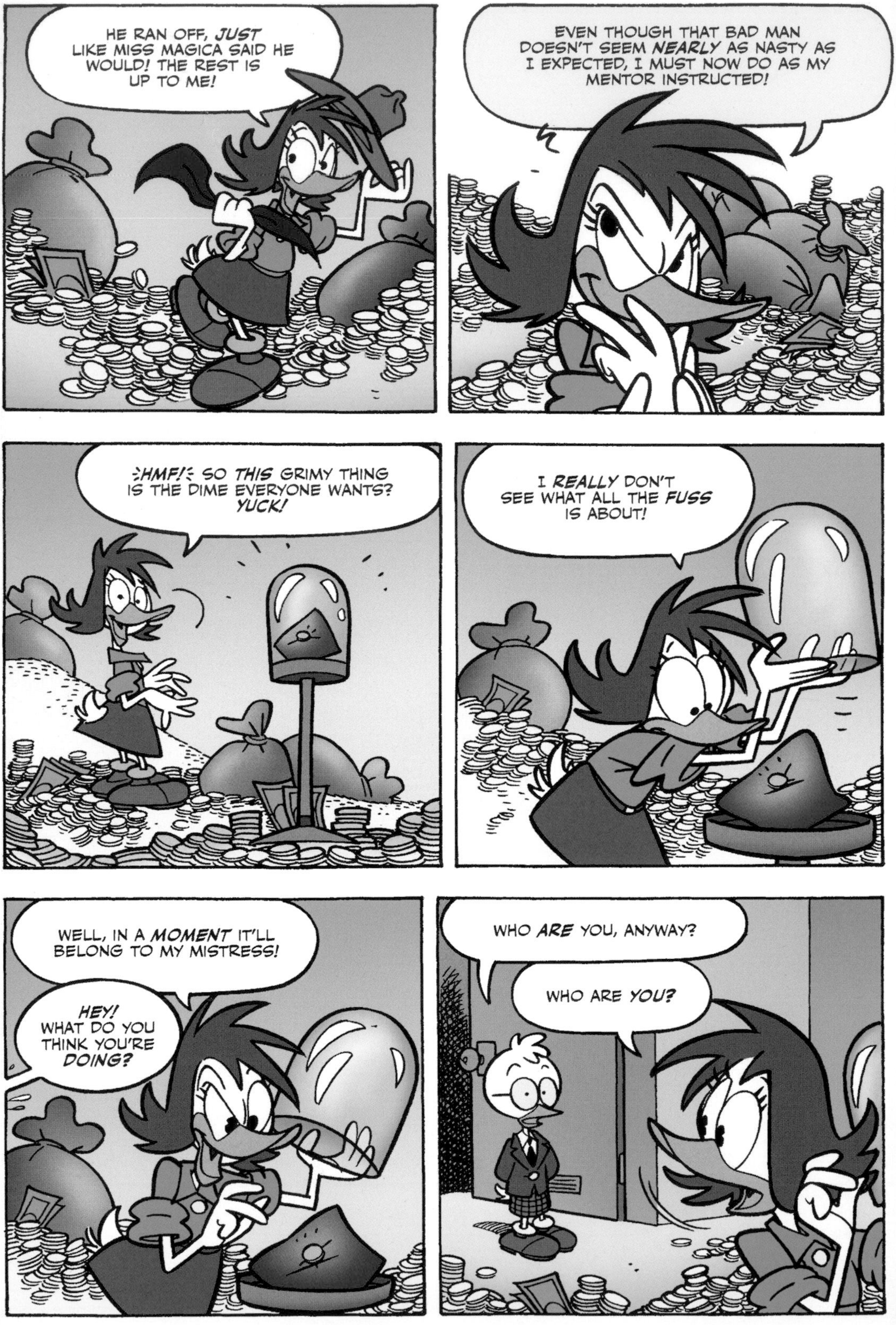
HE RAN OFF, *JUST* LIKE MISS MAGICA SAID HE WOULD! THE REST IS UP TO ME!
EVEN THOUGH THAT BAD MAN DOESN'T SEEM *NEARLY* AS NASTY AS I EXPECTED, I MUST NOW DO AS MY MENTOR INSTRUCTED!
HMF! SO *THIS* GRIMY THING IS THE DIME EVERYONE WANTS? *YUCK!*
I *REALLY* DON'T SEE WHAT ALL THE *FUSS* IS ABOUT!
WELL, IN A *MOMENT* IT'LL BELONG TO MY MISTRESS!
HEY! WHAT DO YOU THINK YOU'RE *DOING?*
WHO *ARE* YOU, ANYWAY?
WHO ARE *YOU?*

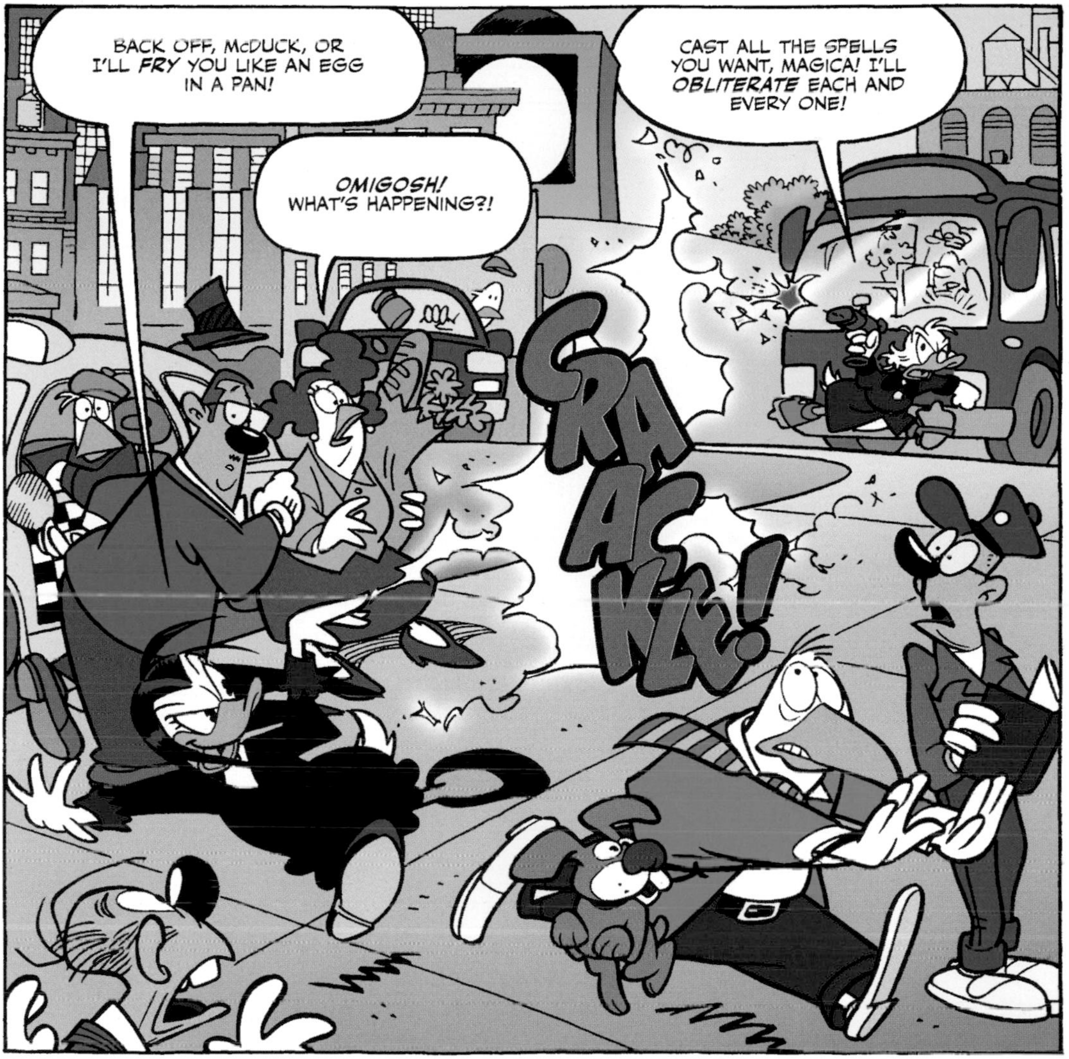
BACK OFF, McDUCK, OR I'LL *FRY* YOU LIKE AN EGG IN A PAN!
CAST ALL THE SPELLS YOU WANT, MAGICA! I'LL *OBLITERATE* EACH AND EVERY ONE!
OMIGOSH! WHAT'S HAPPENING?!
CRAACKLE!

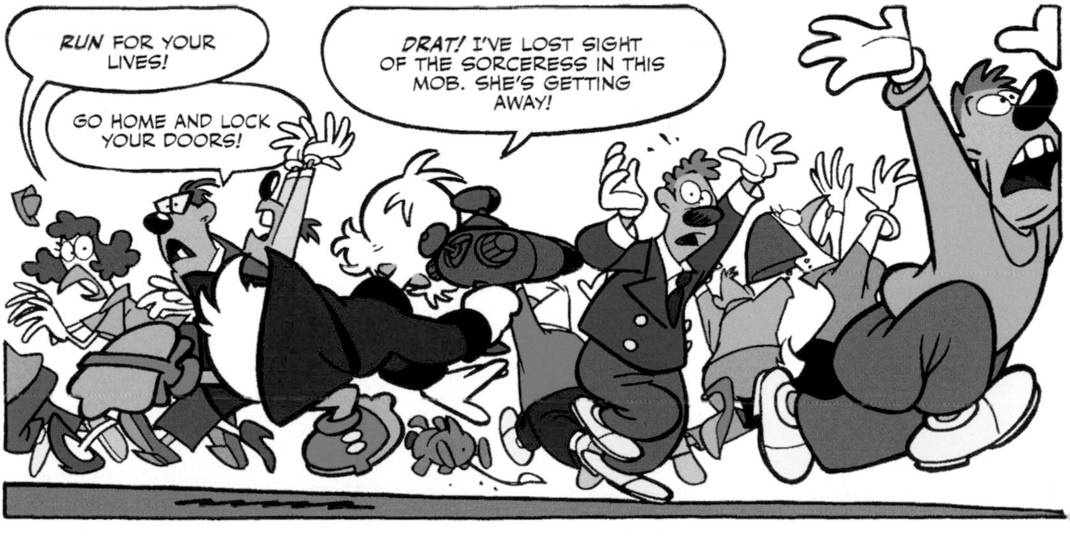
RUN FOR YOUR LIVES!
GO HOME AND LOCK YOUR DOORS!
DRAT! I'VE LOST SIGHT OF THE SORCERESS IN THIS MOB. SHE'S GETTING AWAY!

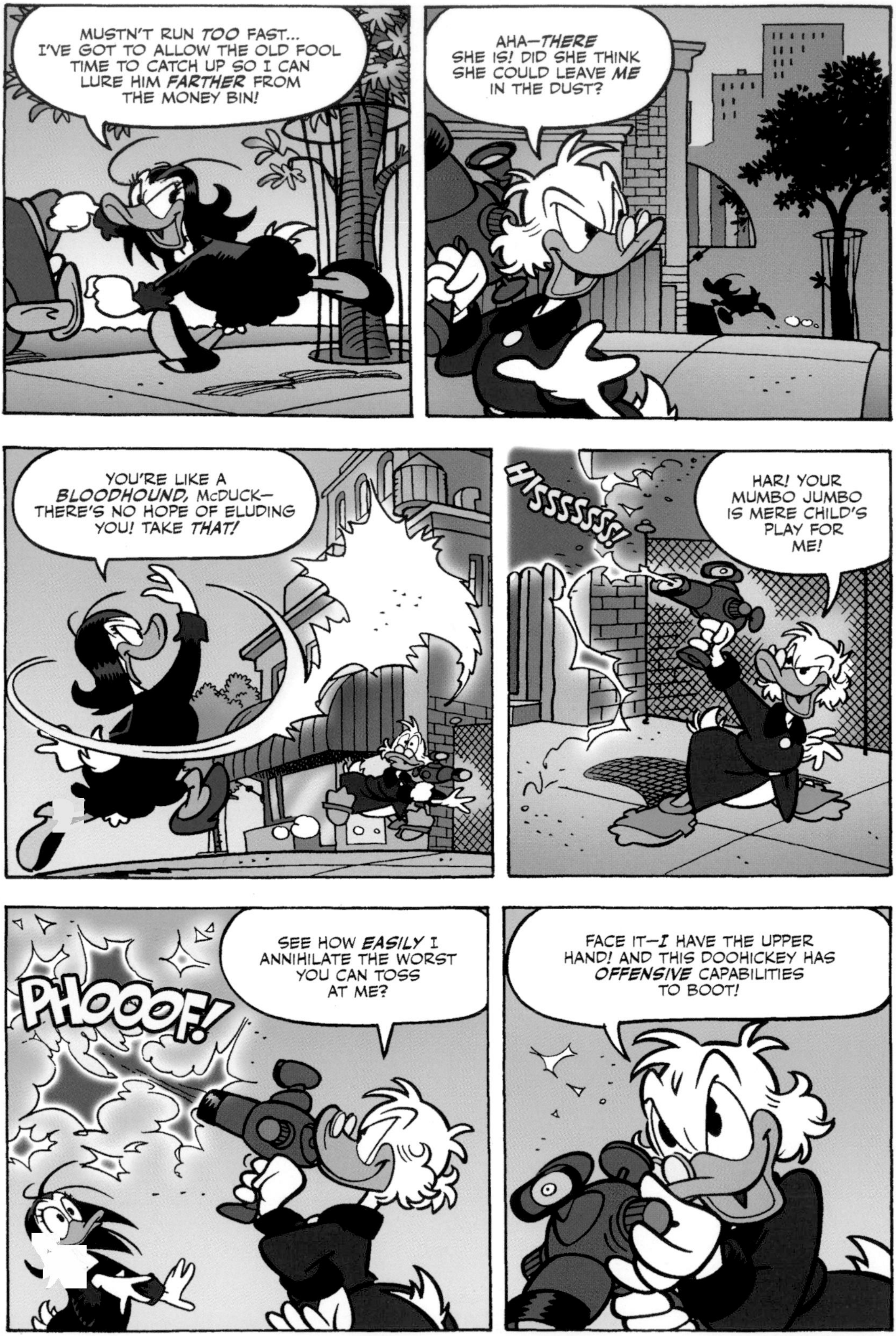
MUSTN'T RUN TOO FAST... I'VE GOT TO ALLOW THE OLD FOOL TIME TO CATCH UP SO I CAN LURE HIM FARTHER FROM THE MONEY BIN!
AHA—THERE SHE IS! DID SHE THINK SHE COULD LEAVE ME IN THE DUST?
YOU'RE LIKE A BLOODHOUND, McDUCK—THERE'S NO HOPE OF ELUDING YOU! TAKE THAT!
HISSSSSSS!
HAR! YOUR MUMBO JUMBO IS MERE CHILD'S PLAY FOR ME!
PHOOOF!
SEE HOW EASILY I ANNIHILATE THE WORST YOU CAN TOSS AT ME?
FACE IT—I HAVE THE UPPER HAND! AND THIS DOOHICKEY HAS OFFENSIVE CAPABILITIES TO BOOT!

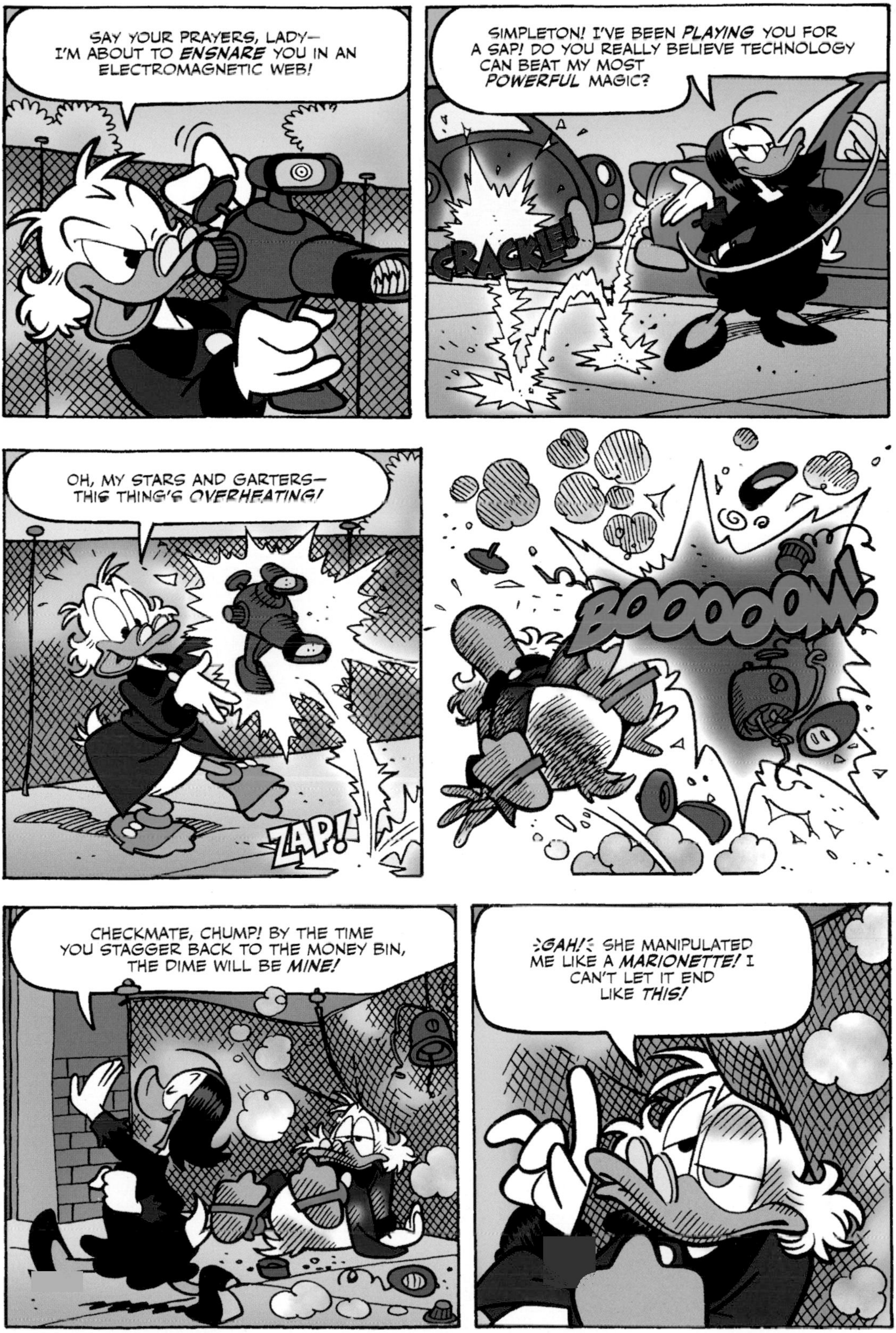
SAY YOUR PRAYERS, LADY— I'M ABOUT TO *ENSNARE* YOU IN AN ELECTROMAGNETIC WEB!
SIMPLETON! I'VE BEEN *PLAYING* YOU FOR A SAP! DO YOU REALLY BELIEVE TECHNOLOGY CAN BEAT MY MOST *POWERFUL* MAGIC?
CRACKLE!
OH, MY STARS AND GARTERS— THIS THING'S *OVERHEATING!*
ZAP!
BOOOOOM!
CHECKMATE, CHUMP! BY THE TIME YOU STAGGER BACK TO THE MONEY BIN, THE DIME WILL BE *MINE!*
GAH! SHE MANIPULATED ME LIKE A *MARIONETTE!* I CAN'T LET IT END LIKE *THIS!*

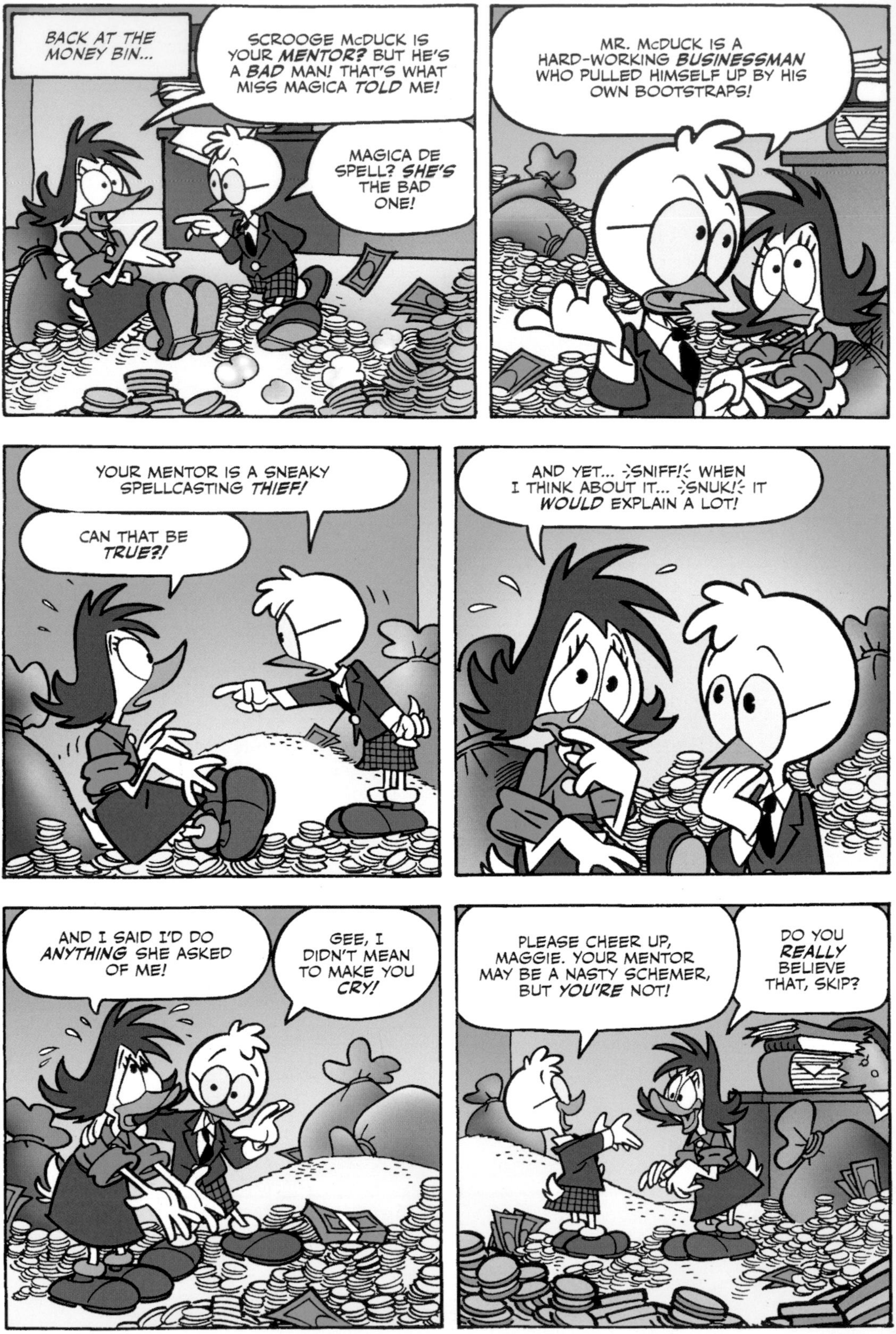
BACK AT THE MONEY BIN...
SCROOGE McDUCK IS YOUR *MENTOR?* BUT HE'S A *BAD* MAN! THAT'S WHAT MISS MAGICA *TOLD* ME!
MAGICA DE SPELL? *SHE'S* THE BAD ONE!
MR. McDUCK IS A HARD-WORKING *BUSINESSMAN* WHO PULLED HIMSELF UP BY HIS OWN BOOTSTRAPS!
YOUR MENTOR IS A SNEAKY SPELLCASTING *THIEF!*
CAN THAT BE *TRUE?!*
AND YET... SNIFF! WHEN I THINK ABOUT IT... SNUK! IT *WOULD* EXPLAIN A LOT!
AND I SAID I'D DO *ANYTHING* SHE ASKED OF ME!
GEE, I DIDN'T MEAN TO MAKE YOU *CRY!*
PLEASE CHEER UP, MAGGIE. YOUR MENTOR MAY BE A NASTY SCHEMER, BUT *YOU'RE* NOT!
DO YOU *REALLY* BELIEVE THAT, SKIP?

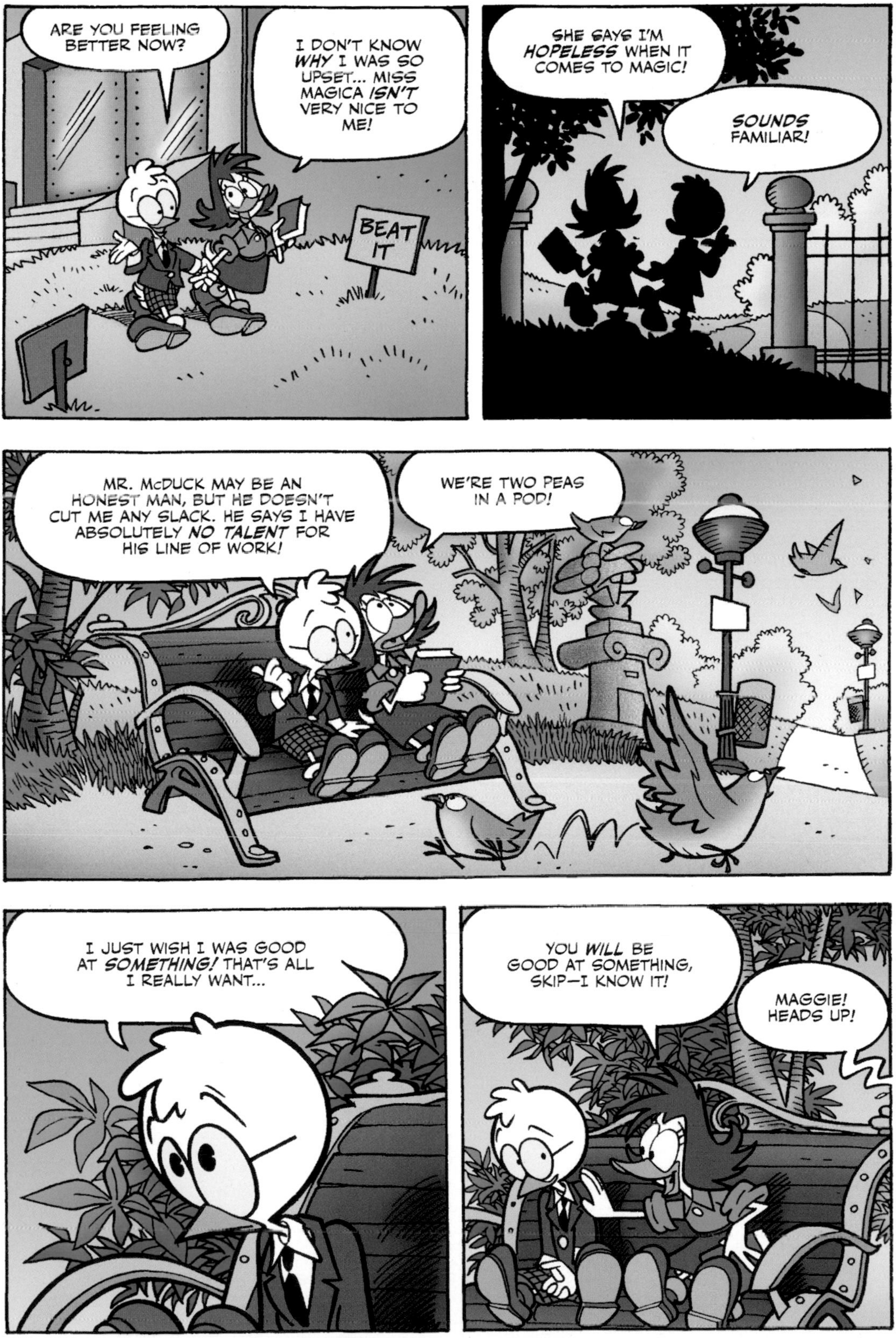
ARE YOU FEELING BETTER NOW?
I DON'T KNOW *WHY* I WAS SO UPSET... MISS MAGICA *ISN'T* VERY NICE TO ME!
BEAT IT
SHE SAYS I'M *HOPELESS* WHEN IT COMES TO MAGIC!
SOUNDS FAMILIAR!
MR. McDUCK MAY BE AN HONEST MAN, BUT HE DOESN'T CUT ME ANY SLACK. HE SAYS I HAVE ABSOLUTELY *NO TALENT* FOR HIS LINE OF WORK!
WE'RE TWO PEAS IN A POD!
I JUST WISH I WAS GOOD AT *SOMETHING!* THAT'S ALL I REALLY WANT...
YOU *WILL* BE GOOD AT SOMETHING, SKIP—I KNOW IT!
MAGGIE! HEADS UP!

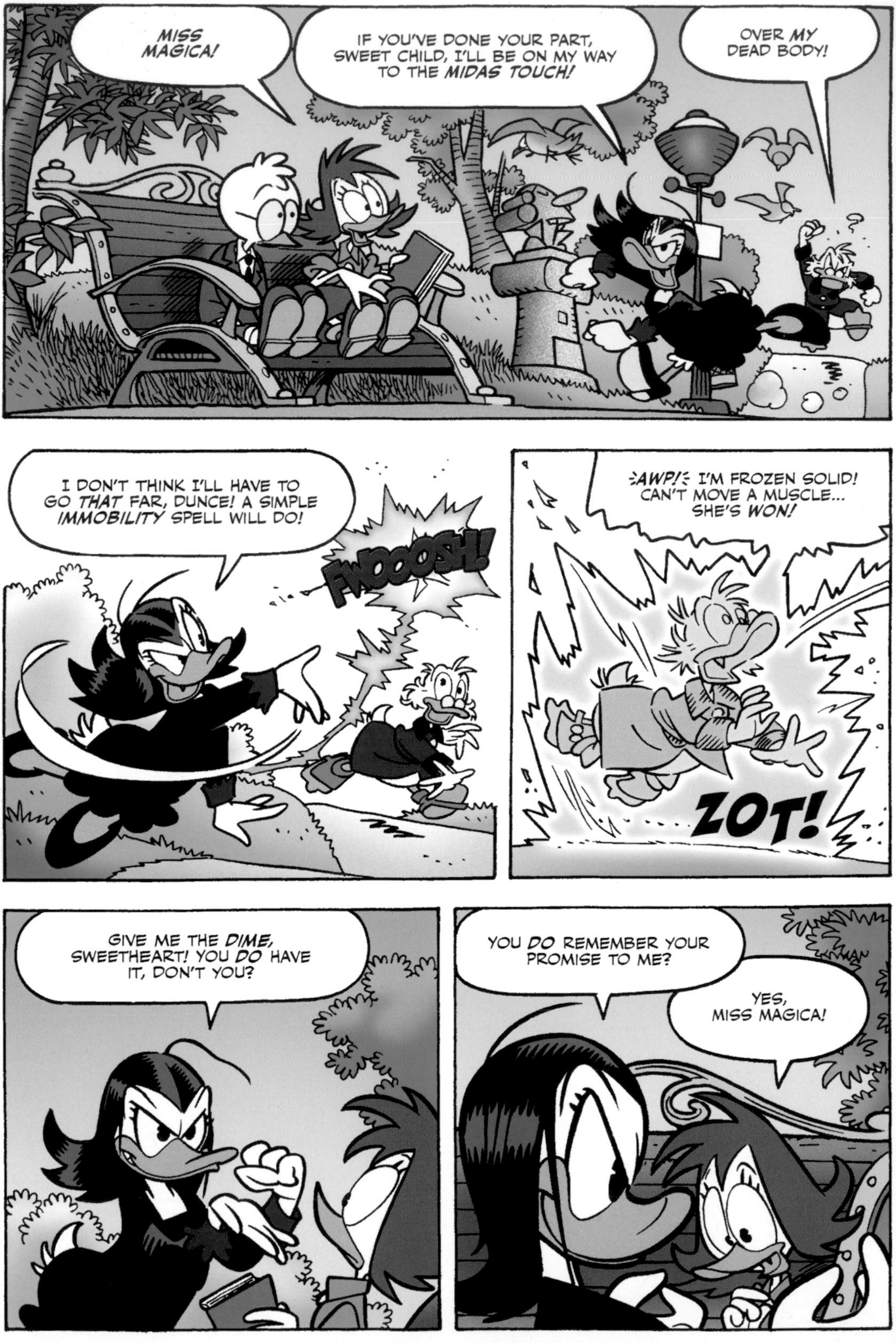
MISS MAGICA!
IF YOU'VE DONE YOUR PART, SWEET CHILD, I'LL BE ON MY WAY TO THE MIDAS TOUCH!
OVER MY DEAD BODY!
I DON'T THINK I'LL HAVE TO GO THAT FAR, DUNCE! A SIMPLE IMMOBILITY SPELL WILL DO!
FWOOOSH!
AWP! I'M FROZEN SOLID! CAN'T MOVE A MUSCLE... SHE'S WON!
ZOT!
GIVE ME THE DIME, SWEETHEART! YOU DO HAVE IT, DON'T YOU?
YOU DO REMEMBER YOUR PROMISE TO ME?
YES, MISS MAGICA!

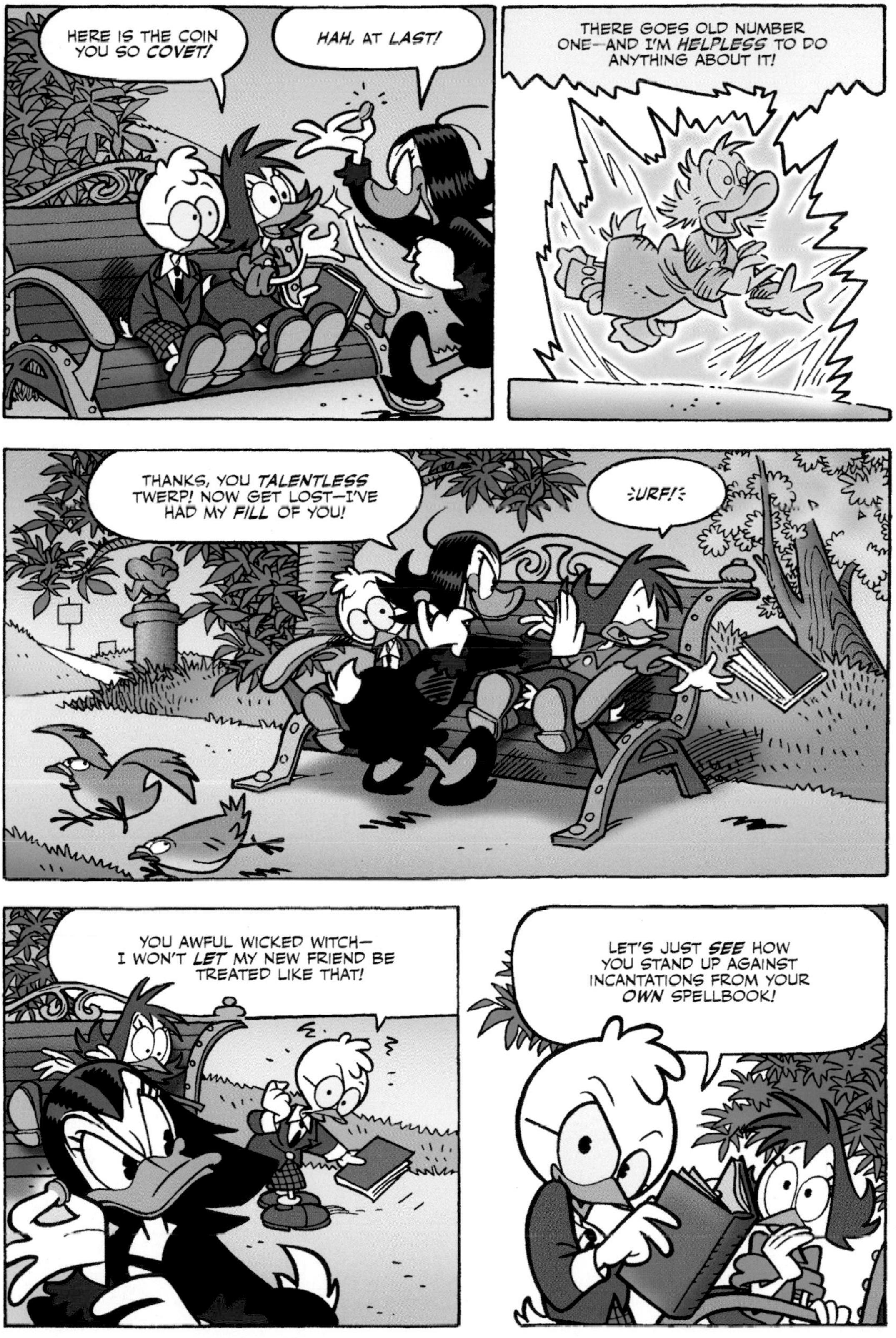
HERE IS THE COIN YOU SO COVET!
HAH, AT LAST!
THERE GOES OLD NUMBER ONE—AND I'M HELPLESS TO DO ANYTHING ABOUT IT!
THANKS, YOU TALENTLESS TWERP! NOW GET LOST—I'VE HAD MY FILL OF YOU!
URF!
YOU AWFUL WICKED WITCH— I WON'T LET MY NEW FRIEND BE TREATED LIKE THAT!
LET'S JUST SEE HOW YOU STAND UP AGAINST INCANTATIONS FROM YOUR OWN SPELLBOOK!

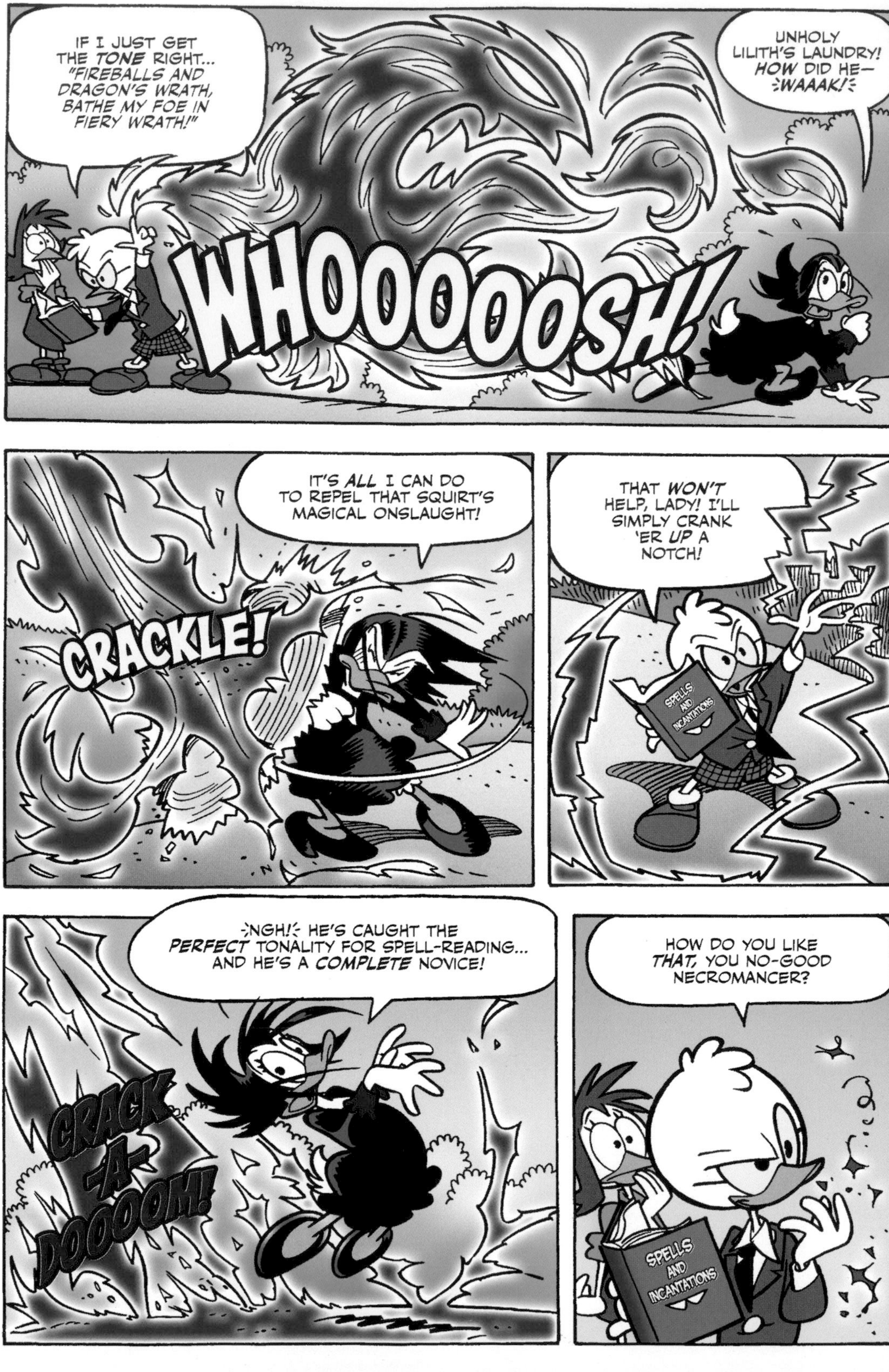
IF I JUST GET THE TONE RIGHT... "FIREBALLS AND DRAGON'S WRATH, BATHE MY FOE IN FIERY WRATH!"
UNHOLY LILITH'S LAUNDRY! HOW DID HE— WAAAK!
WHOOOOOSH!
IT'S ALL I CAN DO TO REPEL THAT SQUIRT'S MAGICAL ONSLAUGHT!
CRACKLE!
THAT WON'T HELP, LADY! I'LL SIMPLY CRANK 'ER UP A NOTCH!
SPELLS AND INCANTATIONS
NGH! HE'S CAUGHT THE PERFECT TONALITY FOR SPELL-READING... AND HE'S A COMPLETE NOVICE!
CRACK -A- DOOOOOM!
HOW DO YOU LIKE THAT, YOU NO-GOOD NECROMANCER?
SPELLS AND INCANTATIONS

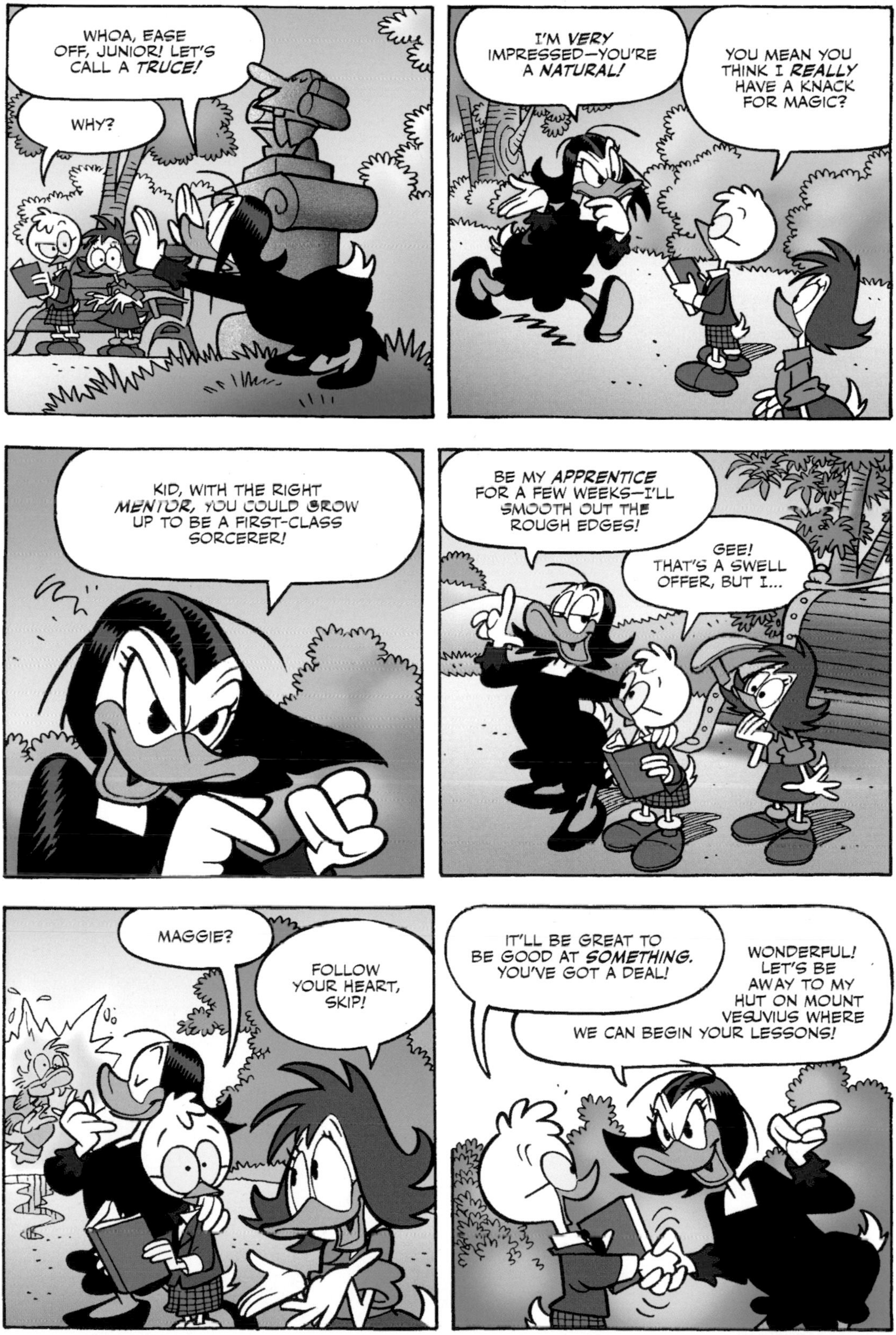

WHOA, EASE OFF, JUNIOR! LET'S CALL A *TRUCE!*
WHY?
I'M *VERY* IMPRESSED—YOU'RE A *NATURAL!*
YOU MEAN YOU THINK I *REALLY* HAVE A KNACK FOR MAGIC?
KID, WITH THE RIGHT *MENTOR,* YOU COULD GROW UP TO BE A FIRST-CLASS SORCERER!
BE MY *APPRENTICE* FOR A FEW WEEKS—I'LL SMOOTH OUT THE ROUGH EDGES!
GEE! THAT'S A SWELL OFFER, BUT I...
MAGGIE?
FOLLOW YOUR HEART, SKIP!
IT'LL BE GREAT TO BE GOOD AT *SOMETHING.* YOU'VE GOT A DEAL!
WONDERFUL! LET'S BE AWAY TO MY HUT ON MOUNT VESUVIUS WHERE WE CAN BEGIN YOUR LESSONS!

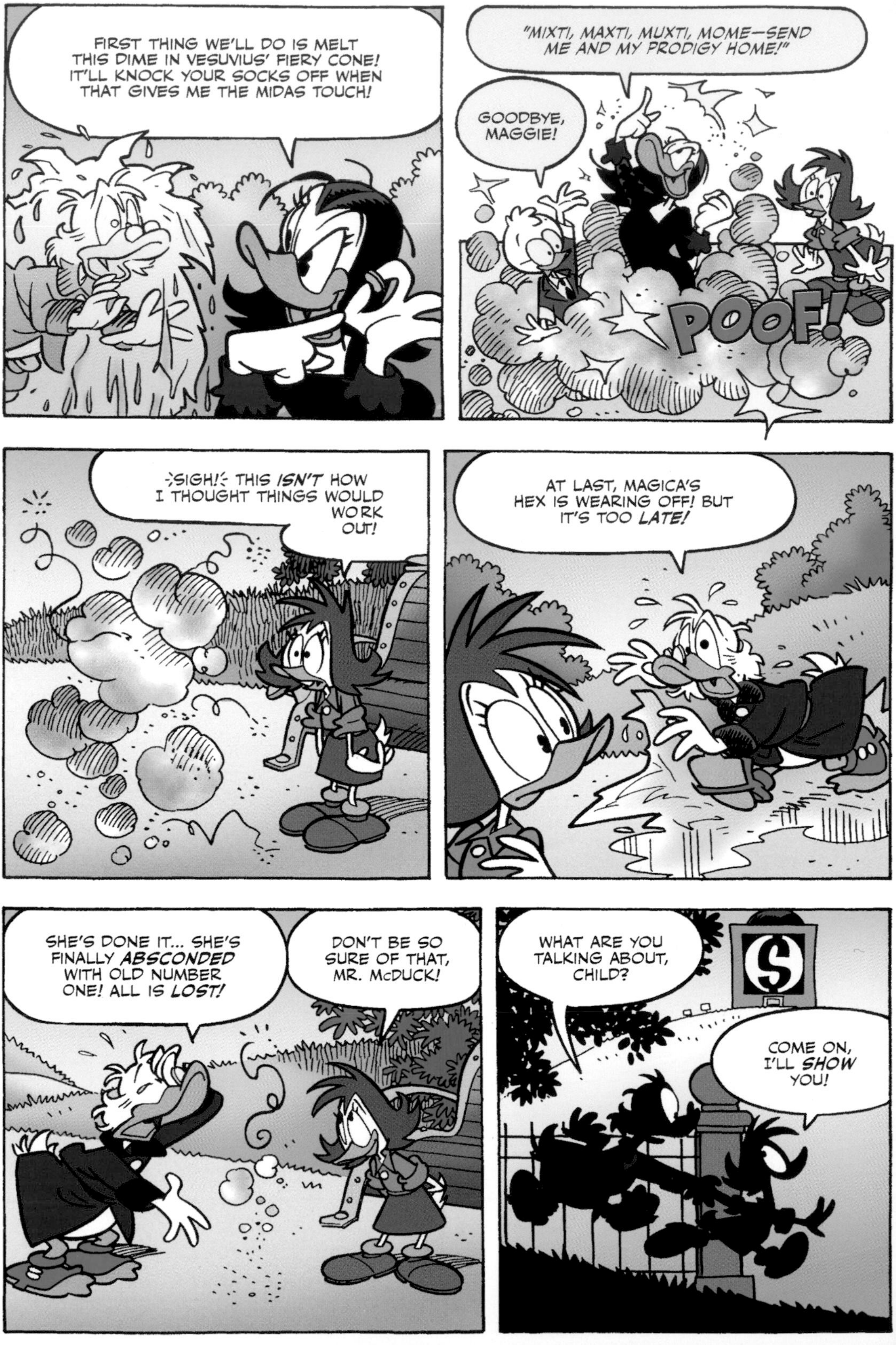
FIRST THING WE'LL DO IS MELT THIS DIME IN VESUVIUS' FIERY CONE! IT'LL KNOCK YOUR SOCKS OFF WHEN THAT GIVES ME THE MIDAS TOUCH!
"MIXTI, MAXTI, MUXTI, MOME—SEND ME AND MY PRODIGY HOME!"
GOODBYE, MAGGIE!
POOF!
-SIGH!- THIS ISN'T HOW I THOUGHT THINGS WOULD WORK OUT!
AT LAST, MAGICA'S HEX IS WEARING OFF! BUT IT'S TOO LATE!
SHE'S DONE IT... SHE'S FINALLY ABSCONDED WITH OLD NUMBER ONE! ALL IS LOST!
DON'T BE SO SURE OF THAT, MR. McDUCK!
WHAT ARE YOU TALKING ABOUT, CHILD?
COME ON, I'LL SHOW YOU!

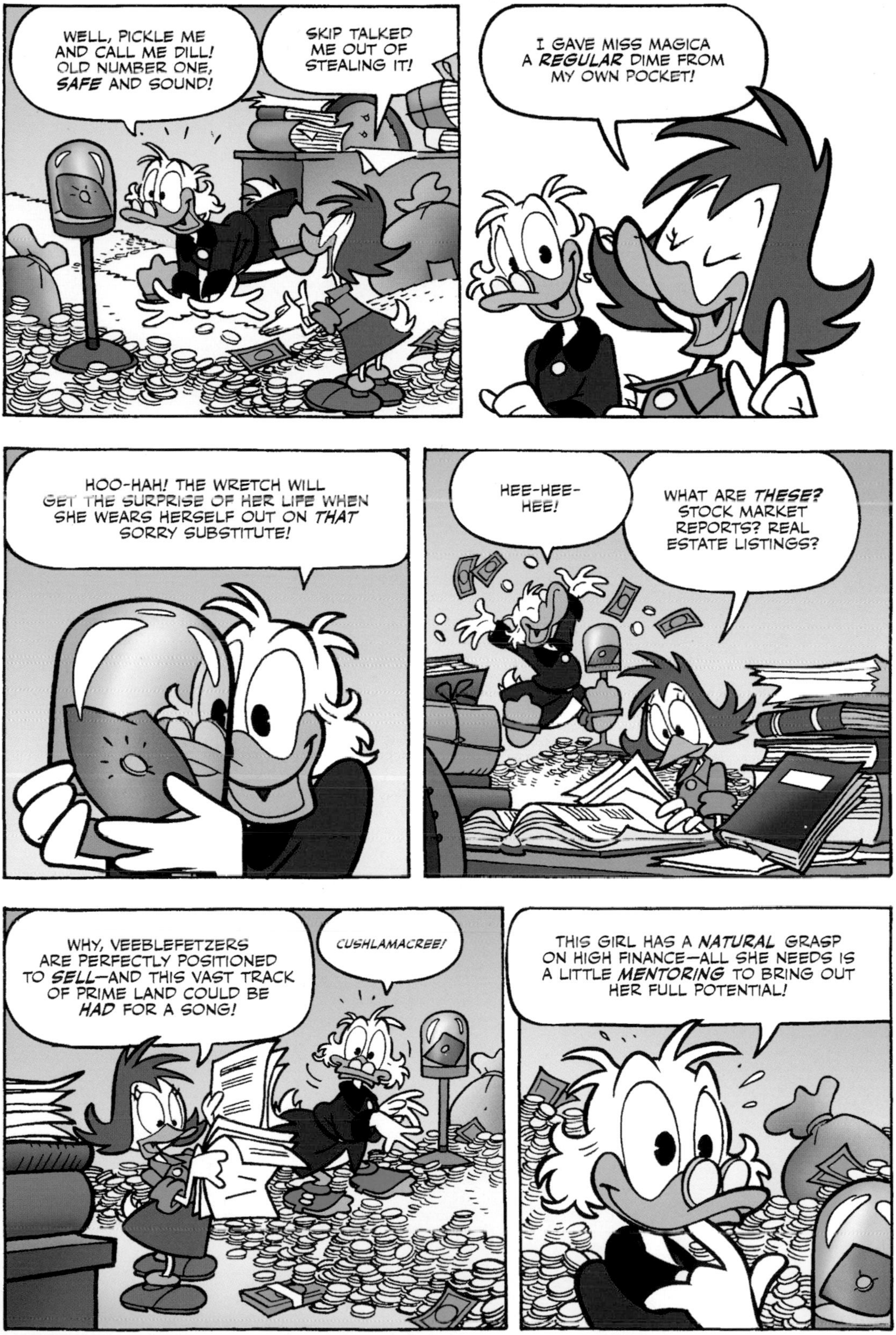
WELL, PICKLE ME AND CALL ME DILL! OLD NUMBER ONE, SAFE AND SOUND!
SKIP TALKED ME OUT OF STEALING IT!
I GAVE MISS MAGICA A REGULAR DIME FROM MY OWN POCKET!
HOO-HAH! THE WRETCH WILL GET THE SURPRISE OF HER LIFE WHEN SHE WEARS HERSELF OUT ON THAT SORRY SUBSTITUTE!
HEE-HEE-HEE!
WHAT ARE THESE? STOCK MARKET REPORTS? REAL ESTATE LISTINGS?
WHY, VEEBLEFETZERS ARE PERFECTLY POSITIONED TO SELL—AND THIS VAST TRACK OF PRIME LAND COULD BE HAD FOR A SONG!
CUSHLAMACREE!
THIS GIRL HAS A NATURAL GRASP ON HIGH FINANCE—ALL SHE NEEDS IS A LITTLE MENTORING TO BRING OUT HER FULL POTENTIAL!

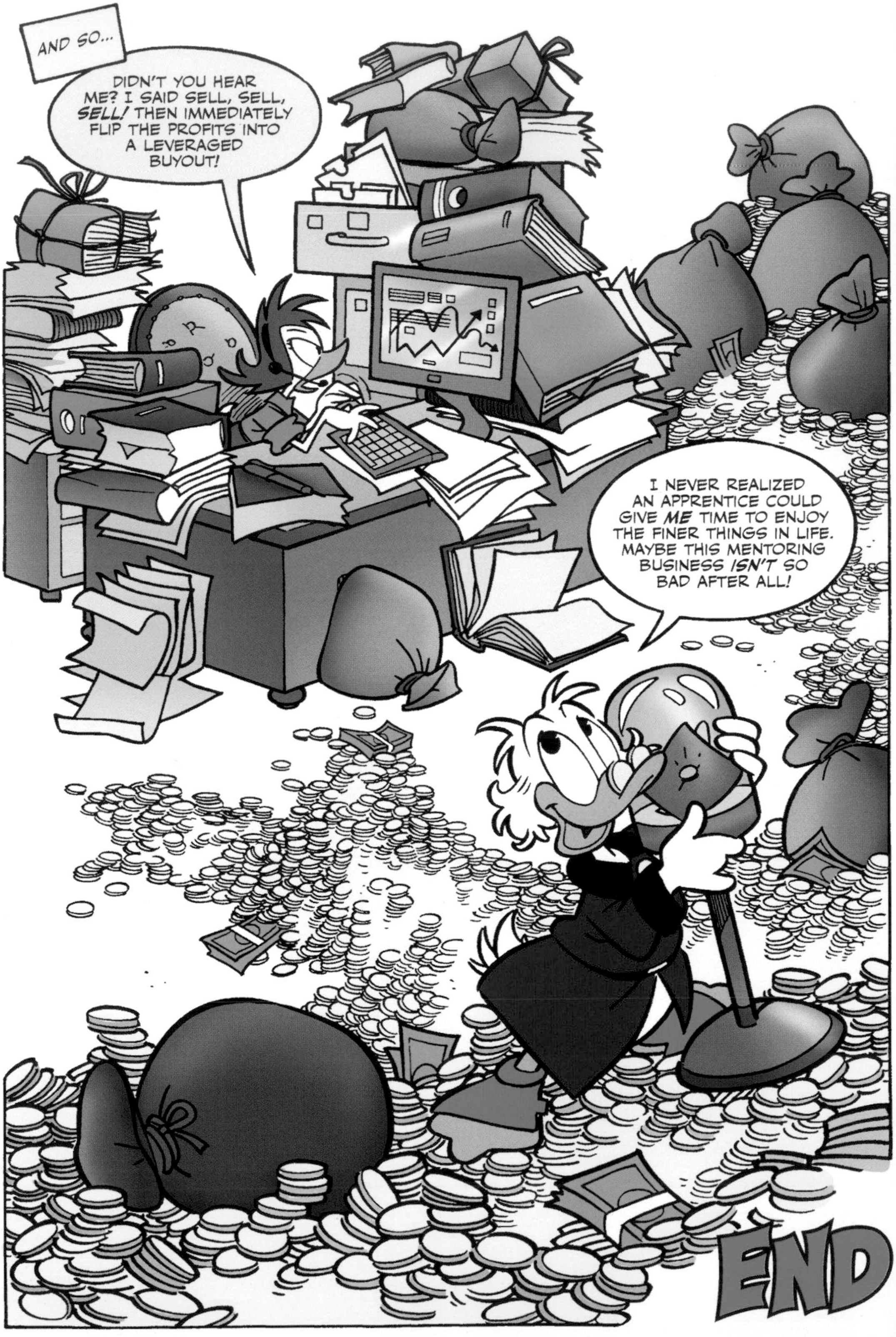
AND SO...
DIDN'T YOU HEAR ME? I SAID SELL, SELL, SELL! THEN IMMEDIATELY FLIP THE PROFITS INTO A LEVERAGED BUYOUT!
I NEVER REALIZED AN APPRENTICE COULD GIVE ME TIME TO ENJOY THE FINER THINGS IN LIFE. MAYBE THIS MENTORING BUSINESS ISN'T SO BAD AFTER ALL!
END

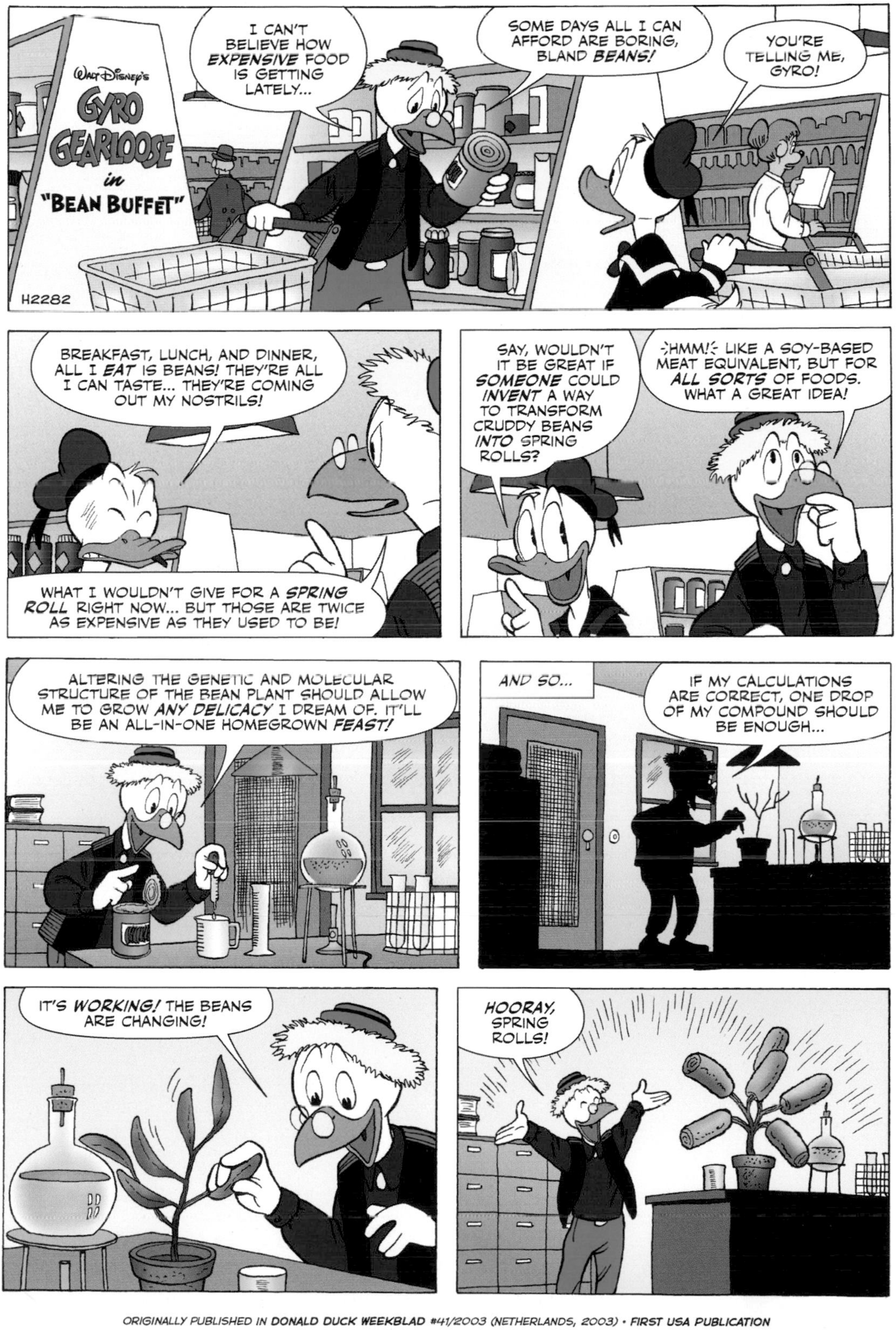
WALT DISNEY'S GYRO GEARLOOSE in "BEAN BUFFET"
H2282
I CAN'T BELIEVE HOW EXPENSIVE FOOD IS GETTING LATELY...
SOME DAYS ALL I CAN AFFORD ARE BORING, BLAND BEANS!
YOU'RE TELLING ME, GYRO!
BREAKFAST, LUNCH, AND DINNER, ALL I EAT IS BEANS! THEY'RE ALL I CAN TASTE... THEY'RE COMING OUT MY NOSTRILS!
WHAT I WOULDN'T GIVE FOR A SPRING ROLL RIGHT NOW... BUT THOSE ARE TWICE AS EXPENSIVE AS THEY USED TO BE!
SAY, WOULDN'T IT BE GREAT IF SOMEONE COULD INVENT A WAY TO TRANSFORM CRUDDY BEANS INTO SPRING ROLLS?
HMM! LIKE A SOY-BASED MEAT EQUIVALENT, BUT FOR ALL SORTS OF FOODS. WHAT A GREAT IDEA!
ALTERING THE GENETIC AND MOLECULAR STRUCTURE OF THE BEAN PLANT SHOULD ALLOW ME TO GROW ANY DELICACY I DREAM OF. IT'LL BE AN ALL-IN-ONE HOMEGROWN FEAST!
AND SO...
IF MY CALCULATIONS ARE CORRECT, ONE DROP OF MY COMPOUND SHOULD BE ENOUGH...
IT'S WORKING! THE BEANS ARE CHANGING!
HOORAY, SPRING ROLLS!

ORIGINALLY PUBLISHED IN ***DONALD DUCK WEEKBLAD*** *#41/2003 (NETHERLANDS, 2003) •* ***FIRST USA PUBLICATION***

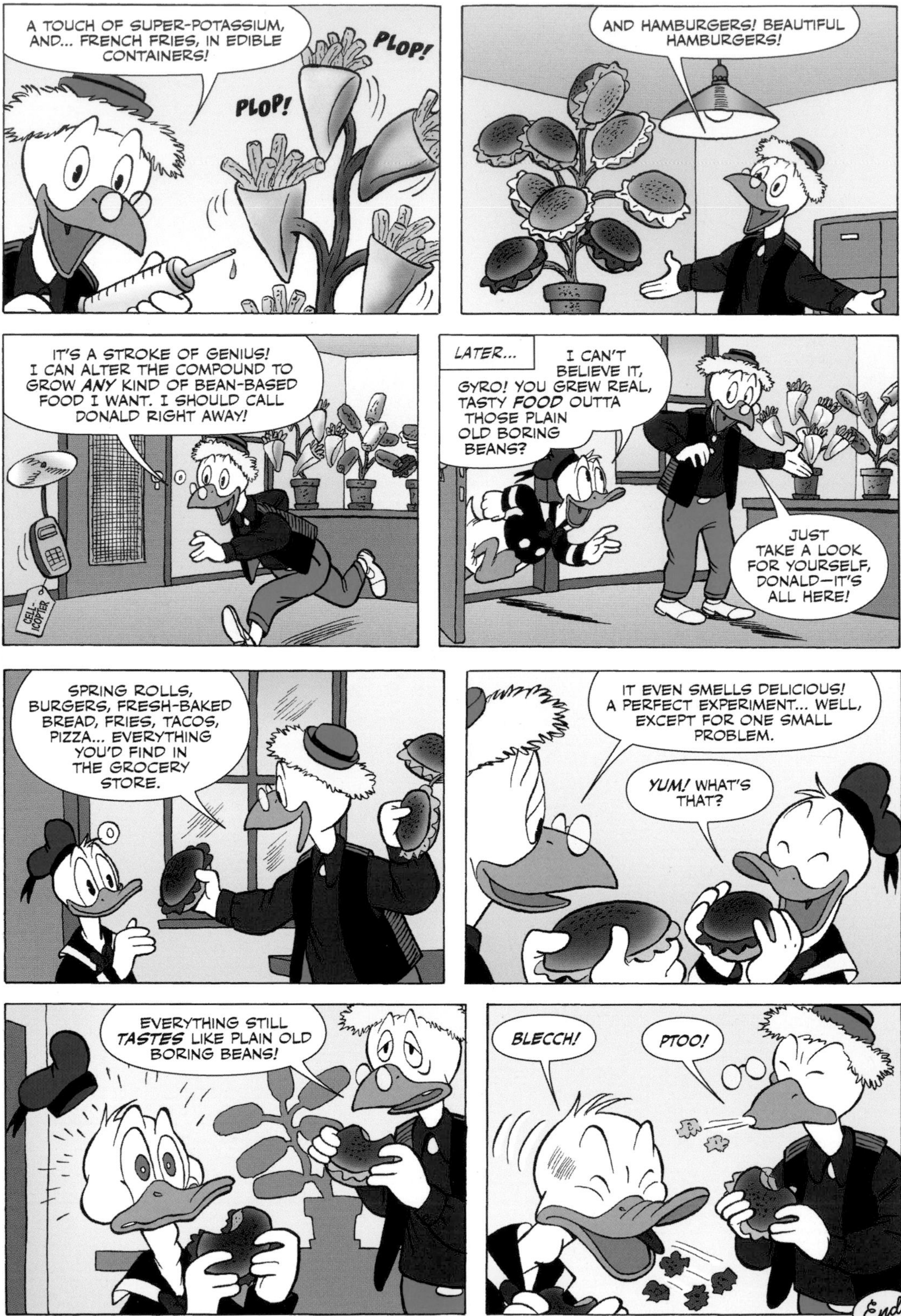
A TOUCH OF SUPER-POTASSIUM, AND... FRENCH FRIES, IN EDIBLE CONTAINERS!
PLOP!
PLOP!
AND HAMBURGERS! BEAUTIFUL HAMBURGERS!
IT'S A STROKE OF GENIUS! I CAN ALTER THE COMPOUND TO GROW ANY KIND OF BEAN-BASED FOOD I WANT. I SHOULD CALL DONALD RIGHT AWAY!
CELL-ICOPTER
LATER...
I CAN'T BELIEVE IT, GYRO! YOU GREW REAL, TASTY FOOD OUTTA THOSE PLAIN OLD BORING BEANS?
JUST TAKE A LOOK FOR YOURSELF, DONALD—IT'S ALL HERE!
SPRING ROLLS, BURGERS, FRESH-BAKED BREAD, FRIES, TACOS, PIZZA... EVERYTHING YOU'D FIND IN THE GROCERY STORE.
IT EVEN SMELLS DELICIOUS! A PERFECT EXPERIMENT... WELL, EXCEPT FOR ONE SMALL PROBLEM.
YUM! WHAT'S THAT?
EVERYTHING STILL TASTES LIKE PLAIN OLD BORING BEANS!
BLECCH!
PTOO!
End

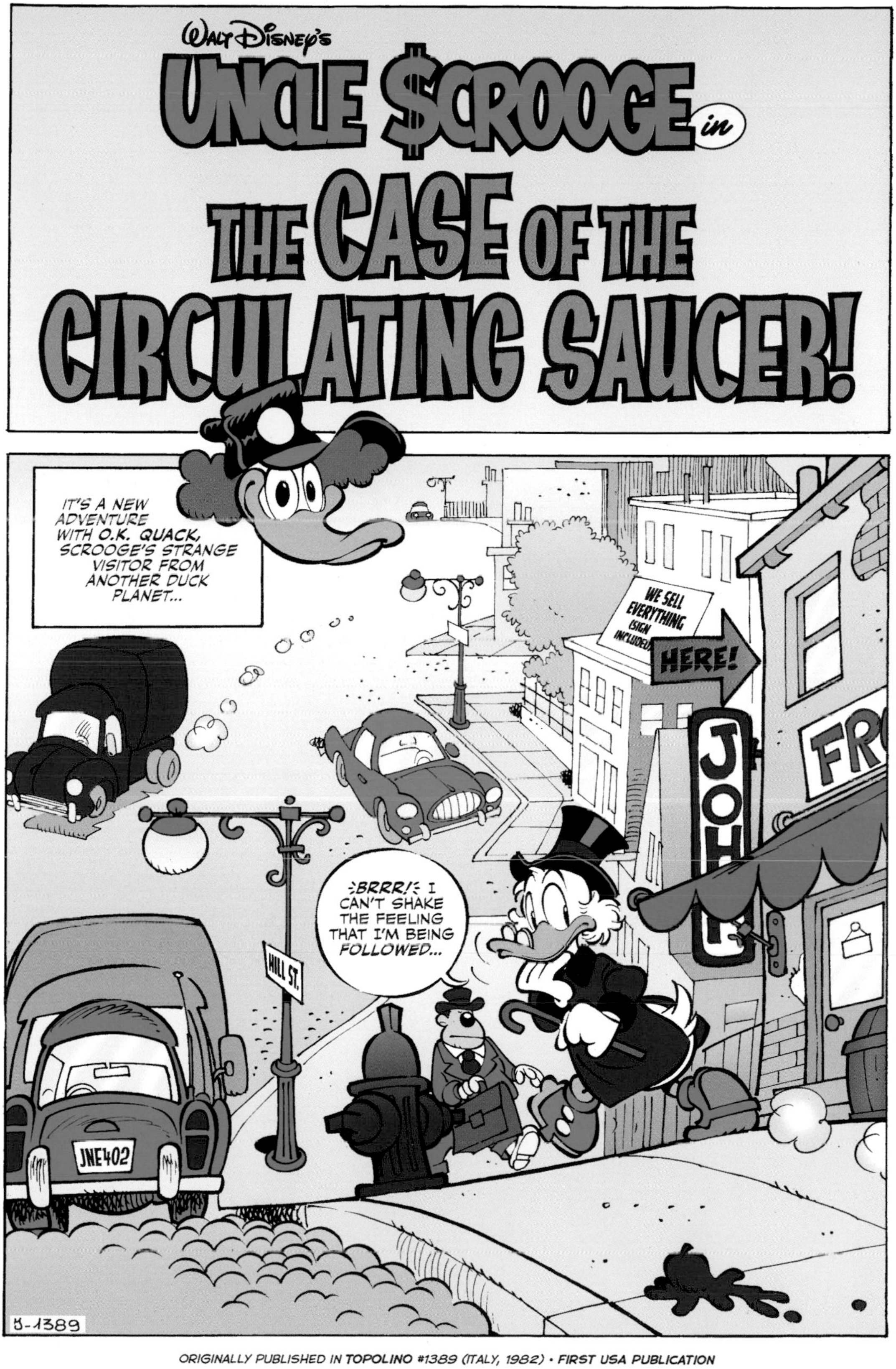
WALT DISNEY'S
UNCLE $CROOGE in
THE CASE OF THE CIRCULATING SAUCER!
IT'S A NEW ADVENTURE WITH O.K. QUACK, SCROOGE'S STRANGE VISITOR FROM ANOTHER DUCK PLANET...
WE SELL EVERYTHING (SIGN INCLUDED)
HERE!
BRRR! I CAN'T SHAKE THE FEELING THAT I'M BEING FOLLOWED...
HILL ST.
JNE402
J-1389

ORIGINALLY PUBLISHED IN TOPOLINO #1389 (ITALY, 1982) • FIRST USA PUBLICATION

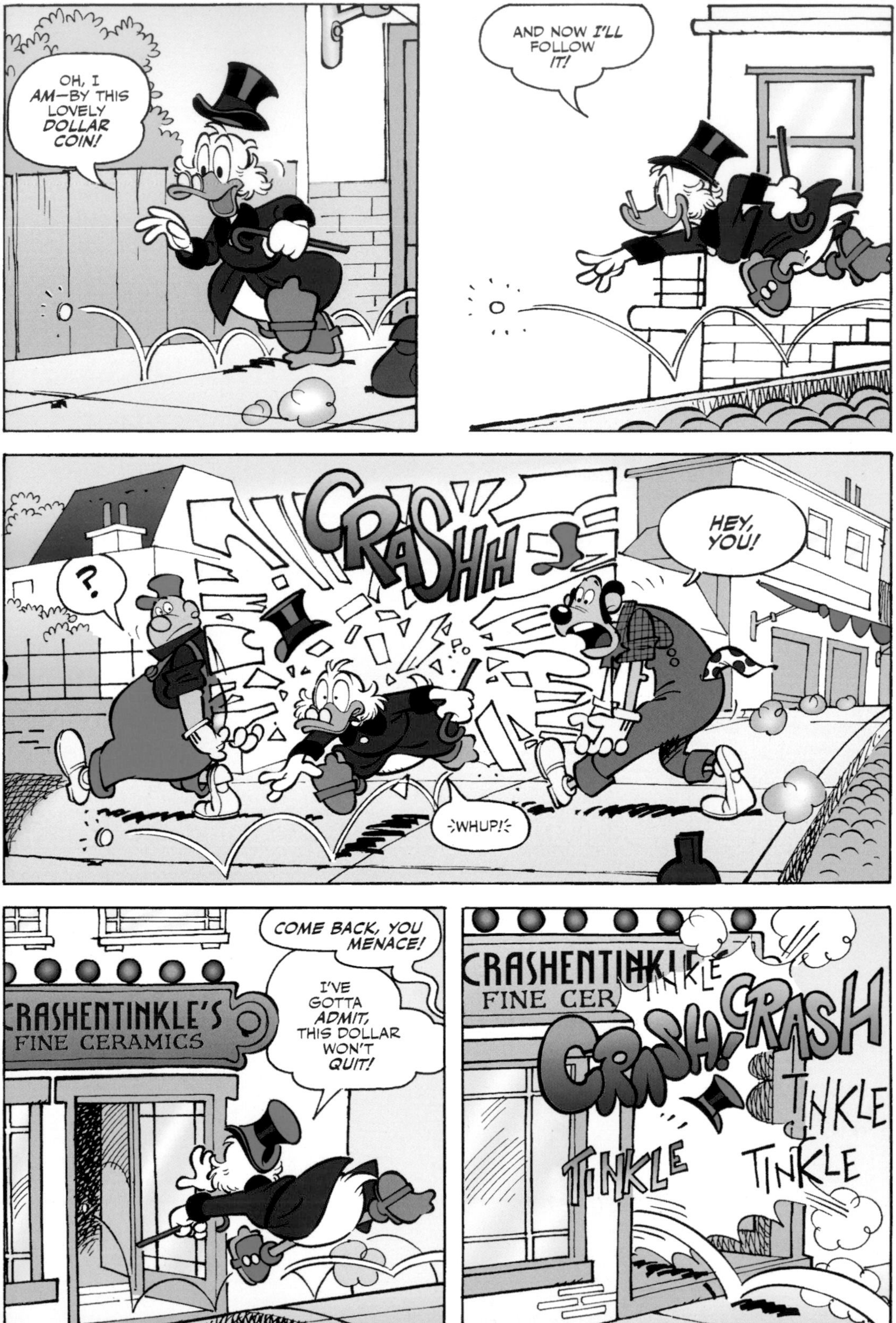
OH, I AM—BY THIS LOVELY DOLLAR COIN!
AND NOW I'LL FOLLOW IT!
CRASHH
?
HEY, YOU!
WHUP!
COME BACK, YOU MENACE!
I'VE GOTTA ADMIT, THIS DOLLAR WON'T QUIT!
CRASHENTINKLE'S FINE CERAMICS
CRASHENTINKLE FINE CER
TINKLE
CRASH! CRASH
TINKLE
TINKLE
TINKLE

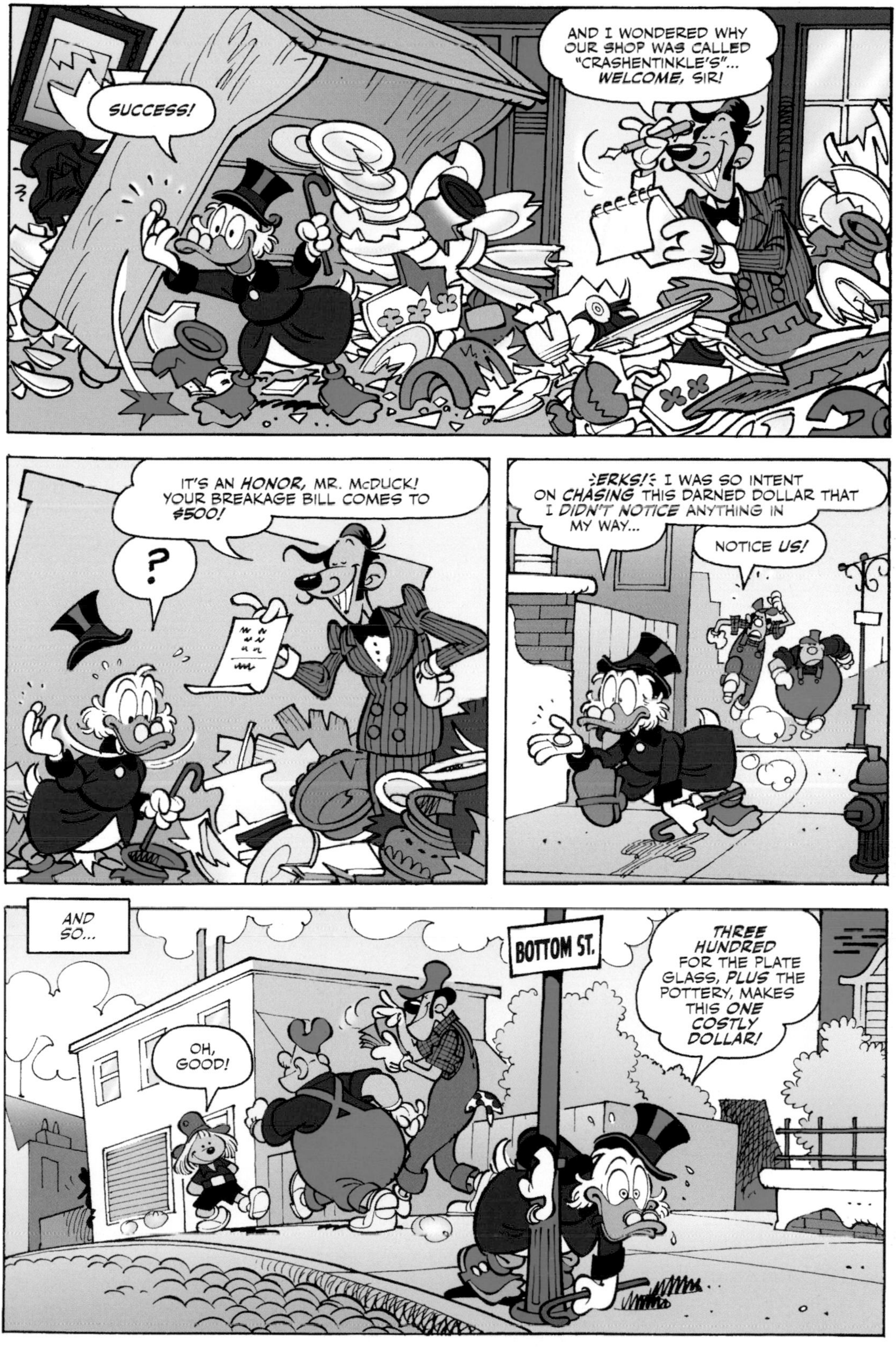
SUCCESS!
AND I WONDERED WHY OUR SHOP WAS CALLED "CRASHENTINKLE'S"... WELCOME, SIR!
IT'S AN HONOR, MR. McDUCK! YOUR BREAKAGE BILL COMES TO $500!
?
ERKS! I WAS SO INTENT ON CHASING THIS DARNED DOLLAR THAT I DIDN'T NOTICE ANYTHING IN MY WAY...
NOTICE US!
AND SO...
BOTTOM ST.
OH, GOOD!
THREE HUNDRED FOR THE PLATE GLASS, PLUS THE POTTERY, MAKES THIS ONE COSTLY DOLLAR!

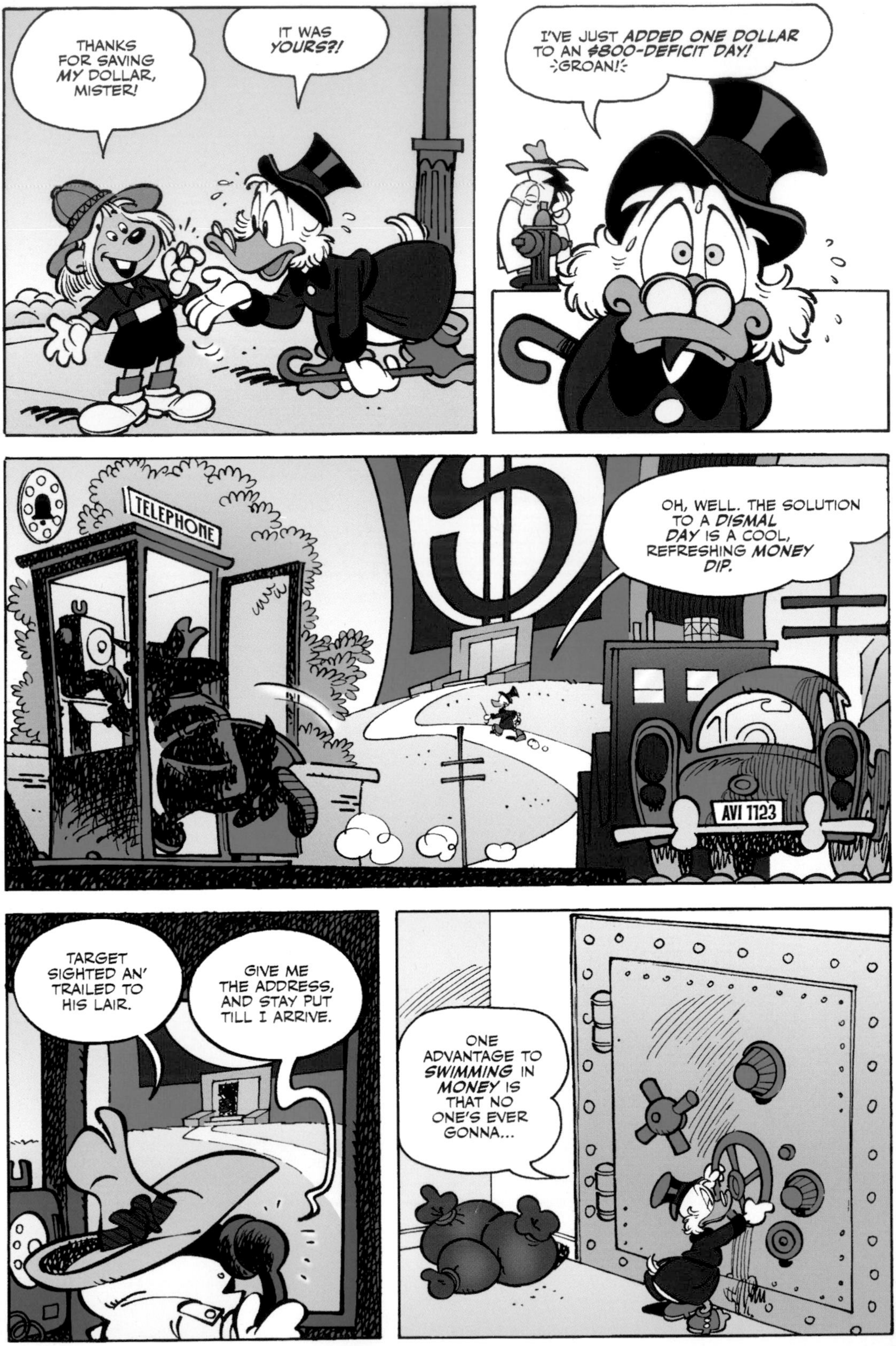
THANKS FOR SAVING MY DOLLAR, MISTER!
IT WAS YOURS?!
I'VE JUST ADDED ONE DOLLAR TO AN $800-DEFICIT DAY! -GROAN!-
TELEPHONE
OH, WELL. THE SOLUTION TO A DISMAL DAY IS A COOL, REFRESHING MONEY DIP.
AVI 1123
TARGET SIGHTED AN' TRAILED TO HIS LAIR.
GIVE ME THE ADDRESS, AND STAY PUT TILL I ARRIVE.
ONE ADVANTAGE TO SWIMMING IN MONEY IS THAT NO ONE'S EVER GONNA...

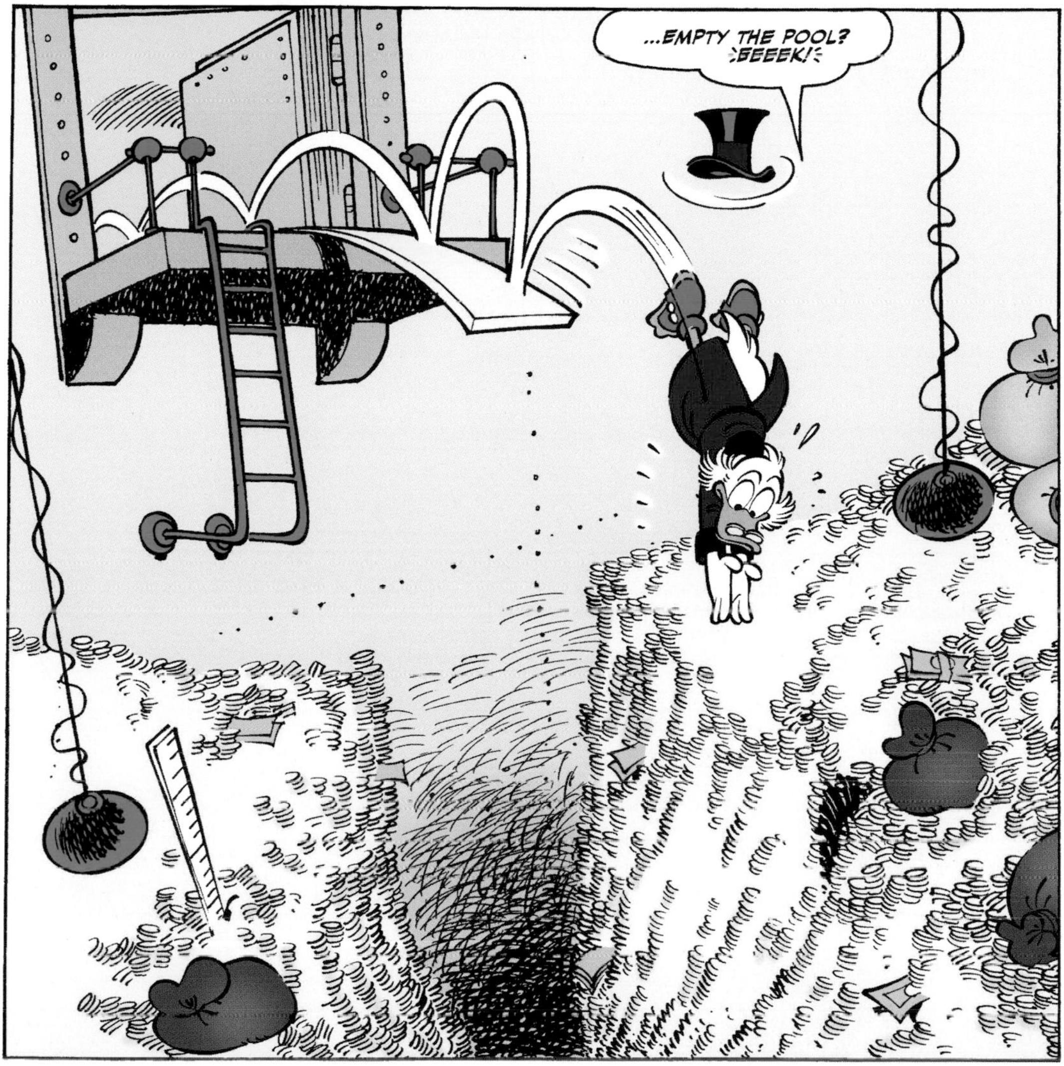
...EMPTY THE POOL?
BEEEK!

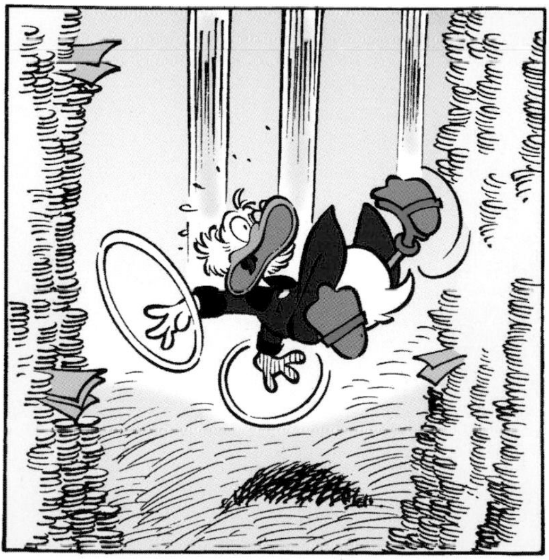

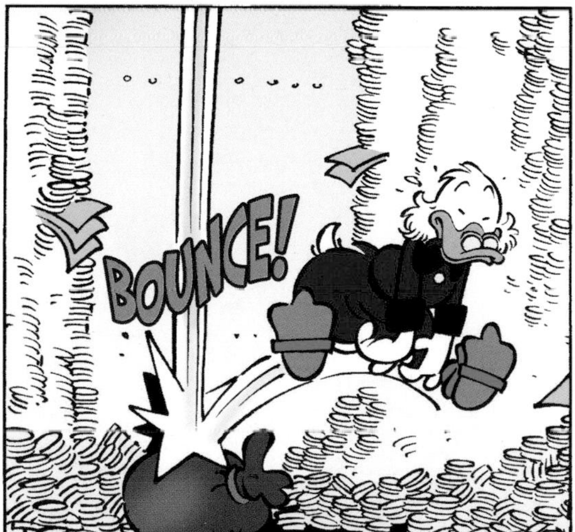
BOUNCE!

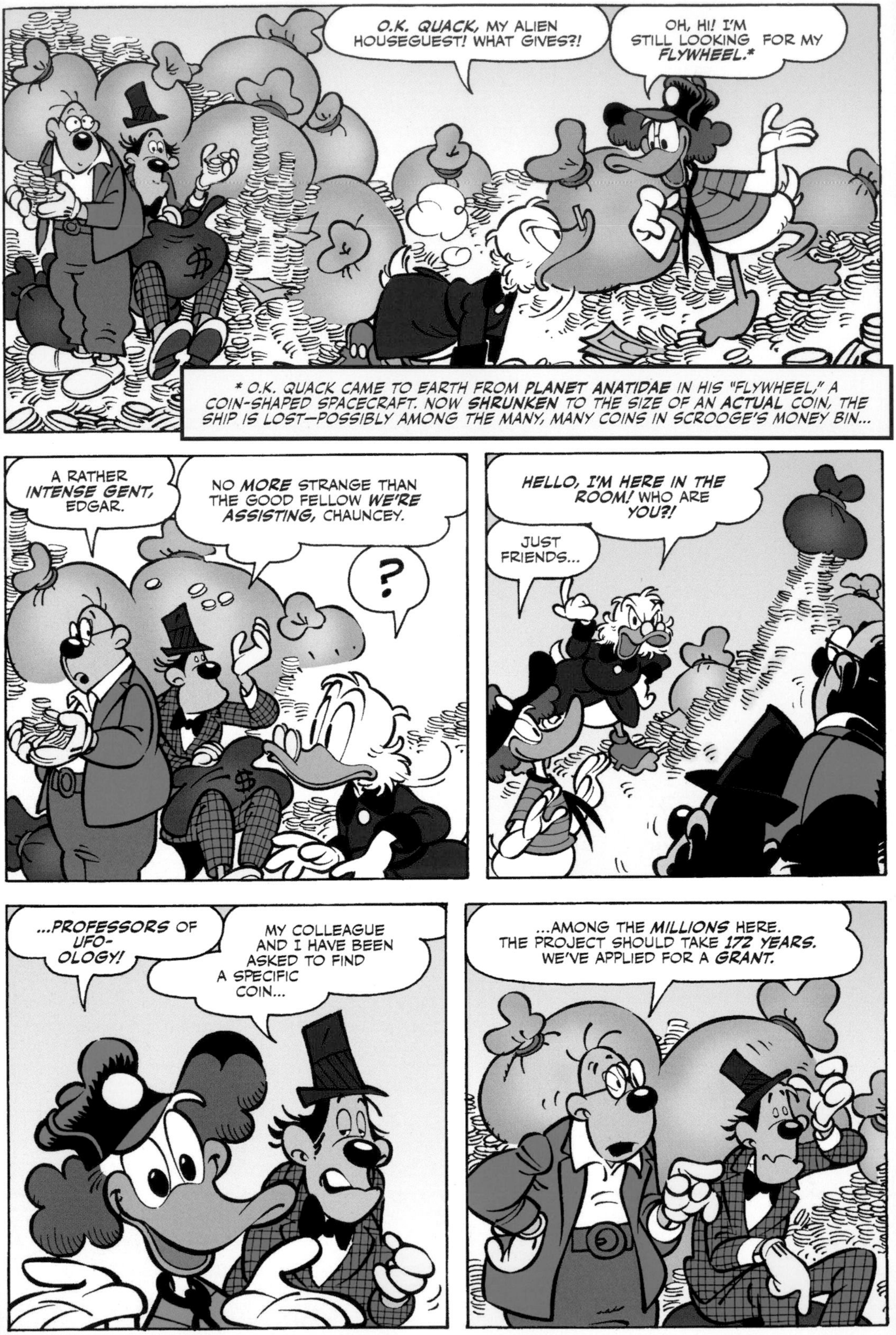
O.K. QUACK, MY ALIEN HOUSEGUEST! WHAT GIVES?!
OH, HI! I'M STILL LOOKING FOR MY FLYWHEEL.*
* O.K. QUACK CAME TO EARTH FROM PLANET ANATIDAE IN HIS "FLYWHEEL," A COIN-SHAPED SPACECRAFT. NOW SHRUNKEN TO THE SIZE OF AN ACTUAL COIN, THE SHIP IS LOST—POSSIBLY AMONG THE MANY, MANY COINS IN SCROOGE'S MONEY BIN...
A RATHER INTENSE GENT, EDGAR.
NO MORE STRANGE THAN THE GOOD FELLOW WE'RE ASSISTING, CHAUNCEY.
?
HELLO, I'M HERE IN THE ROOM! WHO ARE YOU?!
JUST FRIENDS...
...PROFESSORS OF UFO-OLOGY!
MY COLLEAGUE AND I HAVE BEEN ASKED TO FIND A SPECIFIC COIN...
...AMONG THE MILLIONS HERE. THE PROJECT SHOULD TAKE 172 YEARS. WE'VE APPLIED FOR A GRANT.

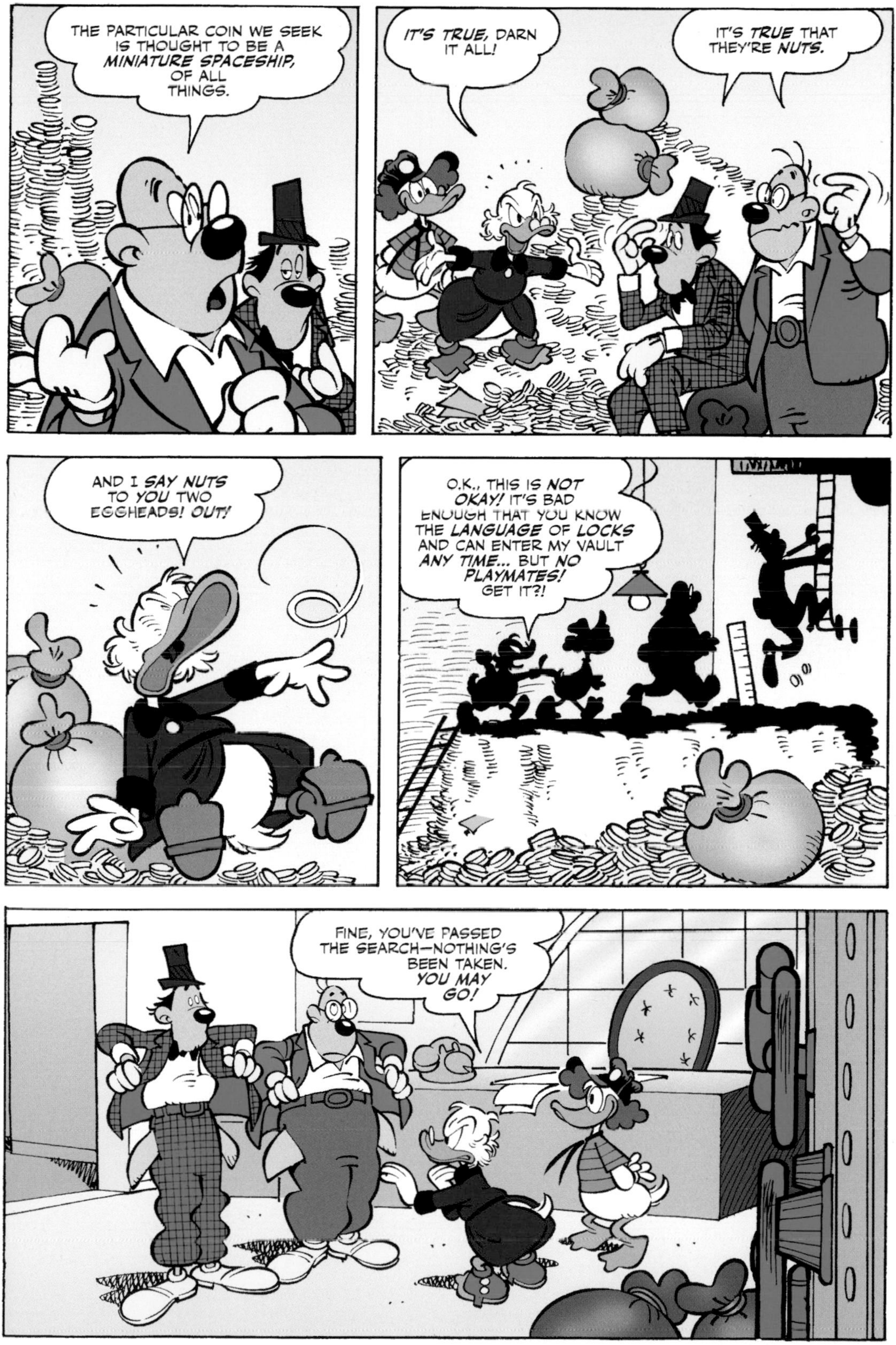
THE PARTICULAR COIN WE SEEK IS THOUGHT TO BE A *MINIATURE SPACESHIP,* OF ALL THINGS.
IT'S TRUE, DARN IT ALL!
IT'S *TRUE* THAT THEY'RE *NUTS.*
AND I *SAY NUTS* TO *YOU* TWO EGGHEADS! *OUT!*
O.K., THIS IS *NOT OKAY!* IT'S BAD ENOUGH THAT YOU KNOW THE *LANGUAGE* OF *LOCKS* AND CAN ENTER MY VAULT *ANY TIME*... BUT *NO PLAYMATES!* GET IT?!
FINE, YOU'VE PASSED THE SEARCH—NOTHING'S BEEN TAKEN. *YOU MAY GO!*

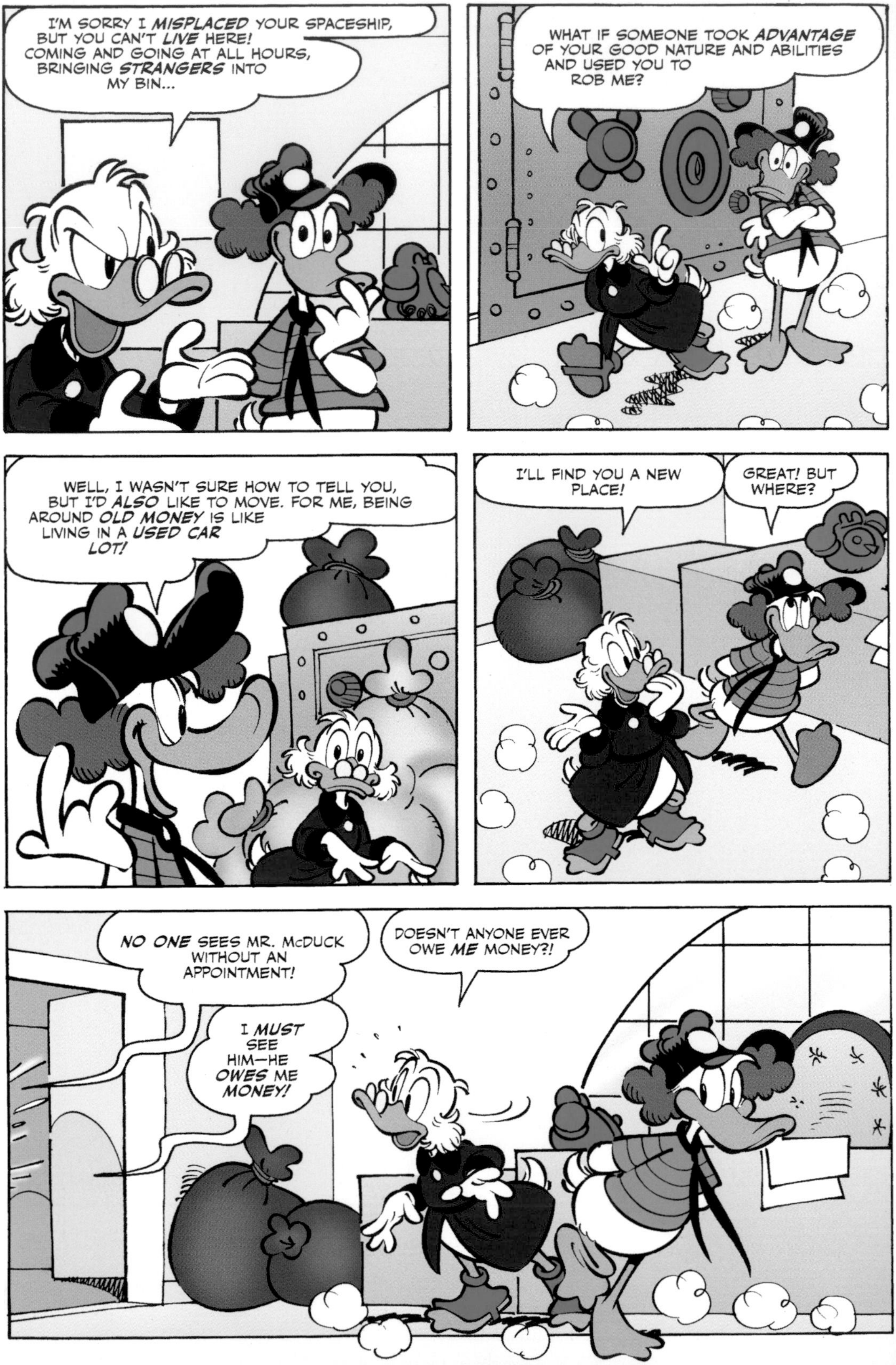

I'M SORRY I *MISPLACED* YOUR SPACESHIP, BUT YOU CAN'T *LIVE* HERE! COMING AND GOING AT ALL HOURS, BRINGING *STRANGERS* INTO MY BIN...
WHAT IF SOMEONE TOOK *ADVANTAGE* OF YOUR GOOD NATURE AND ABILITIES AND USED YOU TO ROB ME?
WELL, I WASN'T SURE HOW TO TELL YOU, BUT I'D *ALSO* LIKE TO MOVE. FOR ME, BEING AROUND *OLD MONEY* IS LIKE LIVING IN A *USED CAR LOT!*
I'LL FIND YOU A NEW PLACE!
GREAT! BUT WHERE?
NO ONE SEES MR. McDUCK WITHOUT AN APPOINTMENT!
I *MUST* SEE HIM—HE *OWES* ME *MONEY!*
DOESN'T ANYONE EVER OWE *ME* MONEY?!

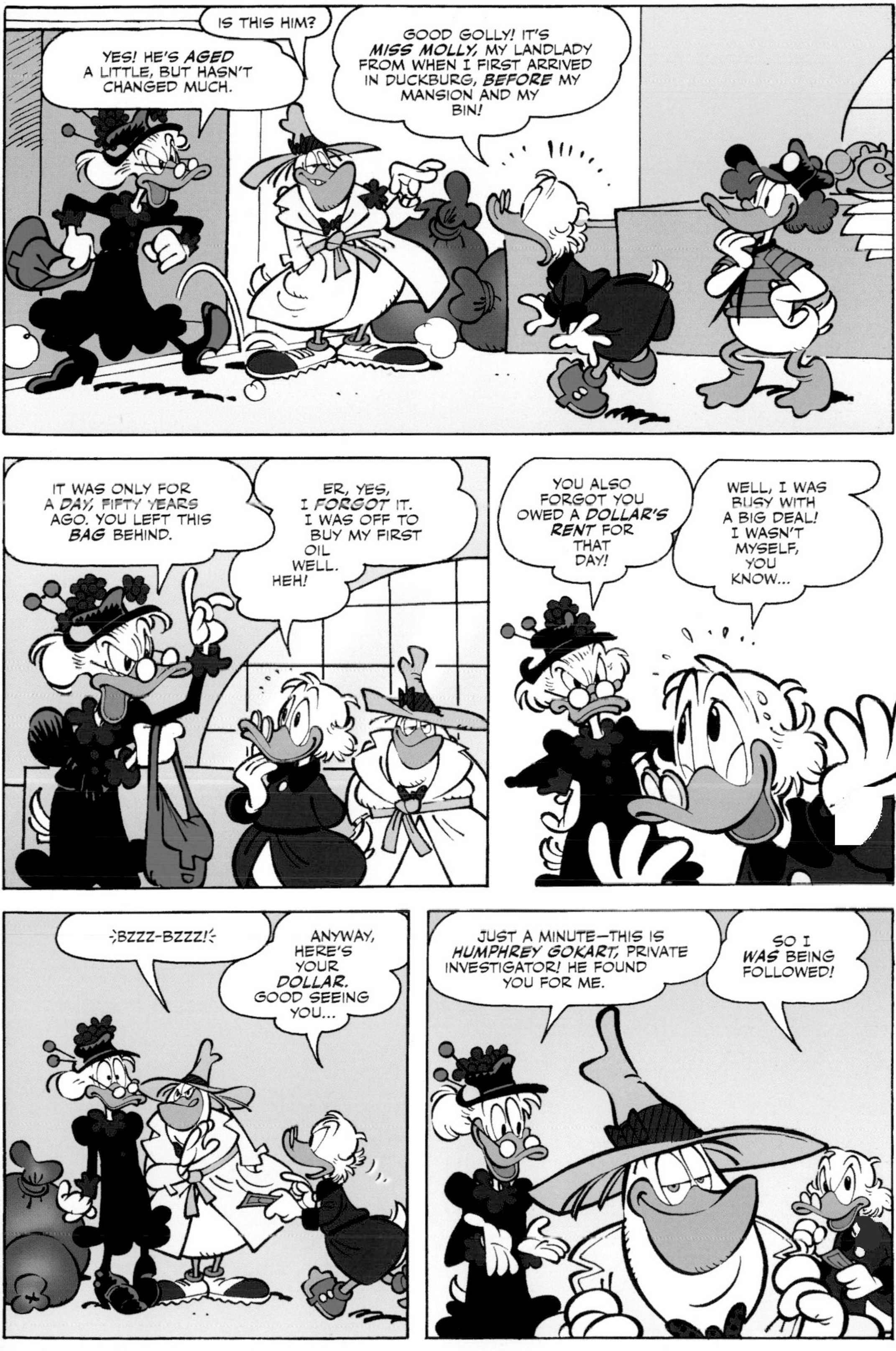
YES! HE'S AGED A LITTLE, BUT HASN'T CHANGED MUCH.
IS THIS HIM?
GOOD GOLLY! IT'S MISS MOLLY, MY LANDLADY FROM WHEN I FIRST ARRIVED IN DUCKBURG, BEFORE MY MANSION AND MY BIN!
IT WAS ONLY FOR A DAY, FIFTY YEARS AGO. YOU LEFT THIS BAG BEHIND.
ER, YES, I FORGOT IT. I WAS OFF TO BUY MY FIRST OIL WELL. HEH!
YOU ALSO FORGOT YOU OWED A DOLLAR'S RENT FOR THAT DAY!
WELL, I WAS BUSY WITH A BIG DEAL! I WASN'T MYSELF, YOU KNOW...
BZZZ-BZZZ!
ANYWAY, HERE'S YOUR DOLLAR. GOOD SEEING YOU...
JUST A MINUTE—THIS IS HUMPHREY GOKART, PRIVATE INVESTIGATOR! HE FOUND YOU FOR ME.
SO I WAS BEING FOLLOWED!

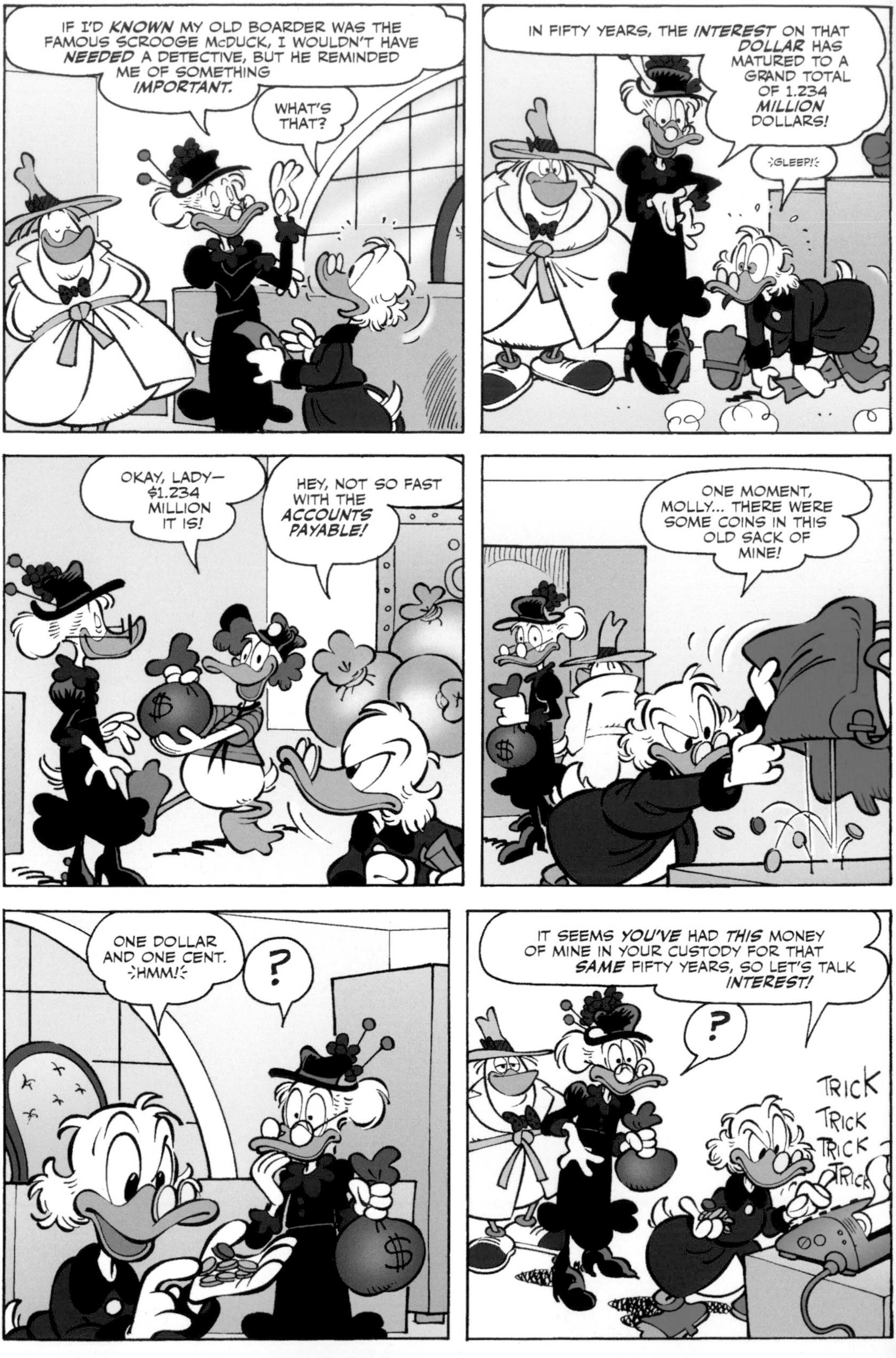
IF I'D *KNOWN* MY OLD BOARDER WAS THE FAMOUS SCROOGE McDUCK, I WOULDN'T HAVE *NEEDED* A DETECTIVE, BUT HE REMINDED ME OF SOMETHING *IMPORTANT.*
WHAT'S THAT?
IN FIFTY YEARS, THE *INTEREST* ON THAT *DOLLAR* HAS MATURED TO A GRAND TOTAL OF 1.234 *MILLION* DOLLARS!
GLEEP!
OKAY, LADY— $1.234 MILLION IT IS!
HEY, NOT SO FAST WITH THE *ACCOUNTS PAYABLE!*
ONE MOMENT, MOLLY... THERE WERE SOME COINS IN THIS OLD SACK OF MINE!
ONE DOLLAR AND ONE CENT. HMM!
?
IT SEEMS *YOU'VE* HAD *THIS* MONEY OF MINE IN YOUR CUSTODY FOR THAT *SAME* FIFTY YEARS, SO LET'S TALK *INTEREST!*
?
TRICK
TRICK
TRICK
TRICK

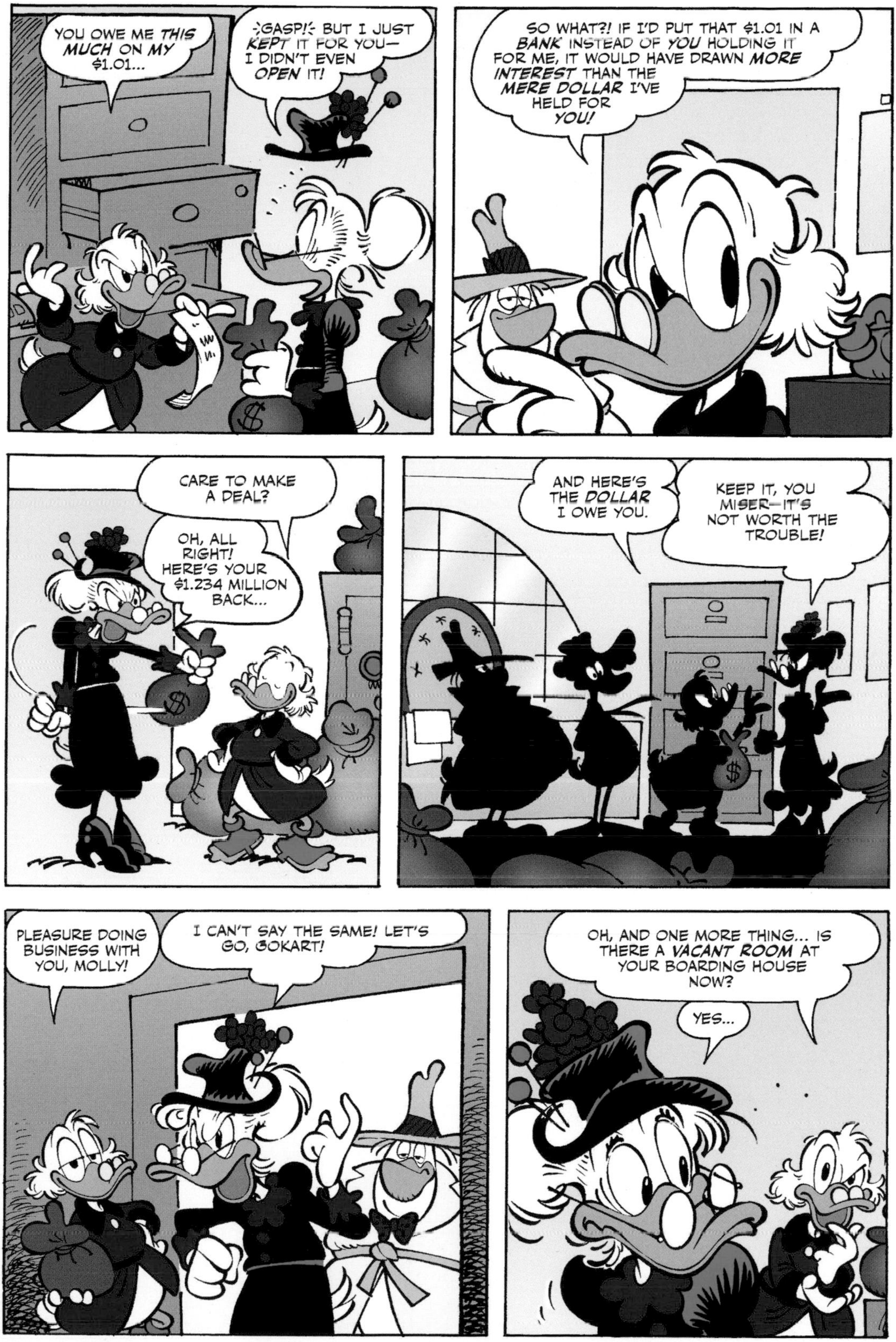
YOU OWE ME THIS MUCH ON MY $1.01...
-GASP!- BUT I JUST KEPT IT FOR YOU— I DIDN'T EVEN OPEN IT!
SO WHAT?! IF I'D PUT THAT $1.01 IN A BANK INSTEAD OF YOU HOLDING IT FOR ME, IT WOULD HAVE DRAWN MORE INTEREST THAN THE MERE DOLLAR I'VE HELD FOR YOU!
CARE TO MAKE A DEAL?
OH, ALL RIGHT! HERE'S YOUR $1.234 MILLION BACK...
AND HERE'S THE DOLLAR I OWE YOU.
KEEP IT, YOU MISER—IT'S NOT WORTH THE TROUBLE!
PLEASURE DOING BUSINESS WITH YOU, MOLLY!
I CAN'T SAY THE SAME! LET'S GO, GOKART!
OH, AND ONE MORE THING... IS THERE A VACANT ROOM AT YOUR BOARDING HOUSE NOW?
YES...

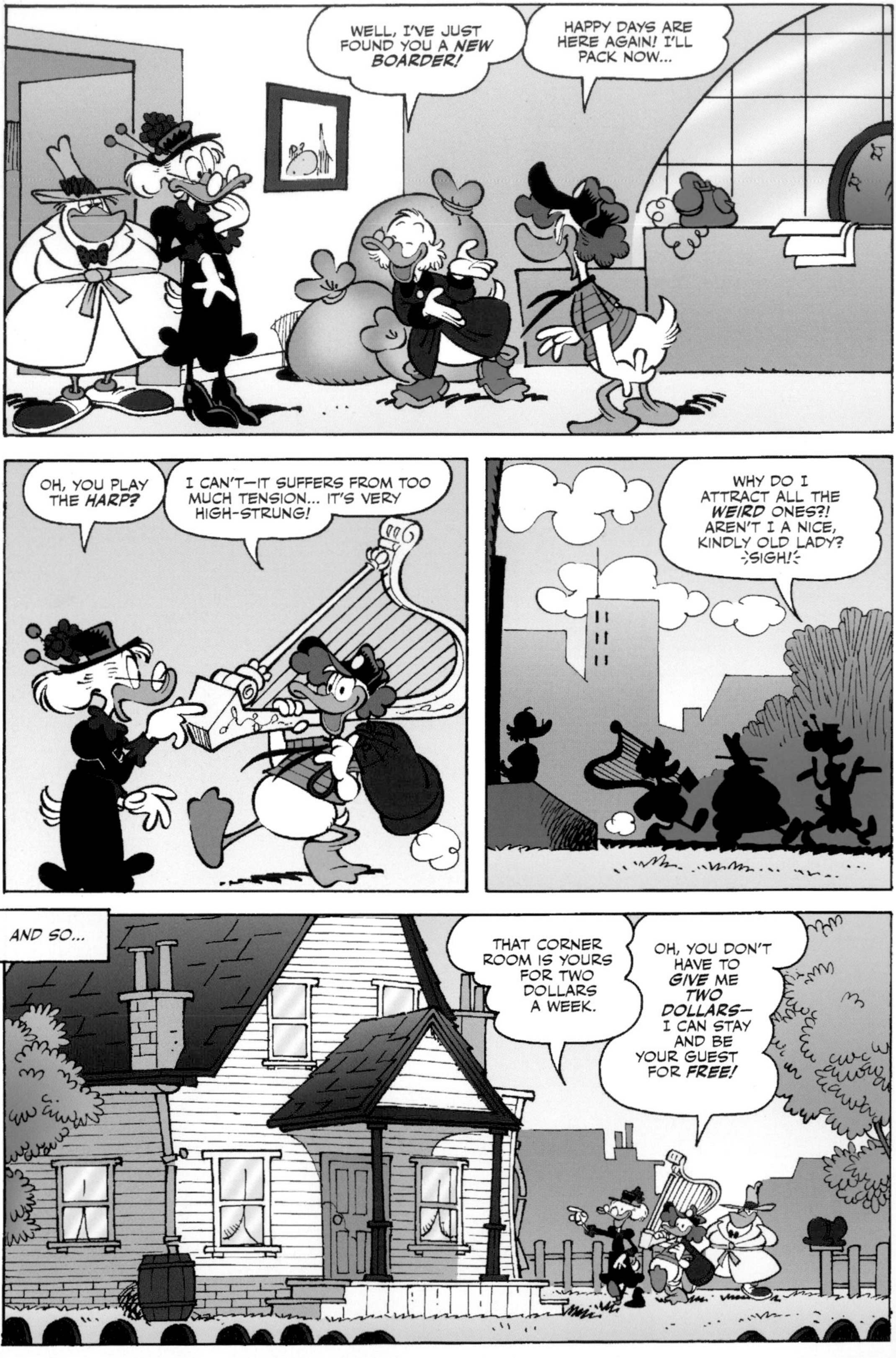
WELL, I'VE JUST FOUND YOU A *NEW BOARDER!*
HAPPY DAYS ARE HERE AGAIN! I'LL PACK NOW...
OH, YOU PLAY THE *HARP?*
I CAN'T—IT SUFFERS FROM TOO MUCH TENSION... IT'S VERY HIGH-STRUNG!
WHY DO I ATTRACT ALL THE *WEIRD* ONES?! AREN'T I A NICE, KINDLY OLD LADY? SIGH!
AND SO...
THAT CORNER ROOM IS YOURS FOR TWO DOLLARS A WEEK.
OH, YOU DON'T HAVE TO *GIVE* ME *TWO DOLLARS*— I CAN STAY AND BE YOUR GUEST FOR *FREE!*

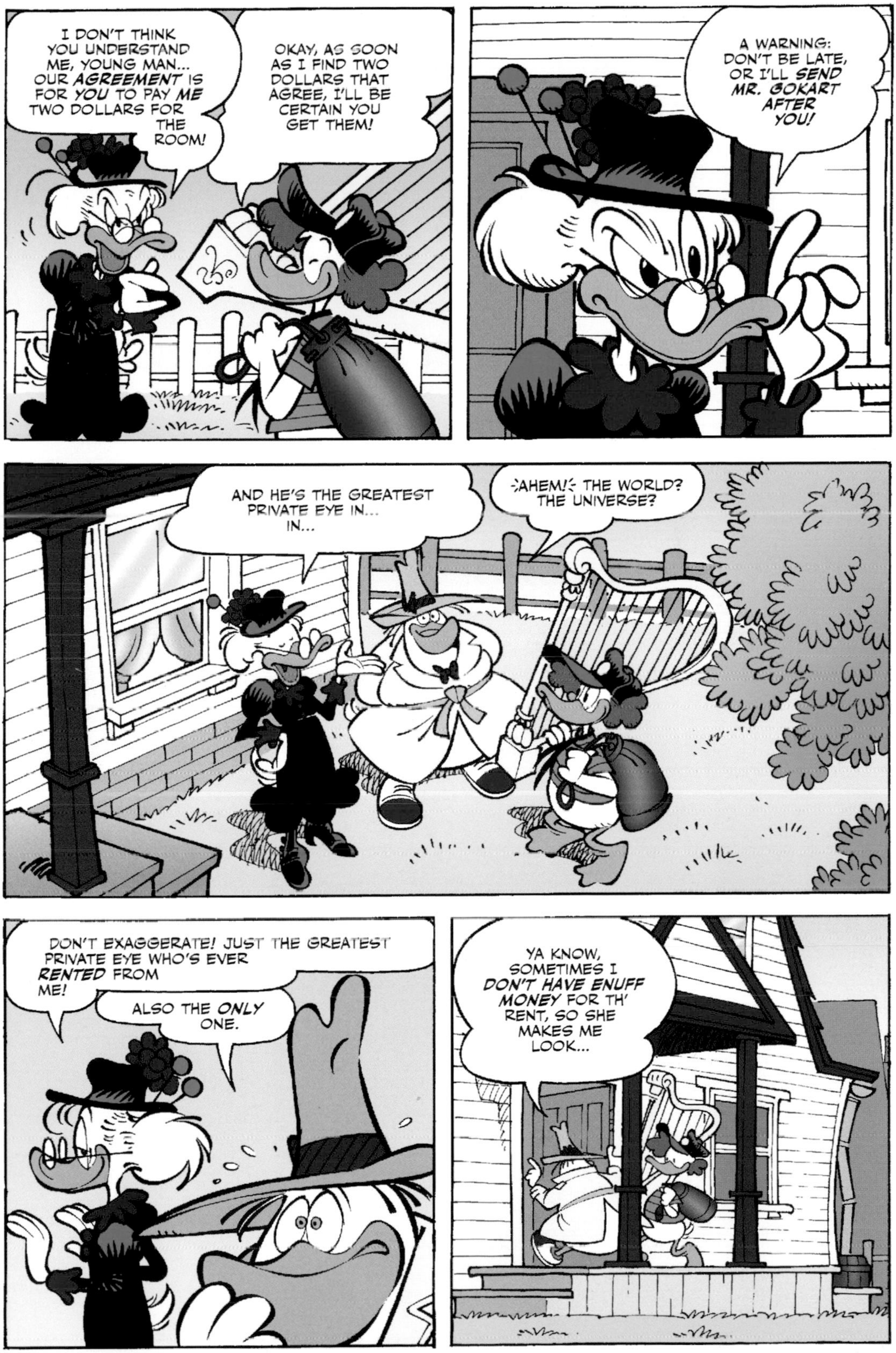
I DON'T THINK YOU UNDERSTAND ME, YOUNG MAN... OUR *AGREEMENT* IS FOR *YOU* TO PAY *ME* TWO DOLLARS FOR THE ROOM!
OKAY, AS SOON AS I FIND TWO DOLLARS THAT AGREE, I'LL BE CERTAIN YOU GET THEM!
A WARNING: DON'T BE LATE, OR I'LL ***SEND MR. GOKART AFTER YOU!***
AND HE'S THE GREATEST PRIVATE EYE IN... IN...
-AHEM!- THE WORLD? THE UNIVERSE?
DON'T EXAGGERATE! JUST THE GREATEST PRIVATE EYE WHO'S EVER ***RENTED*** FROM ME!
ALSO THE *ONLY* ONE.
YA KNOW, SOMETIMES I ***DON'T HAVE ENUFF MONEY*** FOR TH' RENT, SO SHE MAKES ME LOOK...

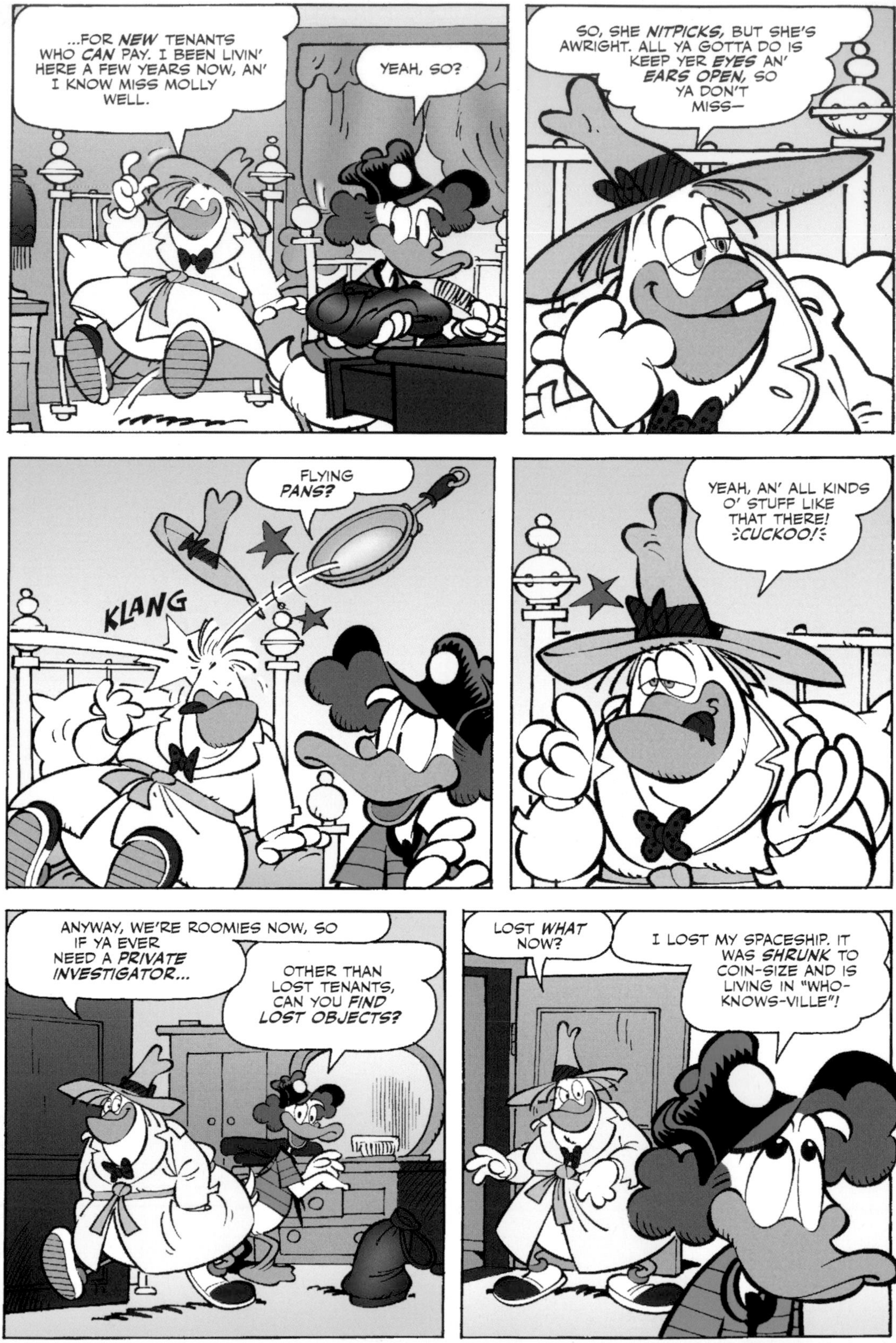
...FOR NEW TENANTS WHO CAN PAY. I BEEN LIVIN' HERE A FEW YEARS NOW, AN' I KNOW MISS MOLLY WELL.
YEAH, SO?
SO, SHE NITPICKS, BUT SHE'S AWRIGHT. ALL YA GOTTA DO IS KEEP YER EYES AN' EARS OPEN, SO YA DON'T MISS—
FLYING PANS?
KLANG
YEAH, AN' ALL KINDS O' STUFF LIKE THAT THERE! CUCKOO!
ANYWAY, WE'RE ROOMIES NOW, SO IF YA EVER NEED A PRIVATE INVESTIGATOR...
OTHER THAN LOST TENANTS, CAN YOU FIND LOST OBJECTS?
LOST WHAT NOW?
I LOST MY SPACESHIP. IT WAS SHRUNK TO COIN-SIZE AND IS LIVING IN "WHO-KNOWS-VILLE"!

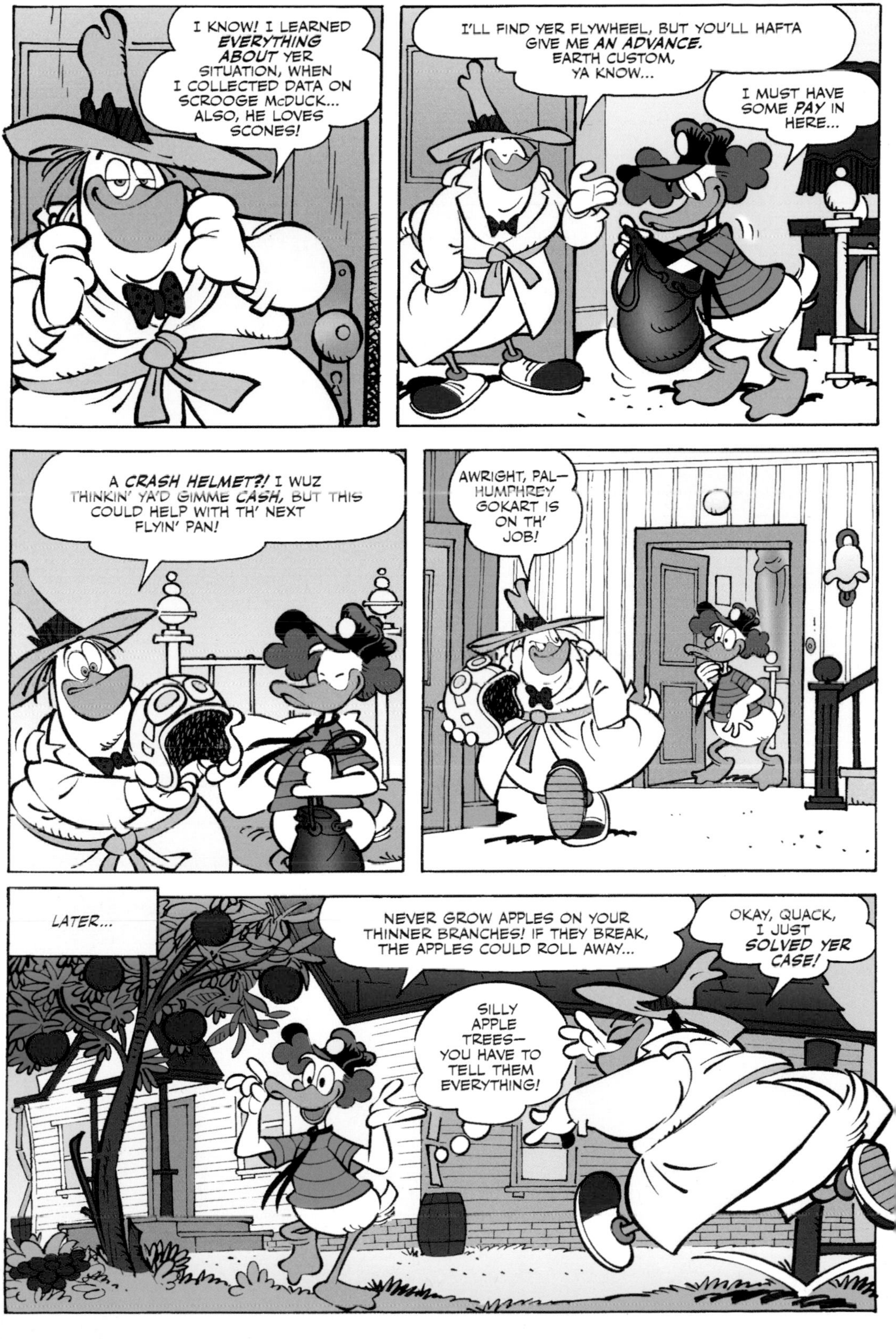
I KNOW! I LEARNED EVERYTHING ABOUT YER SITUATION, WHEN I COLLECTED DATA ON SCROOGE McDUCK... ALSO, HE LOVES SCONES!
I'LL FIND YER FLYWHEEL, BUT YOU'LL HAFTA GIVE ME AN ADVANCE. EARTH CUSTOM, YA KNOW...
I MUST HAVE SOME PAY IN HERE...
A CRASH HELMET?! I WUZ THINKIN' YA'D GIMME CASH, BUT THIS COULD HELP WITH TH' NEXT FLYIN' PAN!
AWRIGHT, PAL— HUMPHREY GOKART IS ON TH' JOB!
LATER...
NEVER GROW APPLES ON YOUR THINNER BRANCHES! IF THEY BREAK, THE APPLES COULD ROLL AWAY...
OKAY, QUACK, I JUST SOLVED YER CASE!
SILLY APPLE TREES— YOU HAVE TO TELL THEM EVERYTHING!

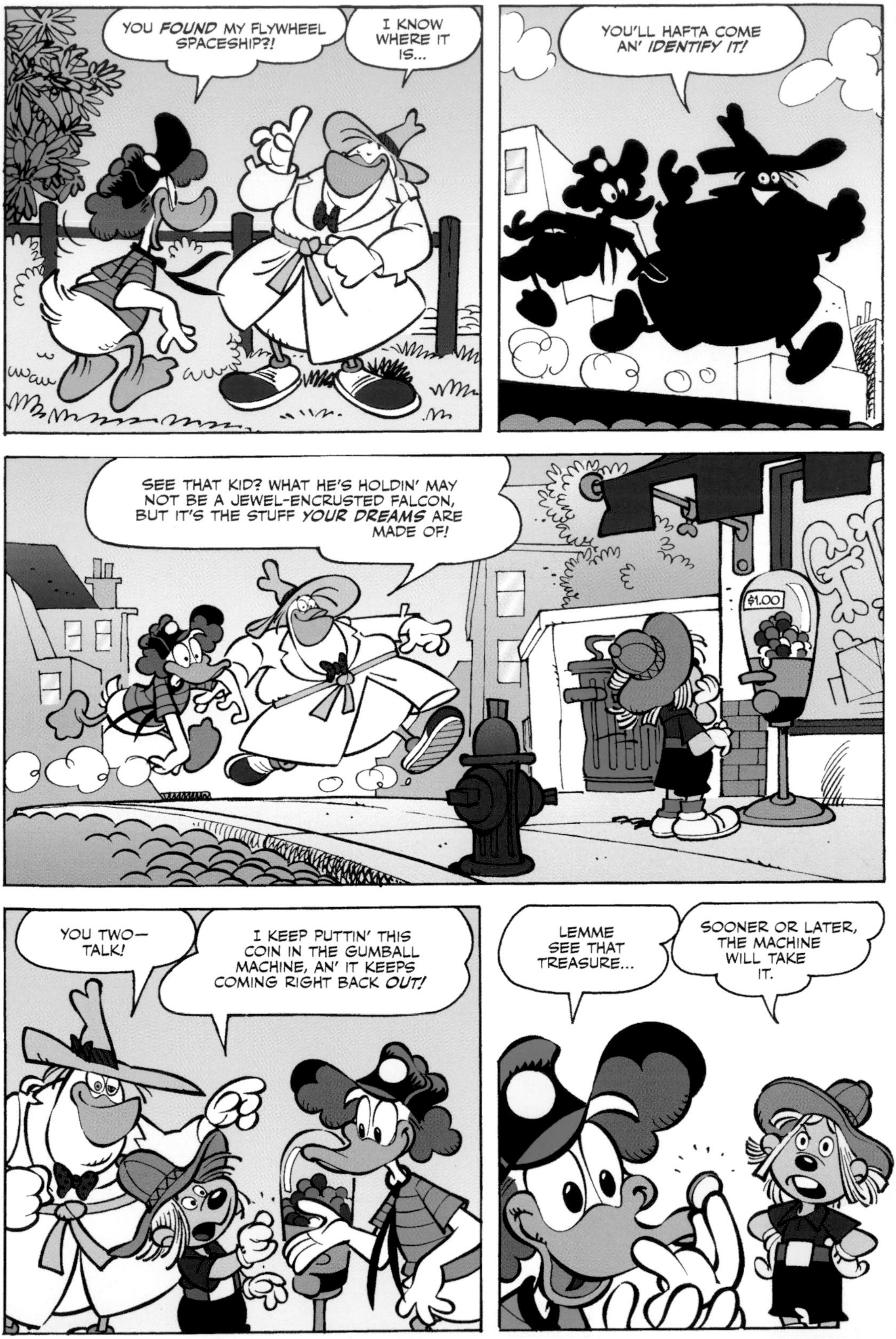
YOU *FOUND* MY FLYWHEEL SPACESHIP?!
I KNOW WHERE IT IS...
YOU'LL HAFTA COME AN' *IDENTIFY IT!*
SEE THAT KID? WHAT HE'S HOLDIN' MAY NOT BE A JEWEL-ENCRUSTED FALCON, BUT IT'S THE STUFF *YOUR DREAMS* ARE MADE OF!
$1.00
YOU TWO—TALK!
I KEEP PUTTIN' THIS COIN IN THE GUMBALL MACHINE, AN' IT KEEPS COMING RIGHT BACK *OUT!*
LEMME SEE THAT TREASURE...
SOONER OR LATER, THE MACHINE WILL TAKE IT.

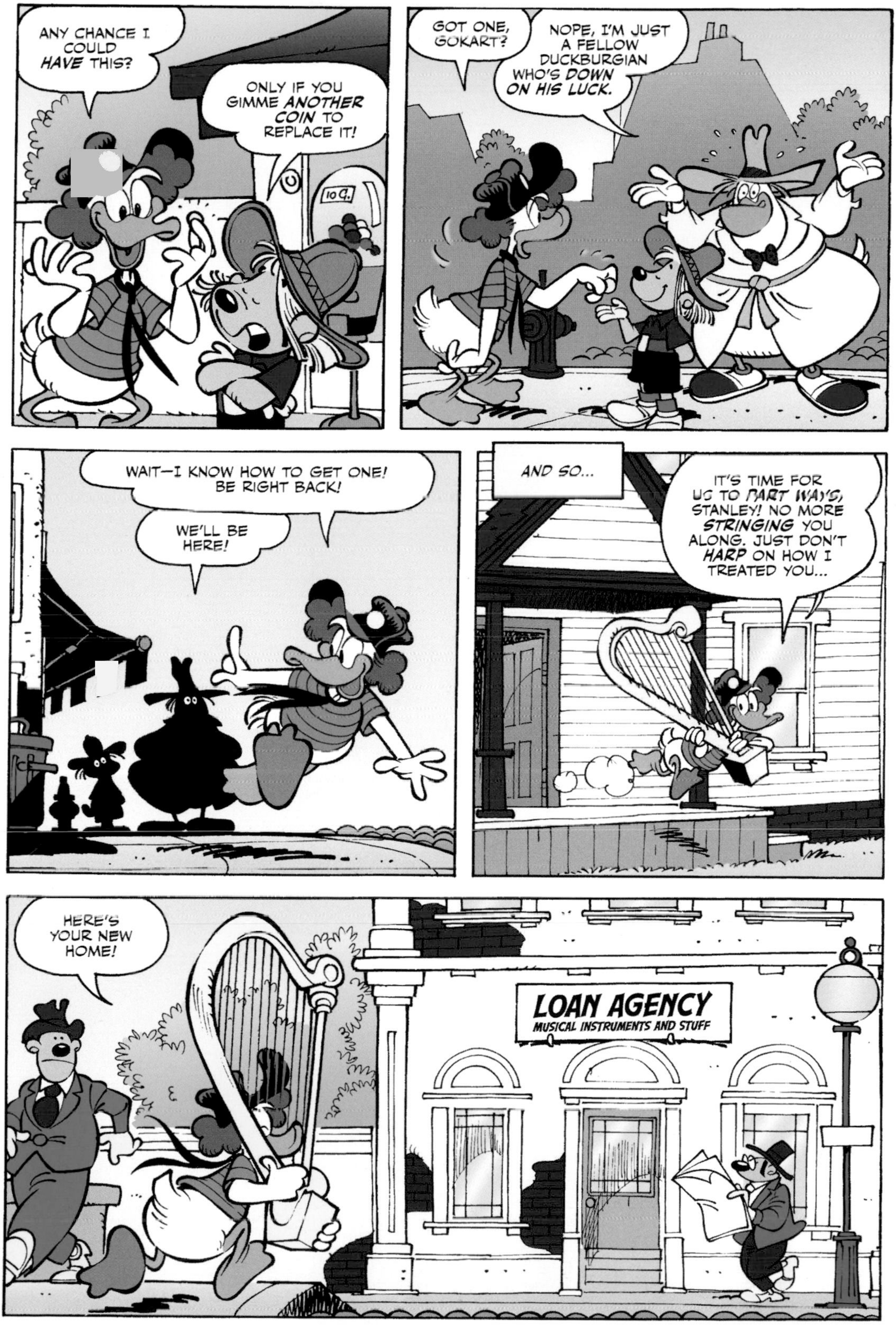
ANY CHANCE I COULD *HAVE* THIS?
ONLY IF YOU GIMME *ANOTHER COIN* TO REPLACE IT!
10¢
GOT ONE, GOKART?
NOPE, I'M JUST A FELLOW DUCKBURGIAN WHO'S *DOWN ON HIS LUCK.*
WAIT—I KNOW HOW TO GET ONE! BE RIGHT BACK!
WE'LL BE HERE!
AND SO...
IT'S TIME FOR US TO *PART WAYS,* STANLEY! NO MORE *STRINGING* YOU ALONG. JUST DON'T *HARP* ON HOW I TREATED YOU...
HERE'S YOUR NEW HOME!
LOAN AGENCY
MUSICAL INSTRUMENTS AND STUFF

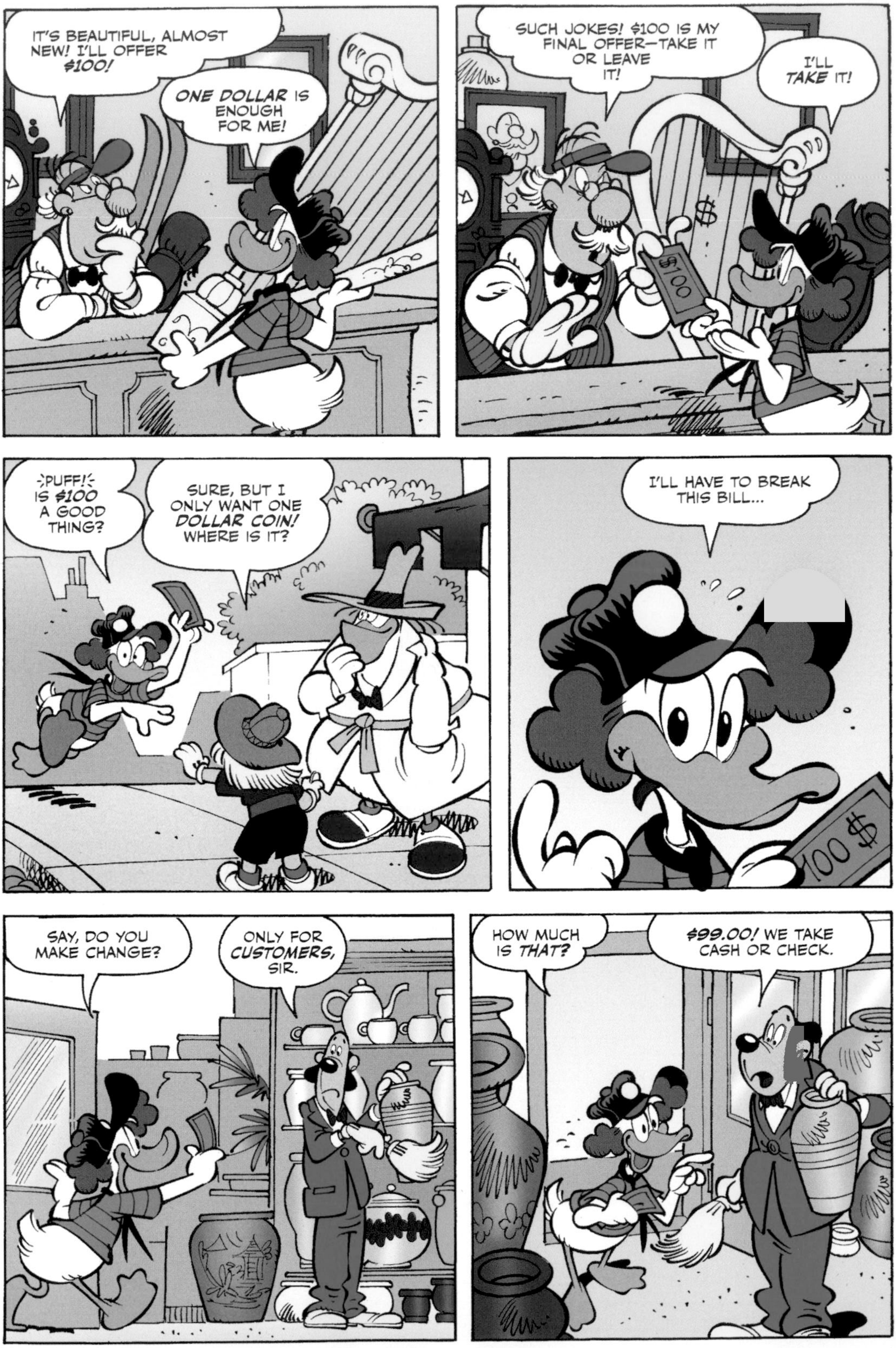
IT'S BEAUTIFUL, ALMOST NEW! I'LL OFFER $100!
ONE DOLLAR IS ENOUGH FOR ME!
SUCH JOKES! $100 IS MY FINAL OFFER—TAKE IT OR LEAVE IT!
I'LL TAKE IT!
$100
PUFF! IS $100 A GOOD THING?
SURE, BUT I ONLY WANT ONE DOLLAR COIN! WHERE IS IT?
I'LL HAVE TO BREAK THIS BILL...
100 $
SAY, DO YOU MAKE CHANGE?
ONLY FOR CUSTOMERS, SIR.
HOW MUCH IS THAT?
$99.00! WE TAKE CASH OR CHECK.

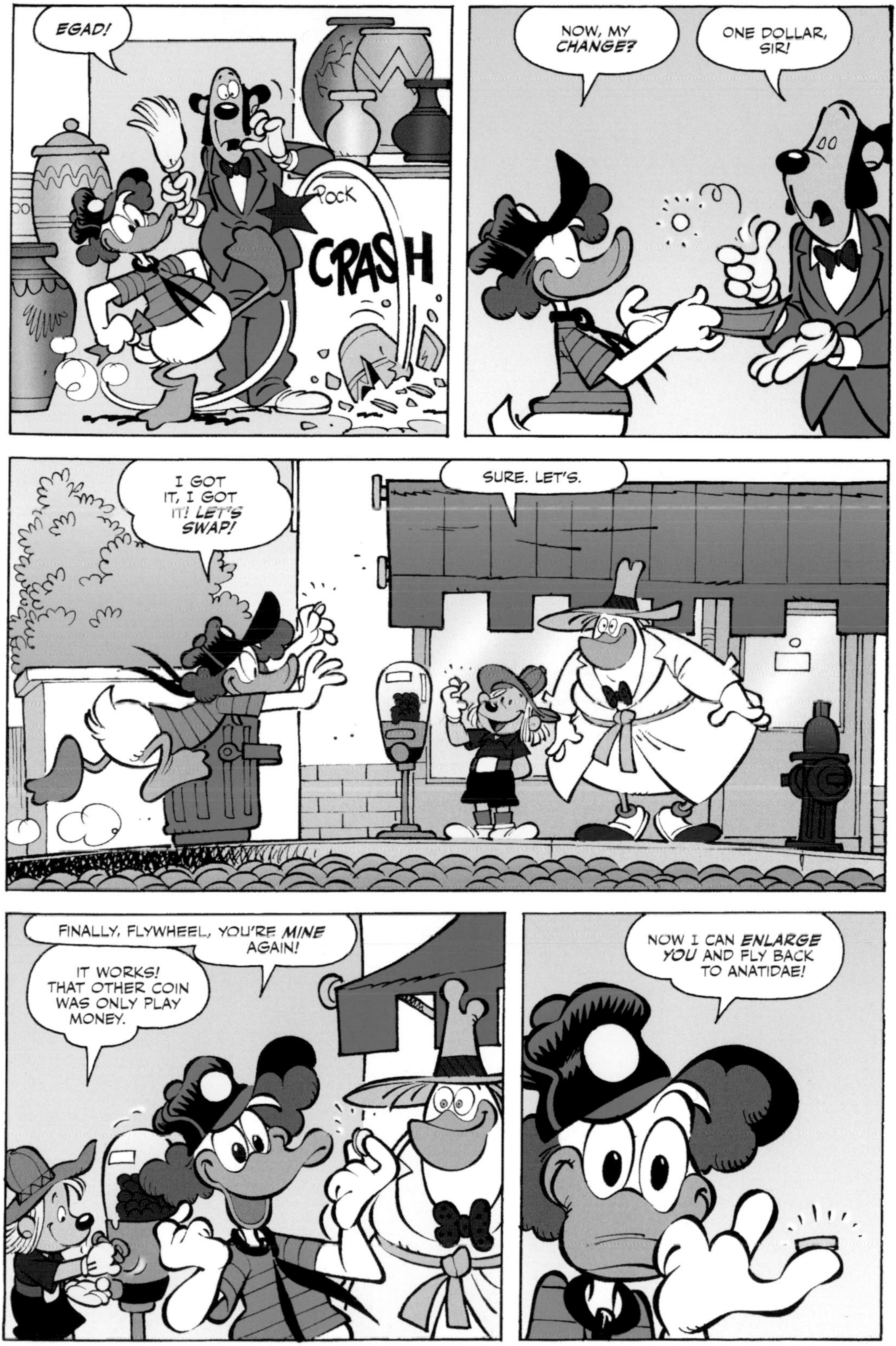
EGAD!
POCK
CRASH
NOW, MY CHANGE?
ONE DOLLAR, SIR!
I GOT IT, I GOT IT! LET'S SWAP!
SURE. LET'S.
FINALLY, FLYWHEEL, YOU'RE MINE AGAIN!
IT WORKS! THAT OTHER COIN WAS ONLY PLAY MONEY.
NOW I CAN ENLARGE YOU AND FLY BACK TO ANATIDAE!

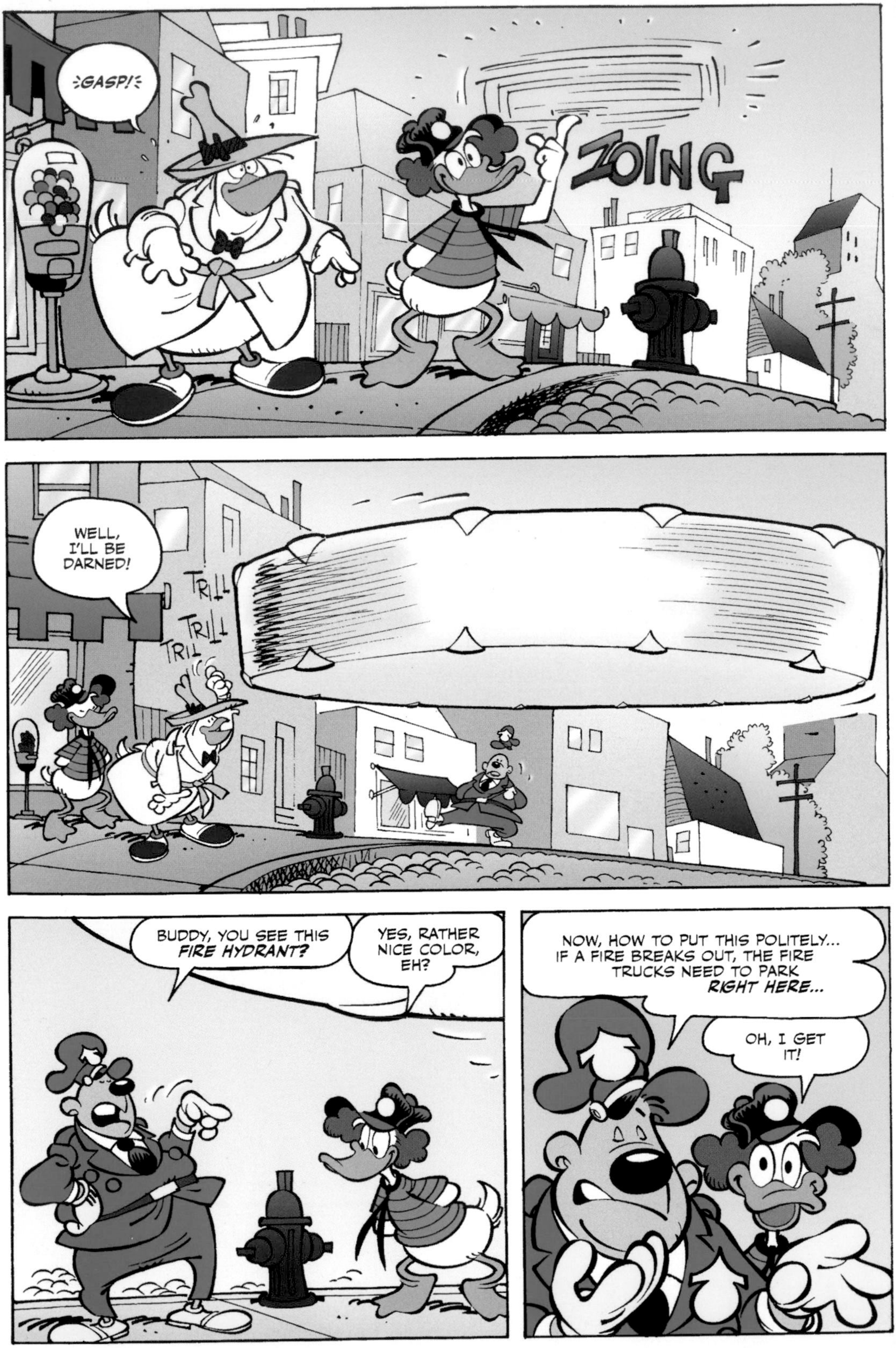

GASP!
ZOING
WELL, I'LL BE DARNED!
TRILL TRILL TRILL
BUDDY, YOU SEE THIS FIRE HYDRANT?
YES, RATHER NICE COLOR, EH?
NOW, HOW TO PUT THIS POLITELY... IF A FIRE BREAKS OUT, THE FIRE TRUCKS NEED TO PARK RIGHT HERE...
OH, I GET IT!

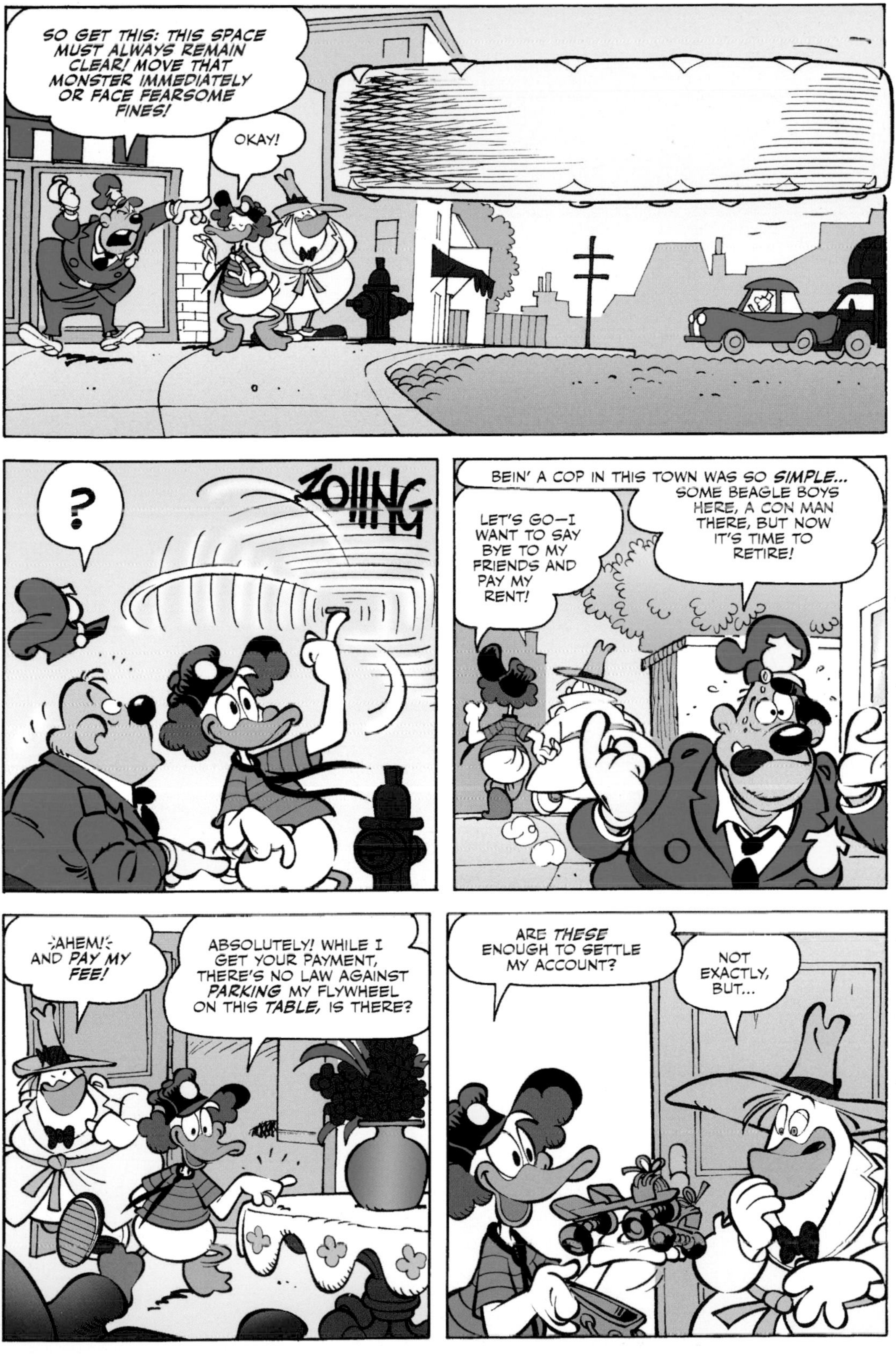

SO GET THIS: THIS SPACE MUST ALWAYS REMAIN CLEAR! MOVE THAT MONSTER IMMEDIATELY OR FACE FEARSOME FINES!
OKAY!
?
ZOIING
BEIN' A COP IN THIS TOWN WAS SO SIMPLE...
SOME BEAGLE BOYS HERE, A CON MAN THERE, BUT NOW IT'S TIME TO RETIRE!
LET'S GO—I WANT TO SAY BYE TO MY FRIENDS AND PAY MY RENT!
AHEM! AND PAY MY FEE!
ABSOLUTELY! WHILE I GET YOUR PAYMENT, THERE'S NO LAW AGAINST PARKING MY FLYWHEEL ON THIS TABLE, IS THERE?
ARE THESE ENOUGH TO SETTLE MY ACCOUNT?
NOT EXACTLY, BUT...

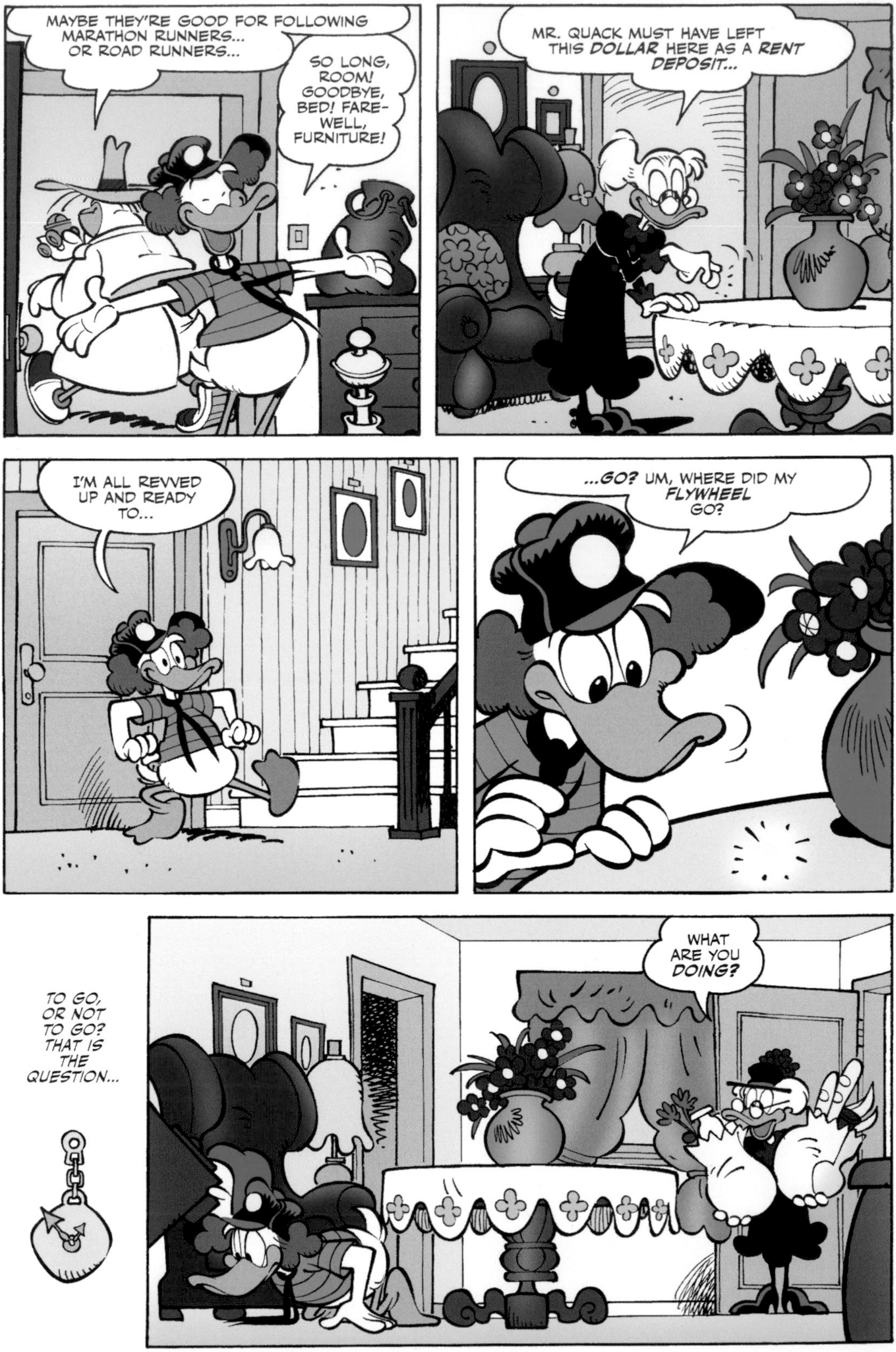
MAYBE THEY'RE GOOD FOR FOLLOWING MARATHON RUNNERS... OR ROAD RUNNERS...
SO LONG, ROOM! GOODBYE, BED! FARE-WELL, FURNITURE!
MR. QUACK MUST HAVE LEFT THIS DOLLAR HERE AS A RENT DEPOSIT...
I'M ALL REVVED UP AND READY TO...
...GO? UM, WHERE DID MY FLYWHEEL GO?
TO GO, OR NOT TO GO? THAT IS THE QUESTION...
WHAT ARE YOU DOING?

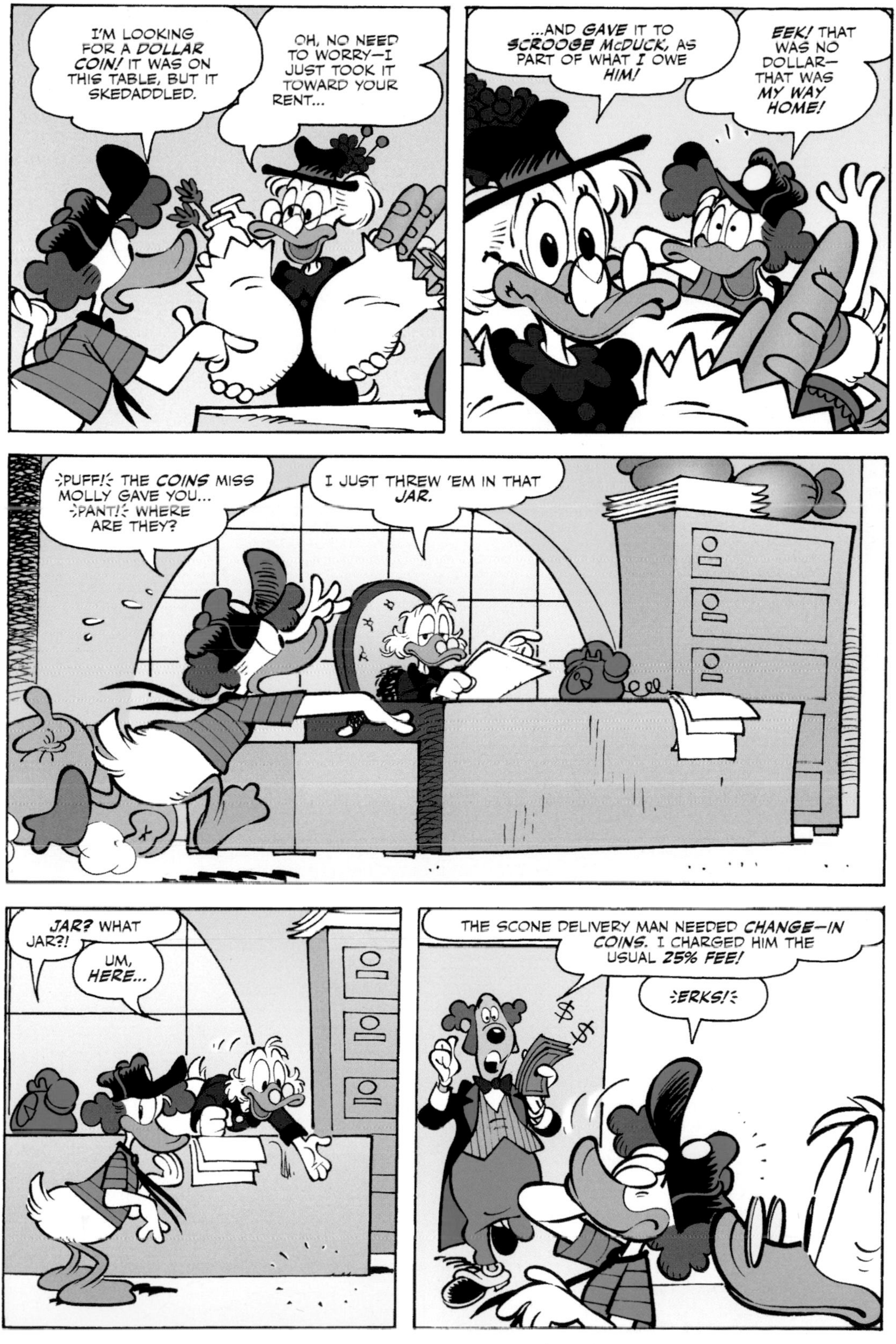
I'M LOOKING FOR A DOLLAR COIN! IT WAS ON THIS TABLE, BUT IT SKEDADDLED.
OH, NO NEED TO WORRY—I JUST TOOK IT TOWARD YOUR RENT...
...AND GAVE IT TO SCROOGE McDUCK, AS PART OF WHAT I OWE HIM!
EEK! THAT WAS NO DOLLAR— THAT WAS MY WAY HOME!
PUFF! THE COINS MISS MOLLY GAVE YOU... PANT! WHERE ARE THEY?
I JUST THREW 'EM IN THAT JAR.
JAR? WHAT JAR?!
UM, HERE...
THE SCONE DELIVERY MAN NEEDED CHANGE—IN COINS. I CHARGED HIM THE USUAL 25% FEE!
ERKS!

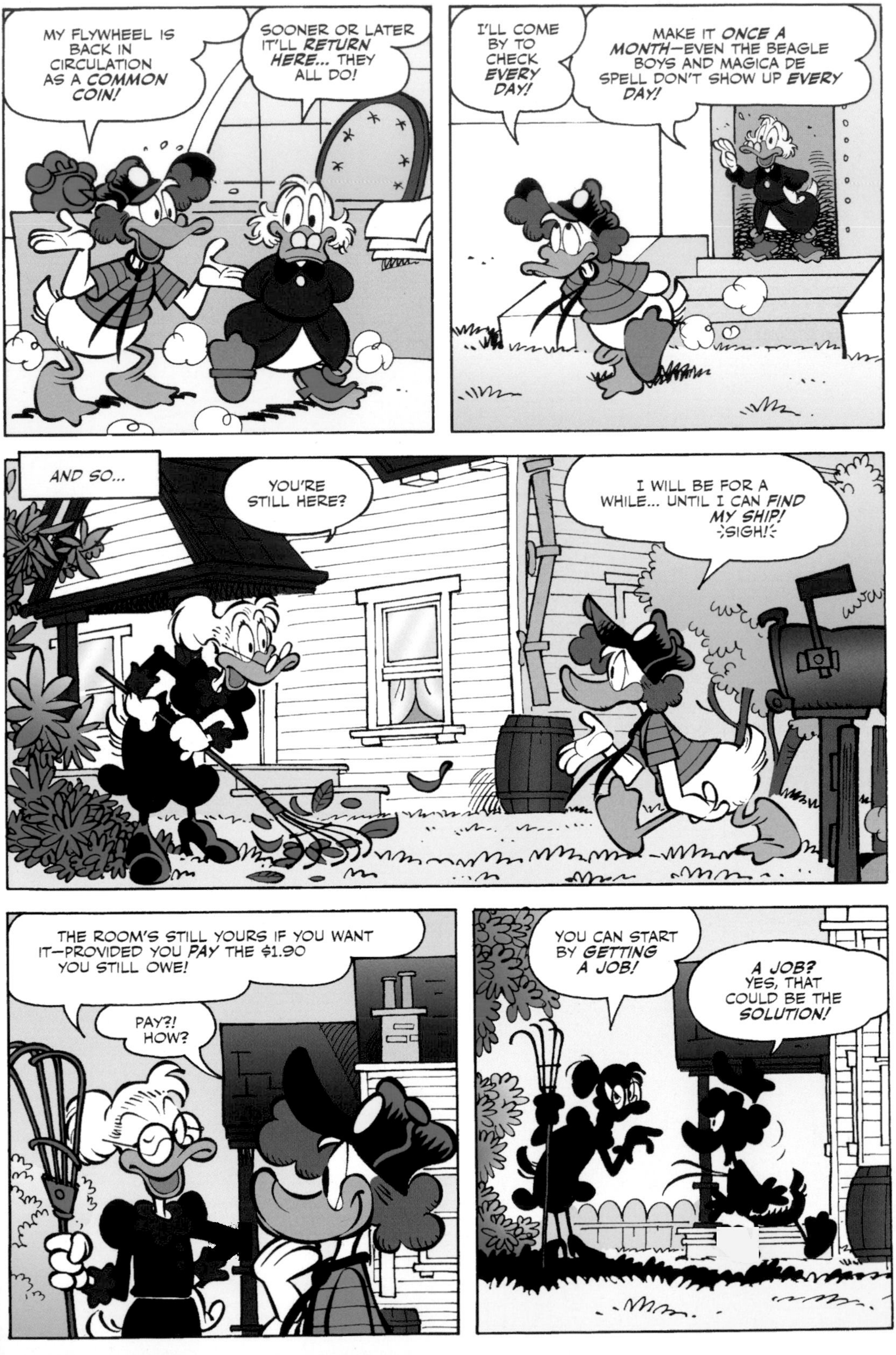
MY FLYWHEEL IS BACK IN CIRCULATION AS A COMMON COIN!
SOONER OR LATER IT'LL RETURN HERE... THEY ALL DO!
I'LL COME BY TO CHECK EVERY DAY!
MAKE IT ONCE A MONTH—EVEN THE BEAGLE BOYS AND MAGICA DE SPELL DON'T SHOW UP EVERY DAY!
AND SO...
YOU'RE STILL HERE?
I WILL BE FOR A WHILE... UNTIL I CAN FIND MY SHIP!
SIGH!
THE ROOM'S STILL YOURS IF YOU WANT IT—PROVIDED YOU PAY THE $1.90 YOU STILL OWE!
PAY?! HOW?
YOU CAN START BY GETTING A JOB!
A JOB? YES, THAT COULD BE THE SOLUTION!

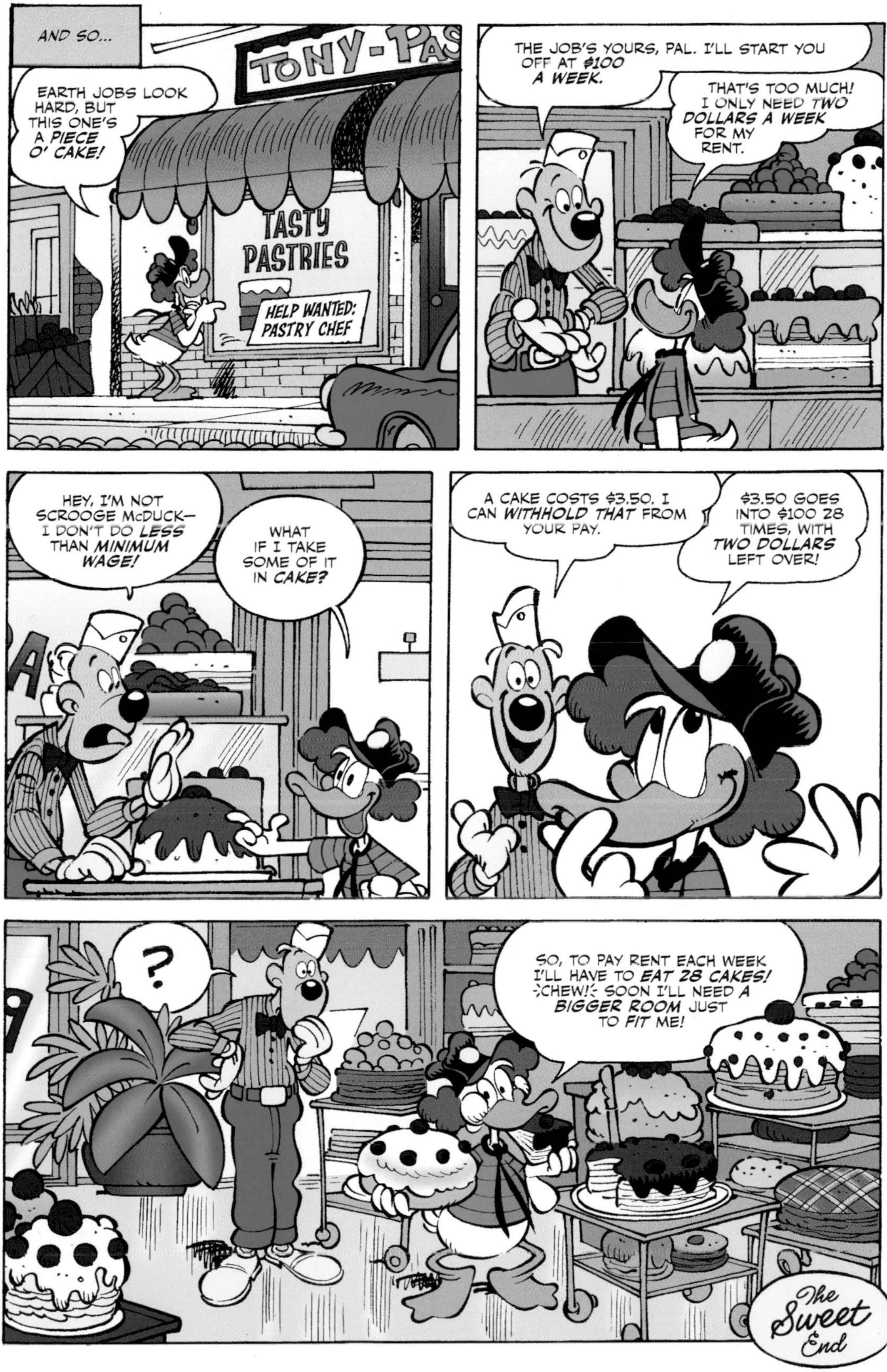
AND SO...
TONY-PAS
EARTH JOBS LOOK HARD, BUT THIS ONE'S A PIECE O' CAKE!
TASTY PASTRIES
HELP WANTED: PASTRY CHEF
THE JOB'S YOURS, PAL. I'LL START YOU OFF AT $100 A WEEK.
THAT'S TOO MUCH! I ONLY NEED TWO DOLLARS A WEEK FOR MY RENT.
HEY, I'M NOT SCROOGE McDUCK— I DON'T DO LESS THAN MINIMUM WAGE!
WHAT IF I TAKE SOME OF IT IN CAKE?
A CAKE COSTS $3.50. I CAN WITHHOLD THAT FROM YOUR PAY.
$3.50 GOES INTO $100 28 TIMES, WITH TWO DOLLARS LEFT OVER!
?
SO, TO PAY RENT EACH WEEK I'LL HAVE TO EAT 28 CAKES! -CHEW!- SOON I'LL NEED A BIGGER ROOM JUST TO FIT ME!
The Sweet End

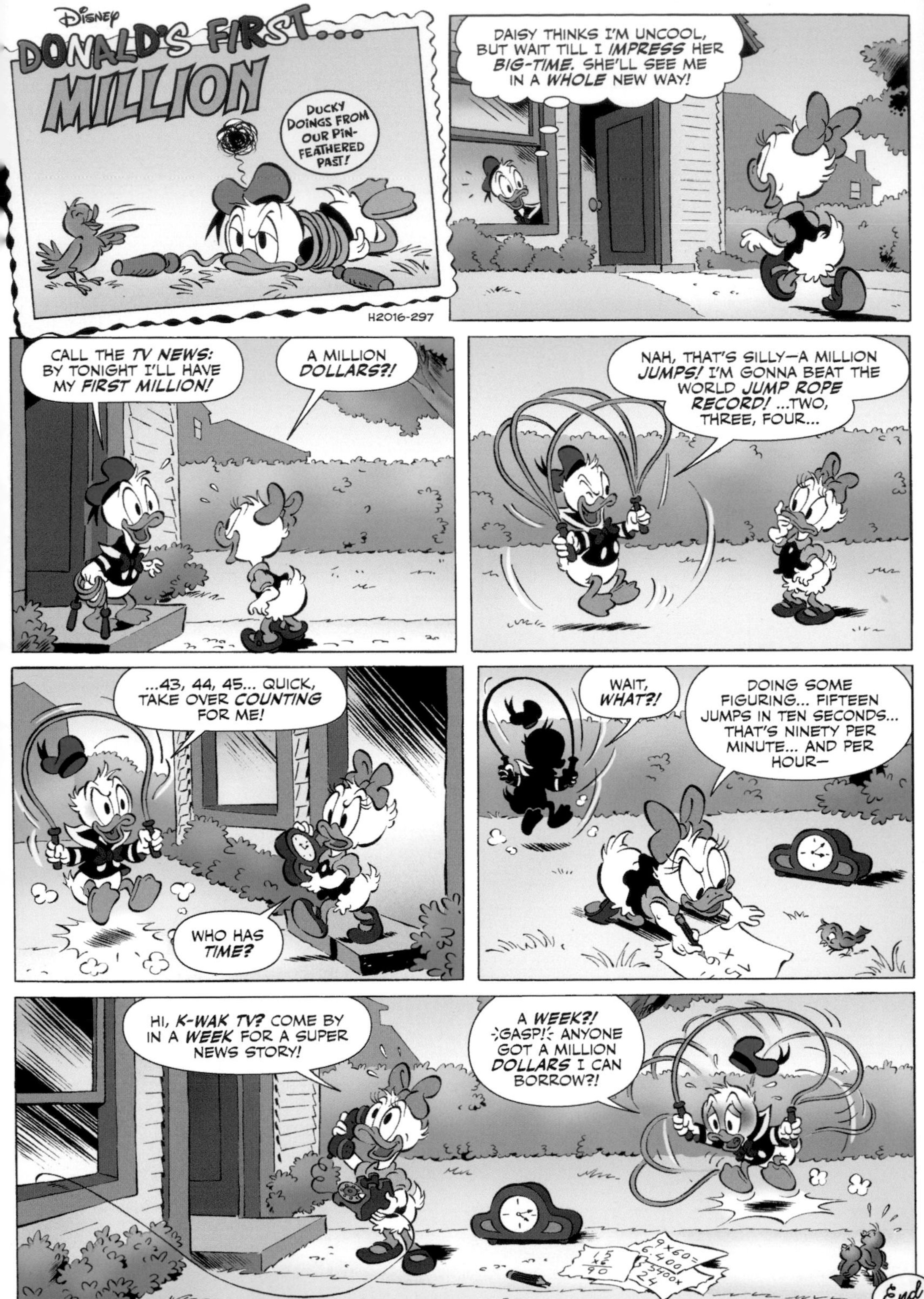
DISNEY
DONALD'S FIRST... MILLION
DUCKY DOINGS FROM OUR PIN-FEATHERED PAST!
H2016-297
DAISY THINKS I'M UNCOOL, BUT WAIT TILL I IMPRESS HER BIG-TIME. SHE'LL SEE ME IN A WHOLE NEW WAY!
CALL THE TV NEWS: BY TONIGHT I'LL HAVE MY FIRST MILLION!
A MILLION DOLLARS?!
NAH, THAT'S SILLY—A MILLION JUMPS! I'M GONNA BEAT THE WORLD JUMP ROPE RECORD! ...TWO, THREE, FOUR...
...43, 44, 45... QUICK, TAKE OVER COUNTING FOR ME!
WHO HAS TIME?
WAIT, WHAT?!
DOING SOME FIGURING... FIFTEEN JUMPS IN TEN SECONDS... THAT'S NINETY PER MINUTE... AND PER HOUR—
HI, K-WAK TV? COME BY IN A WEEK FOR A SUPER NEWS STORY!
A WEEK?! GASP! ANYONE GOT A MILLION DOLLARS I CAN BORROW?!
End

ORIGINALLY PUBLISHED IN DONALD DUCK WEEKBLAD #24/2017 (NETHERLANDS, 2017) • FIRST USA PUBLICATION

Walt Disney's Uncle $crooge in So Dear to His Heart

Part 1 of 2

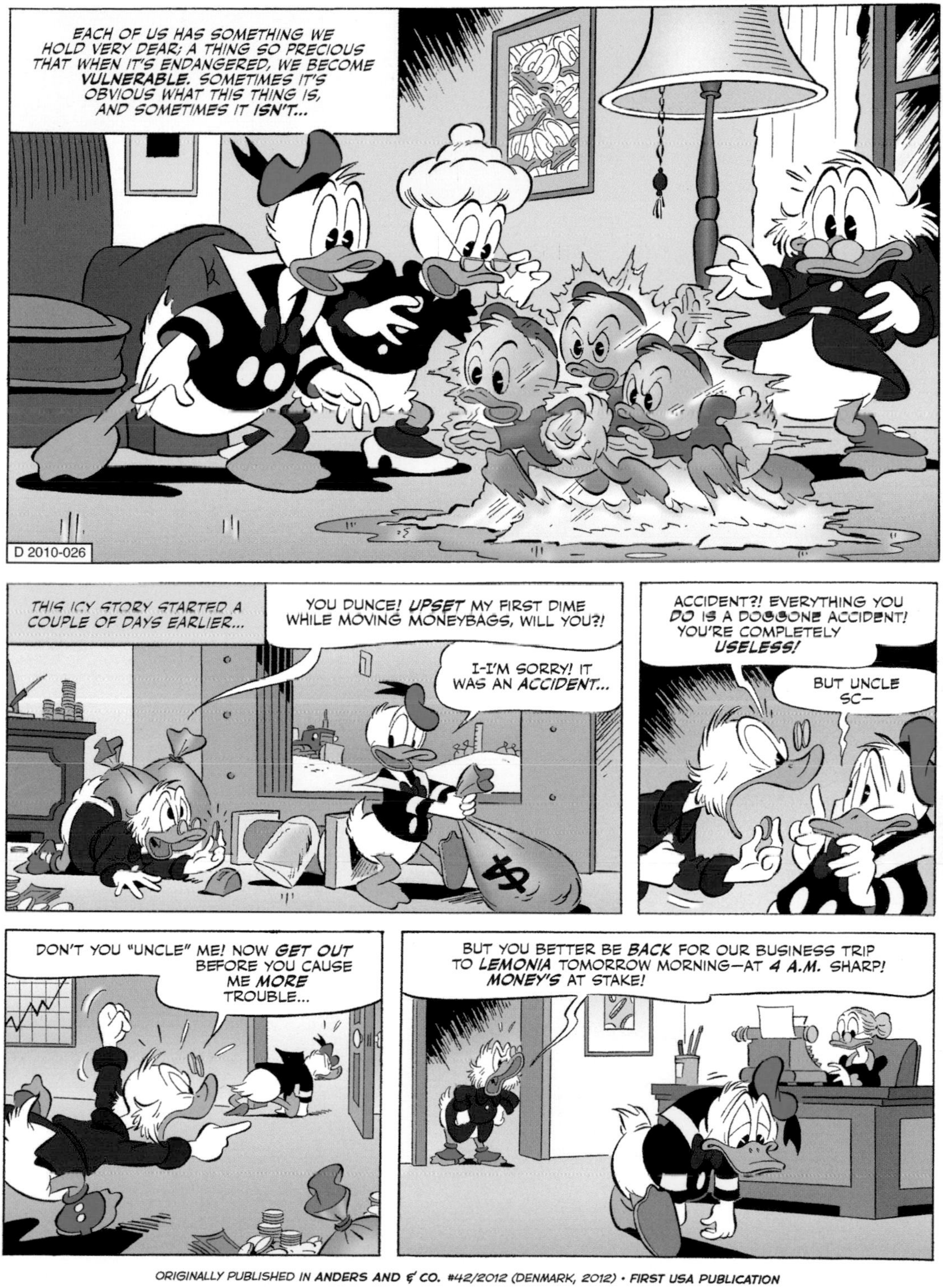
EACH OF US HAS SOMETHING WE HOLD VERY DEAR; A THING SO PRECIOUS THAT WHEN IT'S ENDANGERED, WE BECOME VULNERABLE. SOMETIMES IT'S OBVIOUS WHAT THIS THING IS, AND SOMETIMES IT ISN'T...
D 2010-026
THIS ICY STORY STARTED A COUPLE OF DAYS EARLIER...
YOU DUNCE! UPSET MY FIRST DIME WHILE MOVING MONEYBAGS, WILL YOU?!
I-I'M SORRY! IT WAS AN ACCIDENT...
ACCIDENT?! EVERYTHING YOU DO IS A DOGGONE ACCIDENT! YOU'RE COMPLETELY USELESS!
BUT UNCLE SC—
DON'T YOU "UNCLE" ME! NOW GET OUT BEFORE YOU CAUSE ME MORE TROUBLE...
BUT YOU BETTER BE BACK FOR OUR BUSINESS TRIP TO LEMONIA TOMORROW MORNING—AT 4 A.M. SHARP! MONEY'S AT STAKE!

ORIGINALLY PUBLISHED IN ANDERS AND & CO. #42/2012 (DENMARK, 2012) • FIRST USA PUBLICATION

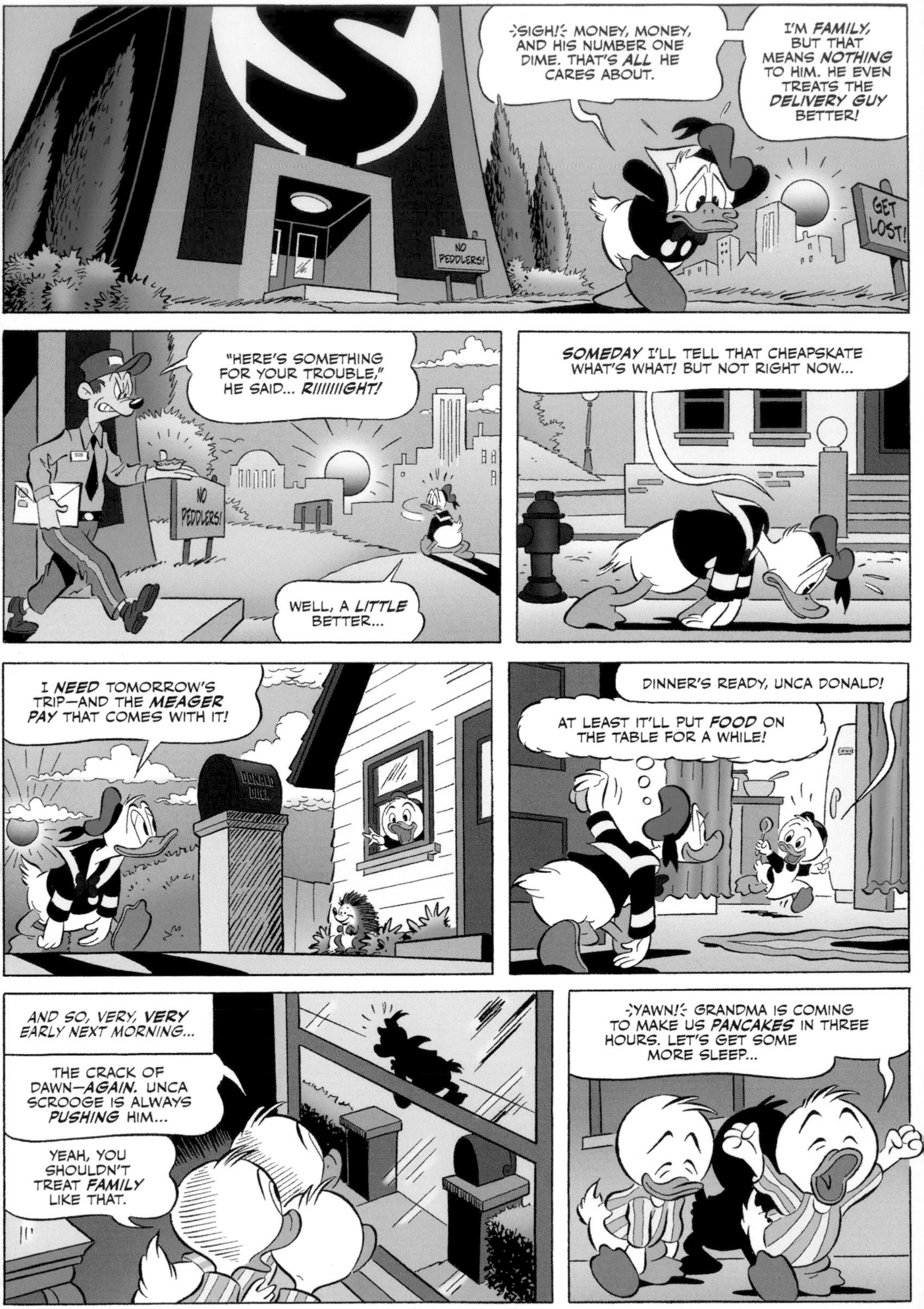

-SIGH!- MONEY, MONEY, AND HIS NUMBER ONE DIME. THAT'S ALL HE CARES ABOUT.
I'M FAMILY, BUT THAT MEANS NOTHING TO HIM. HE EVEN TREATS THE DELIVERY GUY BETTER!
NO PEDDLERS!
GET LOST!
"HERE'S SOMETHING FOR YOUR TROUBLE," HE SAID... RIIIIIIGHT!
NO PEDDLERS!
WELL, A LITTLE BETTER...
SOMEDAY I'LL TELL THAT CHEAPSKATE WHAT'S WHAT! BUT NOT RIGHT NOW...
I NEED TOMORROW'S TRIP—AND THE MEAGER PAY THAT COMES WITH IT!
DONALD DUCK
DINNER'S READY, UNCA DONALD!
AT LEAST IT'LL PUT FOOD ON THE TABLE FOR A WHILE!
AND SO, VERY, VERY EARLY NEXT MORNING...
THE CRACK OF DAWN—AGAIN. UNCA SCROOGE IS ALWAYS PUSHING HIM...
YEAH, YOU SHOULDN'T TREAT FAMILY LIKE THAT.
-YAWN!- GRANDMA IS COMING TO MAKE US PANCAKES IN THREE HOURS. LET'S GET SOME MORE SLEEP...

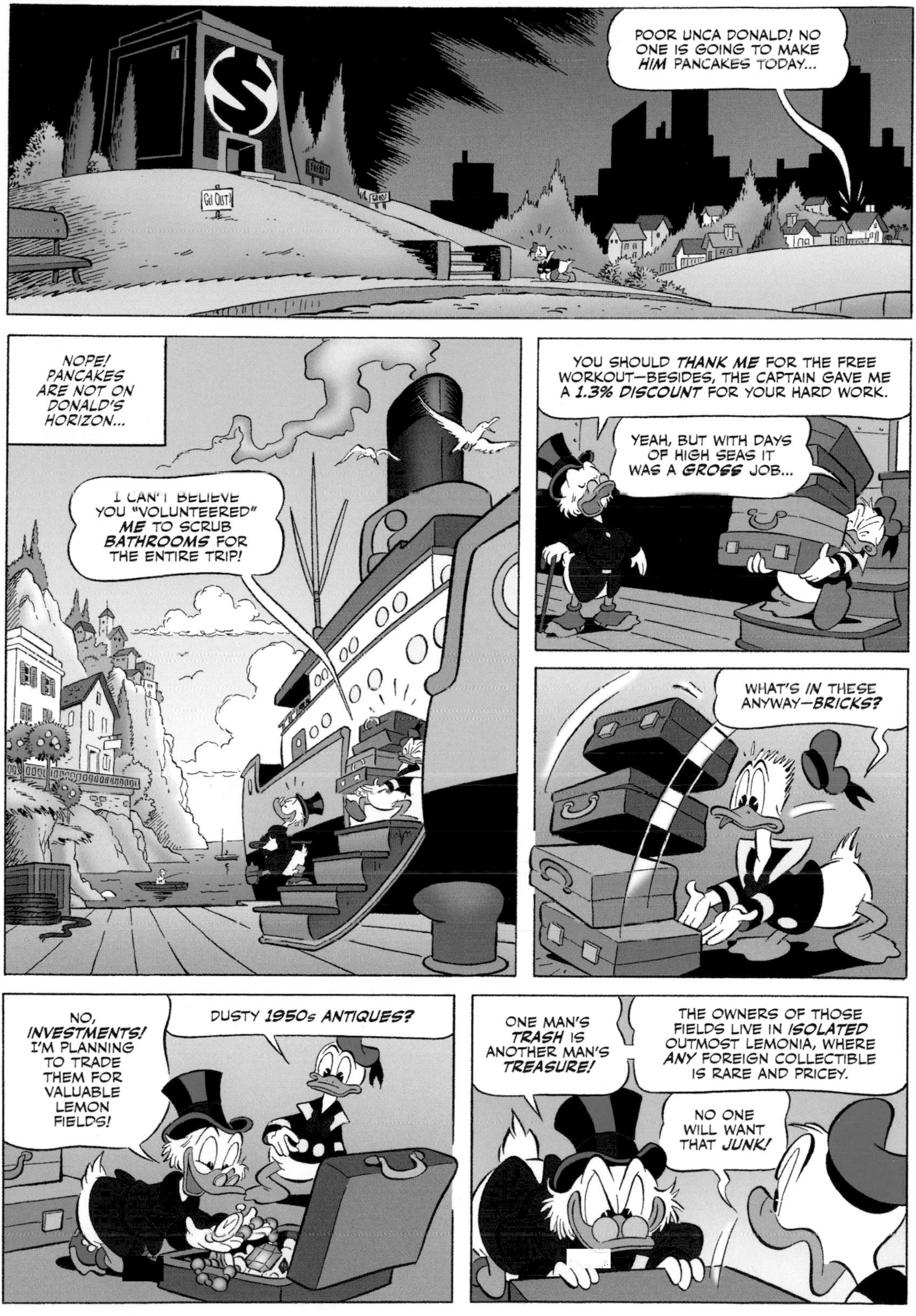
POOR UNCA DONALD! NO ONE IS GOING TO MAKE *HIM* PANCAKES TODAY...
GET OUT!
NOPE! PANCAKES ARE NOT ON DONALD'S HORIZON...
I CAN'T BELIEVE YOU "VOLUNTEERED" *ME* TO SCRUB *BATHROOMS* FOR THE ENTIRE TRIP!
YOU SHOULD *THANK ME* FOR THE FREE WORKOUT—BESIDES, THE CAPTAIN GAVE ME A *1.3% DISCOUNT* FOR YOUR HARD WORK.
YEAH, BUT WITH DAYS OF HIGH SEAS IT WAS A *GROSS* JOB...
WHAT'S *IN* THESE ANYWAY—*BRICKS?*
NO, *INVESTMENTS!* I'M PLANNING TO TRADE THEM FOR VALUABLE LEMON FIELDS!
DUSTY *1950s ANTIQUES?*
ONE MAN'S *TRASH* IS ANOTHER MAN'S *TREASURE!*
THE OWNERS OF THOSE FIELDS LIVE IN *ISOLATED* OUTMOST LEMONIA, WHERE *ANY* FOREIGN COLLECTIBLE IS RARE AND PRICEY.
NO ONE WILL WANT THAT *JUNK!*

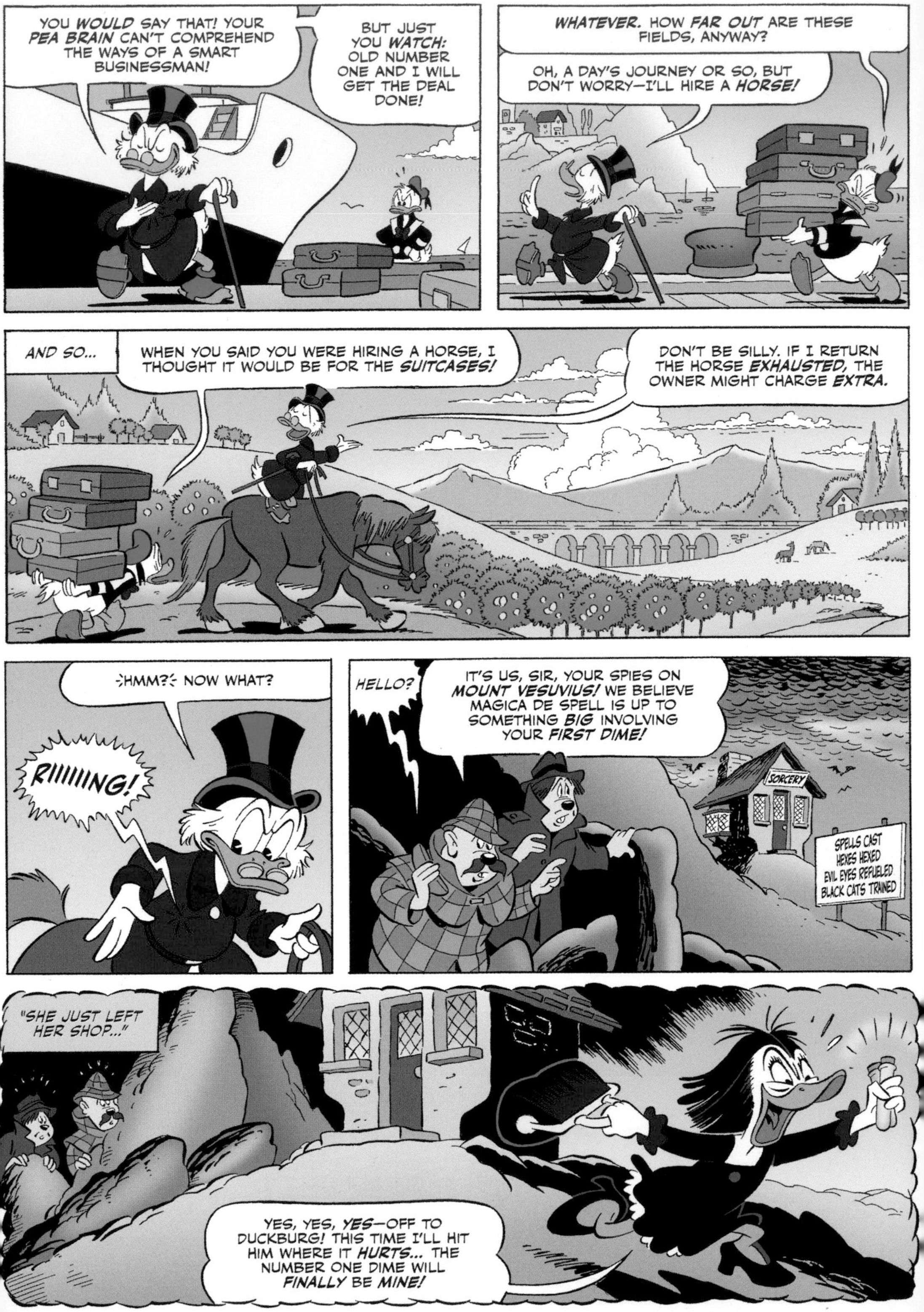
YOU WOULD SAY THAT! YOUR PEA BRAIN CAN'T COMPREHEND THE WAYS OF A SMART BUSINESSMAN!
BUT JUST YOU WATCH: OLD NUMBER ONE AND I WILL GET THE DEAL DONE!
WHATEVER. HOW FAR OUT ARE THESE FIELDS, ANYWAY?
OH, A DAY'S JOURNEY OR SO, BUT DON'T WORRY—I'LL HIRE A HORSE!
AND SO...
WHEN YOU SAID YOU WERE HIRING A HORSE, I THOUGHT IT WOULD BE FOR THE SUITCASES!
DON'T BE SILLY. IF I RETURN THE HORSE EXHAUSTED, THE OWNER MIGHT CHARGE EXTRA.
RIIIIING!
HMM? NOW WHAT?
HELLO?
IT'S US, SIR, YOUR SPIES ON MOUNT VESUVIUS! WE BELIEVE MAGICA DE SPELL IS UP TO SOMETHING BIG INVOLVING YOUR FIRST DIME!
SORCERY
SPELLS CAST
HEXES HEXED
EVIL EYES REFUELED
BLACK CATS TRAINED
"SHE JUST LEFT HER SHOP..."
YES, YES, YES—OFF TO DUCKBURG! THIS TIME I'LL HIT HIM WHERE IT HURTS... THE NUMBER ONE DIME WILL FINALLY BE MINE!

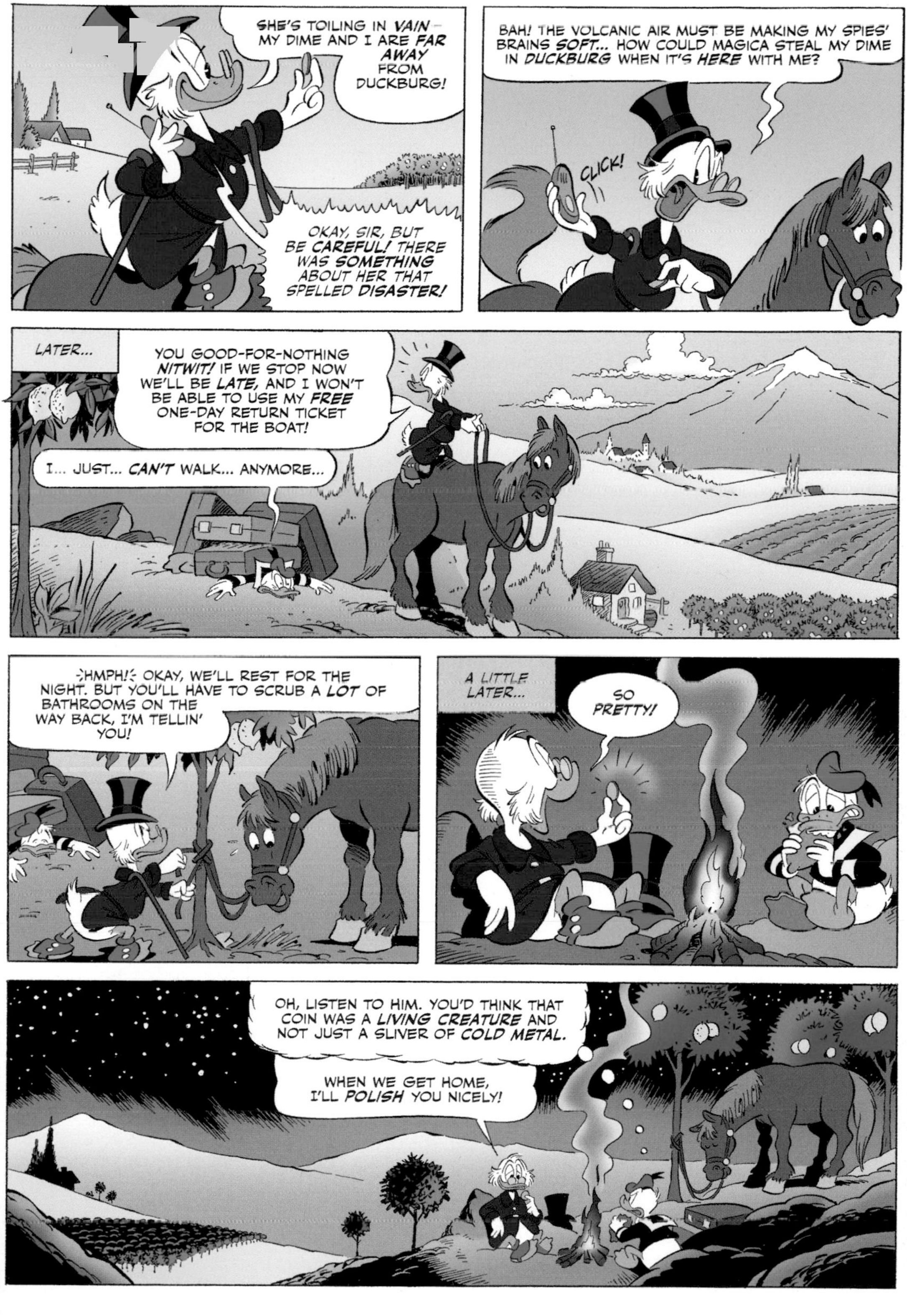

SHE'S TOILING IN VAIN — MY DIME AND I ARE FAR AWAY FROM DUCKBURG!
OKAY, SIR, BUT BE CAREFUL! THERE WAS SOMETHING ABOUT HER THAT SPELLED DISASTER!
BAH! THE VOLCANIC AIR MUST BE MAKING MY SPIES' BRAINS SOFT... HOW COULD MAGICA STEAL MY DIME IN DUCKBURG WHEN IT'S HERE WITH ME?
CLICK!
LATER...
YOU GOOD-FOR-NOTHING NITWIT! IF WE STOP NOW WE'LL BE LATE, AND I WON'T BE ABLE TO USE MY FREE ONE-DAY RETURN TICKET FOR THE BOAT!
I... JUST... CAN'T WALK... ANYMORE...
HMPH! OKAY, WE'LL REST FOR THE NIGHT. BUT YOU'LL HAVE TO SCRUB A LOT OF BATHROOMS ON THE WAY BACK, I'M TELLIN' YOU!
A LITTLE LATER...
SO PRETTY!
OH, LISTEN TO HIM. YOU'D THINK THAT COIN WAS A LIVING CREATURE AND NOT JUST A SLIVER OF COLD METAL.
WHEN WE GET HOME, I'LL POLISH YOU NICELY!

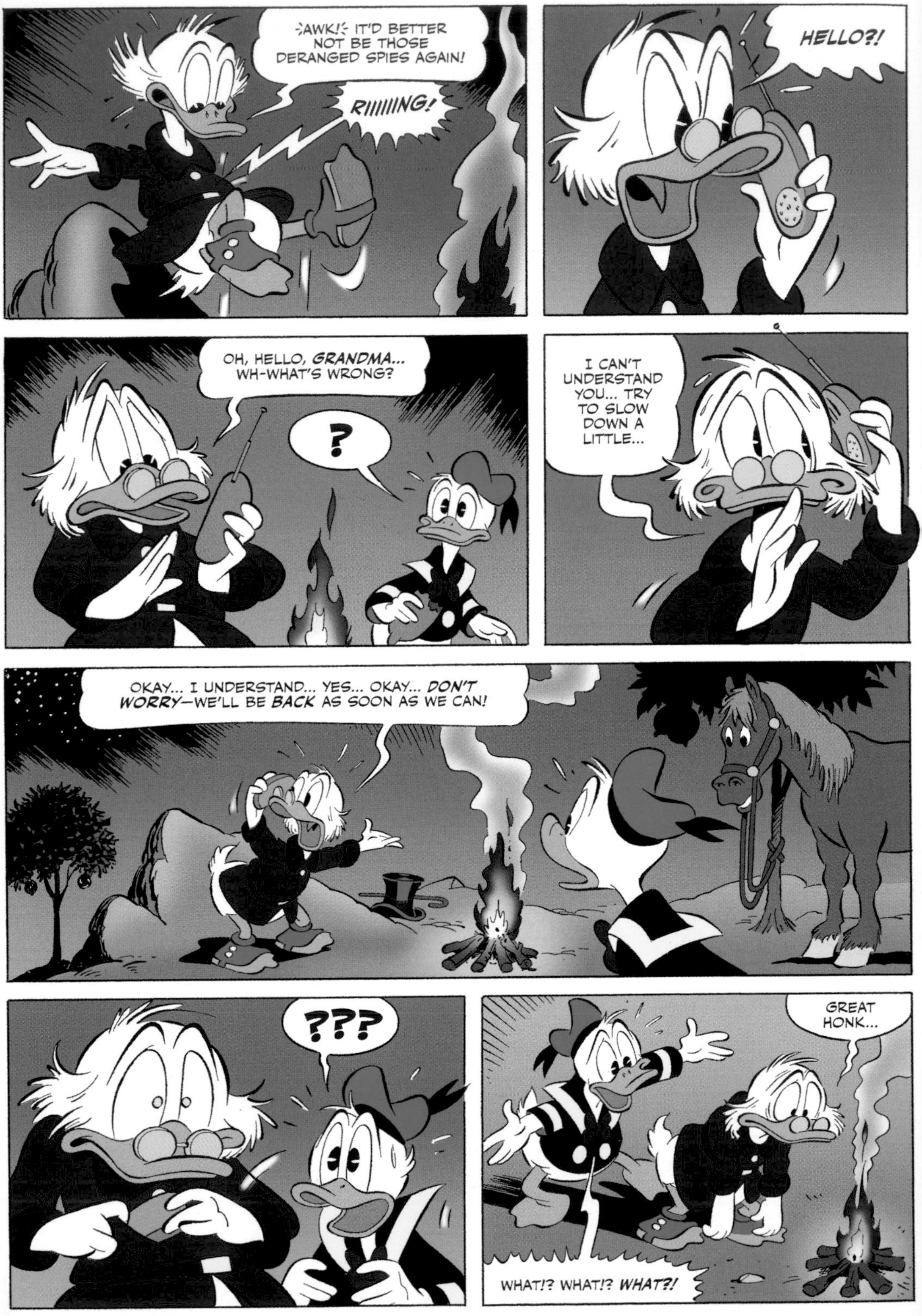

AWK! IT'D BETTER NOT BE THOSE DERANGED SPIES AGAIN!
RIIIIIING!
HELLO?!
OH, HELLO, GRANDMA... WH-WHAT'S WRONG?
?
I CAN'T UNDERSTAND YOU... TRY TO SLOW DOWN A LITTLE...
OKAY... I UNDERSTAND... YES... OKAY... DON'T WORRY—WE'LL BE BACK AS SOON AS WE CAN!
???
GREAT HONK...
WHAT!? WHAT!? WHAT?!

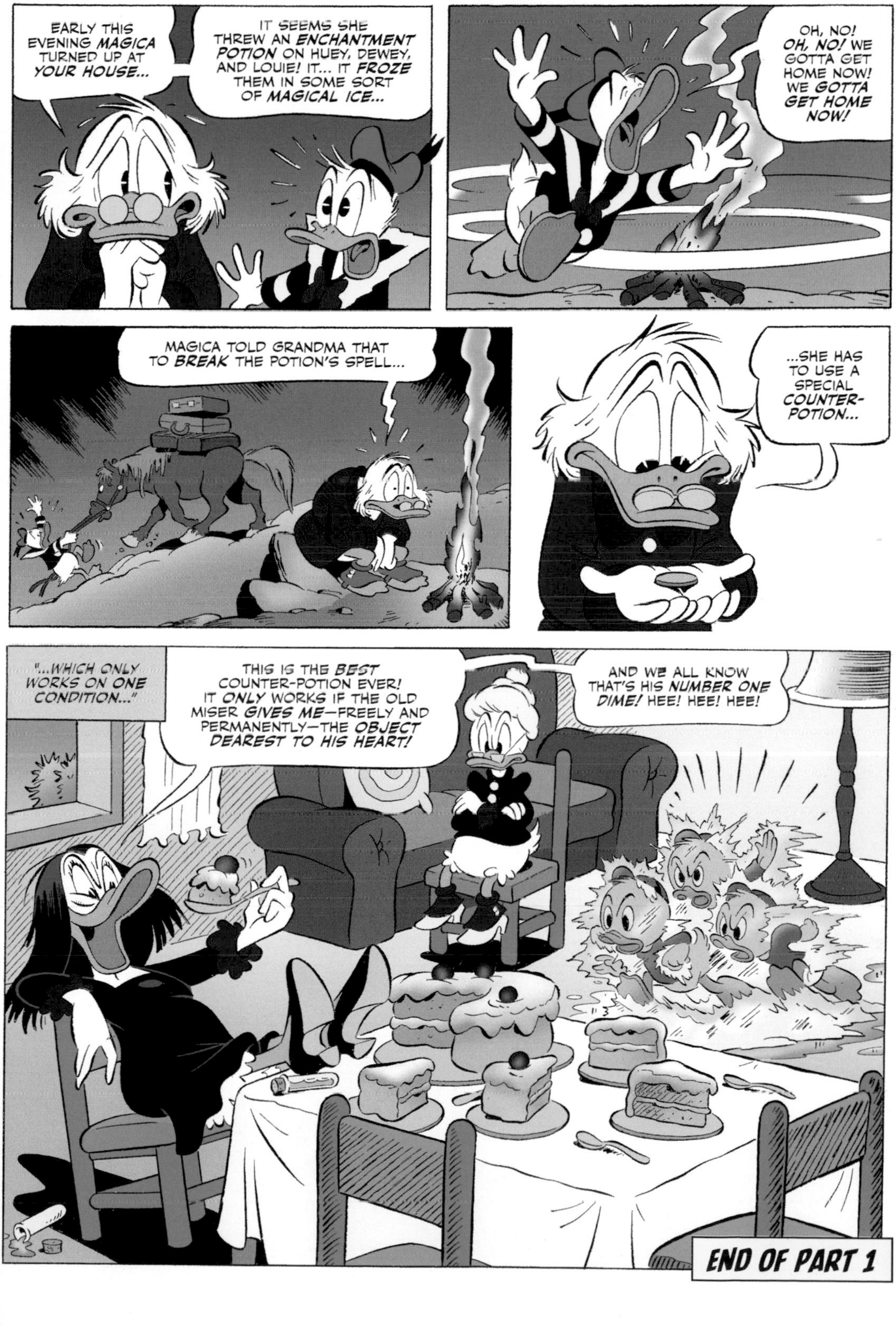
EARLY THIS EVENING MAGICA TURNED UP AT YOUR HOUSE...
IT SEEMS SHE THREW AN ENCHANTMENT POTION ON HUEY, DEWEY, AND LOUIE! IT... IT FROZE THEM IN SOME SORT OF MAGICAL ICE...
OH, NO! OH, NO! WE GOTTA GET HOME NOW! WE GOTTA GET HOME NOW!
MAGICA TOLD GRANDMA THAT TO BREAK THE POTION'S SPELL...
...SHE HAS TO USE A SPECIAL COUNTER-POTION...
"...WHICH ONLY WORKS ON ONE CONDITION..."
THIS IS THE BEST COUNTER-POTION EVER! IT ONLY WORKS IF THE OLD MISER GIVES ME—FREELY AND PERMANENTLY—THE OBJECT DEAREST TO HIS HEART!
AND WE ALL KNOW THAT'S HIS NUMBER ONE DIME! HEE! HEE! HEE!
END OF PART 1

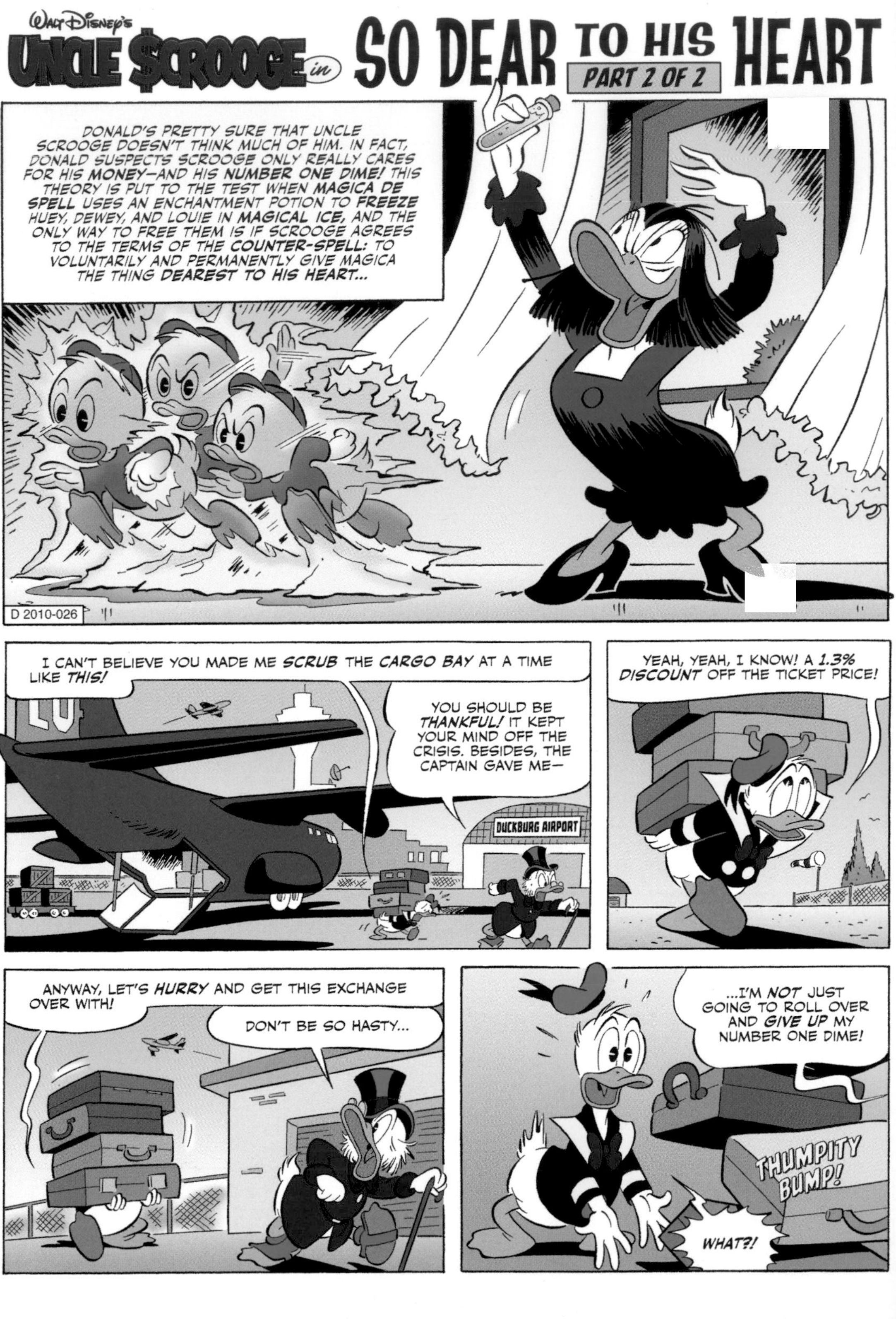
WALT DISNEY'S UNCLE $CROOGE in
SO DEAR TO HIS HEART
PART 2 OF 2
DONALD'S PRETTY SURE THAT UNCLE SCROOGE DOESN'T THINK MUCH OF HIM. IN FACT, DONALD SUSPECTS SCROOGE ONLY REALLY CARES FOR HIS MONEY—AND HIS NUMBER ONE DIME! THIS THEORY IS PUT TO THE TEST WHEN MAGICA DE SPELL USES AN ENCHANTMENT POTION TO FREEZE HUEY, DEWEY, AND LOUIE IN MAGICAL ICE, AND THE ONLY WAY TO FREE THEM IS IF SCROOGE AGREES TO THE TERMS OF THE COUNTER-SPELL: TO VOLUNTARILY AND PERMANENTLY GIVE MAGICA THE THING DEAREST TO HIS HEART...
D 2010-026
I CAN'T BELIEVE YOU MADE ME SCRUB THE CARGO BAY AT A TIME LIKE THIS!
YOU SHOULD BE THANKFUL! IT KEPT YOUR MIND OFF THE CRISIS. BESIDES, THE CAPTAIN GAVE ME—
DUCKBURG AIRPORT
YEAH, YEAH, I KNOW! A 1.3% DISCOUNT OFF THE TICKET PRICE!
ANYWAY, LET'S HURRY AND GET THIS EXCHANGE OVER WITH!
DON'T BE SO HASTY...
...I'M NOT JUST GOING TO ROLL OVER AND GIVE UP MY NUMBER ONE DIME!
THUMPITY BUMP!
WHAT?!

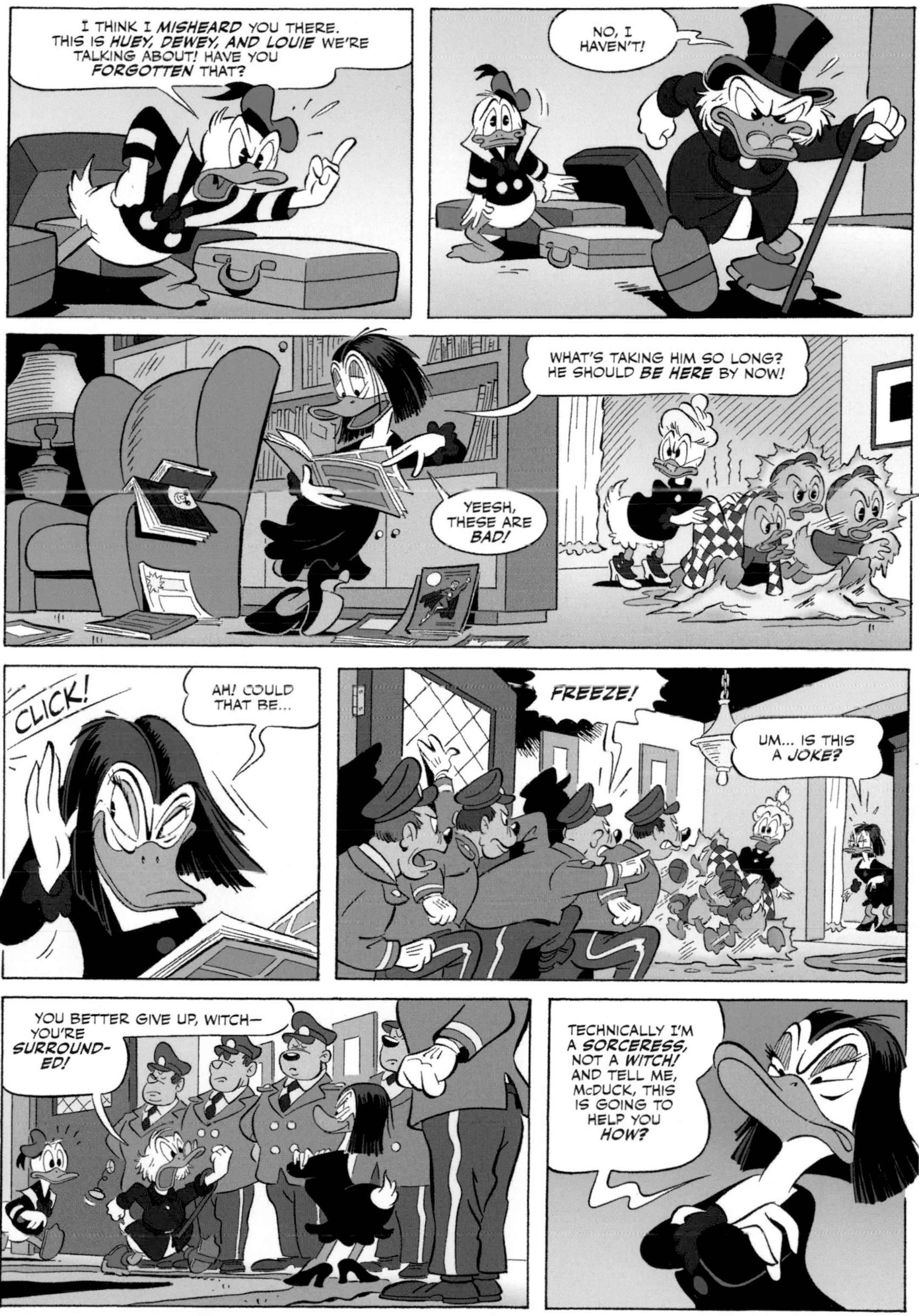
I THINK I MISHEARD YOU THERE. THIS IS HUEY, DEWEY, AND LOUIE WE'RE TALKING ABOUT! HAVE YOU FORGOTTEN THAT?
NO, I HAVEN'T!
WHAT'S TAKING HIM SO LONG? HE SHOULD BE HERE BY NOW!
YEESH, THESE ARE BAD!
CLICK!
AH! COULD THAT BE...
FREEZE!
UM... IS THIS A JOKE?
YOU BETTER GIVE UP, WITCH— YOU'RE SURROUND-ED!
TECHNICALLY I'M A SORCERESS, NOT A WITCH! AND TELL ME, McDUCK, THIS IS GOING TO HELP YOU HOW?

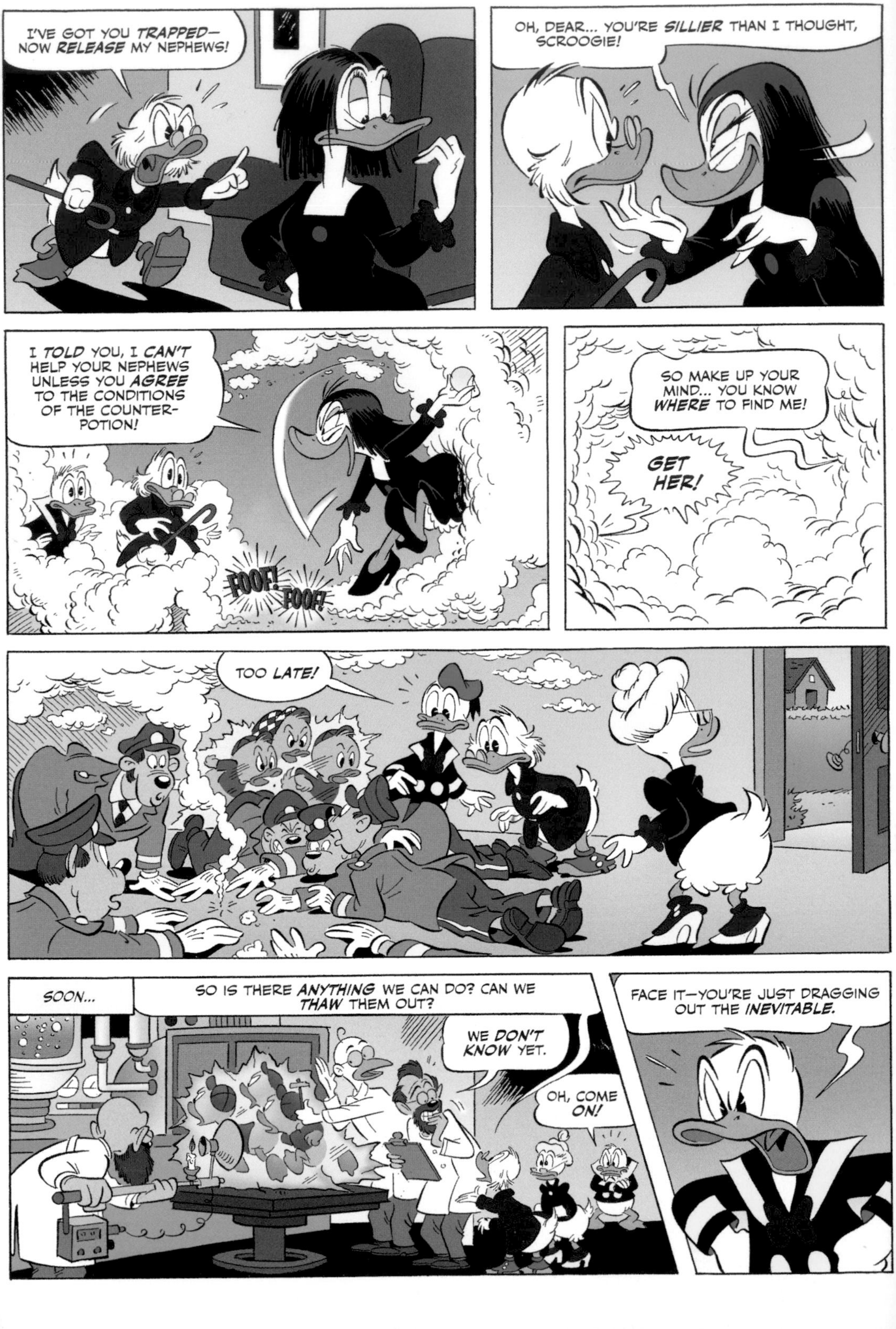

I'VE GOT YOU *TRAPPED*— NOW *RELEASE* MY NEPHEWS!
OH, DEAR... YOU'RE *SILLIER* THAN I THOUGHT, SCROOGIE!
I *TOLD* YOU, I *CAN'T* HELP YOUR NEPHEWS UNLESS YOU *AGREE* TO THE CONDITIONS OF THE COUNTER-POTION!
FOOF! FOOF!
SO MAKE UP YOUR MIND... YOU KNOW *WHERE* TO FIND ME!
GET HER!
TOO *LATE!*
SOON...
SO IS THERE *ANYTHING* WE CAN DO? CAN WE *THAW* THEM OUT?
WE *DON'T KNOW* YET.
OH, COME *ON!*
FACE IT—YOU'RE JUST DRAGGING OUT THE *INEVITABLE.*

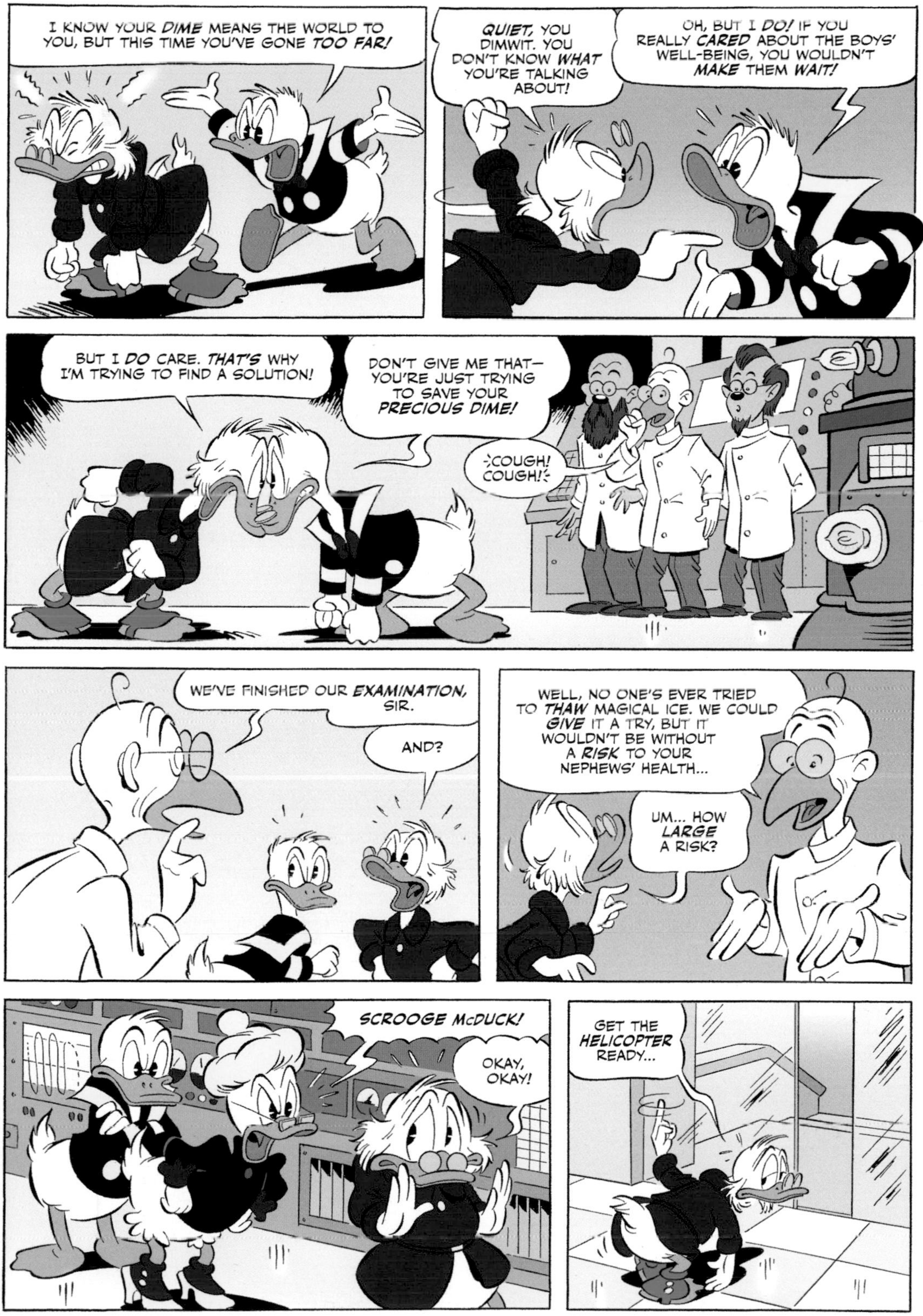
I KNOW YOUR DIME MEANS THE WORLD TO YOU, BUT THIS TIME YOU'VE GONE TOO FAR!
QUIET, YOU DIMWIT. YOU DON'T KNOW WHAT YOU'RE TALKING ABOUT!
OH, BUT I DO! IF YOU REALLY CARED ABOUT THE BOYS' WELL-BEING, YOU WOULDN'T MAKE THEM WAIT!
BUT I DO CARE. THAT'S WHY I'M TRYING TO FIND A SOLUTION!
DON'T GIVE ME THAT— YOU'RE JUST TRYING TO SAVE YOUR PRECIOUS DIME!
COUGH! COUGH!
WE'VE FINISHED OUR EXAMINATION, SIR.
AND?
WELL, NO ONE'S EVER TRIED TO THAW MAGICAL ICE. WE COULD GIVE IT A TRY, BUT IT WOULDN'T BE WITHOUT A RISK TO YOUR NEPHEWS' HEALTH...
UM... HOW LARGE A RISK?
SCROOGE McDUCK!
OKAY, OKAY!
GET THE HELICOPTER READY...

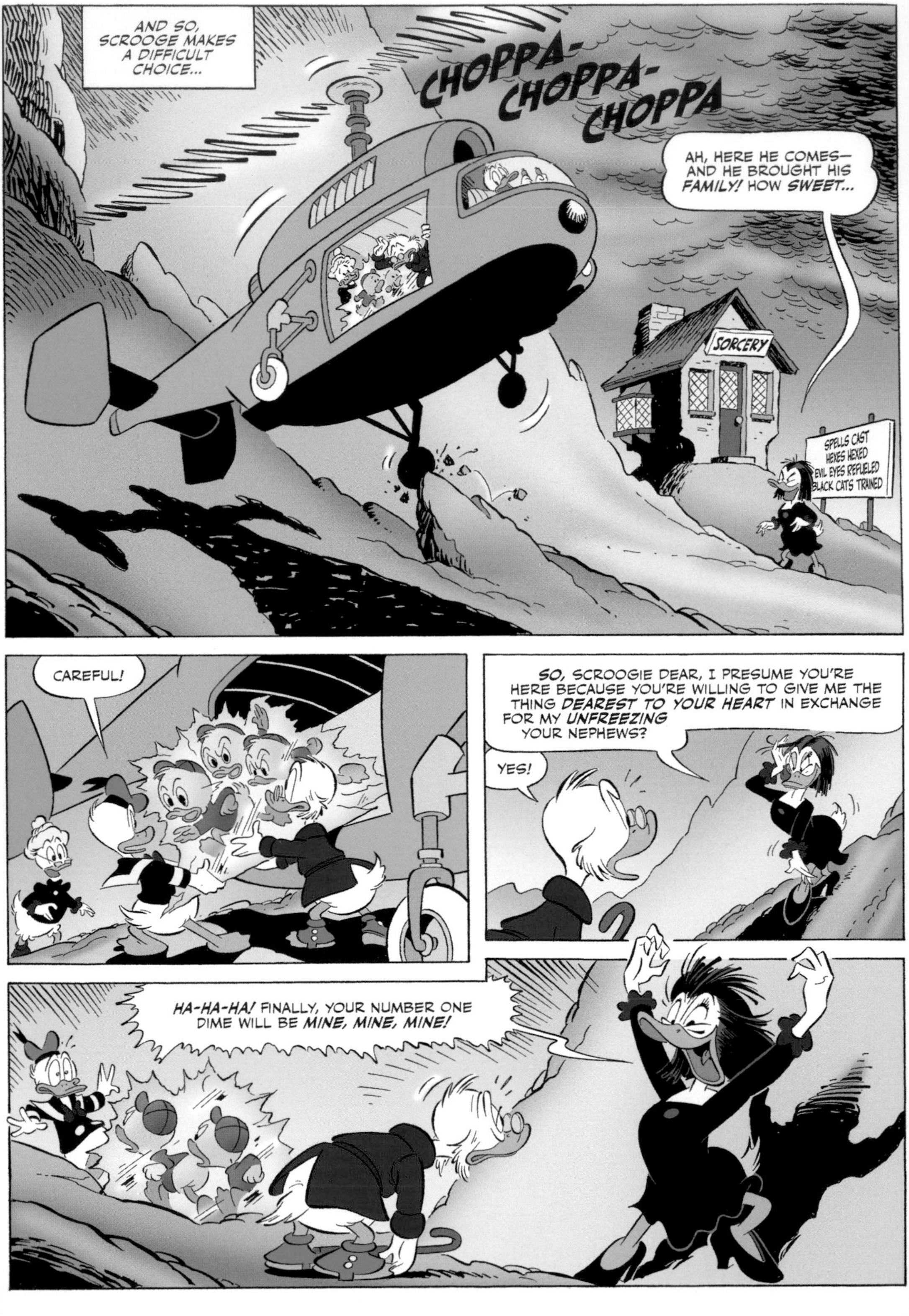
AND SO, SCROOGE MAKES A DIFFICULT CHOICE...
CHOPPA-CHOPPA-CHOPPA
AH, HERE HE COMES— AND HE BROUGHT HIS FAMILY! HOW SWEET...
SORCERY
SPELLS CAST
HEXES HEXED
EVIL EYES REFUELED
BLACK CATS TRAINED
CAREFUL!
SO, SCROOGIE DEAR, I PRESUME YOU'RE HERE BECAUSE YOU'RE WILLING TO GIVE ME THE THING DEAREST TO YOUR HEART IN EXCHANGE FOR MY UNFREEZING YOUR NEPHEWS?
YES!
HA-HA-HA! FINALLY, YOUR NUMBER ONE DIME WILL BE MINE, MINE, MINE!

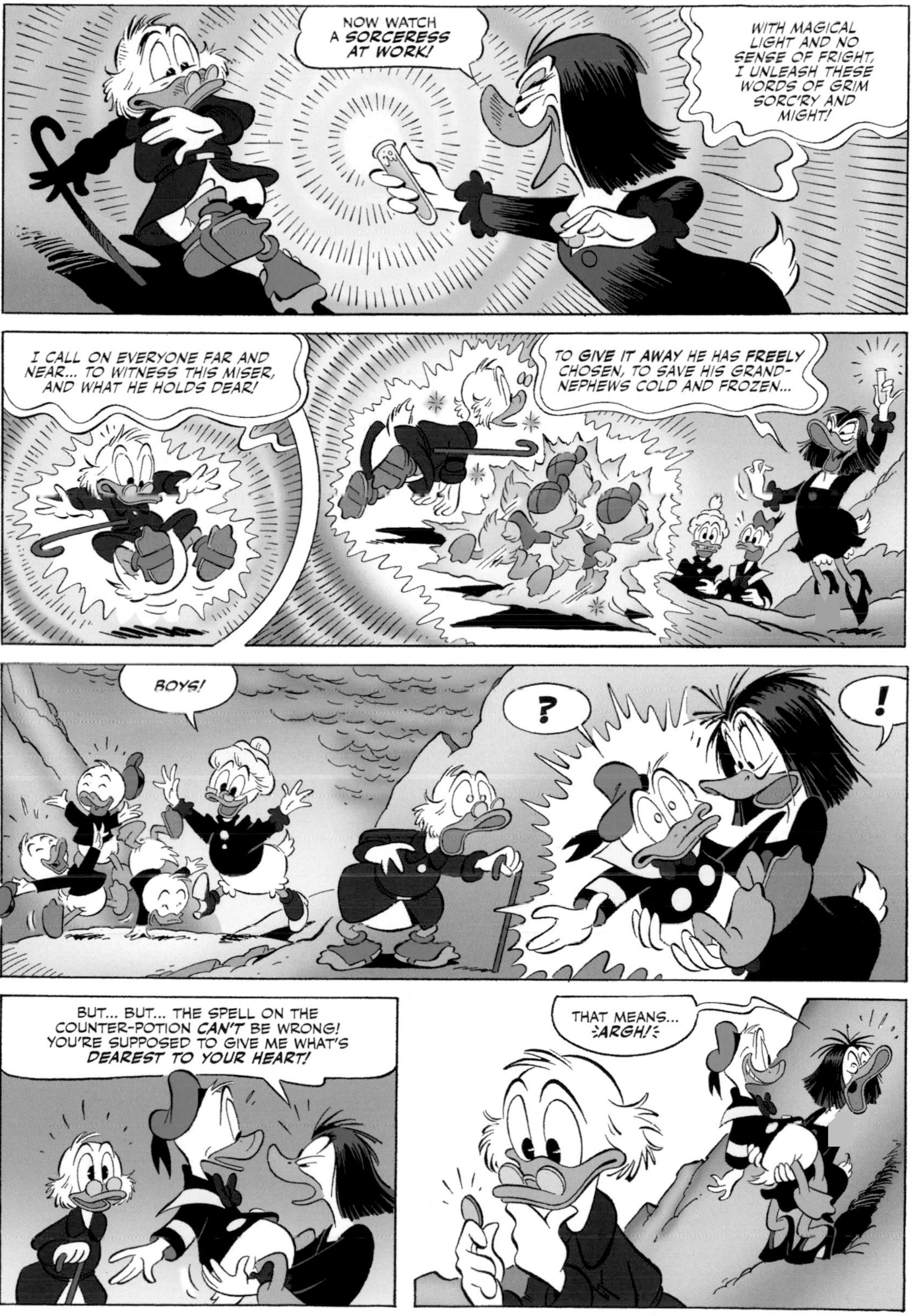
NOW WATCH A SORCERESS AT WORK!
WITH MAGICAL LIGHT AND NO SENSE OF FRIGHT, I UNLEASH THESE WORDS OF GRIM SORC'RY AND MIGHT!
I CALL ON EVERYONE FAR AND NEAR... TO WITNESS THIS MISER, AND WHAT HE HOLDS DEAR!
TO GIVE IT AWAY HE HAS FREELY CHOSEN, TO SAVE HIS GRAND-NEPHEWS COLD AND FROZEN...
BOYS!
?
!
BUT... BUT... THE SPELL ON THE COUNTER-POTION CAN'T BE WRONG! YOU'RE SUPPOSED TO GIVE ME WHAT'S DEAREST TO YOUR HEART!
THAT MEANS... ARGH!

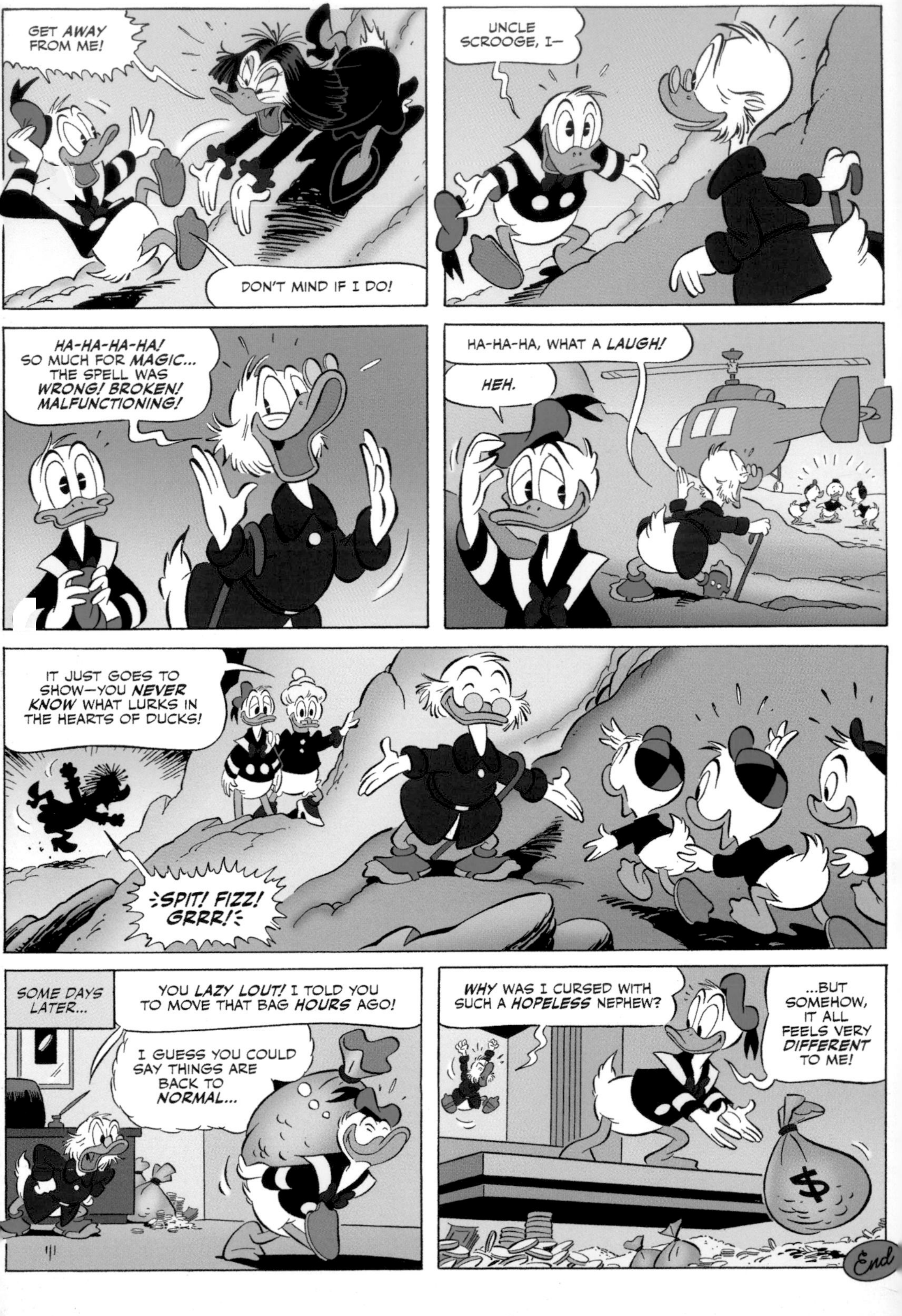
GET AWAY FROM ME!
DON'T MIND IF I DO!
UNCLE SCROOGE, I—
HA-HA-HA-HA! SO MUCH FOR MAGIC... THE SPELL WAS WRONG! BROKEN! MALFUNCTIONING!
HA-HA-HA, WHAT A LAUGH!
HEH.
IT JUST GOES TO SHOW—YOU NEVER KNOW WHAT LURKS IN THE HEARTS OF DUCKS!
SPIT! FIZZ! GRRR!
SOME DAYS LATER...
YOU LAZY LOUT! I TOLD YOU TO MOVE THAT BAG HOURS AGO!
I GUESS YOU COULD SAY THINGS ARE BACK TO NORMAL...
WHY WAS I CURSED WITH SUCH A HOPELESS NEPHEW?
...BUT SOMEHOW, IT ALL FEELS VERY DIFFERENT TO ME!
End

Cover Gallery

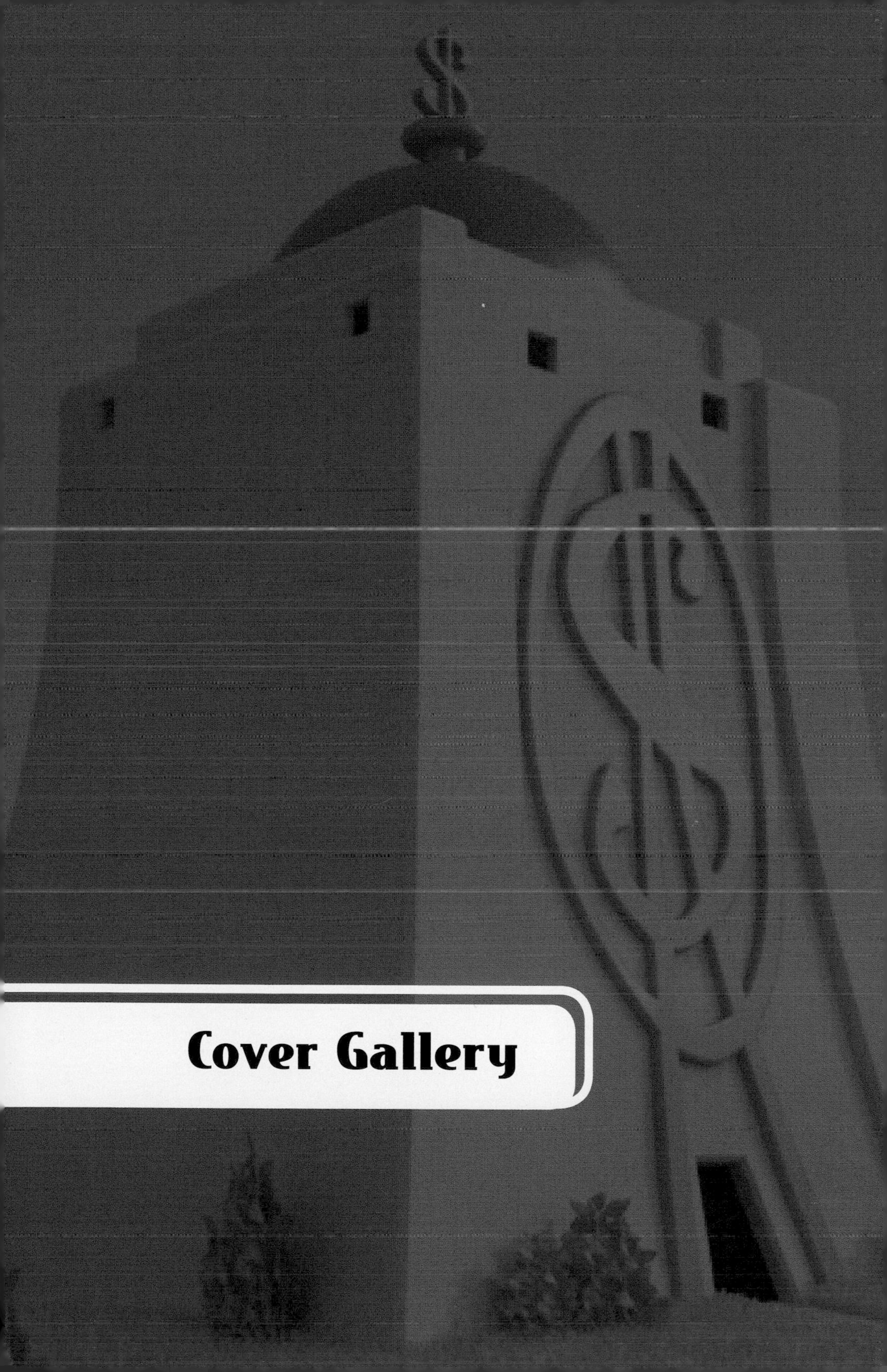

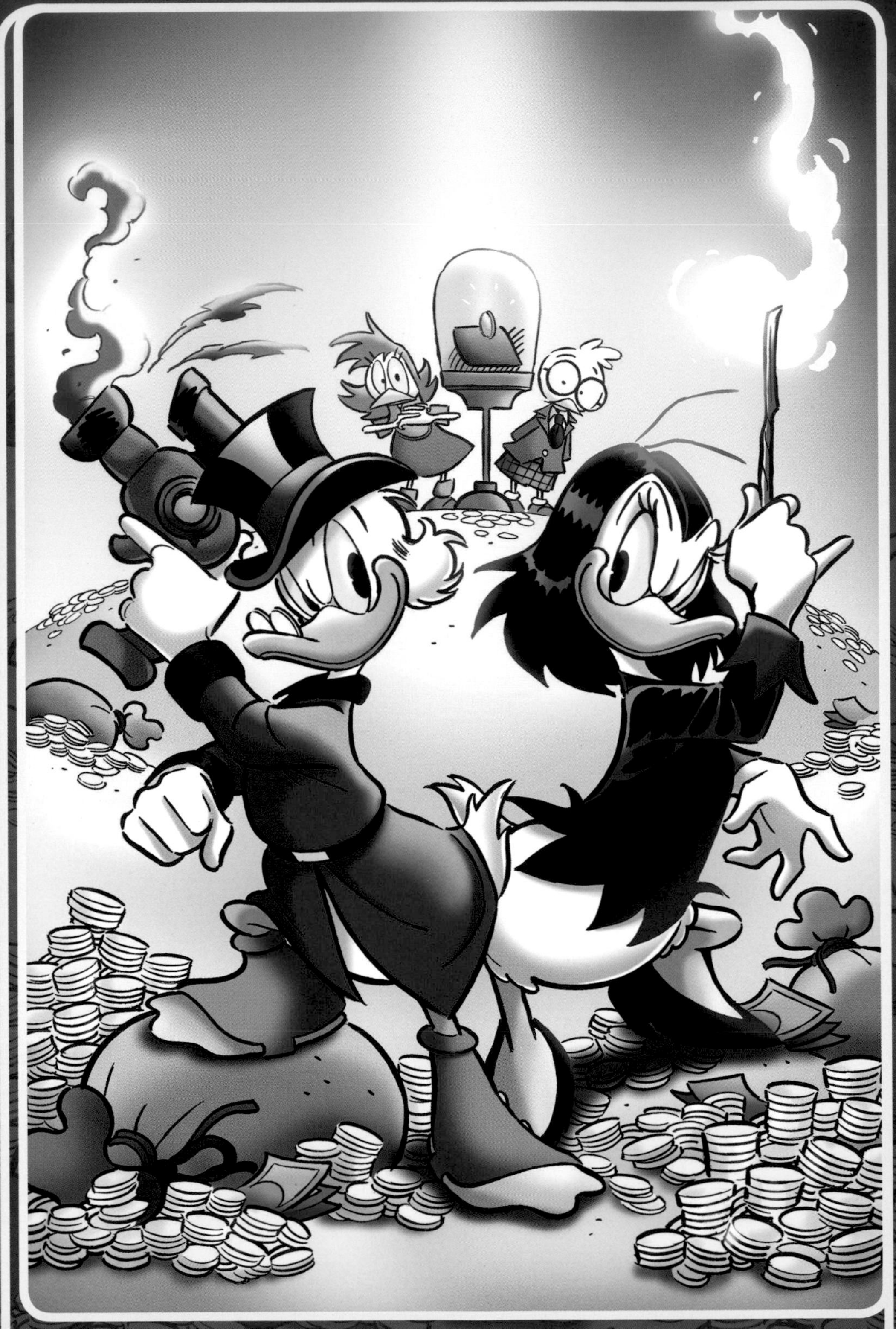

Art by Andrea Freccero, Colors by Marco Colletti

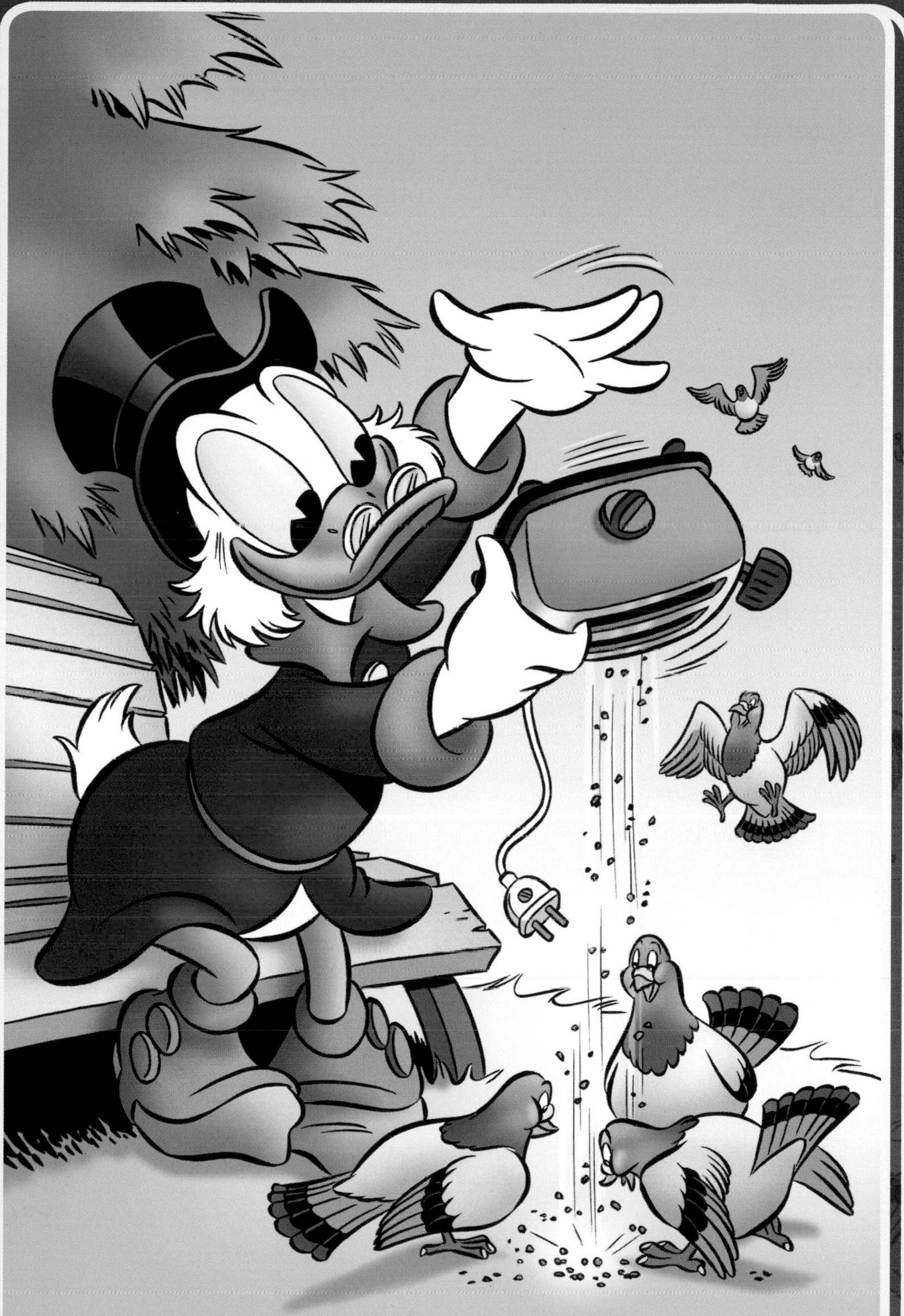

Art by Maarten Gerritsen, Colors by Sanoma

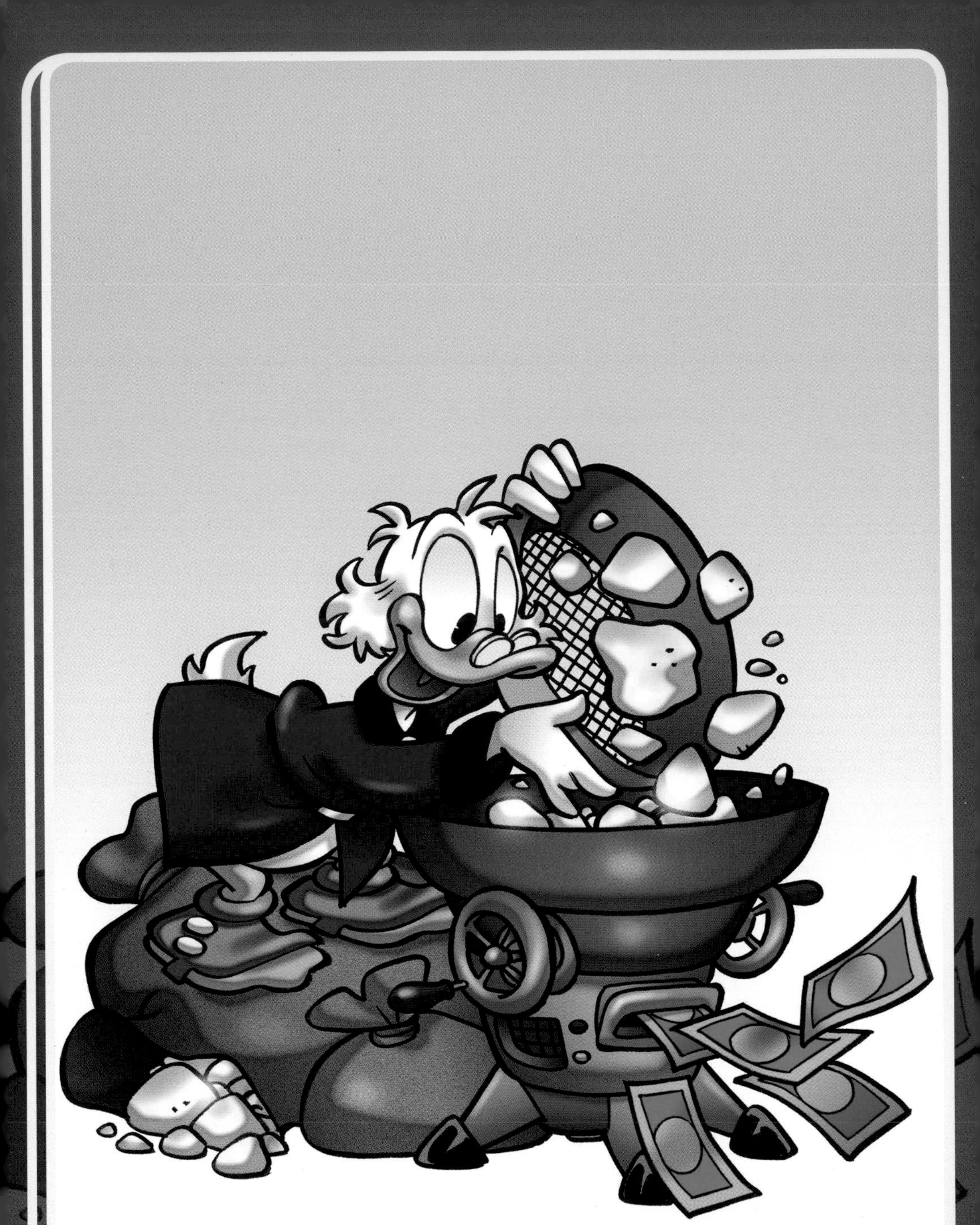

Art by Giorgio Cavazzano, Colors by Max Monteduro

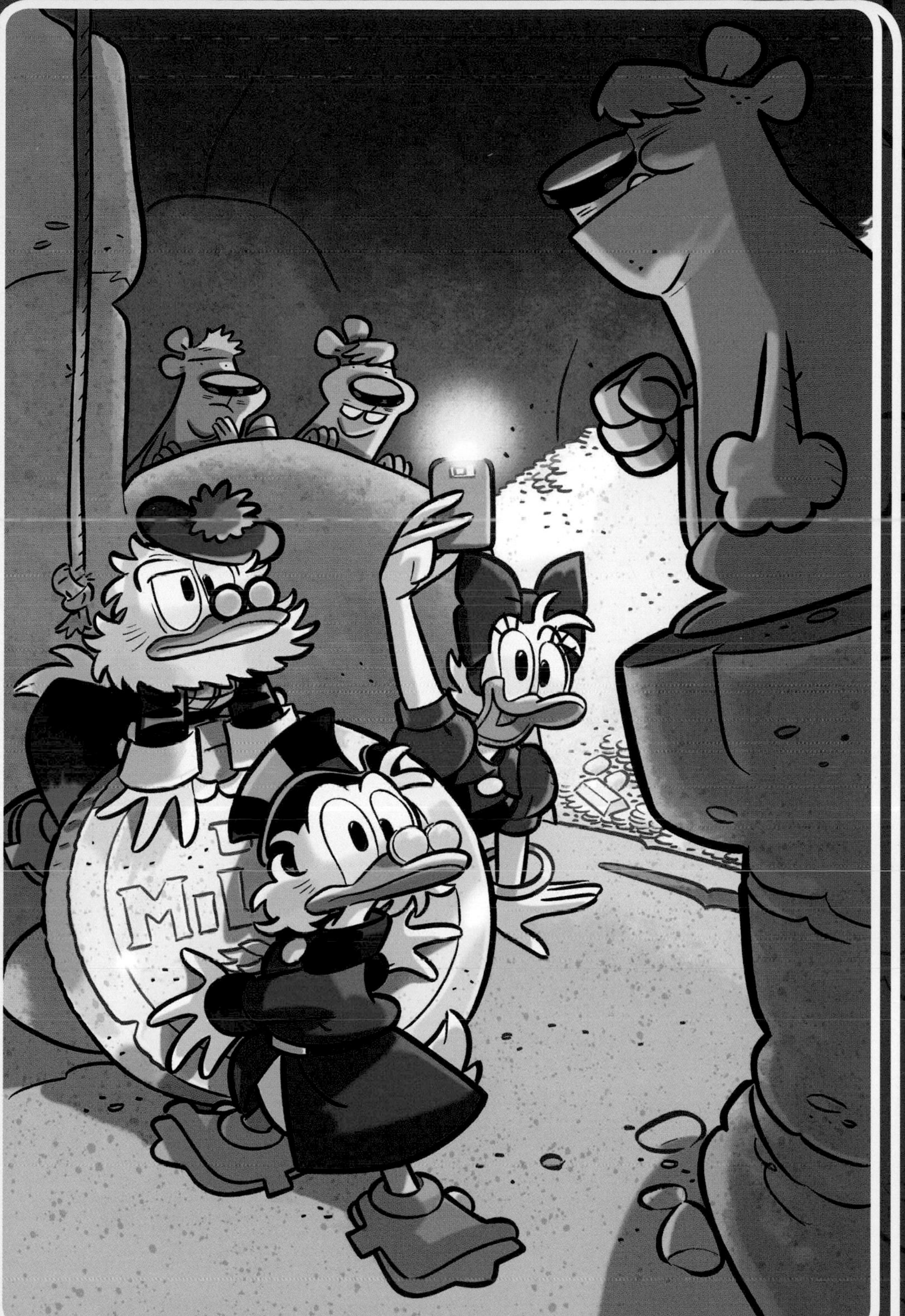
MiL

Art by Stefano Intini

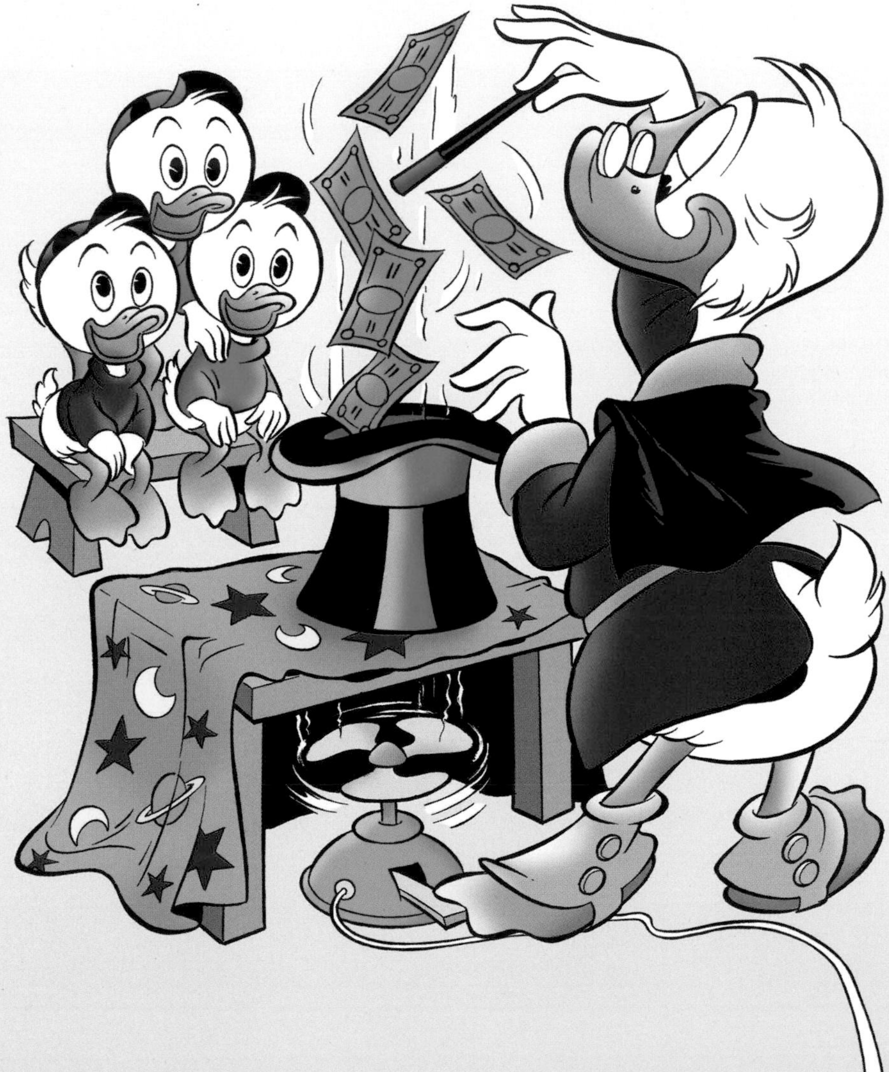

Art by Daniel Branca, Colors by Susan Kolberg

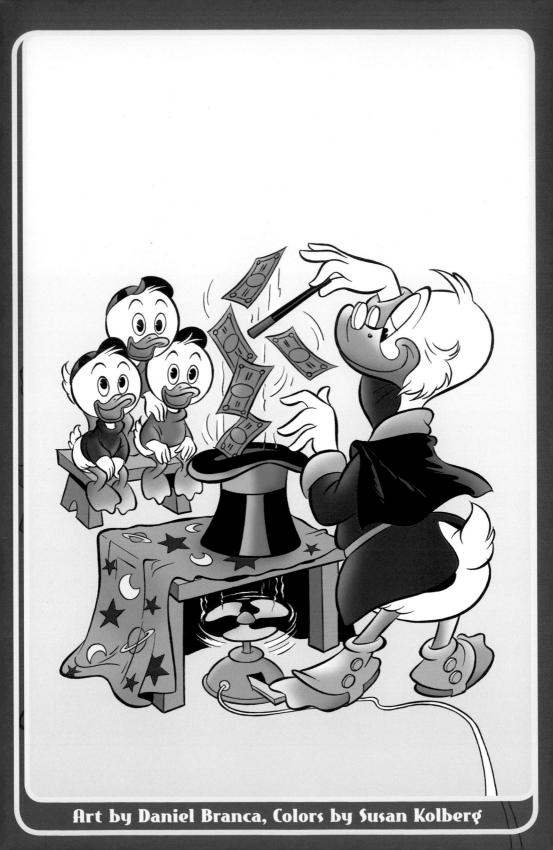

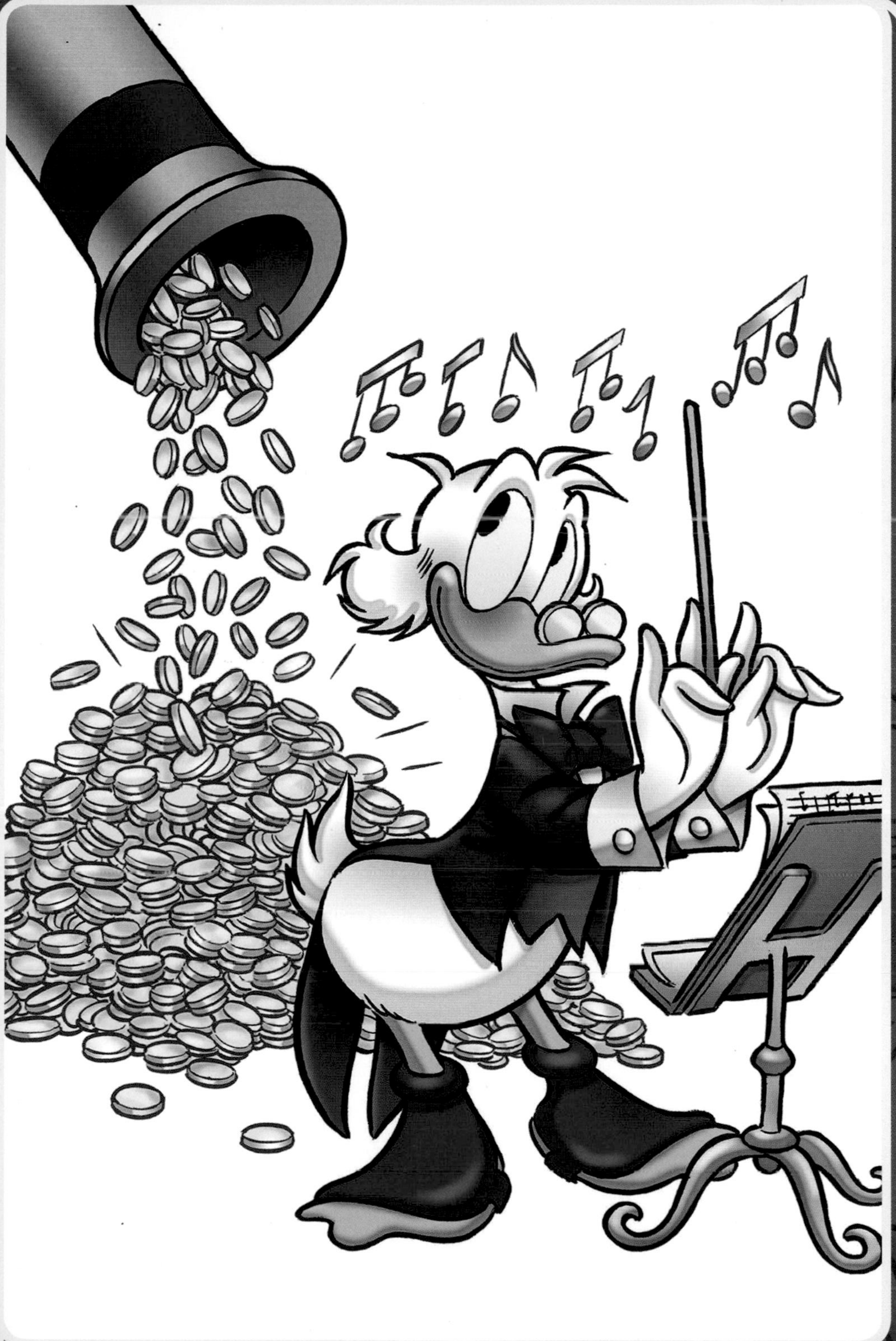

Art by Andrea Freccero, Colors by Max Monteduro

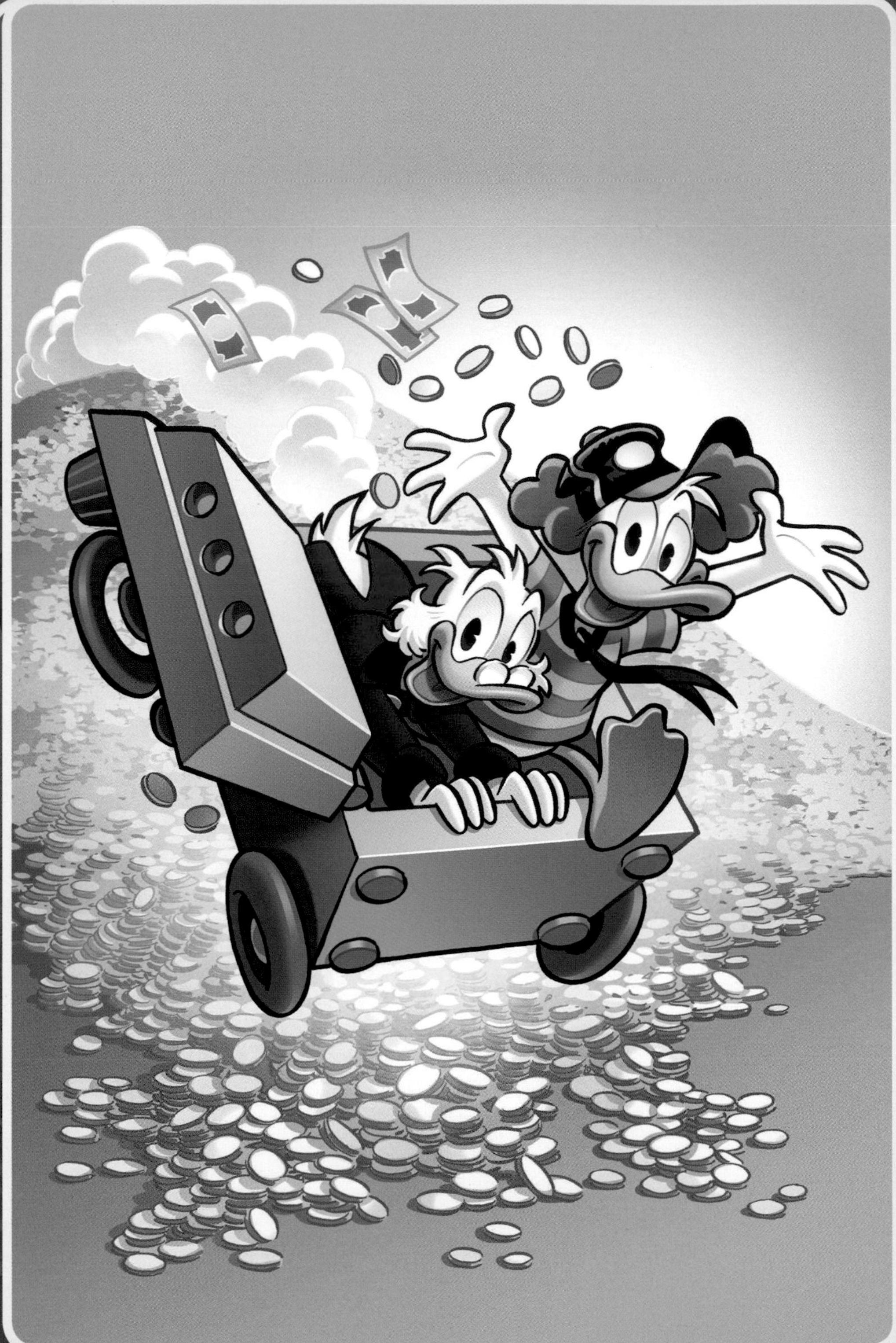

Art by Giorgio Cavazzano, Colors by Andrea Cagol

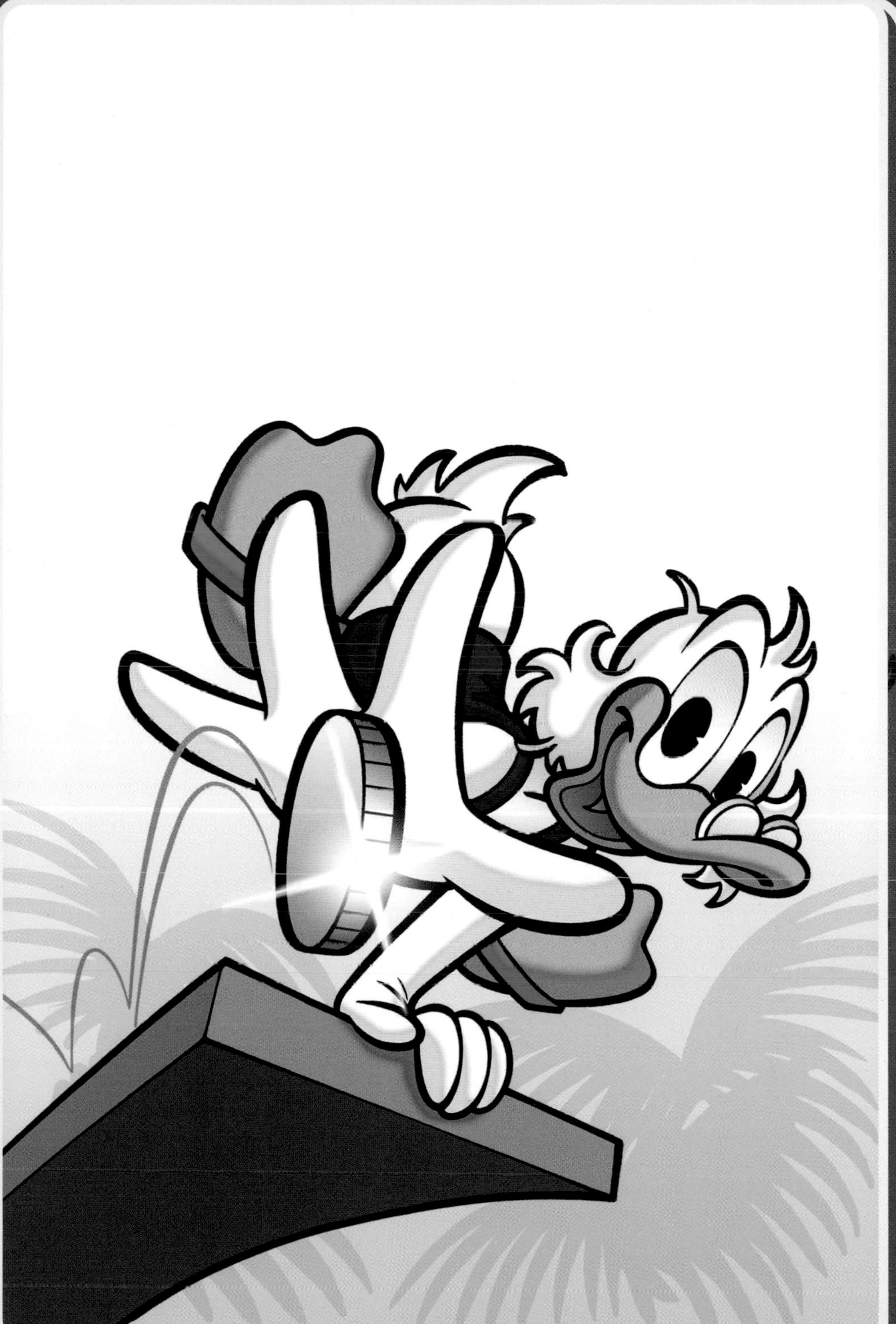

Art by Alessio Coppola, Colors by Max Monteduro

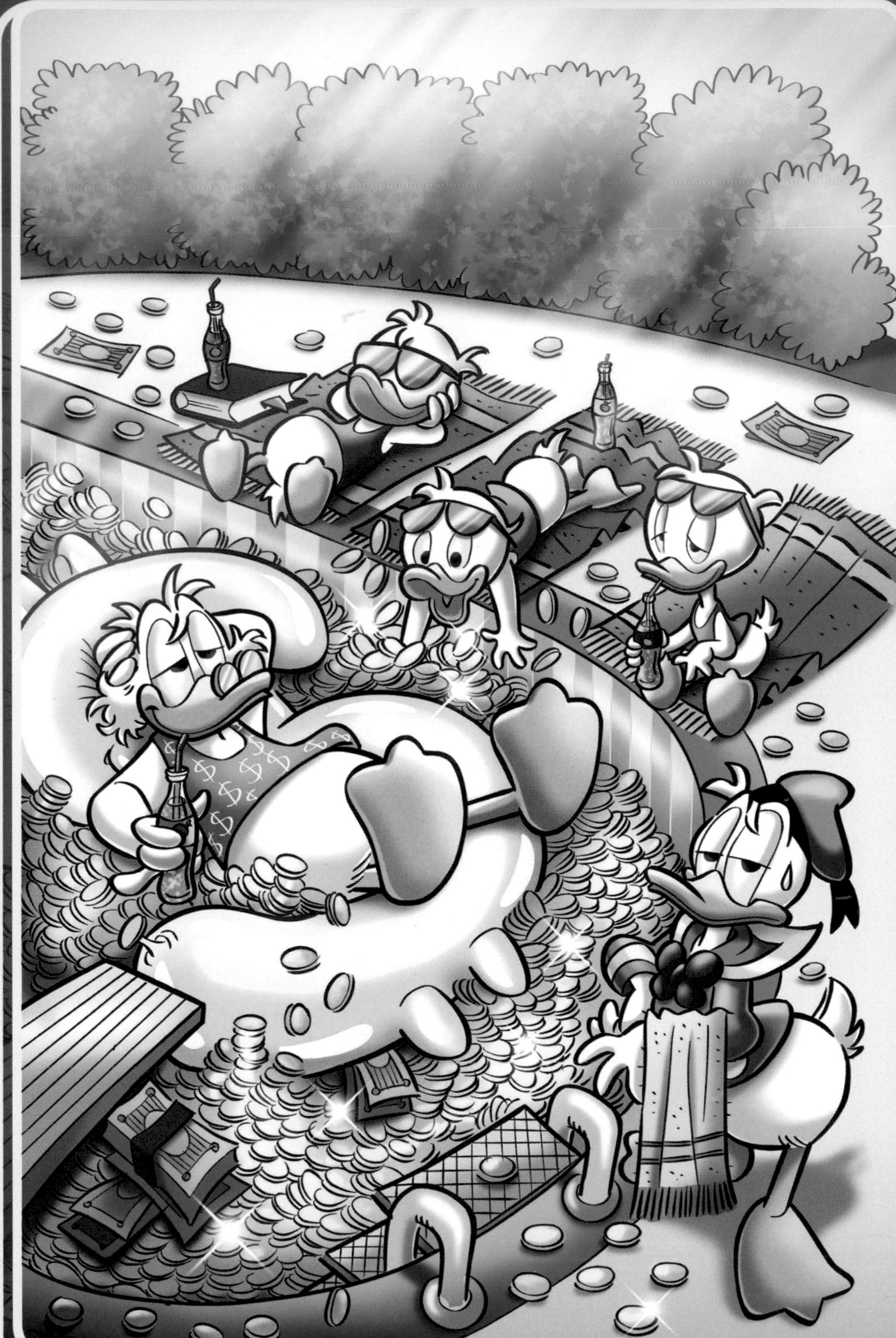

Art by Marco Gervasio, Colors by Marco Colletti

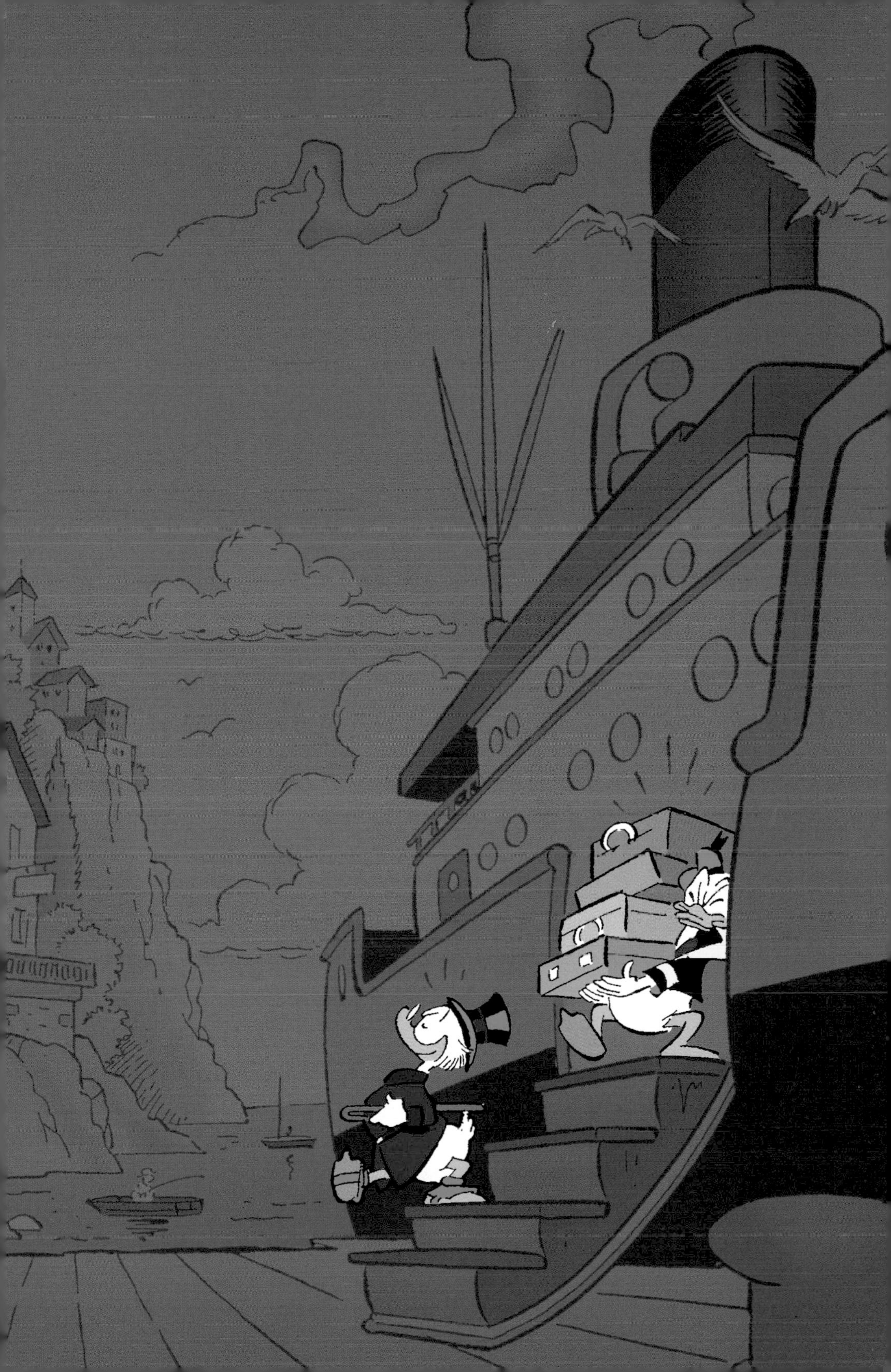

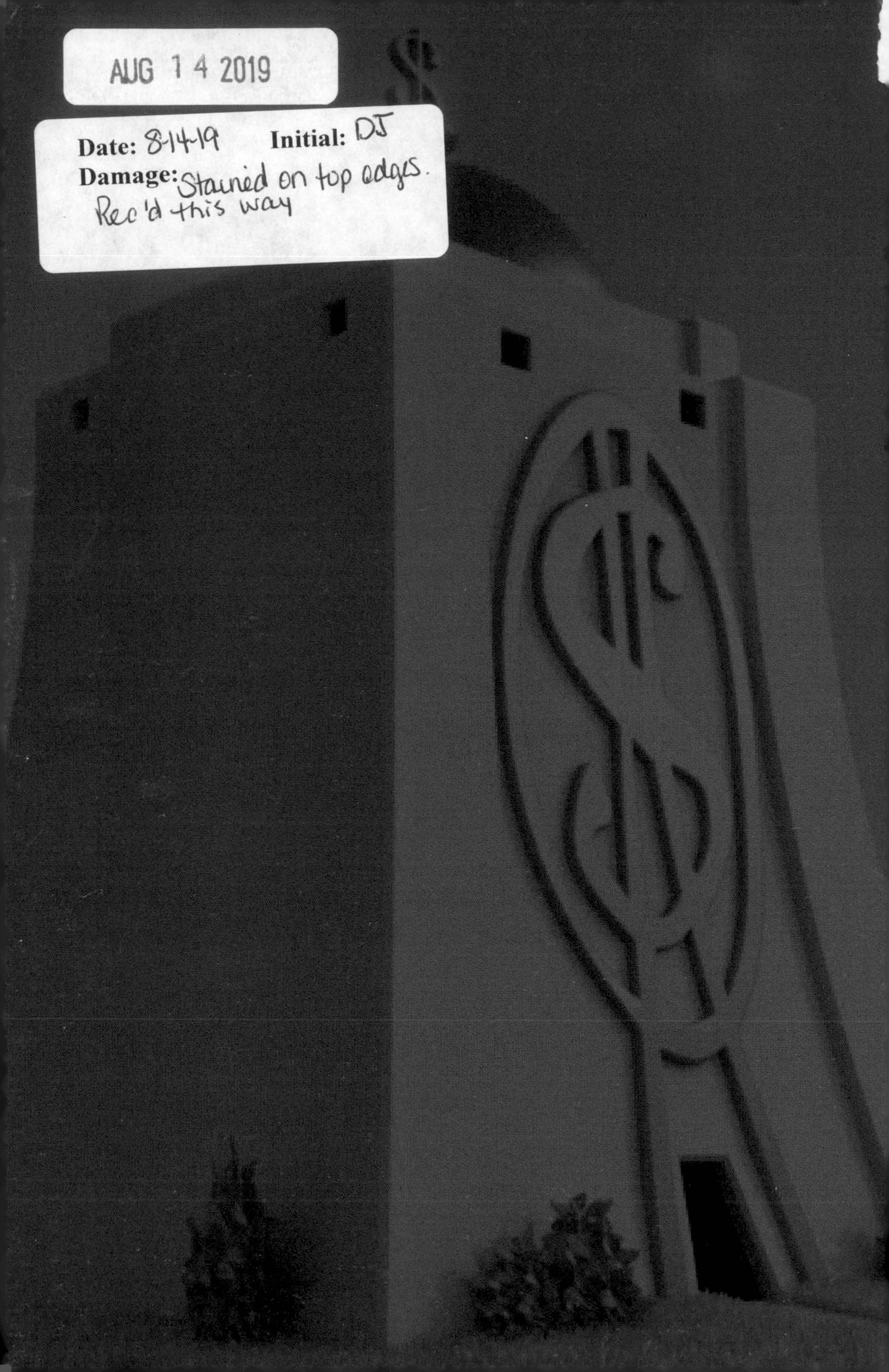